INTO THE
UNKNOWN COUNTRY

Michael McEwen Randall

❈ HOLOCENE PRESS ❈

⌘ **HOLOCENE PRESS** ⌘

First published in the United States in 2016 by Holocene Press.

INTO THE UNKNOWN COUNTRY. Copyright 2016
by Michael McEwen Randall.

For information, address:
Holocene Press,
6533 S.W. 34th Avenue,
Portland, OR 97239.

ISBN 978-0692623312 (Holocene Press)

⌘

Book design by Bryan Wolf, Marrow Design

Cover Photo: 19th Century U.S. Army of the West;
soldiers in their barracks (State Historical Society
of North Dakota: SHSND 1952-0370, detail of image)

For my son, Peter, and my daughter, Libby.
They came from afar, and
trailing clouds of glory did they come.

A Hunkpapa boy came running, and said that soldiers were coming from the East. They were arrogant and tried to cross the river, but we rode with Gall and drove them back. The soldiers who lost their horses fought the hardest, but those who remained mounted ran and we chased them up the long ridge. Some tried to ride back the way they came but we cut them off.

Near the end some killed themselves or shot each other, not wanting to lie wounded and wait for our women's knives. One soldier cried like a child and walked forward and offered his gun to Two Dogs. Two Dogs took the man's gun and shot him in the face. We killed the rest at the end of the long ridge. I found a good knife and plenty of tobacco that day.

I saw no man get away, and I know none did. I heard stories over the years, but they were just more white men's lies. None escaped, but even if they had, where could they ever go?

- unpublished account provided by
Elk Rib near Potato Creek,
Pine Ridge Reservation,
South Dakota, September 1919

FEBRUARY 1931: LIVINGSTON, MONTANA

The evening before the memorial service, Anna's hips ached and her ankles tingled painfully. They were swollen again. She felt as tired as she could ever remember being, for she had traveled nearly four days to get here and arrived just in time for tomorrow's service. She had gone by wagon from Bridger out to Spearfish, then to Billings and Livingston by three different buses. All this was hard, for it was the moon of popping trees, full of snow and bitter cold, but she had come for the purpose of honoring her father and sorting out his few affairs.

The service would be held at his old church. She'd been only a girl when she left for Bridger nearly forty years ago, and had never returned here until now. She would recognize no one at tomorrow's service. "No one will acknowledge me as his family," she thought. "And some won't even see me or the other native people who probably will be in attendance." Sourly, she figured she would hear someone make reference to "prairie niggers," but when she glanced around she wouldn't be able tell who had said it. It often was like that.

Shuddering, she touched her forehead with the fingertips of her right hand as remorse flooded through her for having these bitter thoughts. Coming into the white world always made her anxious, though she knew they were not all bad people. Some were kind and some were ignorant and indifferent, and some hostile. She knew this but was often at war within herself. Too much had happened between her people and the whites to allow it to be otherwise.

Long ago, she had taken on the quiet ways of her Lakota husband's family. The passing years had made her uncomfortable among the restlessly chattering and competitive wasicu. Her husband, Akecheta, always kind, would say, "It is all right, Anna. Mitakuye oyas'in. All these are our family; all of us are related." Still, here among her father's people and the Crows and Blackfeet, traditional enemies of her people, she had to fight back against her fears and her storehouse of anger.

She had written her father once or twice each year. He had traveled to Bridger long ago for her wedding, and a few times during the following decades when his work had brought him near. Now he was gone. The doctor who telegraphed her believed the old gunshot wounds which troubled him at times through his life probably were the cause of his death. By what means the doctor knew how to reach her she did not know.

Her father had been married briefly then was widowed, so he had raised her by himself. His work often took him away and sometimes he had to leave her in the care of friends. But then, when she was fourteen, the army committed its butchery at Wounded Knee. She had become uncontrollable then, so he had let her go to help nurse the Minniconjou and Hunkpapa survivors of the massacre. They had sheltered that brutal winter among the cottonwoods in the valley beside the Cheyenne River, and many had died.

She had met her husband, Akecheta, there. During the massacre he had been badly wounded by shrapnel from the army's Hotchkiss guns. Afterward, he had been carried northward through a blizzard for several days on a horse drawn travois. She had met him there beside the Cheyenne and helped nurse him to health. They had married, raised three children and many horses on land along the river in the village that became known as Bridger. She had spurned white culture, had separated herself from the fat takers. Several times, she and Akecheta had hidden their children to keep them away from the Indian agents who demanded they be taken to the Indian schools where slowly they would have been destroyed.

During her early girlhood, her father had told her very little about his life, and many gaps and holes existed. She looked forward to going through his things, sorting through his life. Her husband would have been too polite to press such an inquiry, but long ago she had developed too many wasicu habits to let Lakota tact put a brake on her will.

That evening, in her father's nearly bare closet she saw what looked like two very old saddlebags draped from a clothes hook. When she pulled them down, the moldering leather shed small bits and crumbles onto the floor. Inside she found that old medal with the eagle and star that hung from a faded ribbon, plus a large envelope addressed to her. She opened the envelope to find a thick sheaf of papers full of his handwriting. It seemed he had written them in segments over a period of time, some pages in pencil, some in blue or black ink.

She looked at the top sheet and saw that it took the form of a letter. She sat and began to read.

Dear Anna,

The time is approaching when I will be gone, and though our contacts have been infrequent over these many years, you always have been in my heart. I have felt you to be my own daughter, and I feel closer to no one else. Much good blood has been shed between our two peoples, and much bad blood remains. I have done my best in my own small way to ameliorate these wounds.

First of all, I want to say that we all are God's children and we are, all of us, quite ordinary people. The liberation of our hearts begins when finally we realize that.

Less than a day after I found you I was shot by a man, and I also met Clotilde. So it was a day of blessing and consternation and calamity, you being the blessing and Clotilde being the consternation. Such days offer the chance to appreciate our Creator's presence in all things. That presence is real, and gives the gift not only of acceptance but also of gratitude to all who have faith in life's goodness.

I never told you about the time before we came together. I was ashamed of much that happened in those few months which played such an important role in the shaping of my own very ordinary life. In these pages I hope to tell you some of what I have omitted before, so that you might understand what I believe about life here in this realm of beauty and struggle.

AUTUMN 1876: BENSON'S LANDING, MONTANA

Clotilde was furious that Caleb rode up after dark with a wounded stranger and a starving Indian brat and presumed to drop them at the door of her inn. There were paying guests to serve and money to be made. Damned if she'd be nurse to a dying man and a prairie nigger. "That nit is going to die if it don't eat. Take her down to the river to Ben Bull Tail's, and tell him I asked can Sarah nurse it."

The stranger had a boy's face, though it was drawn with suffering from his wound. He looked to be aught but a tramp. All he had was a beat up coat and torn gutta-percha, a pair of saddlebags and an old Henry with a battered stock and shine on the barrel. Here it was winter coming and he was little more than threadbare. He did have a sound pair of cavalry boots, but they were beat to hell--in sorriest need of oil. All this she absorbed in a glance.

And the cavalry boots? Maybe he was an army deserter. Last summer, when her Jedro had disappeared along the Yellowstone while selling straw hats to soldiers, the army'd had that big battle over east along the Little Horn, and all those men were killed. She would bet, after that bit of Sioux butchery, some other soldiers broke sweat to skally-hoot. Maybe this boy was such a one.

But, looking at his near lifeless body and the spent horse that carried him, she yielded. "I'll fix up the bed in the big room," she snapped. "He ain't such a big one you can't haul him in."

Caleb grinned. He was too smug by half for a man with such a big nose and no chin. She snapped, "Get him inside and get the brat to Sarah, then brush out his animal and feed it--Bozeman funeral or no."

"But that funeral's early tomorrow afternoon, Clotilde."

Her voice was adamant. "It won't hurt you to ride all night to Bozeman. I 'spect you'll ought to make it before dinner tomorrow, and there'll be plenty of ladies eager to feed the parson."

Caleb took the baby and left. She began to work the wound. Caleb had wrapped his new purple stole--the one with the white doves--tightly around the boy's middle. She muttered, "Aye, God, Caleb!" He'd never get the blood out of that stole now. She unwrapped it and looked at the wound. Caleb had torn up pieces of paper and packed them into the wound for a compress. Pulling away the blood-soaked pages, she looked at them and suddenly realized he'd torn up his Bible. She shook her head and spat on the floor.

The boy'd bled out aplenty for the bullet had passed through his belly, in the front and out the back, spreading calamity along its way. Both his legs shuddered as though they hoped to make him rise, and suddenly he said, "You can't get back, Leo. You'll be killed." His voice was anguished; though benumbed in darkness, some torment ailed him.

He might've been lucky that Caleb heard the gunshot, but as usual

11

luck was too contrary and late. That hole through his gut had sluiced him with his own poisons. Caleb had torn a perfectly good Bible, but it was a waste of gospel, for this youngster would soon slip the crease.

When Caleb came back she pointed to the bloody wad. "You've tore your Bible all to hell and ruined your new stole, too."

Caleb glanced at her. "Under the circumstances I can't think of a better use for the scriptures."

She jerked her head at the unconscious boy. "Well, you've wasted the Word on this one. And look at that stole," she shook her head, disgusted, "Wrappin' him in your new stole!"

At her exclamation the boy's torso convulsed and his knee rose up. She pressed it back down. The boy said, "I can't find Wild--his body...."

They looked at him expectantly, but he lay silent.

Caleb said, "That stole was all I had to use, Clotilde." He looked at her with a bit of spark in his eyes. "I do have three Bibles, and I reckon I know their worth."

She saw with some satisfaction that he'd finally begun to look exasperated.

He said, "Clotilde, I don't think you'd approve good Joseph of Arimathea wrapping the crucified Jesus in fresh linen for his tomb. It might stain the cloth."

God damn, he boiled her! Just because he was a preacher, he expected people--most often her it seemed--to do his bidding. He was a boarder here, but she knew he was interested in her--maybe just wanted to control her. Caleb pleasured himself thinking he drew out people's best, said it was God's will. But it was just his own, and she'd seen enough of God's will to know it didn't impress her.

Caleb's excess of virtue always set her off. "Your parson's airs are swol' as a horse bladder, which is piss enough to drown a cat." Just because he had that poor cut of meat dangling between his legs didn't mean she had to jump on it. Parson or not, a man with only a nubbin-chin shouldn't strut so.

"You best get to Bozeman," she snapped.

But Caleb just grinned. "I've got time yet, with all those ladies and all that food waiting for me."

She didn't take to that lip; he really browned her off. She'd have to break him of such fancies, if he ever did talk her into teaming up. But such a notion--teaming up with Caleb--made her feel guilty, for she knew her husband Jedro still watched, whether gazing down from paradise or wailing up from hell-fire she did not know.

"Sophia, you don't have to go with him." The boy's voice was a whisper, but clear. They watched him for a moment, but he said no more. Clotilde lifted one of his feet and laid him straighter.

She sorely wished to know what happened to Jedro, but most likely the Sioux killed him so it'd be unwise to wish for details. Worse, while she wanted to be angry at God for Jedro being gone, she knew it was really her fault. She'd been wanting to make more money.

She'd nagged Jedro to go downriver and sell her homemade straw hats for two-bits apiece in the soldier camps. Soldier boys had been everywhere this year, looking for Sioux who'd run loose from that big reservation over to Dakota Territory.

She shook her head as she swabbed at the boy's wound: give those Indians a nice big reservation to live on, and what do they do? Just throw it all up and make trouble.

An army expedition, Colonel Gibbon's bunch from Fort Ellis and those from Fort Shaw on the Sun River, had come through the Landing last spring on their way east. They'd snapped up the few straw hats she'd had on hand--paid a quarter apiece. She was taken by surprise or she'd of had more hats made and ready. She hadn't known the soldiers were coming through, hadn't known they hated their cheap felt army hats, which lost all shape in the rain.

But as the soldier boys trooped off down the Yellowstone she'd seen dollar signs--as was her wont, and now her great regret. She'd spent the next few weeks making dozens more hats. And now she had bad feelings in her heart, for it was her who sent Jedro away with hats to find the soldiers and bring back their quarters.

It was almost like Jedro saw a sign. "Tildy, I don't want to go down river," he said. "I just got bad feelings about it."

"We came to this neck of country to make money," she reminded him. But his face wore a worried look until the day he left.

Maybe he'd just been drunk or careless, maybe fallen from the mackinaw in the middle of the river. With pockets full of soldier quarters he might've been sucked down into the flood. In a dream one night she saw straw hats racing along half-submerged on the river's current. At first she thought the dream was a sign from the Lord, but then realized he wouldn't make nothing so clear--for it might cut back the bounty of misery He provided.

Caleb looked at her. "You're angry at God," he said. "I worry about your soul."

"You or nobody else is going to back me away from that battle," she snapped. She had a right to be furious about Jedro disappearing downriver, and she argued with the Lord daily. But of course He didn't answer, for that was His great pleasure: let 'em howl with anguish and despair but pay 'em no mind. She could almost see Him up there walking around, restless with nothing to do. He'd given everybody free will and now was bored, hadn't nothing to do except stir the clouds and destroy a race of people here, create a tornado there, start a plague yonder--just to see what would happen. He ignored her all the while, which made her want to spit.

Caleb went to gather his horse, and when she checked the boy's wound again her fingers brushed his shirt pocket. Something was inside there. If she had a too-nosy interest in other peoples' affairs, long ago she'd decided embarrassment was less painful than boredom--and of shorter duration. From his shirt pocket she pulled a letter that'd been creased and folded many times. One corner was stained, still damp with a bit of his blood. She went across the room to the oil lamp and stood beside it to read.

February 27, 1876

Dearest Mac,

You have been in my thoughts a great deal and I should have written sooner, but due to my present circumstances I have not. You were so good to me when I badly needed a friend, and it was wrong of me to begin a relationship with you of the kind I did. The purpose of this short note is simply to bring you closer to me, at least in my mind, and to tell you I am sorry I left without explanation.

I am not in San Francisco, as originally anticipated. You will be surprised that instead I am living in the village of Bismarck, Dakota Territory. The reasons for my coming to this place are complicated, and I have too little energy or will to explain. Things are not going well.

I truly wish you were here--or I was there--that we might talk. Remember that day in the gazebo when the chickadee nearly took the feather from my hand? When it flew away I looked up and saw you standing there, so faithful and caring. During the short time we had together, I felt a good deal more tranquil than I had for some time, and certainly more at peace than now.

I hope you do not mind me intruding with this letter after my mysterious departure and after the months that have intervened. Although I do not know when--or if--we shall meet again, please know that you are in my thoughts and among my fondest memories. With greatest affection, I hope to remain---

Your dear friend,
Sophia Spence

"Hnnpphhh," she grumped. The letter had many a deluxe flourish, and read like a woman attempting to beguile a man into coming to her, but without coming right out and asking. Apparently she'd coaxed him a long way from somewhere. She must be a one to relish her fancies and glut her whims aught all else.

Later, when Caleb came back she made him read the letter before he left for Bozeman. When he finished she said, "That was quite a trip he undertook--driven by such a thin epistle from a selfish woman. And just look at what it's got him."

Caleb held up the letter to her. "How do you read selfishness into this? It sounds sincere, and the boy must have been filled with good intentions to come so far."

"Considerin' that letter, it was just a bad itch that moved him."

"Good aims moved many a man great distances, Clotilde."

"I don't guess bad intentions kept many to home neither."

After Caleb left for Bozeman, Clotilde looked after the boy's wound a bit more and he moaned, deep in his fever. She was dead-bone weary. She felt too young to be thinking all these gloomy thoughts--and too young to have done so much of this wound tending and corpse cleaning: draining fester born of shit-smeared arrowheads, prettying up drowners from the river, sewing up knife cuts from whore house fights over to Bozeman. And that time Jedro got so drunk and fell down and hit his head on a stone hard enough to split the skull of an ordinary mortal.

The only apparent effect of Jedro's fall that time had been toothsome enough. After he fell, just about daily and without timely notice, his sex got hard. He hankered for her, and in some outlandish locations, whether in the kitchen or on the porch or out back in the shed or fields. And his timing always threatened embarrassment. It was hard to keep a weather-eye for visitors with her heels locked behind his back and crashing around ructious enough to break furniture.

Again the wounded boy's knee rose and she pushed it back down, sighing, then slipped a tangled strand of hair back over her ear. She rinsed the rag, tried to push thoughts of Jedro away, but her throat got tight and though she clenched her eyes shut, tears leaked through anyway. Goddamn' Indians oughtn't to killed him.

She had to calm herself when she got like this, for the vein was pulsing in her neck again, as it always did when God, man, or this bilesome world riled her. Though no one was around to see it wriggling like an inch-worm under her skin, it still made her self-conscious.

She ceased washing the boy and dropped the bloody cloth in the pail, then wiped her fingers on Jedro's old smithy apron. Gazing at the oozing wound, she shook her head, then placed her fingertips over the vein in her neck and pressed down hard. By doing so, she felt a brief dizziness and became less wroth.

⌘

The two of them were talking about the Bible and Jesus, and whoever she was she didn't shy from sharing her views. He just wished for things to go black again, and once or twice they did… *tried to get Holley to stay, but Holley wailed, "I shouldna' run, Mac! I shouldna' run! We got to go back!" But there were Indians beyond the rise…Wild and Burden and the others firing and…*the woman probed at him again like hell lurching across him on a rusty cart.

The woman, Clotilde, had left him in a big icy room at the rear of the house. He couldn't remember what'd happened or why he'd pressed the horse so hard, but there was this great pressure in his belly and a mix of dread and grief washed through him.

Through the window lay fields with open stands of pine that rose up through steeped-walled valleys to snowy peaks. She'd said he would die but his teeth wouldn't stop chattering and he counted that as a sign his body might not yet go traveling.

It was then he remembered laying there on the dusty track. The mare came back and lowered her head over him--and the baby. He couldn't help Sophia now, but.... Some movement woke him again, and waking brought agony. His belly and thighs felt swollen and a metallic, gamy taste filled his mouth; he imagined it slick with blood. As a caution against pain he did not stir, but focused on a bright band of moonlight that shone on the gray blanket. As he looked into the night beyond the dirty window a floor board creaked in the dark. The woman Clotilde was here.

She was feisty, built like a whiskey keg. How could such a woman move so quietly? She said he'd die soon, and though he wanted another blanket, he was afraid to ask. He wondered if, when he passed, would she mail the letters?

She probed at his stomach with her hand and he cried out, saw white light.

The woman said, "Who's Sophia?"

Had he said her name? "She's gone now." His voice sounded hollow, as if at the bottom of a barrel. *Sophia's face intense...she held a small feather toward the bird that hopped agitated flicking its tail only a foot from her outstretched hand...lowering sun backlit her hair...a glow of auburn...faint zephyr brought a scent of lilacs...*His thoughts were confused: in the cold room, were there lilacs?

"She was your sweetheart?"

He couldn't face her intensity and looked away. "Not really, no." The woman, Clotilde: lank hair lay in a half-unraveled bun at the back of her neck. A loose strand lay on her cheek. "If I die, ma'am, will you mail those letters, please." It was one thing he had to be assured of, that he could feel he had done right, letting families know what happened to their loved ones.

She didn't answer his question, but said, "Your name Mac?"

"Yes, ma'am." She had her own ideas of what to discuss.

"What be your kin name, and how old be you?"

"Seventeen, ma'am. My name's Durant. Mac Durant." His teeth chattered and his cheek felt cold from sweat and drool. "I can't get warm."

"I'll get another blanket." She went away and icy wind moaned through chinks beside one window. That forlorn sound made the vagrant drafts feel worse, and drove cold deep into him.

She came back with the blanket. "You wasn't with them goddamn' scalp hunters, was you, Mac Durant?"

"No, ma'am." She didn't have a lot of sympathy in her soul, but his throat began to ache when she spoke his name.

"Why was you shot?" But he started to go away again and...*the two riders--the shooter standing beside him looked into his eyes for several seconds then holstered his piece and remounted. Finally the two rode away... the mare came back to stand over him. Dust rose in small puffs from beneath her hooves as she shifted her weigh then shook herself and nickered a question, quietly lowered her head...her loose reins slid across his brow.*

The woman made a sound of disgust, then: "Last summer when you soldier boys were on the big river, did you see a man name of Jedro? It was hats he was selling, from off an old mackinaw boat."

⌘

Later, Clotilde took up the boy's saddlebags from the kitchen floor where Caleb had dropped them, and turned them in her hands. If a body was going to spend time making a man's last hours bearable, then a body had the right to go through his necessaries. When he passed on there might be family to be notified. Or there might be money, or evidence of past crimes and treachery.

One of the bags' flaps was embossed with the words, "T. Wild, U.S. Army." The boy had mentioned a man named Wild in his delirium, but why did he have Wild's saddlebags?

Inside them Clotilde found a dented locket and a packet of letters tied with dried animal sinew. Some had no envelopes and many had dark brown smears that might be dried mud. The grimy bundle had gotten wet.

She held it gingerly by the knotted sinew with a thumb and

forefinger, squinting at the top envelope. It'd never been postmarked and immediately she saw why. The address was completely illegible from water stain, except for a fragment of the return address that read:

> Pvt. Ottocar Nitsche
> C Company, 7th Regi....
> Fort Abraham Li....
> Dakota Ter....

This was a soldier's letter. Clotilde lay the tattered packet on the table beside her and picked up the dented locket, turning it in her hands. She sort of fancied this pretty piece. The only metal that ever got bent around here was on a smithy's anvil by Jedro with his hammer, then pounded onto a horse's hoof. She turned the locket and decided the filigree was corroded brass, darkened a bit by weathering. The thing had a dent on the top, but the clasp still worked and she unsnapped it.

Inside, fixed into the locket, lay a crisp tintype of a woman's face and bust. Bringing it closer in the shadowed room, Clotilde focused her eyes on the picture. The woman dispensed a smile that challenged the camera--or the photographer. This was the Sophia whose name the wounded boy spoke in his sleep. The woman's lush lips were parted softly and she was dressed in a low-cut dress with puffed sleeves and a small hat with trailing scarf. "Hnnnphh," Clotilde thought, "Struts herself like a harlot."

She snapped the locket shut, dropped it back in the saddle bag, then stood and straightened her skirt and picked up the letter packet. With a dull pair of pinking shears, she gnawed at the piece of sinew that bound the packet. When she finally cut through the sinew and pulled it free, her hands slipped and envelopes and folded sheets cascaded to the floor around her. She muttered and the vein started jumping again, so she pressed her fingers to it. The momentary dizziness calmed her.

Only then did she see that some of the letters were mere fragments without envelopes, and the written pages had been filled with words by many people's hands. Some, while apparently complete, were torn and yellowed. On several, water--and whatever caused the brown smears-- had washed away parts of paragraphs and made them largely unreadable, but still it was clear these were soldiers' letters that had never been sent.

She picked up one letter not enclosed in an envelope and saw that its salutation read, "My dearest sister Margaret,..." One of the muddy smears blotted out the next several words. A shock of recognition hit her: bloody hands had handled these letters. She looked at the paper scattered around her, then slipped from the chair and onto her knees, picking up several sheets. They felt brittle so she handled them carefully, as though they might crumble to powder in her hands.

Gathering her dress front into a pouch, she filled it with the jumbled letters, then settled back in the kitchen chair. For several minutes she spread and sorted them on her table. Then, surveying them silently, she picked up the same one she'd first seen moments before and began to read. Water stains had obliterated some of its words.

My dearest sister Margaret,   *June 23, 1876*

 ...ope this finds you, Robert, and the children well, and... ...ologize for not having written sooner for now we are beyond the reach of mail.

 ...should experience the better part of the last several weeks as I have. At one point in the expedition we stayed for days along a stream that yielded our fellows hundreds of skip jack and grayling. You shall laugh at me, but in these last ten years your brother has become an accomplished cook over an open fire. I must tell you this is extremely gratifying. The very act of cooking well with what one has at hand is essentially an optimistic act, one of faith and hope for, and pleasure in, one's life. In thoughtful preparation of food, one comes to understand that whatever exigencies life may present, one can still find a degree of peace, even grace in...

 ...and... ...am certainly glad you feel Robert is softening his attitude toward me, though I have a hard time doing so myself.
 May all God's blessings come to you, and I shall always be....

         Your loving brother,
         Thomas Wild

Who was this soldier, Thomas Wild? She turned his letter in her hands, read it again. He was a rather fancy writer for her tastes, though apparently he loved his sister. Why did he need forgiveness?

She looked at the other letters, a number of them just fragments. Why were some of them water stained and smeared with blood? Why did some have no envelopes, and here and there a missing page? Wherever Mr. Wild's sister Margaret was, she'd never received his letter.

She looked again at the date of Thomas Wild's letter: June 23, 1876. That was a few days after Jedro left home, and near the time all those soldiers died. These blood-smeared letters were just dregs of men's lives, fragments in the dust. Where these men were now only God knew, and as usual He wasn't talking.

The letters were a mess and not many would make it to their destinations, but she sorted and straightened them as best she could. These sad men had been torn by their own passions, just like her and Jedro. Maybe some--like her Jedro--were already dead, had vanished utterly just as she someday would. It would be as if none of them had ever lived.

Clotilde listened for sounds in the big room, but the boy was asleep and his fever was up.

He was about to die; that seemed certain. But maybe he'd wake and be able to talk before he crossed over. She knew that sometimes a wounded man seemed to recover for a bit, even wanted food. Then he died.

Maybe he'd been a soldier down to the Little Horn last summer. A bit of hope sprang into her breast. Maybe he knew her Jedro, had met him somewhere along the way. But her heart sank in its usual fashion, for in a way none of these things mattered. Any answers this boy might give couldn't bring Jedro back from the dark place. Still, no matter the gruesome tribulation that truth did carry, a body did wish to know.

An excerpt from her father's letter:

...I had left my aunt and uncle's home to try to find and help Sophia. At least that is what my troubled heart told me. Any real understanding was still beyond my reach, for I was young: seventeen. I lacked perspective, but that was soon to be altered by what I would experience, and I....

APRIL 1876: ST. PAUL, MINNESOTA

In late afternoon, when Mac Durant first boarded the train in St. Paul, he was already befuddled from the whiskey he'd stolen from his uncle, but on the wooden seat he drank still more. He slept it off that night and most of the next day. He woke briefly in the afternoon as sleet from a late winter storm lashed the windows beside him. Nauseated and bone weary, his body saturated with alcohol, he woke only to clamber to his feet and find a toilet, then stumble back to his seat and sleep again. He finally woke, stupefied, eyes bleary, mouth dried to crackling--to learn the train was far west of Duluth, but still a day away from Bismarck.

It was in the men's stall he realized with a pang of shock that he'd lost his satchel of clothes. He hurried back to his seat to look, but the search was futile; it was gone. He still had what was left of the whiskey in a string bag, but must have left his entire kit at the train station in St. Paul.

He ran finger tips over his trouser pockets, and through the fabric felt the reassuring crinkle of Sophia's folded letter, felt the bulge of her locket with its picture inside. He probed anxiously for the fold of currency in his trousers--the money he'd taken from the gravy boat in his aunt's kitchen cupboard. Relief flooded through him when he felt it there.

When he stepped outside onto the train's rear platform to take some air, two other men, a civilian and a soldier, were already there. The civilian's shirt sleeves were pulled up and his arms were heavily tattooed. He pointed southwest and said, "Will you look at that?" Dirty snow still filled the draws, and the rises lay gray and barren, covered with winter-killed grass. Far away near the horizon, four horsemen, hardly more than specks on the vast plain, rode single file. "There are the four horsemen of the apocalypse, if I've ever seen them."

The soldier was wide-shouldered, big and lean. His hair was unusual, carrot-orange, and his blue eyes were flat and cold as he gazed into the distance. "That ain't nothing, just Sioux out hunting."

"Well, you can't call the uprising down to the Black Hills 'nothing.' It's something a damn' sight bigger," the man snapped, but he held out his hand. "My name's McGregor. I lead miners and emigrant wagons: Black Hills, Oregon country, California." He gestured toward the Indians. "I wish you army boys would wipe those vermin off the map. I'm to meet a new batch of folks in Bismarck. They're headed for Deadwood to look for the yellow metal."

The soldier nodded. "I'm Burden. Chauncey Burden. I don't guess they'll be much trouble," the soldier said. "I'm going to Fort Lincoln to join a regiment that's about to head west and deal with them."

"It's long past due. They killed my sister and her husband two months ago near Deadwood. Put his head up on a pole and left their bodies on the ground for the animals."

"They don't like us going into the Black Hills for the gold," the soldier said.

"That's too Goddamned bad; the sons of bitches. My father-in-law in Chicago; he's got money. He's put a fifty dollar bounty on every scalp brought to his agent in Deadwood. Man, woman or child: whose hair don't matter."

The soldier looked sideways at the man. "That ought to draw some real hair-poppin' ranahans to the Hills. Glad my hair ain't black."

Even standing in the cold on the rocking platform, such talk made Mac's palms wet, so he went back inside the train car. Days ago, back at Fort Snelling, he'd heard several stories about a rising Sioux war out beyond the Missouri, and for the first time in a year or more he'd had the dream again. He'd awakened in a sweat from it, his heart pounding and his face all hot. When he woke, the release from anxiety was so great that he almost sobbed with relief.

As always, in the dream his mother had hidden him in the slough

23

among the cattails, then thrashed away through the muck. He didn't see her again, but only heard her screams, then saw the tangle of blood-matted blond hair on the war club of the young Sioux warrior who found him hiding moments later. He feared that the dream of the slough would start again, return to bother his sleep in this new place, as it'd done so often when he was small.

One thing was sure: he wanted nothing to do with Indians. They'd brought him enough misery by killing his parents, which resulted in his being raised by his uncle and aunt--and those two had presented him with a whole different kind of grief.

He took a few pulls from one of the whiskey bottles and soon he lay down on another bench across the aisle. As he grew drowsy, he felt a growing nausea and sensed he was floating up into the air. He knew from experience that once he'd attained a certain height he would slowly turn upside down and fall to the ground, so--as he often did--he lowered his left foot to the floor and anchored himself.

As he floated there, a characteristic twinge of uncertainty filled him, a sinking feeling in his heart that had come to him since leaving his aunt and uncle's home to find Sophia. At daybreak when he woke, his eyes hurt deep inside like they'd been poked with a stick. Out the train window the southwest sky bloomed with dark clouds. He sat slack-jawed, head throbbing, and watched a rainstorm slowly approach across the sea of tangled grass.

His head ached and he needed to eat, but felt that food wouldn't stay down. A wind rose ahead of the rain, and battered the dead winter landscape. It buffeted the train, rattling the windows of the car, and for a long while he sat as though mesmerized by mile after mile of withered prairie grass that bent stiffly before the wind. He knew nothing about these plains, but certainly the city was better. Here on the plains a person was surrounded by such emptiness it seemed he could float away and be scattered in bits amid its vastness. His body could just break up like dust and blow away in the endless wind. Maybe this trip hadn't been such a good idea.

The rain finally hit. A wall of wind and sleet slammed the passenger car's windows and slashed sideways along the glass. From the wood stove at the far end of the car a puff of gray smoke belched into the warm compartment like a sinister breath, and a surprised murmur rose among the passengers. For the first time since his trip started, he looked around at other people in the car, and wondered vaguely what brought each of them to such a place.

Ice crystals swept along in the water that ran down the window, and he wished he had his satchel with his clothes. He did have the other sack with the remainder of his whiskey, but right now the liquor didn't seem so appetizing. His dejection deepened as he watched the empty land full of dead, wind-whipped scrub. Icy water flowed past him on the glass. After a time, he reached into his pocket and withdrew his remaining money to count it. Then he opened the locket and gazed at Sophia's picture once more.

She had lived with her grandparents down the road from his aunt and uncle, having moved there with her mother after her father died. She loved animals and they loved her. Once, he had even seen a doe and fawn eat from her hand. Her grandparents were in thrall to her and surrounded her with animals. At various times she had a dog, geese, goats, doves, and a peacock that followed her around strutting and preening.

For several years he had loved her mostly from afar, and she, being older, treated him with a genially superior air. Both of them had lost parents and he thought he saw sadness in her, a grief akin to his own. Because of her manner toward him, he stood a bit on guard when near her, tried to gauge her mood in their first moments of contact. Reading the way in which she strode toward him, he adjusted his expectations and behavior accordingly. Making no special effort to see or spend time with him, he had long known that Sophia, though amiable, was   indifferent toward him.

One day he learned she had gone away to Chicago. She was twenty-one and on her own. He heard no more about her for several months. Then one night he overheard his aunt talking with his uncle in another room. "Sophia's grandmother is at her wit's end with the girl. She is quite willful, and has fallen in love with a man of whom her family does not approve."

His uncle said, "Why don't they approve?"

"The man is ineligible. Ostensibly he is married."

"Good God," his uncle blurted. "Why would the girl soil herself with such an affair?"

"According to her grandmother, the girl has become a handful. She is ruled only by herself. However, she has agreed to return here for a while. They hope for her to recover from the relationship."

These things had been hard to hear, yet Mac could not help feeling excited that she would be coming back to her grandparents' home. When she did return, and he first saw her, the light in her eyes had changed, appeared diminished. Her face seemed older, more somber, her movements more controlled and less buoyant. Her grandmother told his aunt that Sophia seemed to have lost interest in the animals which her mother and grandparents now took care of. But what surprised and pleased him the most was her new attentiveness to him. Before long he had worked up the courage to ask her to accompany him on a surrey ride, and on that spring-time ride she had reached beneath the lap blanket they shared and taken hold of him. She had him tie the horse to a tree and they took the lap blanket back into a darker part of the woodland.

An excerpt from her father's letter:

...If a person is pressed to the wall, he will sometimes make a casual decision that changes his life forever, particularly when he is not clear on what put him in that hole in the first place. At that time in my life, I had some demons at work in me that I didn't even recognize, let alone know how to cast out.

APRIL 1876: BISMARCK, DAKOTA TERRITORY

After arriving in Bismarck, within hours of showing Sophia's tintype around at the hotels and several stores, he stood deflated as though he'd been struck in the gut, for he learned that she had left Bismarck a couple of weeks earlier.

He'd shown the locket picture to an elderly lady he saw mopping muddy plank floors just inside the open doors of a small church. Brushing gray hair back from her face, the woman said, "I remember Sophia. She signed up to go with a group of people who were traveling to the Black Hills to work in the gold fields. She said she was going to Deadwood to work in a store that sells dry goods and equipment to miners."

He didn't know what to make of this information. First, she'd come to Bismarck, and now she'd gone to Deadwood. These detours were far removed from Sophia's original plans to go to San Francisco. He said, "Did she seem all right?"

"She seemed fine, though a rather serious person and not quick to smile. One day she stopped here and she had a black eye. She claimed she'd fallen in the night, but I wondered if that were true or if someone had struck her."

That confused him and made him wonder, for Sophia's smile was radiant and just about always ready. And...a black eye?

The woman sniffed, "I certainly don't know what could draw her to Deadwood. I hear it's not much more than a muddy ravine full of miners' tents and shanties. Not a place for a young lady."

She looked at him more intently. "You a relation of Sophia's?"

He hesitated, but said, "A friend. She wrote and asked me to come." People who eyed him too close made him nervous, and he began to step away.

She said, "Young man," and he stopped. "If you find Sophia, tell her Elsie from the church in Bismarck said she's always welcome back here. She is always in God's hands, but the benefits of that sometimes don't seem obvious to a person."

"Yes, ma'am," he said.

As he left her, his mouth felt dry and his hands tingled, on the edge of trembling. He had too little money to pay his way to the Black Hills as part of some miners' expedition. Why had Sophia come to Bismarck in the first place? And why would she suddenly go to Deadwood? Maybe she'd written to him again, after he'd left his aunt and uncle's home to come find her. There was no way to know.

With the rail line ending here, Bismarck sat perched at the edge of nowhere, with only the Missouri River on its western edge, and empty plains beyond. The town felt like foreign territory, and in fact it was: Dakota Territory. This was the first time he'd ever been out of the states.

But he had to find work that'd get him to Deadwood, possibly working with horses, for the one good thing he'd gotten from his years under his horse trader uncle's thumb was working with horses. A lot of horses passed through his uncle's hands on their way to the army units at Fort Snelling. His mind was a jumble right then: his dwindling money, work with horses, finding Sophia. He didn't know how long it would take, but, God, she had to be there when he got there. He didn't know what he'd do if she wasn't.

Given the Indians out there on the plains, he questioned how safe the trip to Deadwood was and wondered if Sophia had made it all right. He didn't look forward to traveling there. Still, though he only had her locket and letter, he'd come too far to turn back now. And he longed to see her. Besides, there was nothing to go back to. Having taken that whiskey and his aunt's money, he'd burned his bridges. There were plenty more painful reasons he'd never go back, even if they'd want him to, which they did not.

Local people said spring had been cold and wet on the high plains. Though this day started with cold rain, the afternoon brought bright watery sunlight that bathed the town in fresh glory. But the streets of Bismarck were ponds of shallow, wind-ruffled water that lay across long stretches of rutted mud. Mule and ox-drawn cargo wagons cut sloppy wakes, their wheels kneading and deepening the ruts. Standing water reflected dappled sunlight into the shadows beneath the wooden buildings' eaves and under the covered porch ways. At various locations along the street, rough-cut cottonwood planks had been thrown across the mud and water to provide a rickety, narrow passage.

Just then, a small unit of mounted soldiers splashed past, and one shouted, "Hey, whiskey-boy!" A bit shame-faced, Mac lifted his chin toward Chauncey Burden, the soldier he'd overheard on the train. His eyes followed the men as they went along the street. Burden's horse was short-striding, compensating for some problem--maybe a fetlock--that would soon give it more trouble, likely in its hips.

By mid-afternoon, the sky began to gray over and the weather returned to its earlier pattern. Heavy rain clouds boiled out of the northwest. Freezing wind rushed ahead of the coming storm, cutting into Mac's thin suit jacket.

He had two dollars and small change left, and toward evening ate a hand-out meal in the sanctuary of the small church where he'd met Sophia's friend, Elsie. When he saw Elsie serving food he almost turned and left, but instead sheepishly went through the short line and received his soup. When she saw him, she tore off a hunk of dry bread and her eyes bored into him as she handed it to him. "This is the body of Christ, given for you, boy."

He had no idea what she meant--possibly a joke only church people understood. He felt both a bit ashamed and irritated, like he ought to know something and she was trying to embarrass him because he didn't. After he'd eaten, a man from the church directed him to a place he might sleep, a tar-paper shed down a mud-wallow alley behind the church. The first two nights in Bismarck he'd stayed in one of the two hotels, but they charged fifty cents and he couldn't afford that any longer. Humbled that he had fallen so far, he remembered with a bit of shame how when checking in he'd tried to impress the desk clerk, had acted like a visiting swell from the city.

When he stepped inside the tar-paper shed he had to give a nickel to a nearly bald old woman with few teeth and a dollar-sized clump of gray fuzz on her cheek. "Don't be drinking in there," she snapped, "Or you'll be out in the cold and no excuses." She waved him into a back room where several older men, beaten looking, slept on darkly stained burlap bedticks. One of them snored like wagon chains being dragged over iron. Another whispered in his sleep and made vaguely imploring gestures toward the ceiling with one hand.

Heat from the woodstove was intense and magnified a stench of urine, unwashed men and dirty burlap. His impulse was to turn and leave, until he heard the wind moan outside.

He picked out the least stained bed tick and moved it to the far side of the room, then sat on the floor with his back against the wall and his knees drawn up. He had to do something, but didn't know what. He felt at war with his body--so anxious and tight he could hardly draw a breath.

As he grew drowsy in the overheated room his thoughts drifted to his parents, though he could only remember his mother's face so full of terror there in the cattail slough. He couldn't remember his father's face at all, though his aunt and uncle said he'd been killed in the slough just like his mother.

His parents were dead and his aunt and uncle didn't want him. Sophia was the only one he could trust. As he listened to the other men snoring he couldn't think of what might be next. He laid his cap in his lap and wiped his nose and eyes with his dirty shirt sleeve. He sat a long time before falling asleep, his palm upturned in his lap, lightly grasping the open locket.

Mac stayed in the flophouse for several nights. He had to buy a meal or two each day for the church wasn't always feeding people, and he wondered how long the church people would let him eat and not turn him away. So wet and cold, the air was raw each day. He passed groups of soldiers and civilians, all of them rushing about their business or laughing raucously in the muddy half-light under dark clouds and rain mixed with heavy snow flakes. As his money dwindled he felt like hiding from everyone and everything. His anxious fears increased.

He wandered muddy Bismarck, asked for work at the stable, the two dry goods stores, in the saloons and the train depot, all without good result. He remembered the man on the train, McGregor, who said he was leading a group of miners to the Black Hills. He asked around for him, but was told McGregor's group had left for Deadwood several days earlier. Mac hoped to find another wagon master who might be headed for the Black Hills, but nothing materialized. There seemed no way to get to Deadwood, and he was almost out of money.

Over the next few days he managed to get a couple of day labor jobs. He helped a man clean out a shed and load a wagon. The man's wife fed him a meal as he sat on the stoop of their small cabin. "Where you from?" she asked.

"I'm from St. Paul, ma'am." He wished people would mind their own business. All this talk made him feel like he had to earn his meal twice.

"What brings you to Bismarck? The army?"

The army! "No, ma'am." The army'd be the last thing; in fact he'd have to be starving. "I came here searching for my girl, but she's gone over to Deadwood." He put down the pie tin still half full of bread and beans, and took out his locket. "This is her."

The woman took it from him and looked at Sophia's picture. Her face flushed and she touched fingertips to her throat. "Very pretty," she said. "And the kindest soul, I'm sure."

With these day jobs, plus some handouts from local church people, he found he could shelter in the flop and have a couple of thin meals each day for about twenty-five cents, but his money was quickly running out.

After the better part of a week he'd gone through all but a dollar of his money. Rumors flew about the coming army expedition, and one day he heard that more supplies for the army had come to Bismarck's railhead. This was good, for several local traders needed men to help haul equipment and provisions to the cavalry and infantry forts that stood just across the Missouri River south of town.

He found a job loading wagons with one of the sutlers, and accompanied the man south along the shore road to the small ferry. They ferried the loaded rig across to the cavalry fort where he helped unload at the quartermaster's depot. The work was steady for several days, but though the man promised to pay him each day he never did.

Mac finally spent his last bit of money; he felt just about ready to explode with anxiety. In late afternoon as they left the fort and approached the small ferry to cross the river and return to Bismarck, he could stand it no longer. Trying to work up his courage in the face of growing panic, he nervously wiped at his mouth with his fingers. He didn't want to rile the man and lose the chance to work. But what good was work if you couldn't get paid and have something to eat and a place to sleep? He didn't know how he would live. Except for a few pennies his money was gone.

When he finally spoke his voice was a burst. "I've got to have you settle up with me today. I can't even pay for a burlap tick at the doss house tonight."

The sutler eyed him skeptically. "That ain't our agreement. I give you money now, you might not show up to work in the morning."

"I'll show up. I got to eat every day, don't I? I got to have a place to sleep."

"When I get paid you'll get paid."

"Hell, you said you'd pay me each day! I got to eat every day, you know, not just at the end of the week!" This fellow didn't care a whit about his problems.

The sutler leaned away from him, and looked at him from the corner of his eye. "You got plenty of tongue for a young squirt, that's for sure. But the army ain't going to pay me a penny until the goods're brought. Then I have to give 'em a bill. Then they pay slower than molasses drips in winter. I figured you knew that."

"How would I? I don't know this business."

"Well, you ain't going to be doing business with me any longer, neither, if you don't settle down. I don't like a man what gets too noisy."

"Well, I got to have some money or I'm going to be out in the cold tonight," he snapped. "I won't be no good to you if I'm froze to death somewhere."

"You ain't much good to begin with, sprout." The man leaned away and spit over the side of the wagon then flicked the reins at a swing mule that was hanging back in the traces.

Anger burned in him. "I been working hard and I've earned my money. Damn it, I want it."

The man looked at him. "OK, now. You get your ass off my wagon, before I open the side of your head."

"The hell I will!" He couldn't believe this. "You owe me nearly three dollars for the work I been doing." His anger was a powerful release. He felt like punching the man. In fact, he just might. He was fed up with everything going against him and he wasn't going to take this.

The man shifted the mules' reins to his left hand. He reached between his legs and picked up a battered ax handle then turned in the seat and positioned the club as though to strike Mac a backhand blow.

The man said, "Days to come, I got more goods to deliver. I guess I can figure out a way to get 'em loaded and unloaded on my own." He lifted his chin and his voice diminished to little more than a raspy whisper. "Now, you rattle your hocks off my wagon, boy. Just jump over the side 'cause I ain't slowing down."

Mac started to speak, but the driver drew back the club and lifted it slightly across his waist. Mac put out his hand in a gesture of forbearance and backed to the edge of the seat. He climbed down and jumped outward at the last second to avoid the big wheel that brushed him as it rumbled past through the mud.

"This isn't right!" he shouted. The man couldn't just threaten him and dump him out, give him nothing. "I been working for you. I deserve my money!"

The driver dropped the ax handle with a hollow thump then stood in a slight stoop with the reins in his left hand. He fished in his trousers pocket and pulled out a coin. He looked at it, and flung it at Mac.

It landed in the muddy road and Mac picked it up, wiped it against his trousers: a twenty-five cent piece. "You owe me more!" he yelled after the man. "Almost three dollars!" His heart sank and a deep humiliation filled him, as if he was just a victim to whoever came by.

The driver shouted, "Have a good swim and a walk back to town."

⌘

Not wanting to take the same ferry as the wagon driver, Mac walked back uphill to the cavalry fort and wandered alone amid groups of soldiers and civilian sutlers who laughed and cursed as they transferred goods from cargo wagons to the quartermaster's building.

Worry ate at him, but he began to look around. The cavalry fort had no timbered walls. It was just a series of long buildings set around a central parade ground. A quarter of a mile or so north on higher ground stood the infantry fort's palisades. But here rough-sawn lumber and uncut cottonwood trunks, rolled wire, nail kegs and other construction debris lay scattered amid the puddles from late spring rain.

The skinny, sickly looking Indians who hung around the fringes of the fort's economy unnerved him, for they brought back memories of the slough at Lake Shetek. Their children were seemingly immune to the chill, with stringy hair soaked by the cold rain. A few roamed naked in the cold, wandering among the soldiers, teasing half-starved feral dogs that roamed among the construction piles sniffing and growling and fighting over garbage scraps.

Ahead of him in the open stand of cottonwoods, an Indian woman tried to coax one of the half-wild dogs to her with a piece of pemmican. The animal crouched, its ears laid back, but it came toward her slowly, then backed away again. Once more it cautiously approached, quietly snarling, ready to spring away at her slightest threatening move. She squatted on her ankles, one arm extended across her knee. She dangled the piece of pemmican at the dog, teasing it, waiting.

He stopped at a distance and watched them, and as the dog lifted one forepaw to move forward she deftly grabbed its ear. The animal raged and yelped, tried to bite her, and thrashed away. But as she grabbed the scruff of its neck with her other hand, a knife appeared in her freed hand. The dog twisted and tried again to bite her wrist, but her knife hand moved and a gout of red burst from the animal's neck. It thrashed for long seconds then gradually became still.

Her face was hard and unreadable, but when she saw him watching, contempt bloomed on her face. She muttered, "Wasicu," then spat at him and walked away carting the dog by its rear legs. She lightly avoided the puddles in her bare feet and the animal's blood drained into the grass.

As the cloudy afternoon darkened he felt exhausted. Finding a quiet spot beside a huge old willow on the south side of the quartermaster's building, he lay on his back in the grass. He took the locket from his pocket and opened it, gazing at Sophia's picture, but after a minute or so his eyes became heavy and he dozed.

He was dragged from sleep by voices. Three soldiers ambled by. "Harding's ferry's been shut down. They got to winch 'er clear of the river and work on the hull."

"Well, damn, Blevins," another soldier laughed. "They ain't no trips to town nor the red-door house in your near future, 'less you're horny enough to swim."

Mac, still groggy with sleep, suddenly came awake with a shock, realizing the implication of what he'd heard. He was stuck on the wrong side of the river and couldn't get back to Bismarck without swimming. As he fingered the sutler's coin, anxiety engulfed him anew. From the high prairie beyond the wooded hillside, rain clouds began to stream in like a bitter surprise, and out past the fort's ragged buildings he suddenly heard sporadic gunfire. The reports were distant booms followed by faint echoes, but nobody seemed concerned. A sprinkle of rain began, then it started to rain more heavily.

Wet and cold, he looked about for shelter of some kind, then saw a huge willow tree. As he swept aside the willow's drooping branches he took a sharp breath in surprise, for other people had gathered there before him. A small group of Indians, five or six men and women and three small children, huddled beneath the broad limbs beside the massive trunk.

In the semi-dark beneath the great willow, they looked filthy and half starved, soaked by rain. He kept his distance. Among the group were two young boys he'd earlier seen roaming about the fort. Now they stood nearly naked in the rain, arms crossed over their skinny chests, watching him.

One of the older Indians nodded to him then spoke quietly to the others, but Mac couldn't understand what he said. Part of him believed they were not a danger, but a cold finger of fear still prodded his ribs.

35

It was people like these who'd killed his parents in the blood-soaked slough.

While growing up, he'd cried many a time for his mother and father, and though he remembered his mother's scream and the sound of her being struck, he hadn't seen her or his father killed. It had been Mrs. Duley and Mrs. Wright who'd told him they were dead.

Mac never again heard his father's voice after fleeing with his mother and the other whites to hide in the slough. No cry of pain or rage came from his father, no sound of struggle against his attackers. He never saw either of his parents' bodies. For a long time afterward--after the Indians forced the survivors to go with them and they joined with a larger band of Sioux, after their flight westward toward Dakota Territory, after the daily fears of imminent death, after the fierce arguments between Mrs. Duley and Mrs. Wright and their Sioux captors, after the horse soldiers finally came to the place he heard them call "Camp Release," after they all were taken back to Fort Snelling, after he'd gone to live with his mother's sister and her husband in St. Paul--he still couldn't make himself believe his father was dead.

Sometimes, overcome with misery, he wondered if his father betrayed them, left them alone in the slough to be killed while he went to safety. Mrs. Duley told him his father was shot early in the flight through the cattails, in a place that his aunt's yellowed newspaper clippings referred to as 'Slaughter Slough.' But he could never completely shake off the notion that his father was alive somewhere, living with the shame that he'd not been able to save his wife and son, so ashamed that he was unable to come and reclaim his only son from his in-laws.

It wouldn't matter how bad their bodies looked, he wished he'd seen them. He figured if he'd seen them he might not have had bad dreams all these years. He didn't know why, but he remembered the long walk into Dakota Territory with the Sioux. He remembered most clearly how the Indians were fearful that the army would come. They constantly argued among themselves and tried to figure out what to do next. He wanted to hate them, but something in him didn't allow it. Maybe it was the sober look in their faces, and the fear.

He glanced again at these people who shared the willow's shelter. They were poor and sickly looking, not a threat. Hunters had killed off most of the buffalo they relied on. A person would think they'd have had enough of white men without coming to the fort to knock around from pillar to post just looking to get by. But maybe all they could do now was to beg.

Their faces were different than whites' faces: placid and calm, as though thinking or merely observing. They didn't seem nervous or have eyes so restlessly focused like most white folks he knew. Their gaze seemed to probe the distance--as if in their quiet manner they saw things he could not. Even with these people so weakened that they had to hang around the fort, he felt shy around them, and somehow humbled.

When the rain subsided, he left the tree and returned to the quartermaster building where he'd seen several soldiers working earlier. He talked to a big-bellied quartermaster corporal who said he could sleep in a supply shed that night.

"The on'y way for y'all to heigh back to Bismarck is hike north and swim a bit of narrows west of town," the corporal said. But he didn't recommend it. "Some nights, Sioux bands--maybe two, maybe three men--sneak down off the prairie. The sonsuhbitches like to shoot at the boys in the sentry posts there on the rising land," and he gestured, intoning, "One old boy from the infantry fort was shot just last week. His right arm's all crippled up."

As the chatty corporal talked, Mac squinted at the hummocks and hills that rose westward from the river toward the higher plains. He wondered at the empty lands that lay beyond, and the Sioux who lived there.

The corporal brought him a tin of cold slumgullion and two blankets, then showed him a place to sleep inside a small supply shed. The rough-cut board walls were not caulked and though he wrapped himself in the two wool blankets, he shivered all night. He couldn't find a protected spot to escape the cold draft that moaned through the cracks.

When he did doze off, the same dreams came back. *Muck and water. So cold. It sucked at his legs as he lay half submerged curled on his side hugging himself. Mama's mud-spattered, terrified face...she shushed him to silence "Oh Lord--MacArthur! You must be silent or they will find us." She wrenched up fists full of cattail stems, reeds, mud--threw them on top of him. He squirmed and screamed "Mama!"*

For several years after the attack he had dreams in which his mother arrived at his aunt and uncle's home and took him away from them, dried mud from the slough still crusting her face, her pale blonde hair matted and black with drying blood. Waking from these dreams was agony, for his mother had shushed him, tried to quiet him, but he had cried out. She had waded back and slapped him, told him he must be quiet, but he was terrified, couldn't help calling to her again. So many times since, he'd been haunted by a terrible conviction that, because he'd called out to her, the young Sioux had found her and killed her.

The next day, the quartermaster's corporal brought him small portions of food in the morning and evening. The man exhibited a predatory look that he did little to conceal. With no place to clean up, and too little to eat, he felt overwhelmed with a sense of foreboding. Except for the quarter the sutler had thrown into the mud, his money was gone.

He and the corporal stood in the dusty supply shed where he had slept. Wind groaned through cracks in the rough board walls, and a kerosene lamp sputtered and smoked. The corporal's eyes were cautiously appraising. "Why not just go on back home," the man asked.

"It's too far," he said, "And I don't have money." With his finger and thumb he probed at a long sliver that festered beneath one of his fingernails. He'd not been able to remove the thing and the flesh around it was tender and red.

"Telegraph y'all's people for money. Ask 'em for help."

"I don't have folks, just an aunt and uncle. But I can't go back." He wanted the corporal to leave him be, yet he needed the food and shelter this man could provide.

"They'll let you come back."

"No. No, they won't." He felt a catch in his throat at this admission. He remembered his aunt and uncle's anger in bygone days when he was small, before he gradually became aware that his life was an intrusion on theirs. A short burst of hail slammed the shed, and cold drafts of wind carried a smell of horse dung and urine.

The corporal shook his head, "That's real sad." He paused, as though reflecting on the younger man's situation. "Maybe what y'all need is a special friend." He reached out and stroked Mac's forearm.

He flinched, pulled his arm back, and the soldier withdrew his hand.

"So," the corporal said, his eyes narrowing, "What y'all gonna do?"

Mac just looked through the open shed door at the gathering dark, spasms of hunger moving in his stomach, but he didn't answer. Another brief burst of hail pounded the shed.

"Well, you can't stay here no more. Somebody finds you, I'll be in the shit for certain." The corporal ran his hand across his stubbly chin. "If the army's letting in know-nothing foreigners what can't even speak English, they'd sure as hell take y'all."

He shook his head. "I need to get to Deadwood. I've got to see my girl there."

The soldier cast his watery eyes derisively up and down Mac's frame. "Deadwood's a long ways across wild country. And if y'all do get there, how you going to find her?"

"I'll find her. She's pretty much expecting me."

The corporal smirked. "Given y'all's situation, you might consider the army instead of the Black Hills."

He shook his head.

"Looks like that's all the options you got, so I wouldn't make no light of it. You got to be twenty-one."

"What do you mean?"

"Y'all probably ain't even twenty-one, are you?"

"I'm going to be eighteen."

The corporal chuckled. "You're a pretty wore-out lookin' eighteen. They'll probably believe you're thirty when you sign up." He spit on the raw plank floor. "They're gonna want five years from you." The corporal stared coolly at him until Mac dropped his eyes. The man stood aside, gesturing at the door. "Come on out. You got to leave."

He choked back a wave of anxiety. "Maybe one more night...."

"Now, or I'll be in trouble." The soldier handed Mac one of the two blankets. "Take this, but you never got it from me."

Silent, shamefaced, he took the blanket, rolling it loosely as he walked toward the door.

They stepped from the shed into falling sleet. "Understand one thing," the corporal said. "No matter what yuh may think, there ain't really none of us so different when we're cold and hungry and standin' in the snow." He grabbed at the large sliding bolt on the shed door and wiggled it, but it resisted. He pushed it hard, finally slammed it home with a grunt, then padlocked it. "And right now that's where y'all are standin'--out here in the snow."

Mac spent the night under the big willow tree with only the wool blanket and no food. At dawn he lurched anxiously awake, his body aching with cold. He clenched his fists, trying to warm them. Food and the bitterly cold morning were all he could think about. He wrapped himself in the blanket and walked aimlessly for a time, unable to make his hands stop shaking, unable to make up his mind, thinking, "But what other choice do I have?" An hour later, as if in a dream, almost without intention, he found himself standing in front of a sergeant responsible for shepherding new men through the enlistment process.

He knew he didn't look too good. He'd been cold and fearful during the night under the willow, not knowing who might show up if he chanced to shut his eyes too long. He possessed no clothes besides the ones he had on, and he'd worn them for days. He kept his trembling hands in his pockets.

The sergeant looked him up and down. "You sick, sonny?"

"Just tired and a little hungry--from traveling and all--but I want to join the army." His voice sounded reedy and hollow in his head. He felt lightheaded and didn't know if this was from hunger or because of awareness of what he was doing.

"We get lots of fellows when they're hungry. Sometimes they take the bounce after the first few meals. You going to do that?"

"No sir. I want to be in the army." He almost choked on the words.

"Umm. You got anything to show you're twenty-one?"

He couldn't meet the man's eyes. "No, but I am." He wondered how much the sergeant would grill him before they'd let him eat.

"If you join up, you're going to give us five years."

These words stabbed at Mac's soul, and when he heard his own hollow-sounding response it was as though someone else spoke. "Yes sir. Five years--I know that." He looked around, rubbed his forehead with the back of a dirty hand, trying to make the words mean nothing, as though someone else's life was being signed away for five years.

"You ever ride a horse, or shoot a gun?"

He bristled. "I've worked with horses all my life, and I hunt for food. I do guess I know how to shoot." The man was irksome with his questions and his knowing ways.

The sergeant gave a skeptical smile. "All right. You take this paper and go see Doc Porter for him to look you over and see you ain't got more than a few lice. Then come back here."

Mac went to the doctor, and after suffering pokes and prods and answering a few perfunctory questions, the doctor said, "You need some food and sleep, which you'll get. Then you'll be fine."

Because Mac said he knew horses, the sergeant assigned him to the Seventh Regiment of Cavalry rather than to the infantry fort on the hill. He and two other new men, an Irishman named Malachy Spellacy and a sheepherder named Leo Holley, were sworn in together and assigned to First Sergeant Edwin Bobo's C Company.

The Irishman had only been in America a month or two, and had come to Bismarck to find his father. He said that when he arrived here he learned his old man had already left for Nebraska to help start some Irish colony.

Holley had lost a few fingers to frostbite while hunting scattered sheep in the winter. His family had forced him out, he said. There had not been enough food for his little brother and newborn twin girls. He'd walked a couple of hundred miles up the Missouri River to enlist.

Mac quickly learned that together they'd be under the thumb of a buck sergeant named Thomas Wild--though he didn't seem to be a hard man, for his eyes were quiet as he looked them over. He appeared to be in his thirties, had dark hair and a droopy mustache.

"You men are grass-green," First Sergeant Bobo said, "And I want you to learn well from Sergeant Wild. Mark what I say; your lives will depend on what you learn from him."

After Bobo left, Wild told them, "We are what the army calls a "set-of-four." Three of us will fight whenever we have to go to ground, while the fourth man holds our horses. We'll live together on the expedition."

Mac was stunned. The expedition? He and the other new men had to go on that expedition to the west? He looked at the Irish soldier, whose face had turned quizzical. "Sergeant," the Irish soldier said, "If we're so 'grass-green' as Mr. Bobo said, are we not to get a bit o' trainin' before we go gallivantin' into wilderness?"

"There's no time," Wild said. "The expedition leaves in two days. You'll get some training along the way, probably from me," Wild said. "With considerable luck it might be enough to keep you alive." He grinned at them.

As the three of them walked with Wild across the parade ground to get their uniforms at the Quartermaster building, they saw two troopers with their ankles and arms bound. As they drew nearer, Mac was surprised to see that one of the two men was the orange-haired soldier, Burden, he'd seen on the train. The two sat in the middle of the parade ground, near one another but separately bound. Mac shuddered at the spectacle, for each had a short section of tree branch jammed behind his doubled-up knees. Each man's forearms were thrust down his sides and stretched behind the tree limb. Their wrists were bound to their ankles.

How long had they been left here? How long would they be kept here? His uncle had bound him and left him for hours at a time when he was younger, for one kind of misbehavior or another. He'd hated that and cried out at first. But eventually he'd quieted down, not wanting to give his uncle the satisfaction of hearing his screams of pent rage.

Burden sat staring with cold eyes into the middle distance, as though he didn't see Mac and the others passing by, as if his thoughts dwelt on matters far away. But the other man mumbled and sobbed, half out of his head, and smelled suspiciously like he'd messed his trousers. He spoke in a foreign language; Mac thought maybe German.

Wild said, "Those men are Burden and Gunther, both from our C Company. They don't seem to like each other, so they're bucked and gagged here for a few hours to let them cool off--and let others see it doesn't pay for a man to lose his temper in this regiment."

At the Quartermaster shed, the big-bellied corporal recognized Mac and grinned as he handed the men their uniforms. "You decided to come in out of the snow, eh?"

Mac said nothing.

The corporal walked over and stood close in front of him. "I was asking you a question, private." His breath was sour. "You best be answerin' a corporal when he talks to you. Hear?" As he was about to respond, Wild interceded.

"Back off, Sanders, and get these men set up. We've got a lot of work to do to get them ready to travel."

The corporal sneered. "Hey, you bet, Wild. I know you got a world of work to do to get this one ready. He looks a mite blue around his gills."

Wild walked up beside Mac as the corporal went back to his work. "He's right, Durant. You need to answer a noncom when he talks to you."

"Sorry." He felt a spark of gratitude to the sergeant for helping him out of a humiliating situation, but would've liked to say to the corporal, "I don't like being talked down to like that." He didn't relish taking orders from anybody, let alone some pot-bellied fool with two stripes on his arm. He might be in a bad situation right now, but he didn't like such treatment.

Wild took them to get horses. From long habit Mac's eyes ran over the animals in the herd, looking for one most able and healthy. But he had no choice in the matter. Three of C Company's sorrels were cut from the remuda and led one-by-one to Malachy, Holley and him. As his gelding was led toward him he saw with relief that the animal was a good one. It was short backed with a strong hip and moved with spirit. As the horse drew near he felt a bit of warmth bloom within himself, for the gelding had a soft eye.

They stabled their animals and brushed them down. Mac wiped around the gelding's eyes and talked softly to it. When they had finished and were about to leave the stable, he looked out at the parade ground and the formed-up companies of troopers marching past and gave a shudder of anguish. How could he have allowed himself to be so badly caught? He looked at the gelding, stroked its upper lip. Its lips wiggled and twitched, and it nickered softly. When Wild finally called them away, he felt pained to leave the horse there.

He and Malachy and Holley were given some sowbelly and a couple pieces of hardtack. Afterward he felt he would throw up, but fought to hold it down, not wanting to vomit in front of Wild and the two other new men.

In C's barracks, though a couple veteran troopers sneered at them as though they were just fresh meat, most of the older men ignored the three of them. This was a mixed blessing, for while Mac wanted to talk to no one, he acutely felt the mixture of scorn and indifference. He didn't belong here. Worst of all, nobody but himself had put him in this position.

His head hurt badly and he felt dizzy, as though he'd been struck in the face, and his throat had a sharp lump in it that gradually flattened to a dull ache. That night he couldn't rid himself of the image of the two soldiers bucked and gagged on the parade ground. The pained indignity of it. He remembered the impotent rage and humiliation he'd felt when tied up by his uncle. Then he recalled the remoteness of Burden's face, its cold calm.

As he lay coiled tightly beneath his blankets, Mac looked around at the darkened barracks. Torment filled him. Bile rose into his throat and he swallowed, felt he might vomit. For the sake of a few meals he'd signed away five years of his life. How would he ever find Sophia now? He lay a long time in the darkness listening to the other men's snores, then flinched when someone nearby cursed loudly in his sleep. His anguish was the worst he could remember.

The next morning, Wild told the three of them that the expedition might be out a month or two. "We're part of a three-pronged effort to find Sioux and Cheyenne who've left their reservations, and we've got to force their return. Besides us, two other large units of cavalry and infantry will start from Wyoming and Montana Territories. We'll all work our way toward each other. Our expedition is led by General Terry and will head west beyond the Little Missouri River into Montana Territory." They would cross the valleys of the Tongue and Powder Rivers, perhaps go even further west to the Big Horn Mountains. He said not many whites had been in the valley of the Powder before.

Mac glanced at the others. He didn't know about them, but he wasn't at all keen about traveling to such a wild place.

Later, Malachy found another man in C who had a map of the region they would search. He brought it back to show Mac and Holley, saying, "The fellow said this map is a bit wobbly as these things go, for 'twas done by army surveyors ten or twenty years ago."

Mac looked at him gloomily. "I don't care to know anything about that country."

Malachy and Holley looked at each other. "You don't got to be so daunsy, Mac," Holley said. "The good Lord wants a fellow to think about where he's goin'."

Mac snapped, "I don't figure he cares, or even knows one way or other where we're headed, Holley." He didn't have an interest in the project, but had to devote himself to thinking about how he could get out of it. "I don't want anything to do with any Indians." He thought of Mrs. Duley and Mrs. Wright arguing with their Sioux captors so long ago--yet it seemed like yesterday. "I had my fill of them."

Holley opened his mouth to say something, but Mac snapped, "I don't want to talk about it either."

He quickly learned that many of the other soldiers were new recruits, not just Malachy and Holley and him. Some had received training at Jefferson Barracks in Missouri before being sent to Fort Abraham Lincoln, but many others had arrived here on the Northern Pacific only in the last few days. Another group had walked behind a mounted recruiting sergeant for several hundred miles, all the way from Fort Snelling. Mac was glad he hadn't been one of those foot-sore sons of guns.

Many new men were immigrants. Some couldn't speak English, and some couldn't even sit a horse if it moved faster than a walk. During the parade before the expedition departed the fort, he saw a recruit fall from his mount, much to the amusement of other soldiers in his troop. All this seemed unreal and fearful--like men and boys play-acting as soldiers, yet embarked into wilderness to face who knew what hardship and danger. He shook his head, anguished that he was so tightly caught.

He felt confused and anxious about what might come, but wasn't in a muddle about one thing: he wanted out. If they thought he was serious about staying around five years and learning to kill Indians they had another think coming. Others of a bloodier mind would have to handle all that.

Another headache entirely was Leo Holley. The slow-talking, Bible-banging sheep chaser was dumb as a post. Holley stood well over six feet, but was skinny. He looked mostly like a sack of sticks with knobs. Tangled dark hair fell over his forehead and for some reason Mac couldn't fathom, the man's pale-green eyes--so placid and dull-- aggravated him sorely. He couldn't believe it at first, but Holley actually loved the army's food, was always hungry, even though as often as not the bacon was wormy. Holley told him, "It don't matter, Mac. Them little worms get cooked up good, and it all comes out the same."

Holley even relished plain hardtack, though it sometimes had bugs in it--and it was about as tasty as a wood shingle. He was a moocher too, always looking at a man's tin plate and wanting a bite of something a fellow might like to leave himself to eat later. But the sheepherder's Bible-thumping was by far the worst part of him.

That evening, with the expedition due to depart the next day, they almost had a fight. Mac opened his locket and looked forlornly at Sophia's picture. Malachy asked, "Who's that, Mac, your girl?"

Reluctantly he showed the tintype to the Irishman, then to Wild and Holley. Malachy said, "She's a fine looking woman, Mac," but the others acted more subdued, not what Mac had expected. Wild's reaction was completely unreadable; he just nodded to acknowledge the picture.

"The good Lord don't allow dresses like that on women where I come from," Holley said.

"What do you mean?" Mac snapped. He felt his face redden, and this betrayal by his own body angered him further for he wanted these men to know about him only what he chose to tell. "I don't know where you were grown, Holley, but I expect a dress like this is all the fashion." He thought of Sophia in the gazebo, laughing with him as they watched her peacock strut about and awkwardly run at one of her cats. She had laughed and reached out and touched his hand, and he thought now of her goodness.

"I'm from Yankton village, right here in the Dakota Territory. But her dress"--he pointed at the picture--"Is a contrivance of Satan. He uses such things to make us fall."

He sputtered, "I don't know where you got that, Holley, but you can keep it to yourself." He was conscious of the Sergeant and the Irishman watching. "Or you could get some broken teeth." He'd never hit anyone before, but if this sheepherder aggravated him enough he just might.

Holley looked calmly at him. "I expect someone would have to work hard to mash my teeth, and I don't think it is you, Mac."

"Bullshit, Holley. You're so skinny you got to stand up twice to make a shadow. You'd have about as much chance with me as a chicken at a coyote convention."

Holley's face fell, and both placation and disappointment were in his voice. "You needn't ought to swear, Mac. Cursing disheartens a man."

He figured it was useful to know how Holley could be made disheartened. "You shoulda' stayed with your damn' sheep back wherever."

"That's enough, you two," Wild interjected. "Holley, it'd probably be best if you kept your religious ideas to yourself. And Durant, you can stop with the threats. You wouldn't like to be bucked and gagged-- maybe even lashed."

Holley said quietly, "Respecting your rank, Sergeant, but the Lord's word needs telling, not hiding."

Wild shrugged, then turned to study Mac's tintype again, "She's a fine looking woman, Durant. I can tell you're real proud of her. But you won't be laying eyes on her for a while."

Malachy interjected softly, "And how old is Sophia, Mac? Is she back home waiting for you?"

All desire to talk about her had gone out of him and he grumbled, "No, Malachy. That's why I came here--to look for her. She's gone over to Deadwood on some business and wrote me, asking me to come." This Irish soldier was curious about everything. He came up with so many questions Mac wanted to plug the man's mouth with a wad of sacking so he could have some silence.

He darn' sure didn't want to be in anybody's set-of-four, and stuck with people like these, to boot! Yet here he was, with no elbow room at all. He'd rather lose himself for the time being, remain silent and anonymous among the sixty-odd men in C. He'd pick up the minimum know-how to get through each day, then leave the army behind for good at the first opportunity. He just had to get a little organized first.

⌘

Leo Holley lay beneath his blanket in the barracks listening to the other men snore. He hadn't been around so many people at one time in all his life, not even when the family went to Yankton village to sell sheep or produce. After the new twins came, his father talked about Leo going into the army. "Maybe you wouldn't have to do much walking if you joined that cavalry up to Fort Lincoln, that one what rode through Yankton a couple years back."

His parents had his older brother who couldn't talk or feed himself, but he still had to be fed, and now those new twins. He knew they had to get shed of him for the sake of enough to eat for all the rest, so he had prayed to the good Lord that the army would let him in even with the two frostbit fingers missing from his left hand. He knew his mother was concerned.

"Them fingers come in handy for camp work and such," she said, looking doubtfully at his father. "They might want a man to have all ten."

But his father shook his head. "You got you your thumb and two fingers what can hold up a rifle barrel. I expect them's the necessaries. And you ain't shot much before you got the frostbite, so they'll learn you some shooting. Just remember to say that you're right handed, boy. That shouldn't make no difference when you pull a trigger."

He thought to remind his father that he'd always favored his left hand for doing, but thought better of it. He had to go away and didn't want to bother the point. But it was a painful prospect, for the sod dugout was warm and he smelled that bread cooking. He nodded and forced a smile. "I do believe the cavalry is a sound notion. I'll walk on up to Bismarck and become a soldier."

"That's well," his father said. "You're a good walker, boy, and it's a far piece. But once you get there, it'll be easy. They put you on a horse and it carries you right along." He smiled encouragingly and nodded.

The next morning his mother put some bread and two cooked potatoes in a piece of old apron and wrapped it up for him. She waved to him from the dugout doorway as he and his father departed. Together they walked a long way up-river on a game trail, then part-way up a long bluff. Finally, he saw that his father had become winded, so he said, "I got to rest a minute. I got me some spent air."

They said their goodbyes, and he thought his father looked a bit sad at their parting, so he said, "I certainly am looking to serve the Lord as a soldier. I am for certain looking forward to it."

They went their separate ways, but after some more minutes of climbing, he stopped to check the painful thorn that for days had been festering in his bare foot. Looking back down the game trail, he squinted against the sunlight reflected on the Missouri's muddy waters. Far away, his father's small form shuffled toward home. Since the twins came along, his shoulders had become more rounded, and he carried his head down under the weight of new worries. As he watched him go, he hoped that now his father had a little less burden to carry.

Turning northwestward, he squinted at the shadowed river breaks that spread before him toward the horizon. As he began to climb, he wished he could see beyond that horizon to know what would come. It'd be maybe two weeks or more to cover the two hundred miles to the soldier fort. So far, not much in life seemed to be just a short distance off. At the bluff top he turned once more, his eyes searching the vastness for his father, but the landscape had swallowed him up and he was gone. He gave a sigh and gulped at the lump in his throat as he walked down the long slope toward the next bluff. His foot hurt and he wondered what he'd eat when the two potatoes and the bread gave out.

⌘

Late the next morning, as the twelve horse companies left the fort to join up with the expedition's other elements, the band music and rough pageantry of the regimental parade stirred Malachy Spellacy's heart. The day was cloudy and cool. A ground fog gradually overfilled the ravines and slowly drifted along the hillside meadows that rose from the river bottom toward the high prairie.

He'd never ridden a horse until he enlisted two days ago. Now, as the big column moved up the broad hillside toward the high prairie, he was constantly on guard, fearing his horse would veer in one direction while he himself might tilt in another. He wondered if his saddle was cinched tightly enough.

He felt moved by the families waving good-bye, and the barking dogs and such, but he had to ride beside Mac and that ruined a bit of the spectacle, for the man was wearing a long face--a poor bit of gray sausage he was. In the two days he and Mac and the sheepherder, Leo Holley, had been in the army, Mac hadn't said a sociable word. Plain to see he did not wish to be here.

Perhaps he would be one of those soldiers he'd heard about who'd tire quickly of the army and decide to take French leave when no one was lookin'. Malachy hated to think so, for it was important to find some wee bit of goodness in any man's makeup. If a fellow couldn't do that, he got to feeling discouraged, found it hard to find toleration or mercy anywhere close about.

But he'd already found the nib of good in Mac Durant; the man did sit his horse quite well. For a fact far better than himself, or Holley either. And it was clear Mac's horse already liked him, for the animal perked up whenever he came round.

C Company trailed the larger cavalry regiment as it joined with the expedition's other elements in the high meadow and all began to move out. Because C Company brought up the muddy rear, Malachy saw everything spread out before him. Thick ground fog made a strange scene. The whole expedition looked as if it were riding up a bank of clouds into the sky, the white fog curling around its flanks.

Parallel columns of heavy wagons formed the central part of a body of horse troopers and infantry that stretched for nearly a mile. A hundred-forty Studebaker wagons with six-mule teams carried food and clothing, horse fodder, bridge-building equipment, farrier supplies, tents, cooking gear; the good Lord knew what all.

Horse-drawn Gatling guns and Rodman guns preceded the wagons, and ahead of these trudged companies of infantry. Behind the whole squirming array rode civilian drovers on contract to the army. Malachy heard them whistling and howling at the beef herd in such a way as to make one's backbone shiver. As security to all the other elements, the twelve cavalry companies were distributed to the larger body's front and rear and flanks. "For certain, you Americans carry such a lot of cargo," Malachy said to no one in particular.

Several miles ahead, far to the left and right of the expedition, small groups of contracted Arikara and Crow Indians and white civilian scouts felt their way westward. They rode periodically back to the column to report. Malachy was glad he was not a scout, for their work looked lonely and precarious.

The whole body of men and animals and wagons and gear seemed like a huge, unwieldy organism. He wondered how it would look if seen from the sky, for the expedition had a certain splendor--full of human swagger and gritty determination. Malachy said to Mac, "The expedition's parts bulge and clank and bunch and stretch like some great centipede just born to the prairie and struggling to get four thousand legs beneath it."

Mac looked at him incredulously. "I don't see how you get a big bug out of this. It's just a grim bunch of business."

It surprised Malachy to hear so many words at once from the man, but he felt exuberant at the sight that had unfolded before them. "This must be the way Rome's legions looked as they hacked their way across Europe's plains and forests, and headed for England and Ireland back in the hidden times."

"I don't know about all that," Mac said glumly, shaking his head. They rode silently for several minutes. When Malachy saw Mac reach backward and scratch his horse just above the tail and the animal flicked it, he smiled and felt faintly heartened by the dour man's gesture toward his horse.

Malachy stopped trying to talk with him, but just watched the expedition proceed, thinking maybe this was the way all armed men rode out of the mist at the dawn of a new regime, before time passed and their kind lost confidence, began to foresee their own end--and so through their uncertainty brought about the very thing they most feared.

He didn't know why, but such a somber thought made him think of his mother back in Ireland. Tchh. Stone cold she was, there in her grave, not even knowing he'd gone off to America and become a soldier.

⌘

Mac had found the big parade and band music both pompous and aggravating. The big column departed late after that hullabaloo, so they'd not traveled far that first day, and this evening the mules were restless and couldn't settle down.

To his considerable mental pain, in addition to the noisy mules, the day's events had also energized Malachy. By the time the two of them finally crawled into their dog tent Mac was ready for sleep, but the Irishman was wide awake. He was too damned curious, had questions about everything. Mac had to admit he'd encouraged and prolonged the man's chatter by talking about himself--something he would never

51

have been tempted to do if Malachy hadn't started it by sharing a bit of trader's whiskey he'd brought with him from the fort.

Mac felt a bit of sympathy when Malachy told him about coming from Ireland to look for his father after his mother had been killed by stones falling from the roof of the family's church. He'd arrived only to learn that two years earlier his father had gone off on a whim to help found an Irish colony in Nebraska. Malachy's stories and the whiskey--which made Mac hot around the eyes--had loosened his tongue, and when Malachy expressed wonderment about Indians they might run onto, he said, "If I never see any Indians again it'll be too soon."

"And why might that be?"

"When I was three, my parents were killed by Indians in a war back in Minnesota. I was their captive for a couple months." He knew the instant he said this that he'd made a mistake, for Malachy pummeled him with questions until he finally shut him off by saying he didn't want to talk about it anymore. He just wanted sleep, and didn't want to have nightmares.

Then Malachy wanted to know why some troopers rode mules instead of horses, and was it true a mule could outwork two horses? And he'd heard an astonishing fact: over a couple of weeks infantry could travel farther than cavalry, but it made no sense that a man on foot could out-tramp a horse.

This went on until he thought he might suffer an affliction from all the noise in his ears. When the questions didn't stop he finally snapped, "Damn it, Malachy. How do I know? Go ask one of the damn' mule whackers. Let a man sleep."

Though Malachy was amiable, and his questions seemed reasonable for a foreigner, Mac was thinking about how he could get back to Bismarck, and whether he had to worry about meeting some of those Indians who approached the fort at night and shot at the sentries. He didn't know what he'd do for food when he got to Bismarck, and he wondered if the army would send men after him. Even if he found another way to get to Deadwood, what if Sophia wasn't there? All these things set him to worrying.

The Irishman finally fell asleep and Mac was left alone to ponder. He had to get his thinking straight, for he didn't care to visit the places this expedition planned to travel, but unless he acted quickly he'd be stuck. If he waited longer, he'd have further to travel back, and the Sioux might be glad to see him running around alone out there. It was discouraging. He never should've come out to this foreign land, but just stayed back in the states and figured out a better plan to get to Sophia.

He didn't know; maybe even now there were bands of Indians just beyond the low hills to the west. Or maybe they were already on the back trail sniffing at the expedition's leavings. He shuddered at this notion, regretting he hadn't taken off when he had first filled his stomach back there at Fort Lincoln.

An excerpt from her father's letter:

…The beginning of the journey was terribly hard, and I let it spook me badly. I made a wrongheaded mistake that cost me for a long time among these other men. It could've taken me down, but luckily it did not.

MAY 1876: WESTERN DAKOTA TERRITORY

The next morning, as C Company came up to the Heart River, Mac saw that getting the wagons and beef herd across would be a nightmarish quagmire. Water at the ford was four to five feet deep and C Company was assigned as pioneers to break down the muddy banks into gentler grades to and from the ford. As noncoms organized the work, he stood with Malachy and Holley and gazed into the murky water, watching a tree branch drift sluggishly northward on the current.

First Sergeant Bobo yelled, "All noncoms, have your sets grab shovels and picks and start in along here." He pointed along a vertical cut bank about five feet in height that had been created by earlier floods.

Mac groaned and Malachy winked at him, saying, "Mac, laddy. Don't you be shy about pitchin' in now. This'll get us in good shape for the next thousand such jobs, all of 'em certain to be fine examples of courageous soldierin' if I do say so."

They stripped off their shirts and went to work in the rain. Wild had the set accompany twenty other soldiers as they waded across the river to break down the far bank. Troopers from other companies cut and trimmed cottonwood and ash limbs and smaller brush for a corduroy road strong enough to support the heavy Studebakers with their six-mule teams.

But as the wagons lumbered into the water, crossed the ford and tried to ascend from the river onto the west bank, even with the engineering effort that had preceded them, some mule teams found the ascent too steep. It was miserable. He and Malachy, along with groups of thirty to fifty men each, hauled on ropes lashed to each wagon's tongue, and by sheer force helped drag the heavily laden cargo schooners, mules and all, up the corduroyed bank. The branches and limbs of the corduroy road constantly shifted and broke and needed repair. Wagons repeatedly became stuck in the mire.

Horses and mules sank to their fetlocks and one mule's hoof slipped between the shifting ribs of the cottonwood roadbed. The animal's pastern was crushed and Mac looked up when he heard it scream. A civilian skinner in a ragged hat stepped up and unharnessed the animal then pulled it from the line. He pointed his revolver down into the mule's ear and fired. Another mule was brought up and put into harness.

The Irish soldier, Malachy, looked grim, but then winked at Holley and said, "See what's in store for a man if he comes up lame in this caravan?"

Even the civilian skinners had trouble getting their smaller supply wagons to the other side. Hours later, by the time the crossing was completed, Mac was exhausted and covered with mud. The cattle came up next, but some of them saw the dead mule and resisted crossing. A number drifted north and south along the shore, or turned to double back into the herd. But, pressed from behind by their fellows, they tumbled from the higher banks into the river. Two of them broke legs as they fell down the bank. They were hauled out, skinned and butchered.

The drovers and their charges were spent when they finally completed the chaotic crossing, but had to continue fighting to keep the cattle moving through the rain and mud.

After the troublesome crossing of the Heart, he watched the long lines of canvas-covered wagons, infantry, cavalry and drovers move their burdens westward. A panicky feeling started to bloom in his mind, and as each hour passed he felt more fully caught inside this alien creature made of human and horse flesh, bawling cattle, clanking metal and creaking leather.

He wasn't obligated to these people or to the expedition. Hadn't he only joined to keep from starving? Five long years stretched before him, as if forever. And how many times would he be stuck with picks and shovels in the mud, and who knew what else? It was a sentence to hell. Unless he acted quickly he'd be trapped in the wilderness with no way to get to Sophia. He might never find her again.

Once they'd settled in camp, exhausted, he heard the headquarters wagons had milometers on them that measured their travel. They'd only covered five miles that day, which was fine with him for it made his hike back all that much shorter. Yesterday they'd gone only fourteen miles so maybe less than twenty miles separated him from Bismarck and freedom.

Couldn't he walk and run that distance pretty easily? Four days of army life was enough, being told to go here and go there and do this and that, and working in the rain with shovels and all. Backbreaking toil in heavy mud that stuck to your clothes and boots, noncoms shouting and kicking at your nether parts if you lost a step or stopped to get a breath: he wasn't going to take it.

He was in a near frenzy to get away from this tangled trap. He knew others already were thinking about it, too. When they finally set camp that afternoon he overheard Burden advising another man on a possible escape. "When you scarper don't take nothing, and I mean nothing that belongs to the army. Those sonsuhbitches in the Sibley tents'll chase a man clear to Chicago just because he took off with a carbine and a horse."

Burden suddenly looked over at Mac. "Whiskey boy, if you're planning to scoot too, then you better listen. Years back, I was down in Kansas at Riley when a bunch took French leave in broad daylight with all their gear. They chased 'em down, shot some and hung the rest. So hear what I'm sayin': don't take nothing. But if you're gonna go, you better go soon."

He fought back panic, realizing that for him it had to be tonight. If he waited longer, this whole misguided mess would be so far out on the plains the distance would be too great to retrace his path to the Missouri River. They didn't care a whit about a man, and he'd be stuck for months, might never find Sophia again.

She clearly needed his help, and obviously wanted to rekindle their relationship, though he had to reread her letter at least daily to be reassured of her desires. It made him sick to think of how he had badly complicated his journey to find and help her, and claim her for himself.

The huge encampment spread for at least a half mile along what he'd heard was Sweet Briar Creek. The column's left and right wings were arrayed in long rows of facing tents set back from each side of the sluggish creek, which had swollen beyond its banks from the recent rain. Flanking each tent row was a double column of Studebaker wagons that stretched several hundred yards. The long line of cooking fires threw flickering light against the dog tents and wagons' white canvas, and turned the stream's cold water to pale fire.

Pickets were set out for the night just beyond the camp perimeter, while mounted vedettes rode still further out. Mac watched several of these small guard detachments depart into the twilight, but he paid particular attention to those that headed out east along the column's back trail in the direction of Bismarck. As evening darkened, he bided his time, watching the comings and goings of other men who meandered around the cooking fires after the evening meal of bacon and tack.

The cattle herd and remuda, with night guards, grazed off to the south on rising ground. Each company's horses had been strung on long ropes between the two columns of Studebakers. Somewhere along C Company's rope line stood the pretty sorrel mare he'd been issued days earlier, though he couldn't pick her out now in the quickly passing twilight. She was a pacer with a strong, single step gait, and he hated to leave her behind, but he didn't want to give them even a skimpy reason to chase him down. He'd take a bit of sow-belly, hard tack and water, and his overcoat. No bedroll, no gutta-percha, no Springfield or Colt-- nothing of his other gear, nothing of any value.

He'd heard Burden mention a sutler named Henriks in Bismarck who for a price supposedly helped men escape, though he had not a penny. He planned to cover the distance to the river by traveling through this night, and hole up during daylight until tomorrow night. He'd skirt north of the fort, swim the river, then walk into Bismarck. Beyond that he didn't know what else to do. Riders from here, likely a couple of the Crow scouts, would carry a mail pouch back to the fort in a few days, and they'd report him gone. He wanted to think he'd just be allowed to go on his way, but, possibly, soldiers from the fort would go looking for him in Bismarck. His plan was a slim reed to lean on, but he couldn't think about that now. He just had to get away from this trap he'd so haphazardly entered, and he had to find Sophia.

Later, though his clothes and boots were still wet and muddy, he kept them on. He lay on his belly beneath his blanket in the dog tent he shared with the Irishman. Chin on his hands, he gazed through the tent flap at the orange embers of the sleeping camp's fires. A mosquito buzzed near his ear and he moved his hand deftly, crushed it against his cheek. From down the row of dog tents came rasps of men snoring. One moaned twice and called out indistinctly. The light breeze brought a sniff of cold sowbelly and wood smoke as moonlight softly flared then dimmed behind slow-drifting clouds.

Finally, he glanced at the Irish soldier who breathed softly beside him, rose slowly to a crouch, picked up the forage bag and overcoat, and stepped through the open tent flap. He glanced once at the next dog tent where the sheepherder and buck sergeant slept, then strode off between two big Studebakers and away from the camp.

Moving quickly, but bent over, he aimed at a point about a hundred yards east. He thought it half way between what he remembered were two picket positions. His heart was pounding like a steam piston, but once he had passed through that point he stood straighter and picked up his pace, took deep breaths to calm himself.

He almost stepped on the sentry. The man spun around, jerking his Springfield up, "Halt! Jesus!" They stood staring, frozen in front of each other.

"Shit!" Mac snapped. His neck pulsed and his face flushed hot. He lifted his arm to the right. "I thought you were off that way."

The sentry snapped, "The guard sergeant moved us, damn it." He lowered his carbine. "What the hell you doing, sneaking around? Scared the bejesus out of me!"

"I can't sleep. I'm just taking a walk." He had seen this old man earlier in the day. Though he was stooped and his hair was white, he was still only a private in C Company's ranks.

The trooper looked him over skeptically. "Well, go back to camp and walk, goddamn it, or one of us'll shoot you in the ass." Then his eyes fell on Mac's forage sack. "You skedaddling, ain't you?"

Mac looked past him. "No, I just need to walk so I can get some sleep."

"I expect you're thinking to sleep in Bismarck." The old man's voice softened a bit. "You're making a mistake, sonny, and you'll regret it. They'll hunt you down. You'll spend time in the stockade. This outfit's on a war footing now, and you could even be shot or hung."

The old man's kindly tone made Mac's throat ache, and for a moment he couldn't answer the charge. But then, "I'm just going for a few minutes. Shoot me, or whatever you need to do."

"I ain't going to shoot you, boy. I know you. You're in Bobo's C Company, just like me. You're green for certain, but this all will get easier as we go along. It's too quick that you're running for home."

"I have no home and I'm not running for it." The old man's assumptions angered him, especially because they were true. "Why don't you mind your own damn' business? Just turn me in, if you've a mind to!"

The old man snorted, chuckling. "Sonny, I'll pull your nose if I've a mind to."

He wasn't going to take any more of this. His anxiety was pumping; he needed to get going. "You won't pull my nose! Just do what you need to. I'm headed out," and he stepped past the old trooper.

"Well, son of a bitch," the old man said. He shook his head. "I damn' sure will."

Mac kept walking, swung the forage sack over one shoulder and stiffened his back, waiting for the old man's shout to the Sergeant of the Guard. But the shout didn't come and he kept walking, following the broad torn track over which the expedition had come. He stumbled over a rut, fell to his knees in the mire, got up, moved to the side of the muddy back trail and kept heading east.

Then, by sheer good fortune, the breeze dropped for a moment and he heard a horse nicker softly somewhere ahead of him. He dropped to his knees then bent forward and scanned the land ahead. He had no weapon, but thought about the Lakotas who at night periodically snuck down from the high prairie and shot at the fort's sentries. Maybe there were Indians sniffing along the column's back trail, foraging or just observing. He quieted his breathing, tried to think.

Then he saw the horse and rider in a low swale about a hundred yards ahead and to his left, just standing. In the moonlight he could see it was one of the vedettes. He looked around, backtracked a ways and circled downwind of the rider so the horse wouldn't smell him. That detour cost him fifteen minutes or so, then he hurried onward. And as he went, his tension slipped away and he felt giddy, nearly drunk with the idea that he had made it, had broken loose. He wanted to cry out in jubilation at being free after having made such a weak and perilous mistake.

He had to find and help Sophia and wanted nothing to do with the army, had no grudge against Indians, though they'd killed his parents in the Minnesota War. For certain, the Indians the army was after weren't the same ones who'd made him an orphan. They could go about their business for all he cared, and he didn't even like the idea that the government would chase them all over and cage them up. Besides, his uncle hated Indians, and anything that man was against he was for.

Mac recounted these things as he trotted for a time, then walked then trotted again, moving east beneath drifting clouds and moonlight.

He hitched the forage sack higher on his back, and told himself he was finally moving ahead, and in the right direction. He was nearly free of the army, just as weeks before he had made himself free of his uncle and aunt. He put his hopes on finding Sophia, giving her the help she needed, just as in her letter she obviously hoped he would do. She would care as she had before, and they would be together.

Still, a small current of sadness bled through him along a well-worn channel that had been eroded long ago. A hectoring notion sometimes plagued him; it seemed that life was running him in a circle over rough ground where he repeatedly stumbled and fell, then had to get back up.

Just as now: he tripped over a muddy rut and fell into the muck of the expedition's road. He picked himself up, spit out a bit of mud. He began to trot, but then stopped suddenly. Stifling a breath, he listened. The trailing breeze that had helped him onward brought a familiar sound.

Somewhere behind him, not far, he heard the muddy three-beat of a horse's gait. He listened. It was coming closer, at a slow canter.

⌘

Sergeant Thomas Wild came awake when he felt a tug at his blanket and boot nudged his foot. He'd been dreaming of tracking an animal in the snow with his father long ago while still a boy.

"Thomas, wake up."

He went up on an elbow, grimacing as he pressed a finger and thumb into his eyes. "What is it?" His cousin, First Sergeant Edwin Bobo, said, "We've got a trooper who's run off. One of your new boys. Durant."

"Damn! When?" He'd have bet money this would happen.

"About twenty minutes ago. He went out past Cornelius Blosser's post. Headed east."

Wild yawned and stretched, sat up. "Back to Bismarck."

"Only if he has a brain for survival."

"With him that's still an unanswered question." He looked up at Bobo. "I'll go get him."

"No, Thomas." Bobo glanced at the private sleeping in the dog tent beside Wild. "But come outside."

Wild looked at the sheepherder, Leo Holley, still asleep like a stone, undisturbed by Edwin's intrusion. Among the three recruits assigned to his set, at least this one didn't snore or toss around before he slept.

He pulled on his trousers and field shirt, then his boots. This stage of an expedition was often when new men took the bounce, regretting their decision to enlist and seeing nothing ahead but the hardships and dangers of the field. And this time it'd been made worse on their first day out with that nightmare crossing of the Heart River, a five-hour long, muddy melee.

Wild stood up through the tent flap. "Edwin, that Heart River crossing yesterday was a tax on everyone. When Durant showed up to enlist he was filthy and gaunt from hunger. Now his belly's full, and he's not thinking. Clearly he's several years too young to enlist. No use in us--or the officers--killing the kid."

Bobo's face was skeptical. "I looked him over. He can't look a man in the eye and hasn't said ten words to anybody. He's a lost one, I think. Better that he's gone."

"You remember Kansas and the common method, Edwin. If the command chases him and brings him back, it'll go hard on him. At the very least they'll buck and gag him until he shits himself and goes crazy." He pulled out his pocket watch. "I've got four hours before the wakeup at 3:00. Before Reno or Custer or the others wake. I'll go out through old Cornelius Blosser's post."

"But we'd have to discipline him, and while we're on the march."

"Wait a minute." Wild ducked down at the entrance to Durant's tent and saw the young Irish soldier, Malachy Spellacy, snoring softly. Durant's revolver and carbine were beside his blanket. "Edwin, he's left everything. He has no weapons."

Bobo looked at him. "Cousin, I know why you want to do this."

"You gave me a new chance once, Edwin."

Bobo shook his head. "That was different, after the war and all."

"I would've died."

"You had done nothing wrong, Thomas, and everything right. But this boy… I don't remember ever being his age."

Wild grinned. "You were never young, cousin."

"No, perhaps not," Bobo said, making a dismissive gesture with his hand. "Gather your horse and I'll get the Sergeant of the Guard to pass you through Cornelius' post."

⌘

Holding his breath for a moment, Mac listened but heard only his own pulse in his ears. Uncertain he had heard a horse, he stood for a moment to catch his breath, facing back along his path and cocking his head sideways to hear better. Then…there it was again. How could they track him in the dark? Fear rose in his throat at the thought it might be an Indian foraging for food or cast-off equipment.

A last scrap of cloud passed over him and the waning moon shone bright enough for him to be able to see. Suddenly aware that he was a vertical object on the prairie with little cover, he bent forward and ran toward a cottonwood tree. He fell forward into knee-high grass, then twisted around to a position where he could see the way he had come. He lay still for several minutes listening for the horse, but could hear only the slight breeze and the grass that moved nearby.

He hoped the rider was not an Indian. The image of his mother's battered face and the face of the Indian boy with the war club came to him with a sudden chill in his torso. He shivered. A night bird called and he heard a flurry of wings and a shrill squeaking, then quiet. Only the soft zephyr blew through the grass.

A second later a voice behind him commanded, "Don't move even one hair, Durant."

He felt a piece of cold metal against his neck. "Oh, God," he shuddered, recognizing the buck sergeant's voice. His heart sank.

"Just do what I tell you. Keep your face in the grass and move your hands up behind your back." Wild quickly lashed his wrists tightly with a section of rope, then pulled him to his feet. "We're going back, and we're going to do it quickly."

"Why, Wild? I didn't take anything but a little food and my overcoat. That's it." He was caught, helpless.

Wild pushed him forward, walked him over a low hill to Wild's hobbled horse. "The army owns you for the next five years, Durant. You made an agreement."

"I'm no soldier, damn it."

"That's God's truth. You're just a running boy, and you're going to do some more running tonight. But this time in the right direction." He ran the end of a long rope through Mac's arms and lashed it around his chest.

"I'm not going anywhere. I'm not going back there! Why would I?" The man made him furious. Who in hell did he think he was? He was a stupid ass, drunk on the little powers the army had given him.

"I'll drag you if I have to."

"I've got my own plans and they don't include the army." He felt the emptiness of his voice, the futility of his words. He had longings, but not plans. Still, he snapped, "I'm not going back there."

Wild just looked at him in the moonlight. "You put no value on yourself, Durant."

Those words made involuntary tears well up, and he couldn't quell them. He hated that Wild saw this. He snarled, "I value my hide and my freedom plenty!"

"You haven't the slightest notion, boy. We have to hurry before anyone wakes. The only choice you have right now is to run back at the end of this rope, or by God I'll drag you. You decide."

"Shit!" What could he do or say to end this?

"Decide," Wild said quietly. He mounted his horse. "Choose." He spurred the horse, then checked the animal, but the rope went taut and jerked Mac off his feet, landing him painfully on his shoulder.

"Damn it, Wild!" He struggled to rise, but his hands were tied behind him, and he fell once more before getting his legs under him. Sharp pains stabbed his shoulder and neck from the fall.

Wild shook his head. "You don't have a real thought in your brain, do you? You'll never get over running. It'll ruin you."

At this, Mac stifled a sob. Something got at his throat, and it hurt. Why this man's words should hit him so hard was unaccountable, but he felt overwhelmed with a despair that seemed to reach beyond this present indignity. Everything seemed empty and hopeless, his past, present and future. What was the point of any of it?

Wild's voice was quiet again. "Quit running, boy. Make a stand with these men. I don't know where you came from or why you came, but what's best for you now is to stick this out."

The man's presumption was infuriating, but something in his words made Mac's throat tighten up and he fought to keep from sobbing. His mind was in tumult, sadness and anger. He couldn't figure it, but the idea of throwing in with this crowd of pumpkin rollers galled and alarmed him. "You damn well don't know what's best for me."

"Let's go. Move ahead of me. Get moving."

Mac yielded and Wild set his horse's pace at a fast walk. Still, half an hour later Mac lay on the ground beside him exhausted and gagging, snot running from his nose. He choked, "I can't run any more. I've got to stop." He sobbed, the pain and confusion of everything, Sophia, the army, his hopelessness in this moment, and even Wild's words made him want to bawl like a baby. "Just leave me, can't you?"

"I'm not leaving you."

"They're going to punish me anyway you look at it."

"That depends on who's awake and who's asleep when we walk this horse back in. If you deal with First Sergeant Bobo, that's one thing. If the Colonel's awake, that's another. He shot and hung deserters when we were down in Kansas."

"Why are you carrying their water, Wild? Looking for your next promotion?"

Wild climbed from his horse, helped Mac to his feet, and uncorked his canteen. "Open your mouth." He only allowed him a few sips, then pulled the canteen away. Wild said quietly, "You don't know a thing about me, boy." Then he looked into the night and the muddy track ahead. "We'll be challenged by a vedette in a few minutes and then by old Cornelius, the picket you passed by on your way out of camp. He's in C with us, and you should thank him. He put in a word to the Sergeant of the Guard, asked him to talk to Bobo, and not to the duty officer.

The vedette saw them and rode closer, silently waved them through. Moments later, Wild dismounted. Squinting into the darkness of the empty rolling land, he whispered, "This way." They walked until they heard a harsh whisper, "Halt! Who goes?"

Wild grinned, "The Emperor of Siam and his court, Cornelius."

"Come forward and be executed, Sergeant."

As they walked past him, Cornelius chuckled, "That was a long walk, sonny."

Exhausted, but not yet defeated, Mac muttered, "You going to pull my nose for me, old man?"

Cornelius snorted, "Look's like somebody younger than me's been pulling your nose, bub."

Wild nodded at him. "Thanks for the help, Cornelius."

The old man said, "Any time, Wild. Any time."

"Old bastard," Mac whispered, as if to himself.

"This old bastard may have kept you from swinging at the end of a rope." Wild stopped him and untied his hands before they approached the camp. "I'm letting you walk back into camp with me, Durant-- under your own steam."

Mac said nothing, but rubbed his wrists and stretched his shoulder. His arms hurt and his right shoulder ached badly.

"Cornelius helped you by calling to the Sergeant of the Guard. That man helped you by going to Bobo instead of to the duty officer. Bobo helped you by waking me. Each of these men helped you. Do you have no understanding of that?"

"You should've just let me go, Wild." But he could not meet the sergeant's eyes.

"Right now, you can leave again, or..." he held out his horse's reins to Mac... "you can go brush down my horse."

"That's no choice," Mac said, and he took the animal's reins.

⌘

Wild yawned and sat down in the matted grass next to the dog tent he shared with Holley, and leaned his elbows forward onto his crossed legs. The grass was damp with dew. Only moments later, and too soon, he watched a trumpeter in long johns emerge from a dog tent down the way and sound "First Call." Immediately the camp began to waken. Men stumbled from their tents and rekindled the cooking fires. Horses began to stir and stamp, and in the flurry of activity a scent of trampled grass and horse dung, wet earth and wood smoke, rose on the air.

A steer in the distant beef herd moaned plaintively, and others quickly took up the call until the entire herd was a wall of bawling noise in the darkness. Their plaintive cries slowly diminished until finally they fell silent again.

Wild yawned. With half an hour's sleep, this would be a long day in the saddle, but he sat for a few moments more, watching the boy work on the mare. At first the horse wasn't sure of him and it shied a couple of times, but Wild could tell the boy was talking to her. After a moment the mare stood quietly and let him work a sponge around her eyes. He wasted no motion, but was meticulous, and he whispered to the animal all the while. He worked her shoulders and withers and croup with an empty grain sack, then started with a brush around the base of her ears and down her neck. The mare watched him warily at first, but then she settled in to it.

Bobo came up to Wild in the dark. "I see you've finally found someone to take proper care of your horse, Thomas."

"Well, he's not much with people, Edwin, but he seems a fair hand with a horse."

"So what's his attitude this fine morning?"

"He's a bit defeated, but still pissing and sputtering. He's got to change his thinking before he can contribute more than trouble around here."

"Well, I'm going to deal with him. His life's going to be harder than most around here for a while."

Wild nodded and glanced up at Bobo. "Maybe working with the farrier or the horse doc?"

Bobo shrugged noncommittally, then walked away. Wild sat a few moments more, yawning. The hints of first light showed pale yellow on the prairie horizon. About thirty feet off the ground a flat mantle of wood smoke lay suspended, reflecting the flickering light of the cooking fires that fed it with columns of smoke. The smell of burning wood and buffalo chips, fried saltpork and coffee, filled the camp, and this energized him.

The dark shapes of hundreds of troopers, illuminated a bit by the fires, moved quickly about, dressing, eating, pulling down tents and packing. Their banter was a rough grumble amid the clatter of metal cooking pots and plates and spoons. Horses stamped and snorted and mules hawed impatiently, eager to be fed and freed.

As Wild rose and stretched, the young Irish recruit, Malachy Spellacy, came up to him. "What shall I be doing with Mac's things, Sergeant?"

"He'll pack them himself, Private." He could see the inquisitive look in the young man's eyes, but he wasn't going to respond with information.

"Tis a fine morning, Sergeant, if only a fellow could get uninterrupted sleep."

Wild chuckled. "You'll be able to doze on the march." By mid-morning he would be dozing in the saddle himself. "Let's get busy, Spellacy." He rose, glancing once more at Durant. If the boy was smart he'd make the best of this. Of course there was no certainty that he possessed enough wit to tell a workable path from tangled underbrush or, if he could, which one he would choose.

⌘

As Malachy broke down the dog tent, he watched Mac brush Wild's horse and wondered at the other soldier's reasons for running away in the night. Why would he jump into the army only to run off a few days later? Maybe he hadn't listened well when the officers were telling of the campaign's purpose. Searching for Indians, maybe he was fearful that some might be found.

For himself, Malachy had few fears. Just now the only one that came to mind was a fear of missing breakfast. With a cobbler father who'd run off to America long ago, real hunger had too many times made a distinct impression by pressing his belly to his backbone. His father wrote them once or twice a year and talked about a time--never far off--when he would bring them to America. They would have a fine house and live off the fat of the land without England's muddy boot upon their necks. The old man always said he'd send them money, but no money ever came. And the time for his father to bring them to America always stayed just beyond the next bend.

After packing his gear, Malachy sat by the fire and savored his hardtack soaked in bacon grease. He still could hardly believe such a luxury was his on a daily basis. The wonderful smell of the army's bacon grease always reminded him of pig's heads--themselves for certain a measure of God's goodness.

Malachy didn't know what these troubles with Mac Durant might bring, or if Mac would be punished for running off. Clearly unhappy the fellow was, but quite excellent on a horse. Maybe Mac might help him learn to ride better and, in helping him, be helped himself. For certain, the army had provided a horse, but said little about how to put it to use, except to climb up, hold on, and hope to ride. To be sure, it seemed a poorly considered process.

⌘

Leo Holley knew he had a tendency to stare at people, though usually with no more intention or judgment about them than the fact that their bodies moved and so drew his gaze. He found their movements vaguely more appealing than staring at clouds or ponds or stumps--though clouds did move and he liked to watch them, too. And ponds had ripples that moved when there was a bit of wind. What was interesting, though, was when the wind got bigger the waves got bigger, too.

As Leo packed his gear in the growing light he glanced from Sergeant Wild to Malachy. Then his eyes followed Mac as the runaway soldier took the Sergeant's horse from the rope line and led her to Wild, handing her reins to him.

Leo figured Mac was a faithless person, so probably pretty weak and fearful. But then he figured that he shouldn't judge lest he be judged, too. His knowledge of the good Lord was a bit less than perfect, but

God was right-minded and always made a man pay for his wrongdoing--like in the Bible with Job and his sores and woes and dead kin, and God and the devil laying bets on him being faithful or not.

Mac had ought to realize his mistake, but he didn't even come back on his own like that prodigal son in the Bible. Sergeant Wild had to ride out in the middle of the night and hog-tie him. He didn't know what would come of it all, but he'd have to pray on it.

An excerpt from her father's letter:

...Repairing horse's hooves is a noble enterprise, especially for curing the ails in a rebellious young man's thinking. Looking back, Wild and the First Sergeant--Bobo was his name--were both generous and wise to deal with my misdeeds by never letting me rest except to sleep at night, and sometimes the work kept me going into the night while other troopers snored. The army was hell on horses in those days, and there was always lots of mending to be done. I suppose it's not much improved for horses in today's army either.

JUNE 1876: MONTANA TERRITORY

Two weeks passed, and Mac had not a moment's rest. At the time he enlisted, he'd told the army's recruiting officer he knew a little about blacksmithing from having helped his uncle with horses. Now, whenever Bobo or Wild called, "Durant!" he looked about, wishing for a place to hide. It amazed him that he'd received no formal punishment from the army command for having tried to run. At first, Bobo had few words for him, saying, "I'm leaving you to Mr. Wild. Get from my sight."

But now neither Bobo nor Wild would allow him time for anything but the day's march, then extra work in the evenings, and finally exhausted sleep. They assigned him to work with several of the twelve cavalry companies' farriers, and assist the regiment's veterinary surgeon with horses and mules that needed to be doctored. The horses were his only refuge and working with them--just being among them--made his hard labor bearable.

The expedition rode on. Wild told him and Malachy and Holley that the expedition's leader, General Terry had gone easy on them all, not pushing too hard during the expedition's first two weeks. The general was getting the men and animals used to being in the field. But Wild said that as their search drew them closer to the Indians, Terry would press them harder.

The days passed with short marches, and hunting parties brought back plentiful game. The troopers dined on roast venison and breast of pheasant, antelope rib, buffalo steaks and beef stew. For dessert they fried hardtack in bacon grease and sprinkled it with brown sugar. "I think this is the best darn food I've ever had," Holley said.

Mac had to shake his head at the sheepherder. The man was endlessly hungry, always mooching a fellow's leftovers. It was a serious aggravation.

"Hey, Mac," Holley said one morning, eyeing a bit of hardtack that had lain too long on his tin. "You going to eat that biscuit?"

"It's full of bugs, Holley," he lied, "And they taste bitter." He thought that would discourage the man.

"That's all right, Mac," the sheepherder said, and touched his stomach. "I've got a bit of room left down here."

It was nettling that, while he suffered extra work, Malachy, Holley and the other troops were having a good old time. Along the march, troopers and scouts out hunting had acquired fawns, baby pronghorns, wolf and fox pups, birds still in pin feathers--offspring of animals they'd killed, or nests they'd come across. Troopers laughed like boys at these creatures' antics, thinking it hilarious that these young animals thought them to be their mothers and so followed them around begging to be fed.

Mac shook his head; they were just a stupid bunch of pumpkin rollers. It was ridiculous that the officers and noncoms put up with the growing menagerie.

About ten days earlier, a slushy snow had come but it quickly departed; the country now had emerged like an emerald, flush with spring. Cottonwoods leafed out and pillowed clouds drifted eastward in sunlight. Meadowlarks and red-winged blackbirds flitted about and great V's of snow geese and honkers flew noisily northward.

At night the long line of cooking fires was surrounded by soldiers' glowing faces. They were just a bunch of turnip diggers. He'd keep to himself; that was all there was to it. Malachy and the rest could worry about the Indians, though there was no sign of them anywhere. Clearly, this whole outfit was a rabble of dimwits on a fool's errand. It didn't even pay to think about it.

⌘

Several times the expedition camped along streams and the men bathed, something Holley was not used to. "Somebody's getting gamy around here," Wild told him, demanding that Holley bathe himself.

"My kin didn't put much truck in getting wet that way," Holley said. "I ain't sure of the procedure."

Wild shook his head. "Get in the creek, and wash out those socks before they run off on their own."

Prairie rattlers emerged from their winter dens and the men walked shoulder to shoulder through each new camp site and killed them before pitching tents. They caught trout and silvercat by the bucketful.

Mac worked the farriers' fires each afternoon and into the evenings every day while the column moved west. He was relieved that the expedition found no Indians along the Little Missouri where originally they were thought to be. He wanted to believe there weren't any Indians, and that this was all a pointless chase after nothing, but the scouts kept going out and coming back and the column marched relentlessly on. In all this unwieldy but determined movement he felt a vague foreboding.

The column turned southwestward to intersect the Powder River at a point about twenty miles south of its confluence with the Yellowstone. Progress was leisurely, some days covering just a few miles. Wild took small groups of new recruits to train them in field tactics. The weather changed suddenly several times from pleasantly sunny to torrents of rain and roaring northwest wind. On these occasions General Terry had them to stay in camp a day or two.

Mac went about his work methodically, doctoring hoof cracks, tightening clenches, refitting shoes, treating galls. He toiled with quiet resentment, not at the work--which he'd begun to lose himself in--but at the troopers for the way so many ignored their horses' most obvious suffering.

⌘

In days that followed, the expedition left the prairie and moved into the badlands, a place of great dust, jagged conical cliffs and narrow twisting canyons. Mac talked to the others as little as possible. He felt defeated for they'd come a long way since he'd tried to run, too far to walk back now. And if he took the gelding and left again they'd chase him harder than Wild did. It seemed all he could do was keep to himself, do his work, and bide his time until this futile search for Indians ended. He'd be damned if he'd give them the satisfaction of seeing him settle in, try to become a part of all this nonsense. Although Mac was determined to talk to the others as little as possible, he did find himself listening to their conversations. A few times he felt he had some opinion or other that he would have liked to offer, but he didn't want to encourage any of them.

Travel through this terrain was hard and slow, and the land looked like nothing he'd ever seen before. The soil was strangely crusty and crumbling, as though shot through with air bubbles, and it crunched like dry crackers as the wagons and horses passed over it. Passage through these canyons would be hard on the animals and hell on the wagons. It would mean broken axles and bent felloes, thrown shoes and spent horses, all of which meant more work for him.

The companies rotated in service as pioneers, rough-locking the Studebakers down steep grades or working out front of the expedition with picks and shovels to clear passage through narrow bottoms. As the mass of men and wagons and animals levered and forded and bridged its way along, scouts and flankers struggled through adjacent canyons and ridges, for the steep narrow ravines afforded much cover for would-be ambushers and no one could be sure where the Sioux were gathering.

The water they drank was fouled with alkali. With all the pushing and pulling of animals and wagons, by each day's end the troopers were wet and spent and covered with mud. Sentries had a hard time staying awake. "They caught a fellow from "E" sleeping on his post last night," Malachy said, "And now for the evenin's duration they got him bucked and gagged by General Custer's tent."

Nobody relished working as vedettes, for they had to be out beyond the perimeter so far they couldn't sense the presence of their fellows who slept two or three steep and torturous ravines away. Malachy said, "Tis a fact. They might as well be alone in the dark on another world."

Several more days of hard, slow travel came and went. "Damn, we ain't ever going to get to that Powder River," Cornelius Blosser said. Mac rarely looked his way but, when he did, saw the old man's face was gray. Skin hung like sacks beneath his eyes. Although Cornelius rode nearby each day, Mac hadn't spoken to him since the night he'd tried to desert. The old man fell asleep sometimes on the march and his horse had a tendency to drift away from the column, so Wild would take the animal's reins while Cornelius dozed.

The last day on the march to the Powder was the worst. Solitary spruce and scrub cedar adorned the red and brown-layered bluffs and the blooming air was filled with a blustery, warming wind. Whorls of birds veered everywhere. But passage was wet and heavy and the wagons mired, sometimes to their axles. The column traveled down through a narrow canyon of tortured turns and wet, slick gumbo that clung heavily to his boots, and to the wagon wheels and animals' hooves.

But around noon Mac saw the land ahead begin to change. Valleys widened and became shallow, and large areas of new grass quavered in a westerly breeze. Hills to the west rose up in a jumble of piney woodlands and eroded red cliffs. As the column progressed, traveling grew easier. Though tired, the men's spirits' rose and conversations flared along the column. He could smell the fresh scent of pine and cedar on the distant green ridges to south and north. Arid land gradually fell away behind and they descended westward toward the Powder.

The pine trees' pungence commingled with that of horse sweat, and reminded him of riding with Sophia through patches of forest around her grandparents' estate. She was so fresh in his thoughts that if he closed his eyes it could be her riding beside him right now instead of Holley and Malachy. Gazing at the forested hillsides in the shimmering distance, he imagined himself simply riding away from the column with her and losing himself in the dappled shade and breeze and birdsong.

He rode for a long time lost in reverie, allowing his mind to escape from the soldiers' journey into a memory of walking one day with Sophia. She carried a folded blanket and they strolled a twisting game trail that wound through open woodlands of oak and hackberry, pine and maple, where sunlight shifted with the shadows and stippled the woodland floor.

They tripped along the edge of a meadow full of purple phlox and mounds of daisies ready to blossom. There were other wild flowers, each of which Sophia knew by name. They waded a creek that traced its winding channel between old Indian mounds. She grabbed his hand as they climbed the mounds and tried to figure out what they'd been shaped to represent long ago. They splashed in the stream's shallows and he laughed aloud as Sophia hiked up her skirts and chased after water skimmers. In the wake of their passage the lazy stream bloomed muddy clouds that drifted and curled in the slow current behind them. Hearing their approach, box turtles slipped silently from sunny stones and disappeared into the water.

Sophia led him from the stream up a small ravine dappled with sun and shade where they found a sheltered eddy among hackberry trees where wind had nested last year's leaves. Sophia spread her blanket there, straightened and smoothed it. "Like a wife," he thought, stunned by the overflowing feelings in his heart. Right then it seemed to him that they'd always been together, and always would be.

Just then she broke the spell, for she sat and began to undo the buttons on the back of her dress, then glanced up at him and said, "What are you waiting for?" She reached out both hands to his trouser buttons and pulled him down beside her onto the rustling softness. She was five years older than him, always tried to tell him what to do, though right now he didn't mind at all. Dry leaves crackled beneath the blanket as they pulled at each other's clothes, and finally he buried his face and mouth in the sunlight smell of her breasts.

⌘

While Mac still felt trapped within these ranks, and believed Wild and Bobo watched him constantly, his will to resist them peculiarly drained away. He was always tired from the extra work, but the expedition's relentless progress into wilder country made him fear leaving the column.

Most of the hard country was behind them, though once they had to halt as the Rees and Crows returned to confer with General Terry and Custer about the best way to go forward. Finally, the massive unit picked its way across an eroded ridge, and twisted down a steep slope and along a grassy gully, then threaded up and traversed the top of a narrow butte from which, if one of the wagons or mule teams moved too far left or right, it would have tumbled over fifty feet before hitting bottom. This was the only route the scouts could find to get them across the last bit of badlands to the Powder River.

When finally they arrived at the river, according to the milometer on the rear wheel of the headquarters wagon they'd covered nearly thirty miles to traverse a distance that on a straight line Wild told them might have been twenty. During the day several harness mules had dropped in their tracks and been replaced by mules from the reserve. The last straggling wagons finally arrived at the river camp just before dark.

Mac heard a rumor go around that night. General Terry was concerned about not having heard anything from Colonel Gibbon's column up on the Yellowstone, or from General Crook's expedition out of Wyoming Territory. Some of the older men theorized what this might mean. Blosser said, "I don't know how we're goin' to corner no Indians if we don't even know where our own left or right wing is."

The next morning they heard that a detached squad had left before dawn to ride north to the Powder's confluence with the Yellowstone and see if there was sign of Gibbon's or Crook's expeditions.

For most troopers this had been an easy day in camp. The men repaired and cleaned their gear, wrote letters, relaxed, or fished along the banks of the Powder. From Malachy, who made it his business to get around and meet people, Mac gradually heard bits and pieces about different troopers in C, including Burden. He was always in some kind of conflict with Gunther and a couple of the other Germans in C. The Germans spoke little or no English and Mac didn't understand how people could get in such rows when they couldn't understand each other's words.

Malachy had told him that Burden kept writing letters to Travelers Aid Societies around the country, trying to find his brother, from whom he'd become separated years ago during the rebellion. Mac didn't want to know much about the man, for he had an air of menace about him. He did notice that Burden seemed to do nothing else but write letters.

That morning, Wild ordered Mac to work with several of the companies' farriers, including John Rivers, C Company's blacksmith.

He had kept several farriers' fires going, picked and cleaned horses' hooves, and collected troopers' spare sets of shoes and nails that they'd been issued and had carried from Fort Lincoln. He worked methodically as he trimmed and rasped hooves and shod and set clenches. C's usually surly farrier, Rivers, paid him a compliment when he saw that Mac knew how to compensate for bowed tendons, hoof cracks and other conformation problems.

By afternoon he was filthy and spent. He buried his face in the crook of his elbow, wiping sweat onto his long johns. He stopped to rest a few moments and gazed absently at the tents and men and wagons arrayed beside the pale brown river that looked like heavily creamed coffee.

He wondered who bought these horses for the army anyway, for some of them just weren't suited. The army's buyers were a damn sight less able than the horse traders they dealt with.

It angered him to see how many of these animals suffered from troopers' neglect. He cussed out one man who'd allowed a cracked hoof to worsen and caused his horse great suffering. He fumed to the farrier, Rivers, "These people're supposed to check their mounts morning and night. They can't tell a well-set shoe from a hobnail boot."

"Poorly set clenches and galls on a cavalry horse ain't no big news," the man said. "The army goes through horses like meat through a grinder."

Suddenly, from C Company's nearby area he heard cursing and shouting in German and he looked up. Gunther pushed Burden, who fell backward over a saddle and bounded up to advance on Gunther threateningly. But Bobo appeared there between them, "Hold it, you two men. I'll have you sons of bitches bucked and gagged again, or worse, and you'll God damned well regret it. Holy hell if I'll tolerate any fighting in my company."

Mac watched, but nothing more happened. The men separated and went their ways. He just shook his head. It seemed Burden and Gunther couldn't be around each other in camp without getting into some kind of argument. In the three weeks since he'd run off, he'd begun to feel a reluctant respect for C's First Sergeant Bobo.

Bobo was a broad barrel keg of a man, short in stature, but powerful in his middle age, even though his right temple was a smear of twisted purple flesh that he sometimes touched absentmindedly with his finger tips as he talked. His right eye looked like a broken egg yolk and had a jagged streak of red running through it. Cornelius had told Holley and him, "Those scars are from shrapnel wounds he got during the Rebellion."

Holley asked, "How'd he get 'em?"

"In Pennsylvania at a place called Little Round Top."

In Mac's view the man didn't need but one good eye anyway, for he had an extra one in the back of his head. Like many of the other companies' First Sergeants, Bobo had run his own troop for many years and probably would retire in the same place.

Bobo seemed to know most of the civilian scouts and several of the Crows and Rees who came and went as scouts for hire to the army. The Indian scouts' work kept them away during the day, and at night they built their own fire off a ways from the troopers' long line of cooking fires. Often after dark Mac saw their dark shapes moving about near a lone fire in the distance. But they came to C's campsite frequently to trade tobacco with Bobo and silently smoke with him of an evening, seeming to enjoy his company.

Bobo did watch out for his men, and they seemed to respect him. But it was better to avoid Bobo as best as he could, for whenever the First Sergeant saw him it just meant more work. But it was something the way Bobo stepped between those two big men. These thoughts were confusing and Mac tried to scoff them away, asking himself what he cared about the opinions of a scar faced First Sergeant. He probably couldn't hold a real job in the civilian world. Still, he hoped word would get back to Bobo and Wild that he was working hard for the farriers.

That night as he lay beneath his blanket listening to Holley snore, he was puzzled by something else, as well. Bobo treated Wild differently from the other men in the troop, three-stripers and corporals included. Bobo talked with Wild daily, and obviously valued his opinion on various matters related to the company's affairs.

The next morning, Wild was again assigned to lead the training of several companies' new recruits. Mac went with Holley and Malachy and others to a flat meadow above the river bottom north of camp.

Wild taught them to maneuver in mounted formation to set up for a charge. He drilled them on marching by the flank from line with intervals, and how to deploy from fours. They learned how to dismount with carbines slung and hand-off mounts to horse holders so they could form as skirmishers to fight on foot. He showed them how to recover from Indians' flanking movements. At first it was chaotic, but Wild was patient. Yet Mac felt exasperated; some of these cabbage cutters took forever just to learn to get their horses turned and back in line.

The next day Wild taught them the nomenclature of their Springfield rifles, showed them how to clean them, made the men practice sighting and dry firing their weapons from standing, sitting and prone positions, showed them how to lay down enfilading fire. Mac prided himself; he already knew how to handle a carbine, knew that in fact he was a pretty good shot. The whole afternoon was repetitive, tiring. He figured it'd drive him crazy. First Sergeant Bobo showed up and watched for a while.

⌘

The next afternoon two Rees rode into camp with mail pouches from Fort Lincoln. They brought news that spread rapidly among the men. As usual Malachy heard it first and brought it to Holley and him. "Tis a terrible thing. The Rees found the bodies of miners on their way to the Black Hills--all slaughtered with their private parts cut away. Eaten by coyotes and wolves, they were."

"How do they know they're miners?" Holley said.

"How would he know, Leo?" Mac said. "Maybe they were holding onto some picks and shovels."

"The Rees found only men's bodies," Malachy said, "Though clothes and other signs said women had been with 'em. The arrow shafts they found were Sioux." The two Rees had tracked a band of ten or twelve Indian ponies away from the kill site and found three sets of bare footprints accompanying them. The sign led southwestward for several miles to a creek. The two Rees quit the tracks there and rejoined the expedition's trail to deliver the mail.

Mac looked beyond the camp at the empty land to the east. To think that the women might have been taken away as slaves...the thought made his stomach queasy. Years ago in the Minnesota slough, the Sioux had taken Mrs. Duley and Mrs. Wright and him and the other children away with them. He didn't know if those two women had been mistreated or raped, though he doubted it; the Indians seemed almost frightened by the two women's anger. He remembered with admiration that Mrs. Duley and Mrs. Wright exploded at the Sioux on a regular basis, demanding better treatment for the children and themselves.

With the Rees' news, the mood in the camp turned somber. In early evening, Mac overheard one of the buck sergeants, Daniel Knipe, say, "Gold's a fatal lure for fools. I'd rather keep my pecker than a poke of that ore."

Cornelius shook his head. "I guess a man ought to be thankful for fools. If they wasn't gold-hungry, the rest of us wouldn't have no jobs."

Just after dusk, Mac sat with Wild and Malachy and Holley around the cooking fire. A freshening breeze had begun to blow from the northwest and there was no cloud cover. The night would be cold. Mac stood up and without speaking went to the tent he shared with Malachy. He stripped to his long johns and crawled under his blanket where he lay looking out the tent flap at the camp.

He saw Cornelius crawl from his tent nearby and limp toward the sink. In the weeks that'd passed since he'd tried to leave and return to Bismarck he couldn't avoid the old soldier, but he hadn't spoken to him either. One time Blosser had winked conspiratorially, saying, "Guess we're both still stuck here, Mac." It felt an insult that the old man should assume to know his thinking.

But during the weeks since Mac had tried to run his mind had become a growing tumult of confusion. He missed Sophia and needed to make his way to her, but to do so meant either starvation or death at the hands of the Sioux. Also, at day's end he felt an exhausted satisfaction he couldn't recall ever having experienced. The weariness was a result of his work with the farriers and veterinarian at the end of a full day's march, but the satisfaction wasn't something he could deny. He thought maybe it just came from being around the horses, but he had to admit that at times the work itself had provided him some contentment.

He watched Cornelius pick his way back toward his tent from the sink. Though he regretted never giving the man even a nod of recognition--for the old trooper had helped him that night--he just couldn't get around to doing it. Maybe he should at least give him a "Howdy." Tomorrow, if it wasn't too uncomfortable, he believed he might do just that.

Malachy and Holley and Wild and a few others knew he'd run off that night. Bobo, Cornelius, a couple sentries from that night, and maybe Burden knew, too. But he assumed his flight was not a secret any of them felt obliged to keep. He was probably a pariah in the minds of most in the regiment, for they spoke to him only when necessary. But he wasn't sure this was a consequence of his running. Maybe he just struck them wrong--maybe because of his tendency to keep to himself. A shooting star flashed across the sky above the horizon and for a few moments he hoped to see another, but none came.

He didn't like to talk a lot. Consequently, he usually found himself on the outside of any group, feeling irritable at their laughter and jokes--but also a little shy, for he didn't know what to say that might make them welcome him into their circle. His own circle was mostly just himself. But, while he wanted to say, "To hell with that" and "So what?" he knew if he spoke the words aloud they'd be a lie.

Idly, his eyes roved along C's rope line between two of the Studebakers and finally searched out his gelding among the other animals. Wood smoke drifted past and he looked back at the fire he'd left moments before. Wild was sitting there now, talking with Malachy and Holley. He wondered what they were saying. Malachy looked toward the tent, and Mac felt disheartened at the notion they might be talking about him.

Forlorn and weary, he fell to sleep.

An excerpt from her father's letter:

... Those few months in the army had a disproportionately large impact on my life. I hated it, didn't want to shoot anyone or--the good Lord knows--be shot. I learned about hard work, experienced being shot at, dealt with the challenges of getting along with people I didn't know well, and with people I didn't like. And of course, there were the deaths. Somehow, from that time onward I have never feared death. A blessing, now that my own approaches.

JUNE 1876: MONTANA TERRITORY

Because Wild was always giving him extra work, Mac often kept track of the sergeant's whereabouts as he went about the camp. He had resented him for a week or two after Wild chased him down, but his anger gradually dwindled away as he realized the extra work simply was something to be endured.

He guessed Wild was pretty old, probably in his thirties. He definitely was a hard man to know. He never spoke about himself. "Tis a fact," Malachy said, "I've heard speculations that Wild is a man with a past, though for a certainty that wouldn't be unusual among this rag-tag lot."

Wild was not any cleaner than the rest of them, though somehow he seemed to be. He always had water to wash and shave with. He had a couple of books in his saddlebags and was forever pulling out one or the other and reading while on the march.

Mac watched him, but Wild didn't bloviate or puff himself up like some of the noncoms, and he showed how to find bits of plants along the march which could do different things for a fellow. He showed them wild sage and how to dry it and put it on their saltpork. Wild would reach down into the prairie grass and say, "Oglalas use this as a relish. It's like asparagus. I've heard it called knotweed, or maybe smartweed."

Earlier in the trip, when Cornelius had watery humors in his body from the chilly weather, Wild boiled lambsquarter and made poultices from the boiled leaves. He found pennycress and wild onions for salad, told them they'd have chokecherries and wild plums later in the summer. Wild told them how to preserve meat, showed them pemmican he'd made from chokecherries and pulverized buffalo hump, but he wouldn't share any, just laughed and said, "You can damn' well make your own in a couple of months." But Mac saw him slip a hunk to Holley.

Although Wild was only one of five buck sergeants in Bobo's C Company, he seemed to have been accorded charmed status among the men of C, and to some extent throughout the Seventh Regiment. From time to time during the last several weeks Mac had heard several of the older men call out to Wild in greeting, "Hey, Mail Man."

One afternoon while Mac and Malachy and Holley were washing their clothes in the Powder, Sergeant Knipe stood scrubbing out his long johns nearby. Malachy asked, "Sergeant, why is it some of the men are referrin' to Wild by that nickname?"

"It was before I was in the army, back in '66 or '67," Knipe said. "Wild was new to the Seventh, part of a detachment out of Fort Sedgwick down on the Platte. They was eleven troopers carrying mail over to Fort Riley. South of the Republican River forks some Sioux attacked them. It was pretty bad. Folks at Fort Riley heard the gunfire and sent troops out. By the time they got there, eight men were dead, but Wild and two others made it through. He was the only one not wounded." Knipe paused a moment to wring out his longjohns, then said, "Well, Wild did have a wound--of a kind--but definitely not one to complain about."

Knipe said Wild had been carrying a makeshift cloth mail pouch folded inside his shirt across his stomach. "The pouch was filled with letters from some of the men back at Sedgwick." Knipe waded back to shore and shook out his long johns. "In the fight, a Sioux ball passed through the front of Wild's shirt and went through that letter pouch. It bounced off his rib. Knocked the wind out of him pretty good, but that was all."

Knipe grinned, shaking his head. "Some started calling him 'Mail Man' as a joke. But, after that, troopers who was worried about a coming skirmish began to consider it good luck to write a letter and give it to Wild to carry for them until the Seventh came back safe to

Riley. A few gave him a coin or a pocket watch to hold for them--or some other kind of charm."

"Far as I know, he still don't never turn anybody down. He even paid a cobbler to make him bigger saddle bags so he had room to carry all that stuff." Knipe grinned a bit sheepishly. "I been tempted a couple times to write a letter and give it to him before we went into the field." He draped his wet long johns around his neck. "But I decided not. If I give in to such thinking, fate might visit on me the thing I fear most."

Mac noticed that at night Wild had a well-established routine. After work was done and they were settled in, he sat propped against his saddle with a book titled **Meditations**, his back to the fire's light, his face hidden in darkness. As he read he stroked his drooping mustaches with a finger and thumb, lost in thought. Some evenings he penned letters, sitting for long moments staring pensively into the darkness, his face looking a bit drawn, even melancholy. Mac wondered if, like himself, Wild traveled far in memory, perhaps had old regrets. The sergeant tended to speak in leisurely tones, and was genial with them most of the time, but Mac couldn't remember Wild ever speaking about himself.

Mac thought about the night he had run off. Wild seemed to have a clear mind on matters. Life must be easier with a clear mind, and he wished he had such a one.

⌘

Wild knelt against a deadfall pine above the river, packing a small crevice with pine needles and dry leaves to start a fire. He was startled when he heard Bobo's voice behind him.

"General Terry isn't satisfied with what he found out up north."

Wild felt tired and chilled, as though he might be getting sick. He slowly stood up and fished with both hands in his trouser pockets. "What do you mean?" He'd seen Terry's detachment return from a two-day expedition down the Powder to its mouth at the Yellowstone.

"Terry went up to find Colonel Gibbon," Bobo said. "His column's camped on the north shore of the Yellowstone. Gibbon's tried a couple of times to get his men and animals across, but the river's in flood.

Several of his horses drowned, so he pulled everybody back."

"So all he can do is sit?" Gibbon had led cavalry from Bozeman and infantry from Fort Ellis, and was known to be a restless man. For him sitting wouldn't be easy. Wild knelt again and struck two Lucifer matches before the tinder finally caught and a small flame started to spread in the crevice. "Has he heard from General Crook?" He put both hands to the flame.

"Nobody's had word from Crook since he left Wyoming," Bobo said. "Both Gibbon and Crook are supposed to coordinate with us. It don't look real good to me."

Wild gratefully watched the fire grow. Still, he trembled, couldn't get warm.

"Crook started out after we left Bismarck, but neither Terry nor Gibbon nor Crook has sent detachments out to find the rest of us until now." Bobo looked at him. "Are you all right, Thomas?"

"I've got a little chill. Can't get warm." Wild rose up and stood with his backside to the growing blaze. "So no one knows where Crook is or the size and location of the Sioux gathering out there." This strategy of the column feeling its way along like a blind man looking for two other blind men, while maybe blundering into a monster of unknown size didn't suit him.

Bobo said, "I don't see how Terry can correct that lack of information now, except by forging on."

"That seems to be all we've been doing from the beginning, just forging on." Wild felt cranky. His gut was starting to cramp and rumble.

"Gibbon told Terry the Indians have harassed him regularly. A month ago his scouts swam the Yellowstone and went down into the valley of the Tongue. They found a Sioux camp big enough to raise their neck hair. They were trailed by a big party all the way back, but didn't even know they'd been seen until they were back to the river and discovered the crowd behind them. They were lucky to get back across."

Wild shook his head.

"Twice now," Bobo said, "Gibbon's hunting parties and scouts have skirmished with bands of twenty to fifty men. Both those bands had crossed over the Yellowstone from the south."

Wild gave a soft whistle. "Sounds like they still could be gathered along the Tongue, but if they know about Crook coming at them from the south, maybe they're even moving eastward toward us."

"That ain't the worst. A week or two ago, three of Gibbon's men went off to hunt without permission. When they didn't come back, Gibbon sent a squad out to look. They found all three mutilated. Again, the Sioux had come across the river. Gibbon's got to be frustrated that he can't get across and take the fight to them."

"That's what I keep telling these new boys," Wild said, "Don't go wandering off."

"That's not my point," Bobo said. "I don't know who thought this whole venture through at the outset, but supposedly Gibbon's role's to keep the Indians from crossing the Yellowstone and running up into Canada."

Wild threw two pine boughs on the blaze and sparks exploded. "How can he control two hundred miles of river with only two or three hundred men?" He spread his arms to embrace the blast of heat.

"Exactly. The Sioux have already crossed the river several times, killing his hunters and harassing him at their pleasure."

Wild shook his head. "Then it isn't Gibbon who controls the Yellowstone; it's the Sioux." Even with the pine fire's crackling heat, the frigid ache in his torso ate at his energy. Either he was getting sick or was starting to wonder about this expedition's planning. Regardless of the cause, his hands trembled. It was hard to feel optimistic about any of this.

⌘

When Bobo left, Wild called to Malachy and told him to bring Durant and Holley over to the fire. General Terry likely assumed the worst: that the tribes had determined by now that three army columns were coming from different directions with the intent to crush them. Indians might soon send harassing parties to snipe at all three columns, or pick off hunters or scouts, just as they'd done to Gibbon.

When they'd gathered he related what Bobo told him, though he didn't tell them Bobo's judgment about the army's strategy. Custer felt no obligation to keep his men informed, and wouldn't want one of his First

Sergeants talking about what was on his mind, regardless of the effect it would have on the men later.

"You three heard by now that many soldiers and officers scoff at the Sioux's ability to fight," Wild said. He had wrapped himself in his blanket, but still huddled close to the fire.

Holley said, "The Indians don't make a stand, but mostly just run off."

"A lot of these men hold that mistaken view. Most of them haven't been in a fight with the Sioux before, but they still cherish the same ignorant notions."

"What's your meaning, Sergeant?" Malachy asked.

"The Indians tend to fight small scale engagements and withdraw if they see any tactical disadvantage. Some in the army see that to be cowardice, but it's only smart."

"Live to fight another day," Malachy said.

"Of course," Wild said. "Years ago a band of Cheyenne attacked a small group of soldiers I was with down in Kansas. They killed almost everybody, but I was lucky. They only attacked us in the first place after deciding they could carry the day. If they'd have thought otherwise, it's likely we would've never even seen them."

"We heard about that, Mail Man." Malachy grinned.

Wild brushed the nickname away with a swipe of his hand. "'Mail Man' aside, I was damn' lucky that day. Each of you has to hear me on this. You stay close to camp from now on, and stay armed. I don't want anybody going off by themselves over some hill to smell flowers or take a piss. Bobo's going to tell C Company all this, but it won't hurt you to hear it twice."

They all nodded.

"One other thing," Wild said. "Down in Wyoming Territory ten years ago, Indians coaxed troopers out of Fort Kearney into a slaughter. They drew them into ambush and took advantage of the commanding officer's arrogance and inexperience. His name was Fetterman and he thought he was invincible against Indians. The Sioux killed him and all eighty of his men in just a few minutes."

"I got no love for the Sioux," Mac said, "But if they only fight when they think they can win, that's common sense."

Wild looked at him. Maybe the boy was starting to think. "Why such common sense escapes the army is sometimes beyond me," Wild said. He gestured around at the camp. "The fact that a lot of these people think Indian tactics are cowardice and not wisdom casts some doubt on their own judgment."

⌘

Wild had a bad night with the flux, and by noon the next day he was exhausted and chilled by gray drizzle that had fallen all morning. Though he'd wrapped himself in a blanket and his gutta-percha and rebuilt his fire against the deadfall pine he couldn't get warm. Icy gusts swirled around him but the sky was clearing to the southwest and he hoped by afternoon the sun would be warming his shoulders.

Bobo gathered C Company and told them General Terry had ordered Major Reno to lead the regiment's five right wing companies--C, E, F, I, and L--on a ten-day reconnaissance into the southwest to search for the Indians. Terry had brought back a scout from Gibbon's expedition, a civilian named Mitch Bouyer, who would accompany them. Bouyer knew the country where the scouting expedition would travel. The rest of the Seventh, with the infantry and the cattle herd, would move on up to the Yellowstone and camp to await Reno's scouting report ten days hence.

Wild wished he could stay here, but he wouldn't go on light duty or ride in the Dogherty wagon with the other sick men. At this point many new men had come to rely on him because he'd trained them, however briefly and sketchily, and he wouldn't send them off alone.

After Bobo dismissed the men he lingered with Wild and they watched the right wing companies strike their tents and pack their gear for a mid-afternoon departure.

"Until they showed for training I didn't realize how many new men the regiment has," Wild said. "Why didn't Reno get to this training sooner?"

Bobo shrugged and grinned. "Hard to say, Thomas, but it's nice to know the little major has such faith in you."

"A lot of them--Germans, Scandinavians--they can't understand hardly any English. I couldn't do anything but draw pictures in the dirt.

They've got fear and uncertainty written all over their faces."

"It makes for a sorry situation, Thomas, but that's the hand we've been dealt. I don't expect many of them planned to be in the army. Most get past the misery stage, but a few never do." Bobo rubbed his bad eye with his fingertips. "Which reminds me: how do you think Durant's doing?"

Wild kicked two pieces of shattered cottonwood branches into his fire. "He's good with the horses, but keeps his guard up around the other men. He's a reluctant warrior. Says he's seen enough killing--his parents were killed in Minnesota's Sioux wars; he says he doesn't plan on doing any more killing."

"Well, he's picked a poor line of work for being a pacifist. But we can take him off the extra work whenever you say."

"Then let's let him off. Give him some guard duty, but let him have a little free time among the other troops. He won't run off again."

"He'd be a fool to try now."

"He's no fool, probably just ashamed of what he did, though I suspect he hasn't put that into words, even to himself."

Wild watched Bobo walk away to supervise the men's packing, and remembered when he'd been a greenhorn fourteen years earlier in 1862. His experience had been quite different than these new men now faced. Back then he was without experience--didn't even know how to march in step--but he and most others had been committed to their fight.

He'd departed Hopeton, Virginia in 1862, mounted on a big bay gelding that his father had given him. He rode at the head of a spanking new infantry company, all dazzling in gray uniforms tailored by the ladies of the town. Thanks to his family's position, suddenly--at age nineteen--he was made a Lieutenant of infantry in the Army of the Confederacy.

Some of his men were many years older than he, while others were little more than boys amazed at their uniforms and their new role as soldiers. They'd been hungry for glory and proud to protect their homeland from what they saw as the federal government's depredations. But those who lived through Manassus grew up fast, stunned that their first attempt to liberate Maryland from the Union hadn't worked.

He'd been innocent early on, allowing his men to walk to the provo line and give their federal prisoners food and swap tales. In the war's first year, some evenings his men sang two-part harmonies with neighboring camps of federals against whom they fought the next morning. At night his sentries traded humorous insults with Yankee pickets across no man's land. But the blood ran in floods and innocence fled.

The whole sorrowful thing: it still brought him low to think about it, how all that early belief and chivalrous good will was merely illusion. He had to give it up, for it presaged bloody slaughter, a full waste of humanity, a spectacle from which many survivors never recovered. For years afterward his mind could hardly bear the things they'd had to do. He still couldn't evict some of the memories. But he knew he mustn't dwell on them or he'd sink into one of his spells of dejection.

In quiet moments before dark he was inclined to look too far into the past. He had to push back against the memories, for they could overwhelm him. For another man such meditations might not have the same dreary result, might even be salutary and renewing, but what bothered him could never be repaired or made right.

Near the end of the Rebellion, his company had been slaughtered south of Nashville, and he'd almost died of grief and shame. Edwin was his cousin, but had fought for the union. After the war ended Edwin had come and found him at the behest of Wild's own sister, urged him into the Army of the West. He had enlisted, but only with the spirit of a walking dead man. Having been a confederate officer, his enlistment was illegal, though no one but Edwin knew.

Wild tossed a pine bough into the fire and the pitch exploded into flames that leapt high. The men had drawn their horses close to the embarkation point, were milling around, and departure was near. The misty rain had stopped and soon Edwin would send for him.

Over time, younger soldiers had come to see him as a leader. He tried to be a three-striper they could rely on for support and advice-- and for a bit of bucking up under the discouragements regularly faced on any march. Still, how little he deserved their admiration!

He just wished to quiet his mind, to continue as he had, training new men, providing a bit of leadership, feeling he'd earned a little respect. He just wanted to mind his business, and forget.

Bobo didn't like the look on Wild's face as he approached him to tell him they were ready to depart. Bobo was frustrated with Major Reno--and with his cousin, for he was certain that Wild was about to go into one of his bouts of melancholy.

"Thomas, we have to go. You should be ready to mount unless you want to go on the sick list." It vexed him that Major Reno constantly called on Thomas to work with the new men when there were other equally capable noncoms who could've done the job. In many ways Reno was a competent officer, but for some reason he'd become overly interested in Thomas. The Major should have been embarrassed, for he was almost deferential. Bobo said, "All this is weighing you down."

"I'll live, cousin," Wild said.

"Well, I'm certainly glad you'll continue to abide among us, cousin." Bobo slapped Wild on the shoulder. He turned away, saying, "Durant packed your gear and stowed it, and he saddled your horse. Let's go."

Bobo gathered his own horse and mounted, moving to a position that would accommodate his troopers' forming on him. The soldiers led their horses into line. As Bobo gave the command to mount he watched Wild climb into his saddle, his three young charges beside him in the file.

He shook his head at his cousin's plight: able in every respect, but a perpetual victim to unwarranted remorse. As Reno ordered the five companies to move out, Bobo couldn't help wondering if Wild's anguish might someday destroy him.

The following morning, Mac looked up when Wild told Malachy and Holley and him, "Bobo wants me to ride with the scouting detachment today." In the half-light of a cloudy dawn, Mac thought Wild didn't look sick like he had yesterday, and he watched him lead his horse toward the front of the column. Soon after, a command was issued to mount and begin the day's march. Mac looked up to see Wild and one of the Crow scouts ride back toward C Company from the front. Wild and the Indian turned and forded their horses westward across the river, then rode away from the column's flank, disappearing over a low rise.

As Mac rode along he occasionally glanced west across the river, scanning the land for signs of Wild and the Indian, but he saw no one.

The expedition had ridden just past Mizpah Creek's confluence with the Powder when they made a westward crossing of the river. But, at the place chosen to ford, the sloping banks were soft and steep and as the column went into the water several horses slipped and almost fell, nearly upsetting their riders.

Shortly, clouds rolled up from the southwest and the men dug out their waterproofs and overcoats. Malachy pulled the gutta-percha tight around his neck, shivering in the rain. He said to Mac, "Why have we to travel in this mess? 'Tis a galling thing to just ignore the weather and forge on regardless."

Mac only shrugged. He was sunk deep in a funk, trying without success to stay dry. He cursed the monotony of all this motion, for each step the horse took shifted him in the saddle and, as often as not, sent cold rain trickling inside his clothing and down his neck. But the rain squall passed and the sun came back, slowly drying and warming them as curling wisps of vapor rose from the men and horses along the column. Mac took off his field hat and rode with his face upturned in the growing warmth.

In late morning, he saw three Rees ride out southward from the column. A short time later, just as he began to doze in the saddle, a brief volley of gunfire exploded from the south. Some horses in the column shied and whinnied. A large cloud of birds whirled up from a brushy thicket off to the left, flashing white undersides, then dropped from sight beyond the ridge.

From ahead in the line of march he heard a shout and the new scout, Bouyer, and a squad of troopers separated from the column and galloped away, disappearing over a small hill in the direction of the gunfire.

Mac strained his eyes to the south. Was this the beginning of a fight the expedition had come for? A prickly heat flushed his face and he glanced about at the other men, many of whom were fidgety. Their hands moved to their side arms and carbines. Twisting in the saddle, men fussily straightened blanket rolls, secured loose gear, assured themselves their ammunition was accessible. Malachy and many others stood high in their saddles, straining to see. A rush of soldiers' quiet voices rose around him and he heard somebody nearby say quietly, "Sounded like Long Toms."

Cornelius snorted, "That sure as hell wasn't Long Toms. Ain't no infantry out there." A moment passed, then a smaller weapon popped once, twice, three times. Thin snaps, instantly lost in the sky.

The column kept moving. Half an hour later Bouyer and the squad of troopers returned, along with the three Ree scouts, trotting past C Company from the rear. Mac gaped at the lead Ree, who clutched a bloody mass in his right fist. Cornelius said, "They sent somebody traveling. That old boy collected him some hair."

An hour later word trickled back along the line that the Rees had crossed over a small divide and surprised a family of Sioux. A man and boy had been skinning a pronghorn and the scouts killed them both. Searching nearby in tall grass, they found a woman hiding with two small girls and shot them too.

Shortly, a rumor floated along the line: the Rees had wounded the family's one pony, but it'd run off and, too intent on taking scalps, they didn't chase it. Scuttlebutt said Reno was furious at the Rees for letting the pony get away. Maybe it would head back to some larger encampment and draw attention.

Mac was stunned by the event's suddenness and the lack of reaction among the troopers. None of them spoke and he wondered if anybody'd had another thought but that the Sioux family should be shot. Reno and the rest just kept moving forward undeterred, leaving the Indians' bodies to be eaten by animals and their bones scattered.

Holley spoke quietly, "It's a sad notion, but I guess the good Lord wanted to take them folks. Them Sioux helped me one time. They saved my life."

Malachy and Mac looked at him. Cornelius said, "When was that?"

"I was walking up-river to join at Fort Lincoln, and I had a foot fester. It got worse, smellin' real bad with my foot and part of my leg all puffed up. I was out of my potatoes and bread." He put his fingertips to his head, as if remembering. "My face was so hot. It got so bad I couldn't hardly move no more, couldn't hardly see. I figured to lie down by the river and let go of my life. But a Sioux woman out looking for onions found me.

I think her husband wanted to kill me, but she kept him from it. I don't know why. Drained my fester and made a kind of poultice. She fed me." Holley looked around at them all. "Saved my life, you bet. When I was better, she even give me some pemmican to see me up the river a piece."

Mac looked at Holley, trying to see if he was kidding. But Holley never did that. No one spoke for a moment, then Malachy finally said, "Och, Leo. That's just a story."

"It's God's truth, and I don't know why she did. But I'da died right there on the Missouri breaks if it wasn't for that woman. The good Lord and that Sioux lady helped me."

Mac said, "I wonder why."

Holley shook his head. "On'y thing I could ever think of is they wasn't young. Not old neither, but old enough to maybe have their hearts soften some." He paused, his face thoughtful. "I can't help it, but I don't hold no grudges against these people we're after. It's too darn bad about that family what got killed back there."

Cornelius spoke softly. "I expect a bunch of fellas here feel about the same way as you, Holley. But if you come down to the hard nub of it, you'll do what you have to do, boy, and right when you have to do it."

Mac looked at the old man. He didn't know if he could do it in a moment that required it. That God damned Ree scout: to kill like that. The man and boy dead, just like that--and two little girls hiding in the grass with their mother. He still could see the horror on his own mother's face so many years ago when she'd left him there in the cattails, it pained him to think of the hard hearts that lay behind these killings. Those Sioux had done nothing except be away from the reservation where the government had put them. Because of that, they had to face those moments of sudden terror, then death. He felt bitter; that was the world's mercy.

⌘

Later that afternoon, Mac was grateful when the six companies went into camp twenty-six miles south from the morning's starting point. He was tired and grimy, still soggy after the rain and the creek fords.

Reno ordered the column formed into parallel lines to set up camp, and the pack mules were brought to the center and relieved of their loads. The men moved quickly to set up tents, then many headed for the river to clean up.

But all this was interrupted when two of the Rees galloped into the bivouac to report they'd seen smoke to the northwest. Major Reno and Bouyer rode with the scouts to the top of a high ridge, but the rain squall and clouds had dispersed the smoke to a barely visible haze and they couldn't tell its point of origin.

One man said nervously, "Cornelius, you can bet your skinny old ass that the Sioux are letting their brothers know we're coming."

"That's likely," Cornelius said. "There must be small bands out there ahead of us in lots of places, probably all of them riding to join up into something larger."

Mac's stomach tightened at the notion. He looked around at the peaceful camp, smoke rising from cooking fires, men setting their gear out to dry. The Seventh's left-wing companies, the infantry troops, all the Studebakers, the beef herd and the Gatling and Rodman guns had moved far north by now and were settling in along the Yellowstone to await Reno's scouting report. There were maybe two hundred fifty soldiers here, most of them near naked and getting ready to plunge into the creek. They were definitely beyond the reach of any help from the rest of the expedition.

"It seems like we're a large enough number, but I'm not sure how big a crowd we might come onto," Cornelius said to him and Malachy and Holley.

"Well, they can just put me out of me misery," Malachy said. "'Tis a fact I'm so damned wet and muddy and clammy and sweaty all of a once that I've hardly a mind to be caring if a howlin' bunch of Sioux banshees come down on me right now."

Holley looked anxious. "Don't tempt the dark one with no ideas, Malachy. He can think up enough by his own self."

⌘

Wild and the Ree rode back into camp at dusk. Wild took care of his horse then talked with Bobo for a few minutes. When he arrived at the cooking fire he told of seeing the big smoke atop a low butte toward the northwest. "We couldn't tell if it was man made. There was lightning out that way, but the country doesn't seem dry enough to catch fire from a lightning strike."

Holley finished his salt pork and hardtack and walked off toward the river to rinse his tins. "Malachy and Durant, Bobo wants you two on guard duty tonight, midnight to reveille," Wild said.

Mac felt like the wind had been knocked out of him. He'd never yet stood guard, though Malachy'd done so several times.

"Wild," Malachy said, "Tis not enough for a man to suffer mud and rain," the Irish soldier said. "But now he's to get no sleep?"

"You can sleep until just before midnight," Wild grinned. "That's a whole four hours from now."

As darkness became complete, Mac felt increasingly tense and anxious. As he'd done in the past, he'd hoped to hide from guard duty by turning his back and bending over to dig in his forage sack, acting unaware that the selection of sentries was being made. He'd never been certain if his tactic had worked or if they just didn't trust him to perform the work.

Maybe the assignment was indication of Bobo's growing trust. Though Mac felt a little fearful, he also felt guard duty might mean the others had accepted him a bit more, though he scoffed silently at the idea, told himself he didn't care two hoots about that. But guard duty might mean an end to his extra labor with the farriers, for Bobo and Wild hadn't given him any such work for the last several days.

Wild came up to him at the cooking fire. "Let's take a walk. I want to tell you some things about guard duty."

Mac stood and they went along the row of banked fires. "Whatever your post, sit and listen for birds and animals," Wild said. "They have their routines. If anything moves into their area that's unfamiliar they'll let you know by shutting up or calling out or thrashing away from their resting place."

"Eyes play tricks in the dark. If you see something that doesn't look right, don't spook. Push your gaze a bit off center from it; you'll be able to see it more easily and be able to tell if it moves."

After they returned, Mac found Malachy already asleep in their tent. Listening to the Irishman's rhythmic breathing, he quickly drifted away.

But too soon, the guard Sergeant, Bustard, nudged them both awake. Malachy grumbled, but forced himself up, and they grabbed their Springfields and followed Bustard.

Bustard told them the password and reminded them of how to challenge someone and how to call for him or the Corporal of the Guard. He quietly pointed out other sentry positions across the land features that lay black against the sky. The waning moon shed a fair light but was about to set.

Mac went stoically along behind him. Several fires still burned in the camp as they left, and his eyes took a while to adjust to the night. The only camp sounds left were some mules snorting and cavorting, still unable to quiet down. But in the vast country to his front he sensed a great silence and stillness, given emphasis by the buzzing sounds of insects.

Moments later he heard a voice ahead of them say, "Who goes there?"

"The Sergeant of the Guard," Bustard said.

"Advance to be recognized, Sergeant."

They came upon an older soldier from C who Mac had seen often, but couldn't remember his name. Bustard asked him if he'd seen anything Mac should know about.

"I thought I saw something a while ago. It looked light-colored, like maybe an animal"--and he pointed past the trees at the bottom of the ravine that fell away in their front-- "Way beyond, out in the tall grass. But I blinked a couple of times and couldn't see it any more. Guess I need to get a pair of specs when we get back to Bismarck."

Bustard spoke quietly. "Durant, I'm putting you on this high ground above that swale. You're now Post Number Three. This is your first guard duty, so let me tell you a few things. You're on this spot because it's just high enough to afford you a view south and eastward. From there," he said, and swung his arm in a flat arc, "To there. That overlaps the view from Post Four on your right. It also overlaps the view from Post Two on your left."

He gestured. "Gunther from 'C' will be at Post Two along the river bend. Malachy, will be at Four. These sentry posts are on terrain low enough that neither of you will be silhouetted against the sky. But you need to sit, rather than stand or walk. Don't make many movements, and those you do make, make slowly." He gestured down the gully. "Though the moon'll soon be down, even in starlight you and anything else out there will be visible to anybody who wants to look. But if you're still, they may take you as a rock or a bush rather than a man."

As Bustard and Malachy walked away, Mac sighed and sat down cross-legged, the Springfield in his lap. Hours ago night had set in completely to the east and south, but even after midnight a faint afterglow of sunset still lingered beyond the western horizon. He checked the carbine's load and fingered the slugs on the right side of his web belt; then pulled several part way out and pushed them back in. His eyes roved the dark night southward. Far downslope he heard what sounded like crickets. Fifty yards away in the bottom several cottonwoods rose up black against the surrounding terrain.

Time passed slowly. He looked behind him, wishing he could see the tents and horses, maybe hear a snore or two. Mosquitos buzzed near his ear and he sighed, wanting to swat them, but he remembered Bustard's admonition to move slowly if at all. His forehead and cheek began to itch from their bites.

He felt a twinge of longing for Sophia. He'd been gone from St. Paul more than a month, and she didn't even know. Why had she gone to Bismarck and Deadwood, rather than San Francisco? Maybe she wasn't in Deadwood anymore. If not, how would he find her? The thought demoralized him.

Suddenly a rustling noise and a squeaking sound came from the stand of cottonwoods and brush in the ravine to his front, as though something had surprised or disrupted a squirrel or mouse. Had the crickets just now stopped, or had they quieted earlier and he'd only just noticed? He cussed himself for not making note. Did they stop every night about now, or had they quieted because someone was moving near their bed ground? He slowed his breath, taking in only shallow draughts of air, and strained to hear. The breeze blew a cold gust and he pulled the overcoat collar tighter around his neck.

From the corner of his eye, out in front toward the trees he thought he saw movement. He leaned forward, squinting, and brought the carbine's barrel around. Should he call out and challenge? For a long moment he stared into the darkness, then remembered to look slightly away, the better to see what shape was there. But doing this he could see nothing unusual. He saw a movement again. Was it living, or had the breeze just moved a tree branch? It seemed light against a darker background.

The Springfield's loose sling rattled and he extended his left hand to clamp the sling against the rifle barrel. He turned his head toward the camp again, and only thirty feet away the figure of a man stood motionlessly, looking at him. Mac shouted hoarsely, "Who goes!" and wrenched himself around, thrusting the rifle into a firing position.

"Whoa, Durant. It's Bustard."

Mac gulped sheepishly and his hands shook from the sudden shock.

"You need to ask me the password, Private. Maybe I'm not who I say I am."

His mind felt frozen. He could remember nothing. "What's the password then?"

"Rumcake, Durant. I've been standing here long enough to kill you twice."

"Something just moved down in the trees."

Bustard crouched to remove his silhouette from the skyline then moved quickly through the grass. He squatted beside Mac.

"Where?" His voice was a barely audible whisper.

Mac pointed. "Below and to the right of that tallest cottonwood." It moved again, a lighter color. He gulped a breath of air, feeling as if he'd been running a great distance.

But, though they waited several more minutes, nothing emerged from the trees below. Bustard departed, saying, "Keep looking around, Durant. I don't want to have a chance to kill you again."

A bit later, as Mac looked to the east toward Gunther's post, he thought he saw far away a small, light shape moving toward the German trooper's post through the tall grass. But, instead of looking a bit away from it, he turned his gaze fully on it and could see nothing more.

⌘

On Post Two near the river, Private Gunther sat in the grass with his carbine across his lap when he heard a shout from the sentry to his south, and a rush of energy filled his chest. He ran his hand over his chin and filled his lungs, looking hard in the direction of the shout. He heard nothing more for several moments, then a slight breeze from there seemed to carry the faintest hint of voices. He blinked and rubbed his tired eyes, but could see nothing out that way.

As he began to yawn, Gunther heard a slight rustle in the grass behind him. His heart jumped and he turned his head, realizing he'd not looked in that direction for several minutes. He caught the briefest glimpse of a dark shape behind him and a hand came around the front of his face, across his nose and mouth, jerked his head back. Something searing hot plunged deep into his neck and ripped. Strangling and thrashing, arms flailing, Gunther fought to get air, but could only inhale his own blood. Then he relaxed, felt himself sinking into warm water. So warm, so comforting that he didn't mind at all.

An excerpt from her father's letter:

…One of the men on our expedition, a German immigrant soldier, was murdered and no one was ever charged with the killing. However, we all assumed it was Burden who killed him, for the two had repeatedly fought each other. Such hatred seems incomprehensible to me, but humanity seems cursed by it. What lies beneath our urge to kill and devour each other is a mystery. What are the conditions of life in this world that seem to make us relish this?

JUNE 1876: POWDER RIVER, MONTANA TERRITORY

Mac watched a wan, yellow dawn slowly bloom in the east as the Corporal of the Guard and Malachy came to relieve him. They all walked to Post Two but when they got there couldn't find Gunther. "Son of a bitch," the corporal snapped. "Where's he gone?"

Mac saw him first. Gunther lay in a patch of taller grass, stripped naked except for his socks. Stunned, for a second Mac thought he was asleep until he saw with a shock that Gunther's head was laying on his shoulder, almost torn off. Stupefied, all he could think to say was, "He's right there."

"Jesus God-almighty!" Malachy said, kneeling beside the German soldier. "His head's off."

The Corporal of the Guard ran fifteen feet to the top of the rise and bellowed toward the camp, "Sergeant of the Guard to Post Two!" Mac looked at the Corporal dumbly, too dazed to react. He gazed back at the body in the grass and his hands began to shake. The nearly severed head lay askew and Malachy lifted it, positioning it more normally. "Don't touch him, Irish," the corporal said, then yelled toward the camp once more.

Mac could smell the man's blood, a gamy metallic odor, and felt on the verge of retching. He looked toward the camp, trying to clear his head, and saw Bustard and two other men trotting up the rise toward them. The camp was noisy with early morning activity, but in the half-light men stopped their work and stood still, peering to determine what the ruckus was about.

Then Bustard and the others were there, and officers came, including Major Reno. They questioned Mac and Malachy, but having no information beyond what they'd seen, they were sent back to camp to ready themselves for the day's march.

As they came into camp, Wild and Holley stood to meet them, as did Knipe and several other men from C. Bobo asked, "What happened out there?"

"When the guard corporal relieved us, we went to get Gunther, but he was dead," Mac said. He looked around aimlessly at his gear, trying to order his mind to concentrate on getting ready for the march. His fingers tingled, so he clenched his fists several times.

"What happened to him?" Wild asked.

"I don't know, Sergeant," Malachy said, "But his throat was cut so bad his head was almost off, and his forehead and nose was open here and here." Malachy gestured to his own brow and the bridge of his nose. His face looked flushed.

"A hatchet across the nose, that's a Sioux finishing off a wounded enemy," Wild said.

Mac didn't want to listen to this. He should pack his gear, get ready to go, but his eyes drifted to the top of the rise where several officers stood near Gunther's body. Two troopers already were digging a grave. He couldn't shake the sight of Gunther's face; his skin waxy pale; yellow in the dawn, devoid of any animating feature to show he'd ever lived. Something had departed, and his corpse seemed artificial, like a wax statue.

In a few moments the other troopers started to drift away and Mac saw Major Reno walk toward them then stop. The major called to Bobo, who went to him. After a few moments, Bobo called to Wild, who walked over to Bobo and Reno.

Absently, Mac watched the three men. He thought of his parents' deaths in the cattail slough. He'd been snatched up by Mrs. Wright and Mrs. Duley to trek the plains with the Sioux and the other captives. As the Indians prodded them up the trail, along the edge of the slough he saw a dead white woman in the muddy shallows. Naked from the waist up, her skirt and petticoats were twisted about her. She'd been stabbed in the neck and her body was like white alabaster. All that had made her human had departed. Just blank, a mannequin, empty as nothing.

Remembering that moment, he believed he'd been inflicted with a subtle wound, as though he'd suddenly seen some important and terrible truth about life. As years had passed, memory of the woman's pale breasts--her bloody neck--haunted him. And long ago, a painful revelation had struck him: if one life can be so casually and indifferently struck down by another, then what importance does anyone's life have?

⌘

After Major Reno walked away, Wild felt furious. He and Bobo remained apart from the others, and for a moment didn't speak. Wild finally said, "If the Major thinks Burden might have killed Gunther, then what in hell does he think he can accomplish by having the man transfer into my set-of-four?"

"The decision's been made, Thomas. I can't do anything about it right now."

Wild shook his head. "Burden's a renegade, and unpredictable as hell. There's no way he's going to change by being assigned to my set." He felt defenseless at Reno's transfer order. Such a thing just wasn't done when troops were in the field.

Bobo looked thoughtful. "He'd been stripped, Thomas. They took all his gear, but they left his money."

Wild's eyes roved the camp, his thoughts confused, veering between anger and a growing anxiety that he didn't understand. "Stripped? What are you talking about?"

"Gunther. The killer took his clothes, carbine and .45--his belt, boots, ammunition. They left his money belt. There was blood all over him." Bobo paused. "Whoever did it overkilled him."

"What do you mean?"

"The neck wound killed him, according to what the Major said, and it's what the boy Durant implied, too. If an Indian killed Gunther, he knew he didn't need the hatchet work on Gunther's nose to finish the job. That's a ploy; it could be that some trooper killed him."

Wild reflected for a couple of seconds. "Malachy said Gunther wasn't scalped. Indians might not have taken his hair, though. Burden or another trooper killed Gunther and tried to make it look like Indians."

"We know well about the trouble between Burden and the Germans. They've been gnawing at each other since before we left Fort Lincoln," Bobo said. "It's been particularly bad between Burden and Gunther." He crossed his arms and spit. "Bad enough I had to have Burden and Gunther bucked and gagged all afternoon on the parade ground at Lincoln."

"I saw them," Wild said, and shook his head. "I don't relish his presence in my set. He'd be willing to choke on a bone before answering to me." Having to deal with Burden made him intensely uneasy, not from fear, but from something he was forgetting or maybe overlooking. "We've never spoken more than a few words to each other, but he's said a couple of things that leave me uneasy."

Bobo looked at him intently. "Why do you say that?"

"I think we know each other, but I'm not sure from where." Wild couldn't rid himself of the foreboding he felt about Burden, yet didn't know why.

"What's he said?"

"Just called me "Captain" a couple of times when I've had him in a group for training. Maybe I'm putting too much on it, but I keep thinking I should recognize him." He looked down at his front and slapped absently at a patch of dirt on his trousers.

"He calls you 'Captain'? Is he somebody from the Rebellion?"

"I've wondered about that. He looks familiar, but he's an odd enough package that if I crossed his path in the past I ought to remember him."

⌘

Standing with Holley, Mac watched Wild come back. Somehow he looked defeated, but remained silent, clearly not interested in talking.

"So what's going on, Wild?" Mac finally said.

Wild said, "I guess we've got a new man coming into the set."

"Who?" Holley asked. "We're four already."

"Malachy will move out and be part of the company's regular count each day, and Chauncey Burden's going to be with us."

"What?" Mac snapped. "Why Burden?" He couldn't believe they'd push Malachy out and bring Burden in. This set was for new men, and Burden had been in the army for years. Besides, living around him day-to-day would be a struggle. A thought struck him: Burden and Gunther had fought at the fort, and now Reno thought Burden had killed him.

"What's wrong with Malachy?" Holley asked. "He's all right where he is."

"But Burden isn't," Wild said. "The Major has a discipline problem and he's determined to solve it. He wants to separate Burden, shake him up. Burden's had arguments with...."

"With the Germans, including Gunther," Mac said. Could Burden have killed Gunther? He thought about what he knew of the man. It was possible. Apprehension rose inside him.

Wild looked embarrassed, like he'd done something wrong and had brought this problem upon them. "Maybe so," he said, and looked at Mac. "You'll be lashing your half of a dog tent to his."

Mac looked at him in dismay. "What?" He didn't want to be in such close quarters with Burden. "Why don't you take him in with you, Wild?" But the sergeant gave no answer, but shook his head.

"So what about Malachy?" Holley said. "Who's going to watch out for him?"

Wild nodded. "I'll keep an eye on him, and so will the others. He's already connected with McCreedy and McGuire--and a couple of Irishmen in other companies. We'll have him keep on riding with us while on the march, and he can tent next to us at night. He'll be all right." Wild looked at them with an ironic twinkle in his eye that irritated Mac. "You two'll be all right too."

If Burden had killed Gunther then he was a breed apart, someone fearful to be avoided. His heart sank to think Wild would push Burden onto him, make him share his tent with the man. He had a real bad feeling about it.

⌘

Moments later, Burden came into their midst without fanfare, carrying his Springfield and haversack, his saddle bags and poncho, and dragging his shelter-half on the ground behind him. His face was dark, and set with quiet menace. Wild and the others were silent for several minutes as they finished rolling up their dog tents, circling uncomfortably and staying out of one another's way.

Burden finally broke the silence. "Well, it's great to be among new friends and old. Ain't that right, Captain Wild?"

"I'm not your captain, Burden. You're tenting with Durant. Our extra forage for the horses is in Hofer's wagon."

"Well, thank you," Burden said. "I'll blend into this setting just fine, but first let me give you all a little notice. I'll pull my freight, but don't be trying to teach me how to season my meat or clean my equipment or convert me to your right-minded shit, Wild. If you're going to heaven, I'd be pleased to go to the other location."

Mac interjected, "What's the problem, Chauncey?" Wild had done nothing to Burden. They hadn't been friends, but then nobody was friends with Burden.

Burden stared venomously at him.

"Nobody needs to give anybody a bad time," Mac said.

"Sonny boy," Burden spat, "You didn't have the brains or balls to make it out of all this some weeks back, and now I see you buying in. I'll give you some advice. Don't get smug with me or I will make the star-spangled banner float in front of your eyes--or worse."

"Hey!" Wild snapped, and turned to face Burden. "Just take it easy! Calm down and get used to the idea of being here, Burden. You aren't the only one who doesn't like this change."

The call to mount was delayed while troopers finished searching the land beyond Gunther's post, but soon most of them began to straggle back down the slope from the hill to gather their horses. A few wandered along the river bank looking at the muddy shore.

Mac watched the burial party of enlisted men and four officers moving around Gunther's corpse atop the rise above the river. Major Reno and one of the regiment's three surgeons were with them. The doctor moved around the body, then stopped and bent his head. With both wrists crimped tightly against his belly, he appeared to be writing in a notebook.

Along the creek, the horse troopers had finished breaking camp and gathering their mounts. But then, as if some silent signal had been given, most of the troopers stopped where they were and quietly watched the soldiers beside the grave on the rise above the river. The burial party turned over Gunther's corpse, picked it up and lowered it gently into the hole, then filled the hole and began to cover it with field stone.

After a few moments the officers and men at Gunther's grave turned and walked back toward the main body of troops. Seeing this, the companies' First Sergeants yelled orders for their men to mount.

⌘

As Burden led his mount to C's line of march, he smiled inwardly and watched the burial party troopers finish up at Gunther's grave. Several officers stood nearby. They couldn't figure how to pound nails in a dirt bank, let alone find Gunther's killer. And as far as them transferring him to Wild's set, they could move him around like an extra card in a poker deck but they'd never break him. Reno was sorely wrong if he thought that piss-ant, Wild, could tame him like he was doing with Durant and those other two misfits.

It was powerful ironic that Reno suddenly assigned him to Wild, for Wild'd be the last noncom to break him. Like Gunther, Wild was already a doomed man. Obviously he didn't recall their past acquaintance just yet, but with careful prodding a little flame would bloom in his brain and soon enough he'd make the connection.

After so many years of waiting, a man could be patient. He'd relish seeing the realization in Wild's eye when the bastard finally remembered him. His reason to take revenge against Wild was as old as the beginning of the world, for Wild had killed his brother, Lamar, twelve years ago during the Rebellion. And Lamar: just a poor simpleton trying to get away from the Goddamn' artillery noise.

Several men nearby were looking him over, and one by one he stared back until they dropped their eyes. It wouldn't do to let 'em think they could hold his gaze. Few men ever did for long.

His rage about Wild could boil over if he gave himself to it, so he pushed it away by rubbing his eyes with the fingertips of both hands. But he allowed himself a glance at Wild as the sergeant led his horse toward the formation. Wild reeked with a need for other men's admiration. Infuriatingly, many troopers did respect him, though there was solace that a right-thinking few saw he was phony--a man too good to be real. Most considered him Reno's boy, though the Major wasn't no great sponsor to have in a regiment run by Custer.

Wild might play himself up as the generous leader around here, but he'd been a coward south of Nashville in '64 and he was a coward now, too in love with his righteous status and fearful of losing it. When Wild finally did remember him, the good sergeant would find his luck turning bloody. The cover of an Indian battle could give him the chance to finish Wild.

Burden watched as the last of the officers left Gunther's grave and walked toward the camp. The grave was just a small silhouette of stones piled atop the hill. Over his life he'd found out there were a number of ways to point truth to someone who required a bit of pointing. Sometimes--like with Gunther or Wild--it needed a skull-crushing. Sometimes just a poker hand with a third deuce or a second pair would do--or, best of all, a flat-eyed bluff thereof.

The companies were ready to march, except for a few who still straggled in from their search for evidence of Gunther's killer. Well, they could look 'til hell froze. It was times like these, as he strode the edge of a cliff, that he felt nearly immortal. He yawned and looked around. Sometimes he felt like the devil hisself, like he'd always been alive and always would be.

Gunther nor Wild nor Bobo nor none of the rest knew who they was toying with; he could go harder and deeper than any of them. Gunther and the other damn' Germans hung together like Texans jumping on a skinny harlot. They'd been goading him since Fort Lincoln when he caught Gunther rummaging through his goods in the barracks. That son of a bitch had nearly ruined his letter to his older brother, Donny.

That barracks fight got him and Gunther bucked and gagged on the parade ground. The embarrassing thing was not that he'd sat there all lashed up--he'd defeated far worse attempts to humble him. The real humiliation came from sitting beside the dumb German who after an hour or two began to bawl like a baby. Later he'd even shit himself. The weak bastard didn't know no better than to give 'em just what they wanted: a spectacle of collapse and surrender.

Gunther ruining that letter would've seriously set back his efforts to look for Donny, but the German couldn't have cared less. When a man saw such callousness in the world he just had to do something about it, for it wouldn't do to let such a challenge go unmet.

He'd begun trying to find Donny years ago, and with some chance help from a Kansas whore. She wrote the first letter for him and he still remembered her with as much affection as he'd ever felt for anybody. When he went into the saloon, she was the only woman left downstairs, and from the look of her she spent a lot of time alone down there. She was about the homeliest woman he'd ever seen, with stove pipe legs and great big knee bones and a line of black hair above her lip. She hadn't many teeth and no chin to speak of. This world was cruel to her, but she could write words. That was what he needed, for he couldn't write.

He'd felt shy as a virgin, but once she got out of him what he hoped for, what he wanted to do, she figured out the best words to use, then put 'em right down on the paper. Nobody but nobody was going to mess with that letter without they would pay dearly. She'd helped him, and wouldn't take money for it neither. But he made her take it, which got her mad, which gave him about the only twinge of regret he'd ever felt in his life. Thinking about it, that night six years ago in Abilene, that whore had helped lift him up as much as anyone ever had.

He'd known for a long time he ought to recopy her letter and keep a separate sample, then if one copy got lost or wet he wouldn't have to hire another whore to write him a new letter. Over the years the ink grew pale and the paper thin and about tore up, but he protected it on days he knew there'd be rain or a river crossing. He triple-wrapped his waterproof around it. He'd taken many a cold soaking so he wouldn't risk the letter and the list of cities he could write to.

Each month or so, wherever he was, he'd pull out the list of Travelers Aid Societies and cities that said where he could inquire after a person gone missing. He labored so hard at copying the letter that when he finished his neck and arms ached. Every once in a while he hired some other soldier to copy it for him, sometimes he feared they might not be doing it right because they were dumb or spiteful.

Still, doing it himself made him anxious, for he wasn't sure about the way he made those letters. He might make a mistake that he couldn't understand, one that'd make the letter unreadable to the person he sent it to. And that person might be just the one who knew where Donny was. It was a worry, but he kept at it. And whenever he finally did put a letter in the regiment's mail pouch it was like a big stone was lifted off him, and new hope flew out into the world like a bird.

He and Donny and Lamar had always been together, that is until Wild killed Lamar and he and Donny got separated in that Tennessee battle. The one true thing in the world, the one pure thing--was his search for his brother. Long ago, when Mama died, she'd told him he was named Chancellor for a reason. "What it means is 'truth teller,'" she said. "You be a truth teller."

That was several miles from Flat Lick crossroads in Kentucky. They'd built a lean-to shelter thrown together from slabs of sod and tree branches that his mother and the old man had covered with animal skins and blanket scraps she'd brought from Pennsylvania. For two days she lay shivering on a filthy blanket laid beside a cooking fire beneath the lean-to smoke hole.

It was almost spring and his father said it was a shame she was dying for she'd almost made it through the cold time. His father'd been drunk and beaten her again.

"Something is broke inside me," she said. Her cough was loose and phlegmy, and what she had the strength to force up was mostly blood. "You are Chancellor," she wheezed, "keeper of the record. You got to remember, got to tell things straight."

Then she was dead. Their father drank clear white liquor from a gray jug that he stoppered with a piece of her dress, and he sobbed and slobbered in his beard. Donny stared at him with a cold scorn that Chauncey didn't understand. He'd not yet learned to hate the old man.

Lamar never could talk, but he always became excited, afraid at any little thing. When there was trouble he sat and rocked back and forth and hummed to himself, and most of the time there was trouble so

Lamar did a lot of humming and rocking. The old man sat drinking beside their mother's corpse, with Donny's eyes full of hatred, Lamar humming and rocking with his arms crossed high on his chest and Chauncey watching it all.

He helped Donny wrap her body in scraps of old blanket and drag it to a shallow grave Donny'd scratched out with a case knife after the old man passed out. It was Donny always watched over him and Lamar and made sure they did right.

But that night coyotes and coons started digging at the loose dirt they'd heaped over her. The next morning he and Donny found her partly dug up and reburied her. That night while Lamar and the old man slept, they stood watch, throwing rocks at coyotes and badgers that came to eat, but they finally fell asleep.

At daylight, Donny sobbed as he dragged their mother's torn body out of the shallow hole and dug it twice as deep then scooped dirt back on what was left of her. Lamar always cried when he saw Donny cry, so Donny forced his face to hardness. He took the old man's case knife and broke off large branches and underbrush, then piled them over the grave so all but the smallest creatures could not get inside the tangle of limbs and brush to dig her up again. He worked that case knife until his blisters bled.

Burden double-checked his rolled up waterproof, tugging at the knots that held it tightly in place behind his saddle, for inside he'd wrapped the whore's specimen letter and the list of cities. His eyes followed the last couple three troopers as they wandered back along the river toward their horses, their eyes scanning the muddy shore and the water.

He couldn't stop yawning and wished to hell they'd get moving. He'd been on the move much of the night and hadn't slept, but allowed himself an inner smile as he watched the last searchers give up and walk back toward the formation. The search was a wild-goose chase that would turn up nothing, for the dead man's weapons and other gear were lashed with rope and weighted with stone. Unless Reno sent somebody half a mile downriver along their backtrail to a deep, eddying pool on the eastern shore, then dove through silty water to the muddy bottom and got real lucky, they'd never find a thing.

Life was funny. For over a month, since before they'd left Fort Lincoln, he planned to kill Gunther. He'd figured to wait for Indian contact so the German's death would seem part of the fight. But then yesterday the Rees killed those Sioux who just might have vengeful kin roaming nearby. Then the companies rode past that deep pool and it got him thinking. To top it off, there was Gunther assigned to guard duty on the owl shift. Sometimes a problem just got solved by coincidental things coming together in a favorable way.

Here and there, scattered amongst the regiment, there were a number of Jesus-boys. He'd like to tell'em about this, for it was like sweet providence had intervened to help him drain a boil.

An excerpt from her father's letter:

...I did not know myself at that time and I think that is what made me fearful, and I did not know the kind of man I might become. I think the main reason we fear death is because we do not know ourselves. Yet, few elements of our world encourage that kind of reflection and awareness.

JUNE 1876: POWDER RIVER, MONTANA TERRITORY

By late morning, Mac figured the five companies had gone perhaps ten or twelve miles and the entire unit--men, horses, Gatling gun and crew, pack mules--all were covered in white dust. He sweated in the heat, looked over at Wild who seemed mired deeply in misery. Why? Because Burden was now in his charge?

Nearby, the Gatling gun crew cursed and panted and leaned into the gun carriage, prodding the team of stove-in cavalry horses along a series of shallow, eroded breaks that came nearly to the edge of the river. Mac heard one of the crewmen snap, "Them goddamn' Rees, they couldn't give two hoots about us on this gun. Why hadn't they picked another way around this son-of-a-bitching place?"

From a ridge far ahead a small dust cloud arose and drew closer. Several minutes later Mac saw three scouts converge on the column's front. After conferring with these men, Reno put the five companies into a slow lope. Ten minutes later the whole unit arrived at an abandoned Indian camp full of stone tipi rings. Animal bones and other garbage, horse dung and cold ashes from many fires littered the torn and matted earth. The troopers alternately sat their horses for long moments then stood in their saddles to stretch and look around as they waited for an order to dismount.

A faint movement of air brought Mac the smell of charcoal and horse manure and he watched the guide, Bouyer, as he began to walk about and survey the abandoned camp. A white moth brushed past his horse's eyes and the animal jerked its head sideways. Mac sawed absently at his reins. The call to dismount finally came and the troopers climbed down and began to stretch. Mac loosened his saddle cinch to give the horse a bit of rest.

The men were ordered to stay outside the camp's perimeter while Bouyer searched it. Mac admired the man's vest made from the hide of a spotted calf. Bouyer ambled about, stooping here and there, reaching with his fingers into the remnants of a cold camp fire, searching with both hands through a pile of bones, then with his boot he kicked over what looked incongruously like a pile of old newspapers weighted with a piece of field stone.

"That old squaw man is probably leading us right into the jaws of the Sioux," Burden said.

Wild looked at him. "He's half-Sioux, Burden. Sitting Bull put a hundred-pony price on his head because he scouts for us. There isn't any love lost between him and them."

Burden just shook his head. As they rode out of the old Indian camp, word went around that Bouyer estimated maybe two hundred people had been there, with perhaps several dozen warriors among them. Most worrisome, this camp's presence implied that other camps could be close by. But although the five companies followed the wide trail of travois and unshod ponies southwestward they saw no more new sign that day. They did find an Indian pony grazing a mile or two away and Bouyer sent out a couple of Rees who thoroughly scoured the surrounding region, but they found nothing else. The pony was lame and probably had been abandoned, or somehow had wandered off from its fellows.

Mac turned and watched the pony where the Rees had left it cropping grass. The animal lifted its head several times as it chewed, looking after them. This desolate region--in fact the whole world--seemed a place where most things were abandoned. He was feeling low. One thing and another, it seemed like everybody was always leaving. His parents were dead and he was alone. Sophia'd gone off, taking him by surprise in the process. Malachy had left their set and gone out into the larger company among the other men. There was no end to changes, people just going off. It was disheartening.

The column followed the Indian trail all day. By mid-afternoon there was little air moving and they set up camp beside the Powder in a region full of lush grass for the animals and a good supply of fire wood.

Wild spotted a sandy area upriver from camp. He told Mac and Holley and several other young troopers that they might get away from the noise of the troop and find a quick swim, and they could wash out their trail-dirty clothes. Wild invited Malachy and Burden to come along too, but Burden ignored him.

As they departed the main body of the troop, a number of men from "A" and "L" were setting up footraces and placing jawbone bets for "$3,000" or "$10,000" when in fact only pennies and nickels actually changed hands. A three-striper from "L" yelled at Wild, "Thomas, bring those girls over here and we'll see how fleet their feet are!"

Wild grinned and waved away the other sergeant's comments, "John, you all feel free to wear yourselves out, but we're going to wash off the dirt and take a breath."

They were nine troopers in filthy long johns and boots, each carrying his Springfield and ammunition belt and a wad of dirty clothes. Mac kept his distance from all but Malachy and Holley and Wild, still self-conscious about what these others knew about his attempt to run, but the others were in high spirits, kicking at rocks and cracking jokes.

After they'd finished washing, the men started to splash each other and comment on the evident defects of each other's private parts. But Mac mused about what he would do if he were able to get away from the expedition and the army, his thoughts turning vaguely to Sophia. Naked and barefoot, but carrying his carbine and ammunition belt, Mac left the water and the other troopers' boisterous laughter and walked to the rise he'd seen moments earlier. It was covered in thick, knee-high grass. He looked back once and saw Wild glance toward him. He expected to be called back for walking away alone, but Wild said nothing and busied himself washing out his clothes.

Mac lay back drowsily in the warm sunlight and light breeze, daydreaming about finding Sophia in Deadwood. How soon he could get there from here was still an imponderable, but his mind skipped lightly over that challenge and onto the imagined pleasures of having already left all this behind. The late afternoon air began to stir and the grass tickled his legs and arms.

A small breeze rose and shifted, carried away the other troopers' laughter, and he was left with his thoughts of Sophia. He guessed he could forgive her for leaving, though her departure had been a pained confusion.

He was jolted from these thoughts when the breeze shifted slightly and brushed his face with a stench of something rotting and a hint of charcoal. For a second or two it plucked at his nose and he tried to ignore it, but then it was gone on a changing current of air.

He opened his eyes, squinting at the open sky. Several crows flew across his line of vision. The smell of rotting flesh came strongly to him this time and he stood and looked upwind for the origin of the smell, but saw nothing except green prairie grass that waved in the moving air. The light had started to change and the rising ground to the west looked golden. Then, about two hundred feet away to the south, he saw an area of trampled grass and the stench came to him again on the breeze that blew from that direction. He began to walk toward the area of matted grass.

Behind him, Wild shouted, "Durant, come on back!" He turned and saw Wild by the river, pulling on his wet trousers. Mac waved in acknowledgment without speaking, then gestured forward, pointing. He continued toward the area of flattened grass, and from a distance saw what looked at first like three pale logs lying side by side, but there were no trees anywhere in the landscape, except a couple of cottonwoods along the river bottom behind him.

At his approach, several crows squawked and flew away from these forms, disappearing over a rise. The three logs were corpses, a man with tattoos on his arms and chest, and two women. All lay with their elbows bound behind them with sinew. They were naked and bloated and covered with flies.

Behind him Mac heard someone running, and he turned to see Wild loping toward him from the river, his Springfield pointing skyward from one fist. "Durant, when I tell you to come back, you come back." Then he saw the bodies and slowed to a walk. "Jesus." He lowered the rifle barrel and looked slowly around the trampled patch.

Mac struggled to keep his body from shaking and he walked around to the upwind side of the partially decomposed and eaten corpses, barely able to look at them.

Wild stepped carefully, looking closely at each of the remains.

There was no other object in the clearing except the naked corpses, though the grass was torn in several places and Mac could see the prints of Indian ponies that probably came in from the main trail that the column had been following all afternoon.

"We'll get Bobo and Major Reno up here," Wild said. "Don't touch them."

But he had no intention to do that. "There's nothing around here. Where'd they come from?"

"I don't know, but they were probably captives of the people we've been trailing." Wild looked at the body of the woman closest to him. "Sioux did this." He gestured with the barrel of his Springfield at the arrow which protruded from the remnant of one of the woman's two breasts. "See the carved lines on that shaft?"

Mac looked reluctantly at the arrow that protruded from her chest, then back toward the camp. "God, they're a mess." A fire'd been built on top of the tattooed man's stomach but had burned itself to cold ash and charcoal. His blackened flesh had cracked in the heat and his genitals had been cut off and stuffed down his throat with a small piece of burned tree branch that still protruded from his mouth.

"Jesus, how could they do this?"

"They don't hold a patent. I've seen our men do worse." Wild's eyes roved over the corpses. "Look at their feet. They're all torn up. They were marched here barefoot."

Nausea rose in Mac's throat.

Wild looked at him appraisingly. "Don't wander off like that again. I've told you before: we can't have stragglers out here. You could be killed before you even knew somebody was around."

Mac stared blankly at him, neither acknowledging Wild's comment nor the fact that the hardtack and coffee from his lunch was coming up in his throat.

"You better listen," Wild snapped. "You could be filleted on a rock."

Mac vomited into the grass.

"OK. Go get dressed and get back to camp. I'll get Bobo."

Mac spit to clear his mouth, shuddering. "Wild," he said, pointing at the tattooed man, "I know him." Had things worked out differently, worked out the way he'd originally intended, he might be there on the ground with him. It was McGregor, the wagon master he'd seen talking to Burden on the train to Bismarck, whose sister and brother-in-law had been killed near Deadwood and whose group he'd hoped to join up with to get to Deadwood.

Wild looked at him, his face skeptical. "Are you sure?"

"His name's McGregor and I met him on the train, on my way to Bismarck. He was leading a bunch of miners to the Black Hills."

"We need to get Bobo," Wild said.

For the next hour small groups of officers and Indian scouts, left the campsite and trekked two hundred yards to the place where the mutilated corpses lay. Several Rees rode up to the circle of men that stood around the bodies. The Rees looked on, speaking softly and gesturing among themselves.

Major Reno questioned Mac about what he knew, and Mac told him about meeting McGregor on the train.

Bouyer looked at the area around the death scene, but found only hoof prints from several Indian ponies, trampled grass, and pooled black blood, nothing that told them why the three had been killed here. Bouyer said, "They probably been with the Indians from the camp we searched back there. From the shape their feet were in they've come a long ways barefoot." Gesturing at the burnt out fire on McGregor's belly, Bouyer said, "This man here must've wanted some special attention--cookin' him like that."

Bobo assigned Wild's set-of-four--including Burden--and Malachy's set, to bury the bodies. The eight men spelled each other as they hacked through thick prairie sod with picks and shovels. The cooling dusk gradually turned toward night, but the work went quickly once the sod was broken. Mac had never seen grass with such deep roots; some went over two feet deep. No one spoke as they lifted the last full shovels from the holes then stopped a moment to rest.

The whisper of the breeze riffling through the prairie grass and the sound of flies buzzing around the bodies was all he could hear. Three black holes paralleled each other in the gathering night, each one long and narrow and final.

Mac gazed back into the shallow valley at the camp that stretched along the creek for a couple of hundred yards. Clouds were building in the north and a large thunderhead fan blossomed northeastward predicting the track of a storm that should miss them this night. White dog tents lined the camp's perimeter in two long rows, glowing softly in the waning light. Horses and mules stirred along the picket ropes, and several mules brayed resentfully. Troopers moved around the cooking fires like slow, dark moths that bumped the flames then backed away and circled and bumped again.

Mac watched the Sergeant of the Guard begin to walk men out to high points both up river and down. It was a peaceful and ordered scene, but the rot of decomposing corpses gave it the lie.

Wild broke the silence when he bent and grasped an arrow shaft where it entered the woman's stomach. He tugged and the shaft pulled away easily from her with a soft hiss of escaping gas. The arrowhead remained inside. Wild pointed to a piece of animal sinew that had partially unwrapped from the tip of the shaft. "See how this loop hangs off?"

Several men gathered closer to look, stepping carefully around the three pale forms in the grass. Mac felt dizzy from the stench and the swarms of insects.

Wild glanced at each trooper. "I know it's hard, but you need to look at this." He held out the arrow. "This sinew was wrapped in a tight fashion but was looped in a way that when the shaft enters a body, the fluids soften the sinew. When the shaft's pulled out the loop comes loose and the arrowhead stays inside the body. The only chance is to pull the arrow out right away before the sinew soaks up body fluids. Sometimes the Indians smear shit on their arrowhead or arrow shaft before they shoot it, to make infection."

Burden had walked away to relieve himself, and from a short distance away in the gathering gloom he said, "I 'spect these three are about as festered as they're gonna get, Captain."

"I'm not your Captain, Burden," Wild said.

"Well, you look like a Captain to me, Wild. You got you some real leadership potential, knowing about Indian kill-craft and such. A man got that, then he got a lot to offer--if he don't take French leave. Know what I mean?"

Mac's face flushed, and he felt the furtive glances of the other men.

Wild looked at Burden briefly, his face hardening. He tossed the arrow shaft away. "All right," he said, "Let's get this done. Everybody grab an arm or an ankle. Let's do it."

As the men lifted and dragged the bodies toward the graves, flies and insects boiled away from the corpses, bumping wildly into the troopers' arms and faces, tangling in their hair, filling the air around them.

Burden laughed, "A world full of killing, but critters still got to eat."

The troopers lowered the bodies into the holes and began to fill them. They piled the tops of each grave as best as they could with thick pieces of sod to keep animals away, then marked the graves with three rough stakes hacked from the limb of a cottonwood near the river. As Wild said a word or two over the graves, Mac noticed Burden staring intently at Wild, without an ear to the praying. The men finally left the mounded graves and began to walk back to the river to wash off the dirt and stench of death.

⌘

After leaving the three graves, Wild decided he'd had enough. He called to Burden, and Burden stopped to wait. "Why all this venom? Don't you ever just let up for an hour?"

Burden didn't answer his question, but just stared, as though weighing something in his mind. "You don't remember me, do you, Captain?"

"I'm not your Captain, Burden," he said, but memory tugged uneasily at his sleeve. "Remember you from where?"

"You killed my brother, Lamar."

Wild was stunned by the charge, incredulous. "I don't even know your brother, and I don't know you."

"You never knew us more than a mite, but it was enough for you to kill Lamar."

"How am I supposed to have killed him?" Dread rushed through

120

him. The man was crazy, or was he confusing him with someone else?

"We was your prisoners over to Tennessee, near Franklin. You didn't take very good care of us."

Like a lightning bolt, Wild remembered. But his mind couldn't absorb it all so quickly, something that had happened so far away, so long ago. "The three convicts: you were one of them." Staggered by the revelation, he said, "Your brother tried to escape. I didn't kill him; my First Sergeant did."

"You ordered it. You just as well've pulled the trigger your own self."

He couldn't keep his thoughts in order, for it all came rushing back after twelve years. How could this be happening now? Angrily he said, "I gave orders to kill all three of you if you tried to escape."

"Lamar was feeble-minded, afraid of the artillery. He just tried to run away from the noise and danger. You didn't ought to kill him."

"I'm sorry about your brother, Burden, but it was a war. Circumstances were out of control." How could this man be here now, visiting upon him the agony of those few days so long ago when all his torment began?

"Funny I'd run into you after all these years, Wild. We must have been through our own two kinds of hell ever since." Burden's eyes fixed on him, ripping at him like a dull knife. "I lost track of one brother in the woods, and the other was killed because of you. Fact is, if you hadn't interfered where you had no business, none of that woulda happened." Burden chuckled. "I thought of you many a time, Captain, and here fate done delivered you right to my feet."

"Your brothers...." His thinking was addled. "Are they both dead?" What did Burden want from this confrontation? It'd been just one bloody incident in a long bloody war. How could he harbor something for so long?

"Donny and I got separated when we lit out, an' I ain't seen him since. We took off before dawn, just before you ran away and the federals killed the rest of your men."

"How do you know when I escaped or that they were killed?" How could Burden know all this? Wild feverishly tried to reconstruct events in his own mind.

"Donny and me couldn't get out of them woods any more'n you

121

with them federal pickets everywhere. We was right there in the trees. You scooted right by us when you ran off from your men."

"I escaped, Burden. It was my duty." Wild cringed at the hollow righteousness in his voice, meant to shield a larger crime. Still, he wouldn't show weakness to this man. He clenched his fists at his sides to keep his hands from trembling.

Burden smirked, "How'd it feel to sit in them woods and listen to your own men be slaughtered?

He struggled to look into Burden's eyes, and was only able to meet them through great effort.

"You ain't what people around here think, Wild. Your grand airs stink like shit on a griddle."

He had to keep his balance. "My recollection of those events is different than yours, but it looks like it would be a waste of my time to try to change your view."

Burden was silent for a moment. He turned to see how far away the other men were, then lowered his voice. "We get into any kind of heavy stuff with the Sioux, you better be keeping an eye on me, Captain."

"Don't threaten me, Burden. Who in hell do you think you are?" But his words felt empty to him, devoid of any real power.

"Call it a threat if you want, but remember what I said." Burden turned and walked away toward the river where Durant was washing his shirt.

Wild watched him go. He'd anticipated a chance to clear the air and set the man straight, but Burden wasn't having any of that. Now he didn't know what to do. For years, brick by brick, he'd built an edifice to cover his past anguish. But Burden had seen the real events behind his careful construction, and now stood witness to the ancient pain that had cumbered him for so long.

⌘

The other troopers had left the pool and gone back to camp when Mac heard Wild call out to Burden, and Burden stopped to wait. He felt angry at Burden for the comment he'd made back at the grave about taking French leave. It was time he got a little slack, for he'd been paying his dues pretty damn' good. The army'd forgotten about it, and he wanted the rest of them to forget too. Burden could just stop rubbing his nose in it.

He saw the two men stand and face each other squarely and, for a few seconds, though he couldn't hear their words, he sensed they might fight. But, after some words that he couldn't hear, Wild was the first to turn from their confrontation, and he walked to the shore in the near dark, stopping some distance away from Mac. He stripped off his shirt and began to wash, saying nothing.

A moment later, Burden came up beside Mac. He was breathing hard and didn't speak, but waded into the shallows and went to his knees. He plunged his forearms and head completely under water then slathered his upper body all over, as if drowning a fire. When Wild started for the camp, Burden looked after him for a couple of seconds, then waded ashore. He picked up his field shirt, wadded it in his fist and used it as a towel.

"I'd appreciate it if you'd get off my back," Mac said.

Burden looked at him quizzically. "What the hell you talking about?"

"What you said a few minutes ago--French leave."

Burden smirked a small glint of recognition. "Shit. I wasn't talking about you."

Even in the twilight Mac could see Burden's face was dark with anger. Water still ran down his face and neck, and he toweled himself harshly with his shirt. "It's Wild. I recognize the son of a bitch."

"Wild?" Mac was bewildered. Had the two known each other in Kansas? He remembered they'd both been in the army there.

Burden turned his head and looked at Mac for a couple of seconds. "Let's just say I recognize his type, sonny. Let it go at that." Burden shook out his shirt and picked up his carbine. "Wild ain't what you all think he is, the self-righteous bastard. I seen too many like him." With that he turned and walked away toward camp.

⌘

Later, lying beneath his blanket, Wild heard Holley's regular breathing. But no sleep came to him; he felt shaken by the exchange with Burden.

Horses nickered along the rope line in the dark and a breeze repeatedly lifted and dropped one side of the tent wall. For a moment, until the breeze shifted direction slightly, the tent seemed like a living, breathing creature.

The three mutilated bodies above the river were bad enough, but they paled in the face of his confrontation with Burden. The man had promised to kill him, but he worried not so much about that threat as he was by what Burden represented: a witness to that incident in his life of which he was most ashamed.

He realized Burden's charge was true: he had given orders that resulted in his brother being shot. Burden and his brothers were civilian convicts taken prisoner in the chaos south of Nashville in December 1864. After two days' fighting, the confederate attack on the city had been blunted. Federals counterattacked with swarming infantry and cavalry that turned their western flank.

He and his First Sergeant had pulled together ragged bands of remnant Confederate forces that had scrambled up a slope somewhere off the Franklin Pike to take refuge in thick woods. They mustered these troops along the wood line to turn and fire on their pursuers, and the Union soldiers had been deterred from following them into the trees.

The federals withdrew across a rising field and Wild's troops lay exhausted in the growing dark and cold. His men burrowed like animals into fallen drifts of dead hackberry and oak leaves, or sat huddled in twos and threes to gain a modicum of warmth. Slate-dark clouds lay close upon them and the remaining light was slipping away. From the southeast came a clatter of small arms fire and men yelling. Then, from the north, federal artillery commenced firing and shells screamed overhead at targets to the south, toward Brentwood Pass and Franklin. Yellow-white explosions flashed against the low overcast.

Anxiety rose in his chest. Maybe Hood's forces had pulled further south and the federals had swarmed beyond these woods in hasty pursuit. Perhaps he and his men were cut off.

He sent his First Sergeant to make a head count and tend to the wounded. Waiting for the Sergeant's return, he took out a ragged, hand-drawn map and tried to determine where they were--he guessed a couple of miles or so north of Brentwood Pass, but even with artillery flashes to illuminate the dark sky, high ground and a tangle of tree branches obscured his view.

When the First Sergeant returned he brought with him a hatless young infantry Lieutenant. His neck and left shoulder were wrapped in a shredded bandage that was filthy with dried blood, dirt and twigs. The man's face was flushed and his eyes feverish, but he forced three men ahead of him at gunpoint.

Each one, shirtless and dressed in filthy, striped prison pants, was covered with so much soot and grime that Wild could see little but yellow teeth and insolent, red-rimmed eyes. Two were big men, each with a shifting, appraising gaze. The third man had some kind of mental problem, for he immediately sat down on the ground and hugged himself. Rocking back and forth, he whimpered softly with each breath, and one of the others, touching him on the shoulder reassuringly, said, "Hush, Lamar. It's all right." Wild was surprised at the tenderness of this gesture, and wondered if the men were brothers.

The bandaged lieutenant told them that a day ago his company had been pushed back to a small village from which all the people had fled. He said, "The federals walked artillery down the street that hit some shops and a small courthouse building. The courthouse cracked open like an egg and began to burn. He gestured at the convicts. "My captain saw these three jump through flames from the second floor, and told us to capture them."

The three prisoners had been jailed in a Union-controlled village. Why this man's captain would obligate him to hold them under such chaotic conditions was beyond understanding. "Where's your captain?" Wild asked.

"It was my Uncle Charles." The lieutenant's voice cracked. "He was our captain--my mother's brother."

Wild and the First Sergeant exchanged glances. Wild said, "Lieutenant, we can't take these men--"

The young officer's mouth trembled. "Last night, Yankee canister cut us up and killed Charles." He gestured at his neck. "I got this."

Wild nodded. "I'm sorry."

The lieutenant's face sagged from exhaustion and his hands quivered under the weight of the heavy pepperbox he pointed at the convicts. Wild's First Sergeant drew his revolver and pointed it at the three prisoners, saying, "Lieutenant, you can holster your weapon."

One of the convicts smirked, "Yeah, I can hold that for you, Lieutenant."

The First Sergeant looked at the man. "Shut your damn' mouth."

Wild didn't want to shoulder this responsibility that was being thrust at them--an obligation that made no sense in this situation. Still, wounded as the officer was, it was nearly heroic that he'd kept these three men in his custody through today's pell-mell retreat.

Wild looked at the mewing convict who sat on the ground, then at the two who stood before him. Their minds were working hard. One convict grinned at him, then gestured at the man on the ground. "Captain, this here's our brother, Lamar. But he ain't the one you got to worry about."

Ignoring this, Wild shook the young officer's hand. "It's an honor to meet you. I'm very sorry about your uncle." He told the First Sergeant, "Tie these men's hands in front of them, then link them one to the other with a neck rope. Hobble them at the ankles with a four-foot rope that each can carry in a shuffling run if we have to move fast."

The second standing prisoner, who hadn't yet spoken, said, "You ain't got to worry about us, Captain. You can just leave us be and go on your way."

"As long as you do what you're told we'll try to keep you from harm until we can turn you over to a civil authority." He looked each of the two standing convicts in the eye as he said, "First Sergeant, if they try to get loose or escape--or don't instantly obey your orders--kill them. These men will not be a burden to us."

The two grinned at Wild, then each one reached down and hooked a hand under one of their brother Lamar's arms. Lamar looked hopefully into each of their faces, a string of sooty drool escaping over his lip. One of them said, "It'll be all right now, Lamar. Get on up here."

⌘

Just before sunrise the next morning, as the five companies broke camp, Wild decided to seek out Edwin. Only his cousin knew everything about the past. Wild caught up with him as he moved among the men of C. When Wild asked him to walk off a bit to a nearby knoll, Edwin said, "There's not much time, Thomas. We can't be long."

Standing with his cousin atop the rise in the silver light of early dawn Wild could see southward to the confluence of Little Powder Creek and the Powder River. The two streams glowed silver against the darker land, and the first pink hints of dawn began to color a blanket of pale cloud in the east.

"Burden says I killed his brother, Lamar."

"He said what?" Edwin's voice was incredulous. "Chew that a little finer."

"He said he recognized me a month ago, back at Fort Lincoln." Wild looked at him. "Remember I thought I knew him, but couldn't recall from where? Well, last night we were walking back from that burial detail and he reminded me. It was twelve years ago, during that retreat from Nashville." Wild struggled to control his voice, and he saw Bobo nod and look away at the land that was beginning to emerge from night.

"Burden and his two brothers were civilian convicts given to our care. One brother tried to escape and one of my men, acting on my orders, shot him. Burden holds me responsible."

Edwin looked contemplative. "We've talked about that time often, but I never knew about this Lamar getting killed."

"It was just an incident in the war. I haven't thought about it in years."

"Well," Edwin said, looking back toward the camp, "So what's the problem?"

"The problem is Burden was there when I escaped. He saw it all."

Edwin nodded thoughtfully, as though he understood. "But did Burden threaten you?" His tone was careful. "I won't have anybody threaten one of my noncoms."

"Not directly," Wild lied. Telling Edwin about Burden's threat meant he'd have to deal with it as a formal discipline problem. But the ten-day scout had to press on quickly and there was no real means to punish or isolate Burden.

"What'd he say to you?"

"He was careful in what he said, but focused on the idea I killed his brother."

"His name was Lamar?"

"Yes. He was an imbecile, and Burden and another brother--I never knew their names at the time--took care of him."

"Why were they in jail?"

"I never knew, but even with the federals chasing us I remember thinking it would be a mistake to turn my back on them. Funny though, they kept their brother with them and took care of him."

Edwin was quiet for a moment and Wild could see his mind working. "What were the circumstances when you--when your First Sergeant--killed this Lamar?"

"Lamar panicked under the shelling and jumped up and ran off. My First Sergeant saw him go and shot him in the head."

Both men stood silently for a moment, gazing out at the morning. Several dusty coulees fell away from them southward, and doves called softly from nearby. A cool breeze began to freshen from the northwest, bringing a pleasant smell of wood smoke and fried bacon from the camp.

"This thing with Burden's brother--it happened around the time you were wounded--when you and your men were captured?"

"That same day. There were maybe twelve or fifteen of us left." Wild passed a hand over his brow. This was hard to talk about, but he said, "They hit us with Whistling Dick out in the open. I had little judgment left. I...." He felt he had to speak, yet was incapable of giving voice to his crime--even though his cousin already knew all about it.

"Thomas, you left that war behind, just as you should have, like any sane man would've done."

But the old rush of anguish flooded over him and he said, "I ran away, Edwin. Let's call it what it was." He hated this. It was like a ritual litany he felt compelled to repeat, as if for expiation--though none ever came.

"You were weak and wounded, a captive. You'd been at war three years. Most of your men were dead. Your whole corps had been routed, yet after being captured you were able to escape, as was your obligation."

"In my rational mind I think that's so." Shame nearly overwhelmed him as he spoke. "But in my emotions I..."

"You met your responsibility, which was to escape from federal capture." Bobo looked back toward the camp.

128

"Edwin, I never returned to duty."

"You did go back home and try to relate what had happened to..."

Wild interrupted, "How could I convince the entire town when I couldn't convince myself? Only recently has my own sister's husband agreed that she should correspond with me." It was agony to state this aloud.

"Thomas, Margaret's husband is a butter-ass who couldn't lick his upper lip. He spent the war trying to cultivate a limp and make his business prosper. He's not qualified to comment on anything--let alone your actions."

"There are many who agree with him. Their sons and husbands died under my command."

"To hell with them. They know nothing of war." Edwin hesitated, gazing impatiently at his cousin's face. "Isn't it time, after nearly twelve years, that you put this behind you?"

"Sometimes I can forget through burying myself in this life," Wild said, gesturing vaguely at the camp. "But it comes back."

Edwin shook his head. "Thomas, we do the best we can in life. You couldn't know the Federals who captured you and your men would dishonor themselves and kill their own captives."

"I should be long dead with them, Edwin. Burden knows it." Wild felt his cousin's forbearance ebbing, saw his glances toward the camp.

"Well," Edwin said, a mild tone of irritation in his voice, "I don't know what more we can say that we haven't said. You're capable of reasoned thought. But I can't stop a man from destroying himself if he's determined to do so--even my own cousin." In the camp several other companies' First Sergeants had mounted and their men were beginning to fall in.

Even with the urgency of departure looming, Edwin seemed reluctant to leave on such a note. They both let their gaze follow south along the river. Light bloomed across the sky, though a few dimming stars still twinkled in the west. A crow deep in a shadowed gully cawed several times, then several rose into sight and languidly flew eastward toward the treeless horizon where the sun soon would rise.

"Thomas." Edwin put his hand on the younger man's shoulder. "I'm going to talk to the little Major and see if we can't rid ourselves of

Burden, before he tries to deal with you as he quite probably did with Gunther."

"He'll have no opportunity."

"Maybe not today, but he might in a confrontation with the Sioux-- when there's confusion enough that no one will know where the bullet that killed you came from."

Wild shrugged, affecting indifference. "Burden and I will get by for the time being." But if Burden's threat was serious--and Wild assumed it was--during an Indian fight there would be little Edwin could do to help him. He'd have to protect himself as best he could by keeping one eye on the Sioux and the other on Burden.

⌘

As Bobo gathered his horse and formed up his company in the line of march he cast a sideways glance at his cousin, feeling a bit of remorse for his sharp comments moments before. Still, it frustrated him that Thomas could not shake himself free from the past.

When the Rebellion ended eleven years earlier, Bobo had felt completely disconnected from the town and people he'd known all his life, incapable of holding up his end of any conversation. After a year he reenlisted and was made a buck sergeant in the Army's Department of the Missouri, then ordered to Fort Riley with the newly forming Seventh Cavalry Regiment.

Prior to departing for Kansas, Bobo's heart leaped when he received a letter from his cousin, Thomas' sister, Margaret Wild. It was the first correspondence between their two families since before the war, for Thomas and he had fought on opposite sides.

Ever since they were children Bobo'd had a serious crush on Margaret, and still felt great admiration for her. To this day, unknown to his wife, he carried Margaret's letter. Every so often he reread it to remind himself of their connection. She was the kindest person he knew.

The first sunlight nudged above the horizon, and a soft yellow-green glow touched the ridges ahead of the column as it began its march southwestward. Bobo glanced over at the three grave mounds on the rise above the river, each with its solitary cottonwood marker. Turning, he fished in his saddlebag for Margaret's letter, found it and slipped it out. Skimming through it as he'd done many times before, he read:

"…and our father will no longer speak to him, for Thomas' company was composed of local men and boys, all of whom died, save himself. There is more to this story than I can relate in this letter, but most assuredly I know my brother well, Edwin. In our town he is unjustly vilified, the target of misdirected slander. Even my husband, Robert, condemns him as others do, and I must say his severe judgment has hardened my heart toward Robert himself.

I am heartsick and only glad our mother has been gone these years and did not have to see the horror her family has suffered. Now estranged from his father and our community, Thomas has gone away, a lost soul. I know he is in the District of Columbia. Edwin, I wonder if, before your impending departure for the plains, you might travel to see him. I would be so grateful. You both have experienced many terrible events during this most horrid first half of our current decade, and Thomas might listen to you.

In the tangled pain of human affairs, all relationships cry out for reconciliation. My father's break with my brother is only one such example. If you would help my brother--our family!--I shall always be grateful for your kindness.

Although we have not talked during these recent terrible years, I assure you of my cousinly affection, and I ask God's blessing on you, my dear Edwin…."

Margaret and Thomas' father had been a gentleman planter, an owner of slaves, a Virginian who held high expectations for his only son. Thomas had a quiet demeanor, and Bobo always thought him uncomfortable with the rollicking revelry of the other privileged sons of his class. For himself, Bobo considered their courtly manners and droll irony pretentious and embarrassing.

Upon receiving Margaret's letter, he'd immediately gone to Washington. He'd found Thomas hollow-eyed and hungry, living in a flop, lost in anguish at his own actions that he believed had cost his men's lives.

But when Bobo listened to Thomas' account, he could not believe his self-censure should be so severe. He was too sensitive. After much discussion and cajoling, Bobo convinced him to go into the Army of the West and spend his considerable talent and energy on the plains. With a new life among other soldiers, he would forget the past, forgive himself of crimes for which--in Bobo's opinion--he held no responsibility.

But Thomas had found no peace of mind. Having served well both in the Rebellion and here in the Army of the West, he'd still been convicted by fools. But he'd long since also fallen victim to his own thinking, and Bobo felt at a loss of any new means to help him overcome himself.

Also, he would talk to Major Reno about Burden, regardless of how Thomas felt about the matter, for it was himself and not his young cousin who ran C Company.

⌘

Mitch Bouyer stood looking at Major Reno, and every bone in his body ached. As he searched for words to convince the Major, he swore to himself, "I'm too old for this bullshit." He itched all over, for the sweat had turned powdery dust to mud, had worked its way into his mouth and eyes and ears, even his asshole--though that'd been welded to a saddle all the live-long day. And here this gristly hunk of mutton, Reno, was digging in his heels.

Wiping at his neck with a filthy rag, Bouyer tried again. "Major, I'm telling you we ain't going to find those people along the Mizpah or the Pumpkin, any more than we found 'em on the Powder. Even with the three dead folks you buried, that abandoned camp was a sideshow." The little major, was as humorless and indecisive a man as he'd ever seen. The stubby little bastard listened about as good as pigs rooting in a corn crib.

Arrayed in a semi-circle in front of Reno's Sibley tent, the five companies' commanders were attentive to this discussion and Bouyer believed they were in accord with his own view. That he was right was plain as the purple veins on his nose, but the major couldn't tell horse shit from berry jam. Of course he was still big dog in this pack.

⌘

Reno didn't like Bouyer's insolent tone--and he didn't trust the man, regardless of Colonel Gibbon's recommendation. Bouyer was half

French and half Santee Sioux, and the Indians called him "Two Bodies." They'd put a price on his head because he scouted for the army. "Mr. Bouyer," he snapped, "General Terry wants an eyeball search all the way west from the Powder to the Tongue and I'm going to give it to him."

"But we know damn well they ain't anywhere this side of the Tongue, Major," Bouyer said. "We could see clear to Texas from atop that divide. They ain't no smoke, no movement, no nothin'."

Reno scratched his nose in what he believed was a thoughtful way, but his tormented thoughts moved fast and a bit desperately. He was looking for cover and had calculated his next remark with care. "What do you think, Lieutenant Smith?" Smith, whom Custer'd promoted to command "E" last spring over another more senior lieutenant, was one of Custer and Terry's favorites. If Smith favored continuing the course of action ordered by General Terry, and Reno stuck to those guns as well, he knew that when he returned to the rallying point on the Yellowstone, Custer couldn't charge him with being too cautious or too rash.

Conversely, if Smith agreed with Bouyer and supported a departure from General Terry's orders as, truthfully, Reno himself did, then he was covered. When he finished his reconnaissance and returned to meet the main column on the Yellowstone in a few more days, Terry and Custer could have no complaint about his taking the initiative to modify the scouting plan to accommodate the changed situation.

Smith looked surprised to be asked, and Reno figured that was because his junior officers didn't see him as one who normally sought counsel. Instead, like Custer, he kept his officers in the dark about his thinking, preferring just to give orders.

"Major," Smith hesitated, "When General Terry ordered us to scout the Mizpah he was looking at the same map we have here, which has now proved inaccurate. It shows the distance between the valleys of the Powder and Mizpah and Pumpkin Creeks as being much greater than in fact they are. Based on what Mr. Bouyer says, and what we can see from the divide, perhaps we should turn west."

Reno considered Lieutenant Smith an irritatingly confident young officer, but he gave a relieved breath and said, "Well, any other comments, gentlemen?" He paused a polite moment for the junior officers to reflect. "Any disagreement with Mr. Smith's and Mr. Bouyer's view?" No one spoke, but a couple officers shook their heads.

"All right then," Reno said. "Let us assume John Sioux has moved further west." He stepped forward and ran his finger along the unrolled map as though to strengthen his position, saying, "In the morning we cross the Pumpkin and continue to the Tongue. Tomorrow we'll convene again to see if we should deviate even further westward."

Reno dismissed his officers. As they left he noticed C Company's First Sergeant Bobo standing off at a distance, obviously waiting to be invited forward. He pretended not to notice the First Sergeant, but ducked into his tent and took a sizable nip from an uncorked bottle of sutler's whiskey. He coughed and wiped a watery eye, but found he needed more moisture so tipped up the bottle and took a longer tug. Exhaling deeply, he stepped back outside and gestured to Bobo who walked up and saluted.

"Major, I need to talk to you about Private Burden's reassignment to Sergeant Wild's set."

But Reno said, "What about it, man?" Though it had been unusual to intrude into a company commander's and First Sergeant's domain and move a trooper in this way, it wasn't unprecedented. He'd been decidedly bold, considered it beneficial to separate Burden from the several Germans. Happily enough, young Sergeant Wild had the pepper to handle the situation, from everything he'd seen of him.

"There's a conflict between Wild and Burden, one Burden is responsible for, but one that undermines Wild's authority with him. I'm concerned that other men may become involved in the matter, and I'd like Burden moved out of my company."

"First Sergeant, I have no time to deal with any squabbling among your men, and I'm surprised you'd try to thrust these matters on me in such challenging moments as these. You are a senior noncommissioned officer of many years' experience and should know by now how to handle such issues within your own troop." He was in no mood to discuss what he considered minor personnel matters. The decision to transfer Burden had been made several days ago and he had acted resolutely.

Bobo's face reddened at the chastising remarks. "Major," he said, "We have known each other for many years. I wouldn't waste your time with trivial matters."

Reno was beginning to feel the liquor and, as always, it had a curing effect on any uncertainty he felt. He felt his color rise as he snapped, "First Sergeant, I'll not deal with this. I expect you to handle it as you see fit to keep proper order in your company, but keep Burden with Sergeant Wild for now. If there are continued problems, we'll deal with them in a few days on arrival at the Yellowstone."

Reno watched Bobo go with some satisfaction. It always felt splendid to deal so effectively with the delegatory aspects of his office. He surveyed the dusty camp for a moment, saw that all was well in his realm, then retreated to his tent and a bit more of his bottle. There he undertook still another review--though one now more sanguine--of General Terry's written orders.

⌘

The five companies broke camp the following morning at 5:00 a.m. then rode west behind Bouyer and his scouts, crossing over the Pumpkin divide. It was evident to Wild's nose that the Mizpah had offered too little water for washing the night before, for an unusually ripe odor of mingled human and horse sweat hung over the column in the windless dawn.

A couple of hours passed and few troopers spoke beyond making quiet comment about the country they passed. Exhaling and stretching, Wild heard from somewhere far ahead a mouth harp's mournful song, and the distance made the sound silky and rich, like some larger instrument. They passed a blue carpet of blooming lupine, and as they went along he avoided brooding about Burden by composing a letter in his head to Margaret. He described the land and flowers--told her about the things she would understand and appreciate, rather than about his bouts with melancholia, or his anxiety born of Burden being thrust upon him.

From time to time Bouyer and the Rees rode back to the column in ones and twos to report to Reno, then fanned out again far ahead of the detachment, looking every bit as though they were the first humans to traverse this empty part of the planet.

Wild watched two more scouts coming from a long way off, though they raised no dust due to the heavy grass cover and recent rains. They simply appeared at a vast distance as two small dots moving across a green landscape beneath an azure sky. The two riders disappeared behind a rise in the terrain only to reappear minutes later as two slightly larger specks that homed in on the head of the horse column. Wild wished he'd be assigned to scout again soon. Right now would not be a bad time to start.

Late that afternoon in camp Edwin told him that because the scouts had found no sign of Indians along the Powder, Mizpah, or Pumpkin, Reno was going to keep the unit headed west the next day, into the valley of the Tongue. In late May, Bouyer, while scouting for Gibbon, had found a big Sioux and Cheyenne campsite down that way.

Wild didn't know how big the camp was, but wondered if the men of these five companies could handle whatever might come at them. So many soldiers were new and hadn't formed the relationships that would bind them together in combat. Years ago, Edwin had shared his opinion with him regarding what was important in a private soldier. "It's pretty elemental, Thomas. Can a man stay on a horse and control it when it moves faster than a lope? Can he control his fear enough to take careful aim and fire a weapon accurately? Can he develop enough camaraderie--if not friendship--to stand by the men next to him and not run away in the face of gunfire?"

Wild wondered how many in the Seventh had those abilities, given their language problems and lack of training. If they met any kind of numbers along the Tongue, it would be a struggle to keep the five companies of largely untested troopers together. But there was little more he could do. And speculation was useless. Besides, he'd long been a stoic about those he served with or was assigned to supervise. He took what he was dealt--as with his current set-of-four.

The next day Bouyer's scouts found nothing and the column proceeded over another divide and into the valley of the Tongue where the men went into camp along the river. That evening, Wild's spirits rose when Bobo told him he'd ride with the scouts the next day.

At dusk he reported to Major Reno for a briefing about tomorrow's plans. When he got to the Major's tent, Bouyer and Reno and his company commanders were sitting outside on camp chairs around a small fire.

Along with them sat three other enlisted men, a skinny corporal in a sun-faded kepi and two three-stripers from other companies. Like himself, these men periodically augmented the regular contingent of Indian scouts. Wild nodded to them in recognition. Oblivious to the lack of camp chairs, Reno told him to sit so he bent on one knee while the Major and Bouyer presented the situation.

Bouyer summarized the facts. At no time in the several days since Major Reno's detachment had begun its scout had they found recent signs of Indian bands traveling. "That Sioux family our Rees killed was the lone exception, and they likely'd been alone," Bouyer said. "We had the one sentry killed, but that don't indicate any large amount of Sioux or Cheyenne are around."

Neither Reno nor any other officer present challenged Bouyer's assumption that an Indian killed the German soldier. Apparently, no one would offer an alternative explanation of Gunther's death, at least any that might dispel the notion of an Indian having committed the killing. It disheartened him, but Reno did have other matters to deal with beside Burden.

"In my view it's unlikely we're going to find Sioux or Cheyenne here in the valley of the Tongue," Reno said. "However, we'll learn more about that tomorrow by pushing more scouts out in several directions and at greater distances." He nodded at Wild and the other noncoms, saying, "That's why we're bringing you men in."

Bouyer let his gaze wander past each of them, saying, "Back in May I was scouting for Gibbon while we was coming east along the north bank of the Yellowstone. About ten of us crossed over the river and nosed our way deep south into the Tongue River valley. We found a big camp there, Sioux and Cheyenne both."

He reached in his pocket and pulled out a filthy rag, then blew his nose. "It straightened the hair on my neck, I tell you. We skedaddled back north to the river. We'd just swum the horses over and got across in the boats, when about thirty of 'em come up behind us on the south bank. We didn't even know they'd been trailing us." He shook his head. "They coulda had an easy meal."

Wild shifted to ease his knee. He felt anxious at the prospect of them finding a big village south on the Tongue, for they had perhaps fewer than three hundred troops. He said, "What do you know of that camp's numbers, Mr. Bouyer?"

"Fair question, young sergeant, but I don't know. It was damn' big, some several hundred fighters I expect. We saw it and got away fast." Bouyer blew his nose again. "My mama was Sioux and I know'em better'n I know you fellas. The band that followed us to the river paraded back and forth, struttin' like jays at a picnic. They wasn't no flighty bunch, but seemed cocky about anything Gibbon might send at 'em, and that's a fact."

He paused a few seconds. "That camp had hundreds of horses and lots of babies to feed. They can't stay in one place more'n a few days before the grass and game are gone. They may've moved west into the valley of the Rosebud, maybe even back east towards us. We could find 'em anywhere now, and in sizable numbers." Bouyer nodded to Wild and the other new scouts. "They could be up our asses with torch lights before we even smelled smoke."

Wild thought of Fetterman and his eighty men who in a matter of minutes had been killed by overwhelming numbers of Red Cloud's Sioux ten years ago. Bouyer seemed to hold a properly cautious view of things. Supposedly Gibbon trusted him, but how much did Terry and Custer have faith in his views? Custer probably thought him unduly timid.

Reno interjected, "You company commanders know that I have orders from General Terry to finish scouting this valley along the Tongue, and we'll do that tomorrow. Because we anticipate what Mr. Bouyer just said--large numbers of Sioux and Cheyenne somewhere to our south and west--we'll scout upstream in force with squads of flankers and one company to the rear. You noncoms," he looked at Wild and the other three troopers, "will split off in small groups with Mr. Bouyer and his Indians to take in the country ahead."

"Major," a young captain said. "If we don't find these people or their fresh sign, we still have rations for six more days. Will we just go back up the Tongue and meet the regiment?"

Reno said, "I consider it detrimental to return to the Yellowstone with no useful information for the General. I don't want to tell him we found nothing. Consequently, if we find no signs along the Tongue tomorrow I will go beyond my orders and search past the Tongue's far divide and over to Rosebud Creek."

Someone coughed, and two officers looked surprised, exchanging glances. Wild knew it wasn't like the Major to move past the limits of his orders into unmarked terrain. Was the man concerned about criticism from Custer if they showed up back at the Yellowstone with no more information than when they left? In the abstract Wild admired Reno's resoluteness, but didn't know if it was wise in this situation. They were too far from any support or reinforcement, and had no notion of the numbers they might encounter. He looked around at the officers' faces. Clearly some of them felt the same, for the meeting ended quietly, some going away shaking their heads. That didn't leave him with a good feeling.

Wild and the other enlisted scouts walked together back toward their companies' campsites, but stopped together first beside the river. Doves cooed along the bank nearby and a southwest breeze blew the starlit water into white riffles. Though the evening had been balmy it was cooling now.

Wild knew the others, though not particularly well. He couldn't remember if any of these men had been in an Indian fight before, and wondered if they were as concerned as he about charging into a force they knew nothing about, a force that likely had grown in size since Bouyer saw it a month ago.

The common thread the four of them shared--being assigned occasionally to work as scouts--gave them each a bit of pride and they savored these moments amid what they considered privileged company. As if contemplating the next day's events, they looked out at the water and the land beyond. A nighthawk's darting silhouette dove across the blue horizon, swept low over the river, then was gone like a fugitive thought.

"That Major, he ain't got no flash," the skinny corporal said, "But he's OK. He's better than some and not worse than most, what I seen."

Wild knew the corporal had been broken in rank several times, but just recently had been promoted again. Though lower in rank than the other three, he was older-- maybe forty-five or fifty. Small in stature, just skin stretched over bone, his face looked like a skull with sunken eyes and strangely pointy chin. He was an excellent tracker.

"Reno ain't no paper-back," one of the buck sergeants said, "But I don't relish following him into hell neither. It'd be better if old Iron-Butt Custer was leading this scout."

The little corporal removed his kepi and twirled it on his finger. He'd been a heavy drinker and patches of hair had fallen out, leaving random bald spots. He spit and looked across the river. "Hard to know if Reno's bein' courageous or just protectin' his butt," he said. "I'd prefer that it be Custer here, but it looks like Reno's our boy."

Wild kept his opinion to himself, but in his mind's eye still saw the deserters Custer had hung in Kansas, their hands bound behind them, their necks stretched, their trousers soiled with shit. The loyalty Custer inspired in some of these men was infuriating, but there was no point in arguing about it. Like being caught in a downpour or clearing rattlesnakes from a campsite--Custer simply was there to be dealt with, and submitted to.

⌘

Before sunrise Bouyer broke the scouts into several contingents of two and three men and sent them fanning southwestward ahead of the main column. Wild was glad to be assigned to ride with Bouyer. He seemed to have a sense of humor to go with his caution, plus a bit of flair with his hide vest made from a spotted calf. With them rode a renegade Santee Sioux Bouyer had brought with him from Gibbon's expedition.

The three put their horses into an easy lope and rode due west until they were several miles ahead of Reno's five companies. There, for the first time since leaving Fort Lincoln, hair tingled on Wild's neck when they passed over a low rise and suddenly came upon travois scars and dog and pony tracks. The trail was narrow, implying a small group, maybe several families. Travois marks led southwest until obscured in the distance by haze and prairie stubble.

Bouyer turned his horse onto this trail and after twenty minutes or so they came upon a small abandoned campsite in a low area. Six or seven fieldstone tipi rings dotted the landscape as well as ashes from several fires. A pile of dried coyote scat full of animal hair lay beside a pronghorn carcass, its bones picked clean.

They followed the Indian trail southward for several miles and Wild's eyes roamed broadly, watching for smoke or rising dust or figures moving on the wrinkled plain. Along a shallow coulee, buffalo grass was starting to green up, and here and there clumps of prickly pear grew blushing pink with the flush of spring.

In mid-morning they arrived at an abandoned campsite that was much larger than the first one. Bouyer sent the Santee back to Reno with the message that a deserted camp lay ahead. He looked at Wild. "Let's you and me look around while the five companies catch up."

Wild nodded and dismounted, looking out across the plain. As they walked over a slight rise, Wild saw nearby, at a dry streambed, a gnarled cottonwood that stood twisted and bent like an old man. Beside it, made of fallen branches from the dying tree, was a small burial platform. Lashed to the platform with animal sinew was an infant's corpse wrapped in a red trade blanket, the skin of its face desiccated and leathery from sun and wind.

As he and Bouyer walked back through the camp, Wild said, "There's something about abandoned campsites that makes them seem more desolate than the wilderness itself."

Bouyer gave him an amused look. "I don't ponder such things, young sergeant."

Wild looked back at the gnarled cottonwood and the burial platform. Maybe it was just the necessity people faced when having to leave behind a temporary fire and some hut built for the moment. To keep living, one had to move on.

"Young sergeant," Bouyer said, "When Reno arrives, I'll be busy. You keep an eye on that baby back there. I don't want no ears--nor that red blanket--taken as souvenirs."

⌘

After the troops arrived and Bouyer reported to Reno, the five companies left the abandoned camp and rode several more miles southwestward. In early afternoon Reno had them ford the Tongue then dismount again and wait. Mac watched the scouts as they rode out to find what lay beyond a low mesa that blocked their view westward. Bobo told them that before Reno exposed the five companies in the open country beyond the mesa, he wanted information about who or what lay ahead. Mac watched several scouts ride out to find a way around the plateau's sandstone and shale wall. Broken pieces of sandstone and slabs of blue-black shale made a sloping heap along the vertical wall.

An hour later, the scouts returned and reported that the mesa and the region beyond were empty, so the expedition mounted and rode on. Beyond the low hills of the divide lay the valley of the Rosebud, and by mid-afternoon they'd come near the divide. Behind a folded hill full of shadowed coulees the command halted once more to rest. The men were told to unsaddle their horses and eat what they wished, but to build no fires.

Several small groups of scouts headed away from the column and Mac looked for Wild among the mix of Indians, soldiers and civilians but couldn't make him out. Then he saw Bouyer's spotted calf vest and there was Wild riding beside him and an Indian in a ragged calico shirt. They rode over the divide into the valley of the Rosebud.

He watched as vedettes rode out north and south near the divide, thinking that all he had to eat was some Cincinnati chicken and some vinegar he could dip it in. He did so, chewing off chunks of vinegar-soaked raw bacon until he was satisfied.

Moments later Bobo moved among the men of C and told them there would be another hour or two to wait for the scouts to report back. Mac groaned inwardly. All this lying around with nothing to do was getting on his nerves, though he had to admit he was in no hurry to find a crowd of Indians. As several troopers had asserted, there might be a bunch of them--maybe more than their five companies could handle.

The sun dropped behind the low plateau and he was grateful to be in the shade. The land to the east lay vividly yellow in the long light, the shimmering air began to move and cool as the plateau's shadow crept along. Uneasiness settled over him as they waited for Wild and the other scouts to return. He squinted at the western sky and anxiously wondered what Wild and the other scouts would find along the Rosebud. He hoped not much.

⌘

Wild rode west with Bouyer and the Lakota. As they crossed the divide into the valley of the Rosebud Wild looked back and glimpsed the expedition along the bottom of a wide coulee that drained to the northeast. The column of men lay as though disintegrated, a disorderly gaggle among picketed horses, sitting or reclining in small groups along the grassy ravine, taking their ease in slanting sunlight and lengthening shadows on the vast expanse of prairie.

The Santee beside him was the color of an old penny and had his hair tied in a single loose braid with no eagle feathers. He wore greasy deer-hide leggings and a breechcloth, and a filthy calico shirt that looked as if it would fall apart just about any time. Wild had noticed this man several times in passing during the expedition. He gave off a sense of brooding isolation. During their scouting yesterday he'd said only a word or two to Bouyer the entire day.

As they rode Wild said to him, "Do you speak English?" The man looked at him and shrugged, then looked to Bouyer. The two men spoke briefly in Lakota, the Indian grunting only a few guttural syllables. Suddenly, in what seemed an irritable gesture, the Lakota set his horse into a faster lope until he'd pulled twenty or thirty yards ahead, then slowed the animal to maintain the distance between them.

Bouyer chuckled. "He has no words for you, young sergeant. He speaks some English, but he don't like to talk."

Shucking off the Santee's rebuff, Wild grinned. "Maybe he's from the old school: never complain and never explain. What's his name?"

"Name's Caroo."

"Not real friendly."

"He's seen enough of white folks--and his own people too--to last him a while."

"Why's that?"

"In that Minnesota war back in '62, he was in a school for white and Dakota Sioux children run by church people. His clan wouldn't support the war against the whites, so his family had some bad treatment from other Indians. But after the war the army decided to hang his father and brother in Mankato anyway. Trouble was, they hadn't nothing to do with the fight. He don't have no truck with nobody no more, white or brown. We get along 'cause I don't bother him."

Caroo reined in his horse, and Wild and Bouyer caught up with him. The three men let their eyes rove over the green plain ahead. In the far bottom, several miles away they could see a darker band of lush grass and a few cottonwoods that followed Rosebud Creek's meander in a northerly path. Bouyer said, "Rosebud water falls into the Yellowstone 'bout twenty, twenty-five miles north of here." He lifted his chin toward the valley's far margin. "We probably ought to get along and look-see that creek. If any of my mama's kin were in the area earlier they're probably back in camp now."

They rode toward the creek and into a lowering sun, and as they went the Indian sign suddenly began to increase. They crossed several trails, some ten to forty feet wide with travois drags and the prints of dogs and ponies and moccasins. Suddenly Wild saw the barefoot prints of a child. An Indian child likely would have had moccasins. "You think that barefoot print could be a white child?"

"Why would that be, young sergeant?"

"It's barefoot." He was thinking of the three bodies he and the other men had buried earlier, and their raw, torn feet. Could this be a white child the Indians kept?

"Maybe it's just got a mama who ain't good at--or don't care about--making moccasins."

"Maybe."

Bouyer's voice showed a bit of irritation. "What if it was a white child? What would make it special? Mostly, what would we do about it?"

"Not much, that's true. These prints about a week old?"

"A little longer maybe." Bouyer rode silently for a moment. "You a little upset by the notion of a white child livin' with Indians, are you?"

Wild knew he ran a risk of aggravating the man, but said, "Only because it would mean the child was separated from its parents."

Bouyer kept his horse moving forward at a fast walk and said over his shoulder, "More'n a few Indian kids been taken by whites, too, and it's beyond my understanding that such a thing seems sanctifyin' to your people. Puttin' 'em in boots, givin' 'em a white man's haircut and learnin' 'em the good book. Does make a man ponder who the real devils is."

He could think of nothing to say.

Twenty minutes later they crossed a low swale through which many travois had cut parallel furrows three or four inches deep. Caroo reined up and slid off his horse and walked the disturbed earth. He and Bouyer spoke for a moment in Lakota and the Indian climbed back on his horse. They set their animals southwestward at a slow lope.

Bouyer tilted his head at Caroo. "I think this old boy can look at a hoof print and tell you who was sleeping with whose woman, and what horse was the offspring of which another one."

Even though Bouyer's feathers had been ruffled moments earlier, Wild was grateful for the quiet, companionship the man offered. A rolling plain unfolded before them. Sage brush and scrub grass, nipple cactus and prickly pear spotted the land here and there, and in the south the distant ground's rising warmth shimmered and smeared the seam where the far horizon met a milky sky.

He watched Caroo, who rode a bit ahead of them toward another trail that crossed their path on a rise beyond. Two white butterflies fluttered past the Indian pony's eyes. Caroo muttered and the horse flinched and shook its head. Wild's gaze followed the butterflies as they looped around each other and swept past.

Bouyer saw Wild's eyes following the butterflies. "Them's brimstoners."

Wild looked at him quizzically.

"The Sioux shy from that kind of white bug. They deliver ill fortune."

Wild glanced at Caroo. "Apparently he's not too concerned."

"He takes it as it comes. When it's his time to die, he'll go without worrying on no flutter bugs."

"Sounds like an uncomplicated life," Wild said. Caroo's isolation sounded a lot like his own past decade.

"I don't know. 'Bout as happy as a duck in a desert, I expect."

Wild didn't know what it was--maybe his confrontation with Burden back on the Powder after burying those bodies--but he'd been thinking

145

of his father who'd died. They'd had no reconciliation. And there was Margaret and her children, two nieces whom he'd never seen. Edwin was frustrated with him for his handwringing and chronic remorse. Maybe he could forgive himself, even forget the past like Edwin had tried to convince him so many times to do. Maybe someday he'd go back home and see Margaret and her daughters. But first he had to get through the expedition, and deal with Burden's desire to avenge his dead brother.

As if it were yesterday, Wild recalled that last attack where most of his men died. It had come at twilight and his First Sergeant shot Burden's brother, Lamar, when he tried to run from the cannonade.

Wild, full of the stink of gunpowder and layered with dirt and sweat, hadn't had a dip in a creek or clean socks for two weeks--though he'd rinsed them out twice in rain puddles and put them back on wet.

The clouds had begun to thin when the artillery began. They had just started to dig in when the sky screamed as if some huge creature suddenly descended over them. Incoming howitzer and canister walked from left to right along their line. He hugged the ground, averted his face to the blast as stinging debris lashed his neck and shoulders. He never heard the shell that picked him up and threw him sideways, slamming him into darkness. When he opened his eyes he gagged and coughed. His ribs were a wrack of pain. He spit dirt and as his hearing returned he heard a man screaming.

A fragment of memory came back: at the start of the artillery barrage he'd looked up for an instant and seen the feeble-minded convict running north from their position toward the Union lines. His First Sergeant fired and the man splashed face down into dead leaves and muddy water just thirty feet away. How did he get untied from the other two? The barrage had been so intense and unrelenting that the convict had tried to run away, and the First Sergeant simply had followed his orders.

He shook his head to clear it but that only made him dizzier. Slowly he realized the Federals already had swept through their line. He'd been passed over for dead, and all around him lay his men's bodies. Federal soldiers stood silently in small groups, or walked slowly among the corpses, prodding here and there with the toe of a muddy boot or a bayonet tip.

A quiet voice behind him said, "Cap'n, I got no time. You get on your feet now an' I won't kill you. If you don't stand up I'ma put a minie in you." A Union corporal stood looking down at him.

Wild didn't speak, just tried to comply. Muddy water dripped from his hair and ran down his neck. His arms shook badly and for a moment felt incapable of supporting him. The effort to stand seemed almost not worth it. When he tried to rise, immense pain rushed through his torso and he saw that blood soaked the front of his shirt. The pain was instantaneous and so powerful that it flashed through his vision as a white light, but he forced himself slowly to his knees.

"I got no more time, Captain." The soldier raised his rifle toward him, but Wild shook his head, raised his hand in a gesture of forbearance. Panting, he finally struggled to his feet. He was wounded in the ribs but couldn't tell how badly or by what means. He feared his right lung might be collapsed for he couldn't draw a breath that satisfied.

"Git over there," the soldier said. He raised his rifle and tapped Wild's back with the point of his bayonet, nudging him toward a small group of men who stood in the distance. All around, tree trunks were splintered, debarked, limbless, and a burning stump sent flickering light into the dusky gloom. Gunpowder and woodsmoke mingled in the air and blood pooled on the ground. A shattered rifle and pieces of bloody clothing hung from low branches nearby.

Wild stumbled along, holding onto his wounded side. His men's unrecognizable bodies littered the ground, their body parts cast about like limbs of a shattered mannequin. These strange dead, their lifeless corpses bereft of all energy, lay in contorted repose where minie balls, canister, and howitzer rounds had flung them.

In later years Wild thought many times that if he'd known what was to come he might never have had the will to force himself up from the ground at the corporal's command. Instead, he would have lain there and taken the ball.

The remnants of his company were gutted; most of his men lay dead, including the young lieutenant with the head wound who'd brought the three convicts to him. Two of his men, both wounded but able to walk, were being held at gunpoint by a Union private.

The two convicts whose brother his First Sergeant had shot stood aside from his men, but also were being held by the federals. One convict laughed. "Well, Captain, fortune sure do smile upon us, don't it?"

Still dazed, his head ringing and his mouth hanging open, Wild looked dumbly at the man.

The convict smiled bitterly. "You killed our brother. Don't be falling asleep now, yuh hear?"

A painful forced march took captors and prisoners alike a couple of miles further south through dense woods. As they stumbled and fell and cursed the darkness, Wild walked along with one hand held tightly against his painful ribs. He heard other Federal units tramping southward too, and caught glimpses of their movement in pale moonlight through the trees.

Finally, they came out of the forest onto a curving muddy pike that descended a long hill into a broad, marshy valley. Far beyond, on the valley's distant rim, he saw lantern lights. The pike was full of Federal units moving south, infantry slogging along the highway's edge, horses pulling heavy gun caissons and bridging equipment up the middle. In the moonlight, officers and noncoms shouted at the troops to make way for small bands of Federal cavalry that cantered forward through the mass.

One of his men, a forty-five year old private named Monroe, fell beside the road and could not rise. His other three men were too badly wounded to help him carry Monroe so, reaching down to pick him up, he said to the two convicts, both of whom looked strong enough, "Help me with this man."

The bigger of the two laughed. "You gristly son of a bitch. The only thing I'll do is open hell's door and push you in."

A rifle went off right beside Wild and he flinched. Monroe lay dead in the road and the soldier who'd shot him looked at Wild with a cold smile. "Drag him off there, Johnny, or I'll lay you down beside him." Wild dragged Monroe's body from the road.

Later in the night they lay shivering in a small clearing and Wild probed his side and discovered the nature of his wound, not a collapsed lung but a half-hearted bayonet thrust that had forced apart his ribs, possibly cracking one or two without penetrating far.

He dozed but woke repeatedly from the pain in his ribs. Shaking in the cold, he figured he probably had a fever from the wound. Once, late in the night, he looked around. The two convicts were gone. A single soldier guarded them all and Wild, feeling as though he were drifting in and out of delirium watched the man for a while. The guard became Monroe's corpse, but Monroe was dead back there on the road. The guard's head drooped; he seemed asleep. The two convicts must have slipped away a bit earlier. His neck and torso felt like ice and his teeth began to chatter.

His First Sergeant lay panting beside him, still alive, but in the faint light he could see sweat on the sergeant's face. His left foot twitched convulsively. More than any other individual, this man had kept them alive for over three years. Wild thought the soldier who lay beyond his First Sergeant still breathed, but he wasn't sure.

In later years he tried a thousand times to reconstruct his thinking in these few dire moments. His thoughts had been brute-like, concerned only with his own survival. He could do little enough to help himself, let alone save his First Sergeant or the others. They'd die soon enough in prison camp. Why should he die, too? The memory of this craven thought seared him ever after.

In the darkest moments of the night Wild worked loose a rope from his wrists and slipped into the trees. But he quickly realized the woods were thick with Yankee pickets. He stayed for a long time within hearing of the camp, trying to decide what to do, his body shaking with cold, fever and animal fear. If he remained there into daylight, he'd be found for certain.

Moving as quietly as possible, he forced his way into a tangled, brushy area of the woods, and climbed high into a hackberry tree that grew in its midst. Each pull upward with his arms was agony, and every few seconds he stopped to gather his breath. The pain in his ribs was excruciating. But finally he straddled a slender limb he hoped was just strong enough to support his weight. He embraced the hackberry's trunk like a bear cub treed by dogs.

His last two men were killed in the light that came before sunrise. He heard them die, the shouts, the shots. His First Sergeant yelled angrily, "We have a right to be treated as prisoners!"

Someone shouted, "You are, you johnny son of a bitch." He heard the Federals' sharp laugh and the brief snap of pistol fire. Two shots, then silence, then another shot.

He waited until he heard the sound of men and horses moving away through the forest. He waited long after the sounds had disappeared into the distance. He waited longer still, fearful that remnants of federal units might still remain in the area.

As he began to consider climbing down, he heard movement on the forest floor somewhere below. A quiet voice said, "He's gotta be here."

"I know, but shut up."

He heard a shuffle of dry leaves and branches parting, and through a break in the foliage saw one of the convicts move slowly through the snarl of brush below his tree. He suddenly realized that, like himself, they had escaped but had been unable to leave the area until after the Federals departed. They must have seen him in the dark, knew he was alive nearby.

He caught his breath and closed his eyes, trembling, then pressed his cheek against the tree trunk, trying to make no sound.

"Hey, Captain. Come on out so's we can talk."

"Shut up," the other man said.

He stifled an exhausted sob and clenched his chattering teeth, feeling so weak he didn't think he could hold his perch. In the woods there was little sound, for there was no breeze. He was terrified the two men would hear him breathe or move. All they had to do was look up and they would see him. His crotch ached with pain from sitting astride the limb, but with the convicts so close he forced himself to take the pain, for the risk was too great to shift his weight. He nearly swooned, wanting so badly simply to sob and shift his position ever so slightly. His ribs and crotch throbbed and his mind welled with utter despair. He was a small creature, badly injured and hiding, but wishing to live.

Finally, he heard the two convicts move away into the woods. He struggled to control his thoughts, to make his mind utterly blank. He stayed in the tree the rest of the day, falling into a delirium of half-sleep and hallucination in which he saw his sister Margaret as the little girl she once had been. She sat on a limb across from him, legs swinging, petticoats swishing softly. She looked quizzically at him and smiled, but did not speak. Beneath the heavy clouds and gloom of twilight her white dress faintly glowed with its own light.

During the night he came fully awake, but felt so weak he was afraid he couldn't keep his perch. He couldn't remember why he'd stayed so long in this tree, so he slowly slipped toward the ground, losing his grip, almost falling. Once he banged his wounded ribs against a jutting limb. Scarlet light flashed before him and he cried out.

At dawn he woke in thick brush where he had collapsed at the foot of the hackberry tree. He rose and found the small clearing from which he'd escaped, an escape that seemed an age ago. He buried his face in a muddy pool and drank deeply, choking. Shifting bars of sunlight slanted through the trees and yet he thought he could smell rain coming. Soon he found what appeared to be three long trash piles of dirt, a litter of broken branches and pieces of field stone. With fingers stiff as claws he dug into the first pile of loose dirt. He was suddenly confused to hear himself talking to his father, and he shook his head to clear it.

He uncovered the First Sergeant's head beneath a few inches of soil and rock. The pistol ball's entry point was a black hole plugged with dirt beside the bridge of his nose. Gunpowder had blackened the man's face, and the pupils and whites of his eyes stared out at the world through a layer of dirt and grit.

If he'd stayed could he have saved them? He might have thought of a way to convince the soldiers not to kill them. Everywhere there was only death, and his First Sergeant's fate had been no different: another heap of dead flesh on the boundless earth.

He reached out and ineffectually pushed more small scraps of dirt and stone and leaves onto the First Sergeant's grave, then slowly turned and tilted sideways, his face descending onto the mound of dirt and rock. He gagged, choking, then wept, his howls guttural and despairing like those of an injured dog.

Later, he saw Margaret again in their parents' drawing room. She wore a white taffeta dress that glowed in lantern light and held a broad-brimmed straw hat that trailed a wide pink ribbon. Then she stood, her face aglow, beside him in the clearing near the corpses. "Don't die here, Thomas," she said.

He did not die there, though many times since he wished he had, for it would have saved him searing remorse. Having seen such things, having done what he'd done, sinking into such cowardice, he forever wondered what life was worth. Savaged by memory, no pleasure could overtake him, no contentment could stay. That day marked the end of any peace of mind or hope for happiness, save that which he manufactured through leading and serving other troopers in Edwin Bobo's C Company.

⌘

As the three men rode on, Wild asked Bouyer, "You were with Gibbon for over a month. Did you feel he controlled that country along the Yellowstone?"

Bouyer snorted. "He didn't control nothin'. The Sioux came and went--and took their pokes at him--as they chose."

"Will we have enough troops to handle what we find?"

"My gut says not, unless Terry and Gibbon and Crook all come together at the same minute they find the big camp, so they all fight together." Bouyer leaned aside and spit. "That relies too much on coincidence to suit me, but Terry seems to be countin' on it. Hell, he don't even know if Crook's outfit is out of Wyoming yet."

"We don't know the number of Indians we're facing," Wild said, "And we can't coordinate well with Gibbon, or even talk with Crook."

Bouyer nodded. "I'm not sure how Terry thinks he's going to contain these people, even if he could whip 'em with his thousand men, plus Gibbon's outfit. The Sioux and Arapaho and Cheyenne got large numbers and they ain't goin' to take no shit off these nubbins."

He followed Bouyer and the Indian as they turned southwest along a new set of tracks and put their horses forward at a fast lope. Fifteen minutes later they arrived at what had been a huge camp beside Rosebud creek. The creek was bordered with lush grass and scattered clumps of new cattails. At the point where the creek's bank touched the edge of the abandoned camp, clusters of rose bushes still in bud greened the land. He smelled the first hints of fragrance in the few that had unfurled their pink petals. In a few days they'd all be in bloom.

The three men dismounted and separated. Bouyer walked the camp from the center outward in a widening spiral, pausing now and then at a dead campfire or inside a ring of tipi stones to look at the ground. Wild glanced at the Santee periodically, who seemed to have no pattern to his walk. Occasionally Caroo stooped and examined a mark or an object on the ground, but--unlike Bouyer--touched nothing.

Wild walked a zigzag pattern through the camp. Once, when turning about, he almost bumped into the Indian who'd come upon him silently, but Caroo said nothing. Wild stooped and picked up a child's small toy that had been made from bent grass and reeds woven into the rough shape of a tiny horse. He turned it in his hands, wondering about the hands that had made it, and the child who had lost or discarded it. A piece of the reed wrapping had begun to unravel and for a moment he pushed at it and tucked it back with a fingertip. Then, turning the small figurine in his hands, he placed it in the flapped pocket of his field shirt.

A moment later he found several small fossils that looked like the toe bones of some ancient creature. They'd been drilled and strung together with sinew, perhaps had served as a baby's rattle or some other toy. He'd read about the giant lizard fossils that had been found, and thought he'd actually seen the fossils of something like them while on the expedition from Fort Lincoln to the Black Hills two years ago.

Only a light rain had fallen since the Indians departed and hoof prints and moccasin prints were still clear indentations in the ground, though slightly fluffed and cratered by rain drops. The warm breeze brought a faint reek of animal carcasses and horse manure. He shook the stone bones in his hand and gazed about at a vast expanse full of tipi rings. Several hundred lodges had stood here. How did that translate into population? He wanted to get Bouyer's view on it, but their sheer numbers made his heart sink. How would the army ever force these people to do anything? He dropped the fossil toy on the ground.

He heard a distant yell and looked up to see Bouyer wave at him as he and Caroo went toward their horses on the far side of the camp.

They set their horses at a gallop, heading back east to the point where a couple of hours earlier they'd left the column waiting hidden behind the divide.

"How many people do you think were in that camp?" Wild asked.

"I don't know, young sergeant. I figure four hundred lodges, so maybe a thousand warriors, maybe less."

"That many?" Wild felt a chill fill his chest and he shivered as in a draft of cold air.

"Take two or three fighters for each lodge. That's what we got to face so far." Bouyer ran his hand over the grimy stubble on his face. "It won't be no picnic. Them what was in this last camp won't be the onliest ones the army's got to face."

They rode in silence the rest of the way back. Sentries on high ground had seen them approach and by the time they entered the broad ravine, the five companies had stirred themselves. Men were saddling their horses and stashing their gear. Troopers led their animals into formation, falling in on their First Sergeants' positions. With much cursing, gear clanking, mules bawling--and after a short report from Bouyer--Reno signaled the column to advance at a lope.

Less than two hours later they all arrived at the abandoned campsite. Reno called a brief halt as dusk was turning to dark. Though all signs were that the Indians had left this camp several days earlier, instead of going into camp now Reno turned his companies southwestward into the coming night to follow the heavy trail.

Wild and Bouyer and Caroo led the way while two squads from C were detailed as left and right flankers. The other Rees and soldier scouts fanned out a mile or so ahead and to left and right of the column to see if any campfires loomed on the horizon. None did, and by eleven o'clock darkness was so complete that they could no longer follow the trail, so went into camp. Reno allowed no fires and the men grumbled as they ate cold sowbelly and hardtack, then fell into exhausted sleep.

By five o'clock in the morning all scouts were riding the furrowed trail again. Bouyer and Wild and Caroo traced their way southward along a broad highway of ground torn by hundreds of travois. They stopped at several abandoned camps, briefly walked the ground, then rode on again, keeping a couple of miles ahead of the main troop.

"The trails between the camps look like they were made more recently than the camps themselves," Wild said.

Bouyer looked glum. "More people are comin' along after the ones what were in camp earlier. New people coming in all the time. They're puttin' together a pretty big social somewhere out ahead."

He didn't know how many men Crook was bringing up from Wyoming but they'd be needed--every one--or Terry and Gibbon's men would have hell on their hands.

All along between the campsites, the ground was plowed five or six inches deep by the passage of so many travois, and the trails and camps had begun to overlay one another. Bouyer stopped and sat his horse, looking uneasily about.

Wild glanced at their backtrail, hoping to catch sight of the main column, but it was far to their rear beyond the rise of land. He didn't like being so far ahead of the others.

Bouyer gestured broadly at the scarred earth around them. "This's maybe three thousand people--figure maybe a third or more of them fighters. That's more than this piddlin' bunch of soldier boys can handle," he said. "The sign is variously fresh or old, but none of it more'n a week. We best not get too far ahead of Reno, and we best hope we don't run up on them people somewhere ahead." He looked to the southwest. "Some of 'em will be out hunting and we don't need 'em puttin' no eye on us."

Three times through the morning they rode to and from Reno's command. To Reno Bouyer reported his fears about the growing number of Indians that the trail signs indicated, and his concern that the five companies were drawing too close to the Sioux. They could be seen at any moment and attacked by what he was certain would be a much larger force. Reno looked anxious, but each time told them to go back out again.

Finally, in late morning the three men rode back to Reno one more time and reined up at the head of the column. Bouyer confronted the Major. "This ain't no damn' good. Even though their big camp and these lesser ones we've been passing were abandoned a week ago, the trails in between camps have been traveled in the last few days, some less than that."

Wild watched Reno gaze toward the southwest, as though to divine what lay beyond the low hills. The Major ran two risks: either being caught out with a force too small, or being dressed down for overstepping his orders and showing initiative.

"Maybe there's even more of them coming along," the Major said.

Then, quietly, as if musing to himself, "If they see us we could have problems."

Bouyer gave Wild an exasperated glance. Then, apparently wanting to make the decision as easy as possible for Reno, he said, "We got to stop rolling these dice and head back to Terry to report what we've found."

Reno's florid face streamed sweat in the heat. Wild remembered that Terry had ordered Reno to return to the mouth of the Tongue. The regiment's left wing companies, the infantry units, the Studebakers and the beef herd all waited there. Instead, the Major said, "We'll not retrace along the Tongue, but go straight down the Rosebud to the Yellowstone."

Wild and the other soldiers from the scouting detail were told to return to their respective companies. As the column turned to head north for the Yellowstone Wild sat his horse, savoring for a moment his last bit of freedom. He watched Caroo and Bouyer splash through the creek to get in front of the column again. The grass was lush and green along the creek and he smelled again the first hints of rose fragrance that in a day or two would fill the entire creek bottom.

He reached into his shirt pocket and took out the small grass horse figurine. It reminded him of something clean and pure, of himself in another time. Then, for a few sweet seconds, something like grace descended on him and he sensed what his possibilities might be: to see Margaret, to feel whole--a man in full once more.

Even as he mulled these thoughts, a number of troopers along the column greeted him with friendly catcalls and genial derision. Then C Company emerged from the dust. Wild sighed, clicked his horse forward, and was swallowed back into the ranks.

⌘

Burden was hot and filthy after the six-hour ride, and the Yellowstone was a welcome sight when they all came over the last high ground and saw it below them in the distance. He watched two Rees depart from the column and ride off downriver, likely headed for the mouth of the Tongue to notify Terry and Custer and the rest of the expedition that they'd arrived.

The worst part of the whole damn' ride had been the last, for as Rosebud Creek neared its mouth the ground grew rough. The last part of any journey or major chore was always hardest to endure. But he'd long ago learned the last part was most important, for if he could get through that, he just became stronger.

He had to laugh at the sorry sonsofbitches on the Gatling gun. They just about broke their asses on the rough ground, the gun carriage slipping sideways and nearly spilling many times in the dry ravines and little water channels that drained at odd angles across the column's path. They fumed and cursed--a waste of energy--and when they arrived at the river drenched in sweat and choked with dust they just dropped to the ground, sprawled out right where they'd halted in the formation. Other troopers dismounted and began to lead their mounts to the river, but the gun crew didn't move an inch.

A First Sergeant finally barked at them, "Get those damn' animals unharnessed and watered." Burden grinned as the Gatling troopers groaned and swore, then slowly rose and did as they were told.

He kept to himself as the expedition set up dog tents and put the horses out to crop grass. He'd spent much of the day, since Wild returned from scouting duty and the column had turned back north toward the Yellowstone, not speaking to anybody except when he had to. Ever since he could remember, when his mood bordered on rage, silence had been his discipline. Sometimes that was a tall order, for much of what he heard around him in the ranks was the purest kind of bullshit and worthy of being skewered as caustically as possible. This world was peopled with fools, and frauds like Wild who just delivered misery.

Unless he could find Donny again, he'd always travel alone. If he could only find Donny they could stand together against the world's assaults. They understood each other's thinking even without words passing between them; it was this shared understanding that drove him to send out the letters--and that filled him with longing.

Burden scratched himself, thought he'd head for the river in a few minutes to wash, but then--there went Wild, taking Durant and Jesus-boy Holley and the Irishman with him down to the water--probably for a baptism. He'd hold off on the swim, for he liked this time to himself and hoped Wild would keep his eager apprentices on the river a while.

He'd find relief from the memory of Lamar's death only when he finally got rid of Wild. The only problem was good timing.

He knew he'd kill Wild when they found the Indians, for surely then there'd be a big fight. If the battle was chaotic enough then Wild's body'd be found among the unfortunate casualties. Damn' sure, Wild would never strut around Fort Lincoln no more.

Burden saw Bobo approaching him and he bent to tighten the stakes on his side of the dog tent that he shared with Holley. "Burden," Bobo said, "You'll stand guard duty tonight. The Major wants C to provide vedettes on the high ground to the south. I want you to ride midnight to reveille."

Burden nodded, but didn't speak. He liked his sleep, considered guard duty a pain that had to be avoided or simply endured. He'd learned long ago to let his displeasure show, however subtly, for these noncoms would sometimes think twice about hitting him again too soon with the same pain.

But Bobo snapped, "You hear me, soldier?"

Burden straightened and looked him squarely in the face. "I hear you, First Sergeant." Just to let the man know he didn't fear him, he added, "Clear as a tinkling bell."

Bobo returned his gaze. "You need to go dig C Company a couple of sinks," and he gestured, "Right down there by those cottonwoods. Give us all a couple of nice deep holes to shit in."

Burden felt his face grow hot. He glared at Bobo. "I'll gratefully take that on, First Sergeant, right now."

"Good. Hop to it."

As Burden walked away his hands trembled with a wrath hardly endurable and he felt Bobo's eyes as a tingling spot on the back of his neck. He didn't turn around to look at him, but went to one of C's Studebakers and grabbed a shovel.

He strode to the place Bobo had indicated near the river and began to dig, aware of Bobo's eyes on him, thinking, "Plague me, you son of a bitch. I'll destroy you faster than hell fries a feather." He gripped the shovel tightly in both hands to stop them shaking. Grunting, he bore down hard and thrust the blade deeply into the soil, as if jamming it into Bobo's and Wild's necks.

⌘

Bobo kept watch on Burden until he started to dig the first sink, then turned away. He was sore and tired from the ride. His head ached as it often did when he faced much work and had little rest. He was tired of his responsibilities, had begun to wish he could be released from them. However, he was still four years away from retirement and he had a young wife to provide for back at Fort Lincoln. She wanted children, too. The fact they had none was a bigger disappointment to her than to him, for he felt he had to deal with enough children in C each day.

He walked among his men, automatically checking how they looked and what shape their gear was in. Among the men of C Bobo always had his share of problems, troublemakers who made careers of stirring up one bit of bedlam or other, Burden and the Germans being counted among them. Along with the other complications Burden presented, he was also a fairly skilled gambler and kept several slow-witted troopers from various companies in chronic poverty. These men should have stuck with euchre or whist, but they were drawn like moths to the flame of a betting game.

Cornelius Blosser rose stiffly from the ground where he'd dumped the contents of his haversack. "Edwin, I got enough of this angel cake to feed a choir. You need any?"

"No thanks, Cornelius. That old biscuit binds me up. I'm hopin' that steamer gets here tonight or tomorrow and has a few canned goods on board." However, it wasn't constipation that bothered him, but something else.

In the last few days, since they'd seen the big Sioux trails south along the Rosebud, a sense of disquiet--even dread--had begun to creep into his head, a sense of his own impending death. Bobo touched the twisted scar on his temple. He'd experienced fear many times prior to battles: the years of the Rebellion, that raid on Black Kettle's village along the Washita in Kansas and a dozen or more other skirmishes here and there in recent years.

And during the Rebellion, at Gettysburg--where he'd gotten this scar and the destroyed eye, the terrible headaches--he'd had a premonition about that as well. Looking back, he considered those fears normal. He was first a soldier, and he'd behaved well back then for the sake of his friends, and for his own dignity and pride. For many years now, as a First Sergeant, he controlled his fear for his men's sake.

But this time things felt different. The immensity of the last Indian camp they'd inspected, and the deep and widely furrowed ground that composed the Sioux trail leading southwestward from that camp, filled him with dread.

It was almost as though something worse than death might come, but he didn't know what that possibly could be. Maybe the possibility of torture, for the Sioux often mutilated wounded enemies so they'd arrive disabled and disfigured in the next world. He didn't consider himself a very religious man, but it was a wonder what might lie beyond the grave; a mystery. He thought of his wife, Lydia, of her desire for children, and couldn't shake off his fear.

⌘

Late the following morning Wild heard someone shout, "Steamer!" He and the others looked up from their work to see a trooper pointing downriver.

Around a sharp bend, beyond some low bluffs, two pillars of gray smoke boiled into the sky. The steamer Far West was approaching. Moments later, a shout went up and men pointed southward up at the rising land beyond the riverside camp. The regiment's six left-wing companies were picking their way in column-of-fours down a wide ravine toward the river encampment. Wild made out Custer in pale buckskins at the head of the column, two of his hunting dogs swirling around him.

Raucous greetings and genial insults flew when the dusty soldiers arrived. Wild and several other men from C went out to greet old friends. Wild grinned at the melee, for although Reno's scouting expedition had lasted only ten days, the men from the regiment's right and left wings welcomed one another like they'd been apart for years. Milling men and horses and mules spread for hundreds of yards along the river in a happy cacophony of laughter, shouts and cursing and cordial insults. Soon enough, the greetings trailed off to scattered conversations among small groups of men as they filled each other in on the last ten days. The new arrivals led their horses to the river then unsaddled and brushed them out and set them out on picket pins to graze.

A couple of hours later Wild sat spraddle-legged, leaning forward to shave over a mirror glass, when he saw Daniel Knipe heading toward him. Right now he didn't relish a conversation with Knipe or anyone else.

"Thomas, guess what I just heard? Terry considers Reno's scouting expedition a failure, and Custer's furious," Knipe said.

"What do you mean?"

"I was walking by Custer's headquarters tent and heard Custer dressing down the Major. He said if he had his way Reno would stand before a court martial when they returned to Fort Lincoln." Knipe looked rueful, as if a little embarrassed at having to relate all this. "Custer even called Reno insubordinate, and a coward to boot."

"A coward?" Wild's mind leaped angrily at the word. "What--how in hell does he get that?"

"Custer says Reno disobeyed his orders by taking his companies over the Tongue's divide and into the Rosebud Valley. He ran the risk of being seen by the Sioux."

"Reno departed from his orders, but it was a reasonable thing to do if Terry wanted to know where the Indians were." He took another slow scrape at his chin with the straight razor.

"Not according to Custer. He said if Reno was seen--and that was likely--then by now the Indians have probably run south or east out of harm's way. Custer claimed Reno should have pursued them."

Wild felt his face flush with irritation. "Not damn' likely." Everybody thought the Indians would run, but why would they, with their huge numbers and what they would suffer by submitting? Still, Wild controlled himself. "I rode with Bouyer for two days, scouting. We followed that Sioux trail for miles, and it was wider than a platted section. Bouyer said if the Sioux had seen us they'd've wiped out our companies with little trouble--and I agree. I was with him when he passed on his views to Reno."

"Then, in your mind, Reno was wise to disregard his orders?"

Wild felt edgy, like he was blundering into treacherous terrain. But he was angry, and at bottom he didn't care. All Custer's second guessing just browned him off. "Hell, yes, Knipe."

Wild had seen enough of Reno's actions and decisions over time that his esteem for the Major had narrow limits. And, though Reno kept pressing responsibilities on him that he didn't always appreciate, he felt modestly grateful to the Major for being valued. "I'm not going to second-guess Reno for exceeding his orders. It was a calculated risk, and as far as I'm concerned he did the right thing. Besides, he faces problems I'm glad I don't have."

"What do you mean?"

Wild looked at Knipe. The man was dense. Wild knew he was in no position to comment on what went on among the officers, yet his fear of Burden's threats to expose him--all his concealment of the past--infuriated him. He was bone weary of hiding, of being timid and careful.

"Hell, what do you think?" Wild barked. "Working for a hot head: Custer. A man who tears him down and who always puts himself forward first for praise and publicity. A man who doesn't listen to the views of his subordinates when he damn' well might benefit."

Knipe looked surprised at the force of his words. "That's quite an indictment of Custer."

"You can take it however you want. I'm not the first to think or say it. He's my commanding officer and I've served under worse. In my opinion he pleasures himself too much to carry out his role the way he should."

"Well," Knipe said, "Custer thinks Reno shouldn't have taken us beyond the Tongue at all, and I agree. But if he did exceed orders, then he should have gone further. It does seem Reno expects to have it both ways."

Wild paused to calm himself. Knipe wasn't the brightest torch in this parade, but that didn't stop him from having opinions. "Realistically, what do you know? Reno doesn't want anything both ways. He's not the one picking the fight. Probably he just wants to be left alone to do his job." He could only surmise what might be on Reno's mind, based on what he himself might feel in similar circumstances. This conversation was pointless.

Knipe looked angry as he said, "I guess maybe I don't know much, but that's why I came to you. I thought you could enlighten me."

"Yeah, well," Wild said, cooling off a bit, "Look. Custer should simmer down and give a thought to what we did find out."

"What do you mean?"

"There are a couple thousand fighters down southwest of us somewhere, maybe in the Rosebud valley or over toward the Big Horns. Maybe only a few days from here. That's worth knowing."

"True," Knipe allowed. "That ought to be worth something."

"Custer expects Reno to live up to the old saw: 'If you're going to eat poison, then lick the plate.' That sounds real good, but just because Custer relishes that last lick doesn't make it smart."

Knipe's grin was conciliatory. "I guess with Custer sympathy is about the scantiest of emotions."

Wild folded his arms and nodded, waiting for Knipe to leave. "For him, mercy's a stranger." Knipe was always looking for a bit of excitement. In the next few days he ought to find it, for there'd likely be hell to pay--enough for all of them, including Knipe.

⌘

The next morning was overcast and before dawn Wild saw faint flickers of lightning far to the southwest. In the last of the darkness, infantry troops hoisted supply boxes and pork barrels from the hold and onto the deck of the steamer, then hauled them ashore to distribute their contents to the twelve cavalry companies that prepared for departure the following day.

They'd learned last night that all companies of the Seventh would load up for a fifteen-day push right back down the Rosebud Valley where they'd just come from. Only this time the entire regiment would be there, over six hundred men--plus one hell of a lot of pack mules. General Terry and the rest of the expedition were going on west to the Big Horn River, then south into that river valley, intending to meet up with Custer's regiment in about two weeks.

Wild and other buck sergeants from C supervised as their troopers were issued fifteen days' rations of hardtack, coffee, sugar, and bacon. Wild made sure these necessaries were repacked properly into the leather and canvas allforches, then tied to the mules' crossbucks. The men all went to a second line for ammunition, and then another to be issued two extra horseshoes each.

Faint light glowed in the east, but a lantern still hung above the Far West's deck. Wild watched as Custer and several other officers stepped gingerly across a tangle of mud and matted grass and onto the Far West's pontoon bridge, then clumped across the deck to meet with General Terry in his cabin headquarters. Two mules picketed near the boat's stern brayed loudly, complaining about not being able to reach the river to drink.

Wild watched each of his men receive a hundred rounds of carbine ammunition and twenty-four rounds for his Colt. He left Burden to his own packing, but made sure Holley and Durant each had a full web belt and that each man's Dyer pouches were balanced with the bulk of his ammunition. Such little things, done improperly, could turn a new trooper's first fight into catastrophe. Also, into their allforches the cavalry companies packed twelve pounds of oats for each horse, as well as bags of rock salt in case the march went longer than fifteen days and they had to butcher and cook mules or horses.

As the infantrymen broke open more boxes on the shore Wild heard one of their officers tell a First Sergeant the Seventh would take no tents or wagons, for Custer wanted the regiment to travel fast. Wild looked at the big Gatling Gun with its carriage lashed to the deck. He'd already heard that Custer would leave that gun behind, it being too unwieldy for the uncertain terrain they'd cover.

An hour after a cloud-covered dawn crept up, after the steamer had been unloaded and the twelve companies had replenished their stores, many of the men finished their personal packing while others wrote letters. Wild sat in the grass, leaned against his saddle, and began to write to Margaret. Far to the southwest thunder rumbled quietly, and the sky in that direction was dark. An east wind kicked up as dark clouds bloomed beyond the table lands. Out past the river's furthest curve lightning flashed.

Just as he finished his letter, the wind dropped. Then from the west came a cold blast of wind that carried the smell of rain. Suddenly a brief torrent of marble-sized hail drove upon the camp but as quickly as the hail started it stopped and was followed by a cold, heavy downpour. To the southwest Wild could see lighter sky, so this wouldn't be an all-day storm. He stood on a small hummock of turf as a small, rain fed torrent rushed by. When he turned toward the river he saw another slicker-wrapped trooper with his shoulders hunched only ten feet away. The trooper turned and Wild found himself staring at Burden. The nearest soldiers were twenty or thirty feet beyond them and oblivious to everything but the pounding rain. Burden looked equally surprised for an instant, but then stared back at him from beneath the dripping edge of his gutta-percha, his big fists clamping the rubberized fabric close around his chin. Rain streamed down his face.

For the better part of two days Wild'd had nothing but silence out of him, but now Burden said, "Well, Captain, here we are. It's a fine day to find a few Indians and confront your fate. You ever think them Sioux was just fate waiting for you?" Burden stared at him for a few seconds as if to let the thought sink in. "Maybe they're just carrying a bill you owe what's been ignored too long and now's gotta be paid."

Wild ignored this, just stared at Burden. There was something oddly intimate about them being stuck there in the rain with no one else close by. He said, "What happened to your other brother, Burden? There were three of you at Nashville."

Burden looked at him without speaking. His eyes traveled slowly about in the downpour, as though to assure himself that others were at a distance and that rain would continue to fall. He said, "We got parted after you killed Lamar. Federals picked us up. I 'spect they didn't trust us to behave proper. Donny was took away with some, an' I was took away with others."

Wild considered that for a moment, then said, "You never found one another again?" He doubted he could defang Burden's intentions but a calm conversation couldn't hurt.

Burden's brow furrowed, but then, as though he'd made a decison, he said, "Twice I think we just missed. I 'spect he was looking for me like I was looking for him."

For a second Wild thought maybe it was discomfort from the cold rain, but he saw something like pain replace the anger in Burden's eyes. His rancor, at least for now, had declined. Wild said, "I've heard about other troopers copying letters and envelopes for you. One told me you're writing to places around the country looking for your brother."

"People's got big mouths. If it was any of your business, Wild, I'd be first to say."

"I'll take that to mean you're still looking for your brother."

"Take it how you want."

Hoping to prolong this moment of what he considered reasonable conversation, and not knowing where it might lead, Wild said, "I didn't kill your brother."

"The hell you didn't. You might as well have pulled the trigger your own self, instead of that son of a bitch First Sergeant. I was glad to see them Union boys make a hole in him. I'da killed him myself, but slower." Burden spit into the rain. "Always regretted I didn't."

Wild decided to take a further chance. "I'm sorry about Lamar, Burden. It was just the chaos of battle that made him jump and run."

Unmistakable anguish spread across Burden's face. "You never had to shoot him. He was just a loose package and there wasn't no harm in him running off--'cept to his own self. Lamar wouldn't never got far without me and Donny, and he couldn't hurt nobody."

"Well, I'm sorry he died."

Burden looked at him and Wild could see the anger mount again in his eyes. "He didn't die. You killed him and sayin' you're sorry ain't changing a thing between you and me."

Wild shook his head. He didn't want this trouble but there was no reasoning with the man. "It doesn't look like you're open to a different perspective on the matter." His calm words belied the growing hopelessness in his gut. He really didn't want to worry about Burden when the Indians came at them hot, for he'd be impossible to keep track of.

For a moment Burden didn't respond. Then he said, "Lamar was a lost soul wandering this world. He rarely knew a moment's peace or a mote of comfort. You seen him rock back and forth, whimpering like a dog."

"Those letters, the ones you send out looking for your brother? I'd be glad to help you with some of those." But even as he spoke, he knew it was a mistake. He didn't intend for his words to sound like weakness, but they did.

Burden's face turned deep red as the rain slackened. "You coward son of a bitch. You ain't going to help me with nothing." He looked around at the other men, as though to reassure himself they were beyond hearing. "You and me's got a reckoning coming soon, and there ain't no way for you to avoid it."

Wild's throat and chest were tight, but he forced himself to speak calmly. "I'm not interested in battling you."

"I don't expect you are, but you ain't going to have any more to say about it than that German bastard, Gunther, did."

Wild looked at him, trying hard not to betray the sinking feeling, the futility, in his heart. He was not physically afraid of Burden, but felt overwhelmed by the man's venom. He didn't want this trouble, but could see no way out of it. "So you did kill Gunther." Another bolt of lightning struck above them on the bluffs and thunder exploded, smelt of burning metal.

As though oblivious to the noise, Burden glanced around at the other men then leaned forward. "That's right," he said softly. "I cut him and dumped his gear in the Powder."

"I figured so."

Burden's voice was still little more than a whisper. "Of course, we ain't had this conversation." As the rain ended, Burden lifted the gutta-percha away from his head and pulled off his soaked and shapeless field hat. Absently, he plumped it. "I only tell you so's you know what's coming on your own dance card."

"It's too bad you feel that way, Burden, but don't underestimate me." His words felt devoid of any force or conviction, and he was sure Burden sensed this.

"Underestimating you'd be hard to do. You're a hunk of white liver what needs to learn this life ain't worth so much that a man should act the coward." Burden looked at him. "Tell me, Wild, what's so fine about living at the cost you pay?"

"You and I are stuck together right now, thanks to the Major's wisdom. You pull your weight and I'll pull mine."

Burden ignored this. Orange hair lay matted on his forehead except for a cowlick that stood up stubbornly against the wet. "I'm gonna show you for what you are." He spit, then wiped his mouth with the back of his hand. "Then I'm gonna do to you what you did to Lamar."

Wild forced a smile. "Sounds like we're both going to be a little distracted when the shooting starts."

"I'll hold up my end," Burden said, then rose to his feet and walked away.

There was no way to forestall any of this. Burden had admitted he killed Gunther, and Wild had no doubt about Burden's threat to kill him too. He thought for a moment to tell Edwin, but Edwin had no means to help. There was no other answer but for him to take care of himself during the coming fight.

An excerpt from her father's letter:

...I loved horses all my life, felt a kinship with them as do the Lakota people. Mules are another matter. They are stubborn and unreasoning, and full of themselves; too much like men. One of my worst days in the army involved too many mules.

JUNE 22, 1876: YELLOWSTONE RIVER, MONTANA TERRITORY

In late morning, Mac lay down to doze by a small cooking fire, but Bobo prodded his foot. "Durant, get your butt up and get your gear packed. When you're done, start packing C's mules. You and Holley are skinners today when we head south."

Mac's heart sank. Holley and he--along with men assigned from the other companies--would have to coax and bully one hundred seventy-five mules southward toward the Sioux. He hated the prospect, for having to fix supplies to those mules' backs brought all hell within arm's reach. The animals hated the cross bucks worse than death, and they bit, jumped away, tried to bolt. Most had to be blindfolded before the work could proceed with any success.

Finally the sun came out, but even though the air rose fresh and crisp after the rain, Mac and Holley and the other skinners were drenched with sweat after they finally finished packing the mules.

As he and Holley finished 'C's' last mule a shout went up. Several men pointed upriver at a battered mackinaw boat drifting along the south shore toward camp. In the boat's bottom some kind of goods lay covered with a couple of old blankets. As the craft came in close, the man on board tossed a bow line to a soldier on shore. The trooper snatched it, dug in his heels, and the mackinaw swung around in the current. The trooper lashed it to a small boulder just upstream from the Far West.

The boatman jumped ashore. "I'm Jedro Dothan out of Benson's Landing," he roared, "And I got you the best straw hats in Montana Territory! The best sun cover money can buy! My sweet Clotilde made these items an' I personally guarantee they'll keep old sol off your brow or you git yer money back!"

One soldier shouted, "And where'll we find you to get our money back?"

"Up to Pardee's in Bozeman," Dothan yelled, laughing. "Drinkin' and gamblin' your money away!"

A friendly jeering rose from the soldiers, but many stopped their packing and other preparations and drifted toward the boat as the civilian pulled the blankets off his stacks of hats. Although the hats had no strings to hold them on in a big wind, a number of officers and men dumped their shapeless, army issue hats and snatched up the straw hats at twenty-five cents apiece.

As Mac and the others put the mules along a rope line, he ignored the crowd that started to gather around the mackinaw. He had no money and who cared about a straw hat anyway? When some time later he glanced absently at the boat, it had cast off and was disappearing downriver past the steam boat. Many a soldier wore a new straw hat.

He and Holley and two dozen other men from the other companies who'd been assigned as packers now stood by their horses among the braying herd and watched the regiment's horse companies pass before the commanders in review. It was a rag-tag display, and all for the benefit of the commanders' self-puffing. The parade was just another bunch of army rigmarole, and he had no patience for it.

The commanders had ordered all companies' trumpeters to gather as a band to toot their horns and thump a drum or two as General Terry, Custer and several other officers sat their horses and watched the regiment ride past in fours. The unit's horses went their way half helter-skelter thrashing through tangles of sage brush and puddles from the morning's rain.

Mac was surprised that despite their pomp--the band's trumpets blaring "Garryowen," the long, creaking column of horses and men, the burdened mules' braying complaints as they waited to join the mounted companies in train--all this noise seemed meager for it was swallowed by the empty land, drowned by the wind and the river's rushing murmur. The trumpeters' notes came tinny to his ears and evaporated in wisps along the barren ravines and sandstone cliffs, then into the empty vastness. It felt vaguely disturbing that, as big a bunch as they were, their noise was muffled and thin, as if blown through a reed.

As the companies finished parading, he and Holley and the other packers mounted. They goaded the mules forward, falling in behind the regiment in a huge clamor. The ground already was drying and dust from six hundred fifty horse troopers, plus the following train of pack mules filled his mouth and nose and eyes and sent him into periodic sneezing fits.

Rosebud Creek was only a few feet wide, and luxuriant clusters of wild roses had begun to bloom beside it. Lush prairie grass stretched a ten or twenty feet from its banks before thinning into sage and hard-pan, rock and weed.

Lush grasses and stands of cottonwoods and willows along the creek bottom concealed ditches and small channels that impeded travel and made the animals tire faster, forcing the regiment to cross and re-cross the creek numerous times. The mules hated the water and, given any chance, veered away and had to be driven back into line. Due to sloppy packing, several lost their loads and troopers had to stop and recapture each animal then repack and catch up with the column.

By mid-afternoon the expedition rode along high ground at some distance west of the creek. The heat was intense, pressing on Mac's head and shoulders. Holley and he and the other packers coughed and sneezed and cursed the balky mules and the long column's dust.

At 4:00 o'clock, Custer finally called a halt, the expedition having traveled only twelve miles.

⌘

After sunset, Wild and Holley and Burden and Mac sat beside the banked cooking fire and watched Malachy play with a three-footed coyote pup that a soldier from "I" had given him. The tiny animal was a male, perhaps six or seven weeks old and barely old enough to be weaned, but Malachy had already named it Phinney. "It's me father's nickname. This pup's nose is black and me father's has many a dark vein as well. They both share a willingness to eat or drink about anything and raise hell's portion."

Mac saw that the pup had been born with four legs but its right front leg was slightly shorter than the others and parts of its right forepaw were missing. The deformed foot was but a single pad and claw. They all laughed at the small creature and the way it went after hardtack soaked in bacon grease. The pup limped but seemed only a little slowed by its debility, and several troopers from C had wandered over to watch it cavort and yip.

The coyote pup was restless in Malachy's arms, trembling and whimpering. Wild said, "Malachy, how are you going to take care of that animal on the march?"

Malachy's face fell. "I don't know. I carry it inside me shirt for the time bein', but I don't know what I'll do if things get hot up ahead." He'd tried to get Wild to put the thing into one of his larger saddle bags, but Wild only laughed and said, "Irish, if you want that pup then carry it yourself."

The little animal had already wriggled free once today and fallen to the ground. Malachy's horse had almost stepped on it. Malachy turned his mount out of the formation then dismounted to pick up the animal. Bobo had seen this and said nothing, but to Mac it was clear that Malachy's ability to keep the pup would last only as long as Bobo's patience.

⌘

Daniel Knipe asked Wild to go for a walk. Sentries and vedettes had been sent out and the camp's perimeter snugged up tight. Troopers sprawled beside the fires or moved languidly along the creek bottom on small errands. Wild and Knipe nodded here and there to acknowledge a greeting.

"At officer's call tonight, some officers say Custer seemed low," Knipe said, "Kind of like he'd been whipped."

Wild looked at him. "What gives you access to this information?"

Knipe just grinned and shrugged.

"I've rarely seen Custer be anything but curt and commanding," Wild said. "Even when he's relaxed--or deigns to josh a man--he still acts like there's a stick up his ass."

"Well," Knipe said, "Tonight he implied that during the last couple of days some of his officers had tried to undermine him with General Terry."

"I don't know who would try to do that." That was an interesting idea, but one Wild wouldn't have expected from any of the officers he knew. When it came to Custer, many of his subordinate officers fell to bootlicking.

"Supposedly everybody at the meeting looked around at one another but said nothing. Except Captain Benteen, who got his dander up at the suggestion."

Wild bent and pulled a stem of grass, feeling irritable. Somehow, since Burden had said he was going to destroy him, he'd felt less reticent, more free to assert himself. Ruefully, he thought, maybe he owed Burden some thanks. "I've never seen Benteen reluctant to speak his mind. That's probably why he's still a Captain and not a Major."

"Well, he challenged Custer to point a finger at the man he was accusing, and not make remarks that seemed to condemn them all."

Wild said, "It's a known fact that Benteen and Custer enjoy each other about as much as fire loves water."

"Yeah, but Custer as much as apologized to Benteen."

Wild looked at him. "Custer doesn't apologize for anything." He started to walk again and Knipe followed along beside him. "I always assumed he didn't know the meaning of regret, let alone feel any."

"It's just interesting that Custer would show something that looks like doubt," Knipe said. "Makes me wonder if he's uneasy about where we're headed."

Wild realized Knipe was scrutinizing him closely. "Why talk with me about all this?"

"I thought maybe you'd have some insight into the situation."

Wild let a little impatience show in his voice, for he didn't like Knipe's manipulations. "Why would I have insight? The only tales I hear about the officer corps are what I hear from you."

Knipe's voice was suddenly quieter when he said, "Well, you having been an officer once yourself, and all...."

So that was it. Wild stopped and faced him, feeling his face redden. "Where in hell did you get that notion?" He reversed his course and began to walk back the way they'd come.

But Knipe turned and walked briskly beside him. "I'm just looking for your perspective, Thomas, and the story going round seems to fit you well. I'm not surprised you've been an officer before."

He didn't need such trouble, but here it was, like a brown bear poking its head inside his tent. "I have three stripes on my arm, Daniel. That's all."

"Maybe right now, but you didn't back in the Rebellion."

"Where'd you hear about this?" It had to have been Burden, setting about to tell his tale.

"Andy Grimes over in 'E'," Knipe said. "We were talking about how some of the men in the regiment first came to be in the army. He said Burden told him."

"Shit!" There was the answer. Wild shook his head disgustedly, but, oddly, felt more in possession of himself now. "I don't like such nosiness, Daniel."

Knipe raised his hands in a conciliatory gesture. "I meant no offense."

Wild shook his head, said, "I'm done talking," and walked away. He felt Knipe's eyes on him, as well as those of several other troopers. He needed to think, had to get out of here.

Knipe's revelation had staggered him, but the surprising blow had as quickly provoked a righteous anger. Why should he care what any man thought of him? Though he knew others would judge him, none had lived his own experiences, so how dare they? He wondered what the army might do with the information that he had been a captain in the Army of the Confederacy.

He strolled the length of the camp. The half-buried campfires reflected little light off the surrounding terrain. The coming fight made it likely some men now standing beside these fires could be dead in a few days, but their present actions indicated little concern for that possibility.

Custer would say they were here because of his leadership, doing their duty for their country--for the army. The government would say this expedition was only just, given the murderous devastation the Indians had wrought, and to which so many whites could point. But many of the newer men wouldn't be able to say why they were here, about to enter a conflagration that might end their lives. Durant and Malachy and Holley were among these, had come into service because they were hungry--and Burden perhaps because he fit nowhere else in human company.

Wild soon found himself at a remove from the long line of companies' campsites and banked fires. At the end of the horse herd he found another fire, solitary in the high plains' darkness, and built in a concealing hole like the rest of those in the bivouac. Squatting around the fire were Ree and Crow scouts. Among them was Mitch Bouyer who sat cross-legged, chewing on a piece of jerky.

Wild stood at a distance and watched. One of the men rose and picked up his rifle and blanket and moved away into the darkness, and Wild suddenly recognized it was Caroo, the Santee outcast.

Looking up, Bouyer saw Wild and rose to his feet, saying, "Hello there, young Sergeant. Come on over and take some warmth."

"Well, I didn't mean to push in here, Mr. Bouyer."

"You ain't disturbing, young Sergeant. We was just discussing what might be coming in the next few days."

"What do you think might be coming?"

"These boys are pretty worried. They're paid to help find the Sioux, but nary a one wants to be part of the fight." Bouyer picked at his teeth and flicked something into the fire. "I ain't too partial to the idea neither."

"Why should any of you fight when you're paid to scout? You'll be released when we come on the big camp, won't you?"

"I imagine Custer'll release us then--if he has time. Likely some hunting party will see us first and go warn the rest. If such a thing happens, there won't be time to give us no cheery send off with handshakes all around."

Wild had the same fear. The speed with which Custer now pursued this trail unnerved him. If they came upon the Indians in force, there likely would be no time to react or try to negotiate. Wild already knew Bouyer's reaction to the massive trails, but he wanted to draw the man out further. "If we're six hundred fifty men or thereabouts, do you think we can handle what we find?"

"Come on, young sergeant. You ain't got three stripes on your arm for being all green."

"I've been in a few fights, but never when we've been badly outnumbered."

"Then you're about to have a new experience."

"Is it your view that we can handle them?"

"I don't believe it will be the easiest thing, but possible. I don't care what your Colonel Custer's reputation or experience says. I'd like to see a little more caution in the man." Bouyer fumbled on the ground beside him and came up with a greasy leather pouch, then pulled open the string top and thumbed some tobacco into his mouth. "But, that's just my view. I'm gettin' on a bit in years for this work, and I'm prone to take things on the safe side."

"That's not a bad view."

"Well, some might say so. But if a man's warring," he laughed, "You want to kill with gladness, or you want to be killed."

"That's good advice for many things, Mr. Bouyer." The scouts' faces were impassive, but a couple of the men glanced at him, then got up and wandered away. "I need to let all of you get back to your evening."

Wild could understand the Rees and Crows' presence here with the expedition, for the Sioux had been their traditional enemies. And the Sioux usually had gotten the better of them, too.

The government considered the time for talking was pretty much over and Indians' voices, no matter how loud or righteous, were no longer heard. That'd been the case years ago in the village of the Cheyenne leader, Black Kettle, in Kansas. As peaceful as Black Kettle had tried to be, the army's--the government's--indifference and cynicism killed him. After the Seventh's attack Wild had seen Black Kettle face down in the shallows of the river, shot in the back. Wild couldn't remember that battle with anything but shame, for much of it had been a massacre of women and children.

Walking back in the dark to C's area of the bivouac, Wild wondered how many other men had heard Burden's story about him, and how the story had been changed and embellished as it was spread. Oddly enough, his worst fear, that of being exposed, had been visited upon him, and he didn't know what the consequences would be, legally or otherwise. But he suddenly felt that, whatever the outcome, he could live with it. And it'd been Burden who'd pushed him to the wall, exposed him and made him think. He'd done his best, sacrificed food and sleep and safety many times, to protect his men. So who was qualified to judge him?

For a moment he had the pleasant thought that perhaps when this campaign concluded he would take leave and go home to see Margaret. To hell with what her husband and the rest of the town thought. He would deal with them when the time came. And when his enlistment was up he might just say good-bye to the army.

First there would be the Indians to deal with, and in the middle of all that would likely be Burden. Being threatened by such a man did have a tendency to concentrate one's mind. It was odd how Burden's actions, and his wish to kill him, actually had helped clarify his thinking, had helped strengthen him.

⌘

The next morning the expedition rode out in a column of fours. Mac and Holley, freed from yesterday's assignment to shepherd the mules, rode on the inside between Wild and Burden, the four of them at the extreme end of C Company. Mac shook his head, for C rode the regiment's drags. They were the last four men at the rear of the entire regiment, except for the pack mules. They'd eat dust again today.

By late morning, torturing heat had burst forth again. Around him dirt-crusted horse troopers sweated in the hot sun of late June, unrelieved by any sign of breeze. The pale blue of his field shirt was little protection against the sun, which seared his neck and shoulders. He'd hoped to doze in the saddle, but his teeth grated with dust and cinders, and grimy sweat chafed and abraded his sunburned neck. Although he'd plunged into the cold Yellowstone only two days earlier, his clothes stuck to him now and he longed for a splash in cool water.

The regiment's column stretched far ahead in a long, awkward file of men and animals. He smiled absently as Malachy stood up in his stirrups for a long moment and craned his neck, looking at the land and the long horse column ahead. The Irishman was curious about everything and seemed to stand in the saddle about as often as he sat. Heads drooping, troops rode stolidly, dozing at the edge of sleep, their faces ghost-like with chalky grit. In the rear, the pack mules jounced heavily along beneath their burden of ammunition and rations, periodically braying in complaint. From time to time several simply turned off the trail, and troopers assigned to the mule train had to bully and curse and kick them back into line. Finally, his eyes heavy, Mac's head fell forward and he drifted off.

The expedition passed into a region where dozens of new Indian trails came in from the east, then converged southwestward along Rosebud Creek. Through the steaming afternoon, the regiment traveled in the wake of a massive movement of people and animals, and Mac felt a growing unease. Quiet murmurs and whispered conversations rose along the column of tired men. Horse manure littered the ground and everywhere the earth was plowed with the scars of travois poles. The massive, furrowed trail--ponies' hooves, camp garbage, moccasin and dog prints--moved up the creek drainage in the same direction the regiment now traveled. Hoof prints of what must've been thousands of unshod ponies had torn the ground for hundreds of feet to the left and right of the column.

"There's been a lot of people through here," Mac said. He was almost afraid to say out loud what they'd all heard at breakfast that morning. Bouyer thought the warriors might number fifteen hundred to two thousand. It was hard to imagine what so many Indians would look like in a big bunch, and he shuddered to think the regiment was a little over six hundred men since splitting off from General Terry and the others back on the Yellowstone.

Wild said, "We might end up wishing Custer hadn't left the Gatling guns back on the Yellowstone."

Burden spit and said, "Those temperamental sons–uh–guns ain't worth nothing in this kind of a fight. It's good he left 'em."

Holley looked up. "Maybe we shoulda brought 'em. The good Lord mightn't be inclined to help those who overlooked the obvious to protect their lives."

Burden said, "Hauling those sorry bastards around this country is worse than useless, a close-up vision of Hell, too, which might interest you, Holley. Dirty damn' grease buckets, tons of ammo. Miserable, played-out horses. Pushing those wheels through the mud, up and down, up and down."

Wild said, "The voice of experience."

Mac looked at Wild and saw his face smoldering with anger. Besides hearing Burden hold forth, what had got into him?

Burden seemed oblivious to this. He snapped, "Damn' right. Fire a hundred rounds and the damn things jam. They're a nightmare. I spent a month on one such crew and I know what I'm talking about."

Wild turned in the saddle, leaning his head toward Mac and Holley, his jaw muscles working in the side of his face. He lifted a hand and pointed languidly over at Burden. "This man's got a lot to tell us. He's just a soldier of the first order."

Mac was surprised by the sarcasm; he'd never seen that in Wild before. Anxiously, he wondered how Burden would take it.

Burden's face flushed and he glared at Wild, but his anger momentarily mingled with confusion. He snapped, "Anyway, you get into running fights with these people. They ain't inclined to stand still while we turn that goddamn' gun on 'em."

Wild had spoken in a quiet, mocking way and Mac couldn't account for this talk coming from him. Still, Wild wouldn't let it drop. "You understand," he said, looking at Mac and Holley, "Burden thinks he knows a lot about fighting, but maybe all he understands is rampage. That doesn't make him a soldier."

Burden, his face dark red, looked ready to explode. "I am who I am, Wild. But unlike yourself, I ain't confused I should have some statue erected to me." He gestured at Mac and Holley. "An' I may not be one uh your runny noses here, but I ain't ever run from trouble, nor pretended to be some plaster saint when I'm really just a cowardly piece of shit such as you, Wild."

Wild said, "You're so damned disagreeable you couldn't get along with an old dog. You're not much of a soldier, Burden, and for certain you're not worth a damn as a human being."

Cornelius Blosser, riding just in front of them, chuckled.

Burden turned his gaze at Blosser. "You dried up old son of a bitch." Then, to Wild: "Just remember what I see in your future."

A black mark fell across the sky. Mac turned toward it as a goshawk hit the ground in a dust explosion. The bird, flapping hard, lifted into the air, its talons gripping a small form that trailed a slender tail. The hawk glided onto a dead cottonwood limb and bent its beak to its meal.

Cornelius said quietly. "This ole world ain't got remorse for nothing no how." Cornelius winked at Mac and waved a hand toward the hawk, then stared at the back of Burden's head. He said softly, "That old bird yonder, he don't give killin' a second thought, but at least he does it upright."

⌘

By early afternoon Wild rode in a half-doze, but came awake when he heard the horses ahead pick up their gait to a slow trot. For what purpose he didn't know, but he set his horse forward with the rest.

The lead companies had just forded the Rosebud for the fourth or fifth crossing of the afternoon, when Wild heard a great caterwaul of blue language explode behind them and turned in his saddle. Back at the ford troopers goosed and bullied the pack-laden mules toward the water, but suddenly they had wide-spread mutiny on their hands. The mules balked and started to scatter. Bolting between the horsemen, they jolted heavily away through the clumps of prickly pear and sage brush, while others reversed course and lumbered onto the regiment's back trail, anything to keep from having to cross the creek again.

The pack train soldiers, cursing and yelling, chased down the mules one by one then dragged them back with lariats and rope halters, finally forcing them across the water. Once across, individual mules suddenly turned placid, flicking their ears and shaking themselves. They trotted peaceably forward toward the rest of the column that by now had dwindled into the distance ahead.

Wild said, "Custer's ignoring his own orders about not leaving stragglers."

Holley asked, "What orders?"

"The orders he gave night before last at Officers' Call," Wild said.

"He's putting Benteen and the others back there in a bad spot where a force of Indians might be able to cut them off." Wild figured that, regardless of what Custer had ordered, the man just wasn't capable of restraining himself from an effort to close in on the Indians. The massive gathering of Sioux and Cheyenne and Arapaho sure as hell wasn't going to run from six hundred soldiers, so what was the hurry? Wild said, "His regiment's just crossed a creek ford and he knows he's got a balky mule train in the rear. So what's he do? He picks up the pace without a thought for the pack train being cut from the rest of us."

He knew it was reckless to criticize Custer so openly, but he didn't care. He felt as if a new freedom was being born within him for the first time in many years.

As he rode, Wild noted they were passing the farthest point south where days before Bouyer finally convinced Reno to turn back north and not pursue the Indian trail further until they told Terry and Custer what they'd found. It was clear that, though they now had more men than they'd had while on Reno's scouting expedition, the apparent number of Indians that lay before them still made their numbers insufficient.

Through the afternoon the regiment came upon several more deserted campsites, each very large and separated only by a mile or two. Wild saw hundreds of stone tipi circles and vacated wickiups made of bent limbs and brushwood. Larger and larger areas of prairie grass lay trampled and torn. Dried blood, fly-blown viscera and the bones of butchered buffalo, deer, and pronghorn littered the ground. Crows fought over these remains and the stench of human shit and rotting flesh drifted on the hot breeze.

Wild heard nervous conversations jump back and forth along the horse column. Just ahead of him, old Blosser said, "I do believe they're only movin' as far as it takes to find fresh grass for the ponies. That herd's got to be mighty big."

The trooper next to Blosser said, "Whatever they're doing, these large camps been home to several bands. They're just lally-gaggin' along-- and not too far ahead neither."

A short time later, a party of six scouts rode out of the west and converged with the front of the column. Among the riders Wild made out Bouyer's spotted calf vest. With a pang of yearning he wished to be riding with the scouts once more, but events were coming together too quickly now, and the officers weren't likely to pull any soldier scouts from the line to supplement the Crows and Rees. Custer would be wise to hold his troops together, for he had no idea how big a force he faced.

Wild anticipated that some new men, possibly even Holley or Durant, might freeze up at first, maybe even be unable to act. He'd seen an odd phenomenon before in combat: inexperienced men facing a dire situation, transfixed by a brutal and immediate necessity for action but mentally and physically incapable of making their fingers load and fire their own weapons. A number of times early in the Civil War he'd seen dead men with multiple loads jammed down the barrels of their muzzle loaders. They thought they'd fired each load before reloading, but had not.

Though a few newer men had expressed hope that Custer would try to talk with the Indians, Wild knew that wouldn't happen. Custer was not a man who believed in negotiation, and Terry was not available now to constrain him. For Custer's worst traits, there'd likely be a bill come due. From evidence all around them on the ground, that bill might have to be paid in the next day or two.

⌘

That evening Wild walked over to Malachy, who sat apart from the other men playing with his coyote pup. "I don't imagine Phinney comes when you call him, does he Irish?"

"Och, no, Sergeant. He's got a rough little mind of his own. He'll not tolerate orders from any man."

"What are you going to do with this thing when the regiment finds the Indians?" Wild asked. "There won't be time to tend a coyote." The Irishman had a tender heart for animals, but he was setting himself up for trouble.

"I've no room in me Dyer pouches, and this little bugger tries to chew his way out of me forage sack, so I don't know."

"I suppose you want me to take him into my saddlebag."

"The thought of your fine assistance has crossed me mind, Sergeant."

"If we get into trouble I'll take him, Malachy--if there's time to do a hand-off."

Malachy grinned. "Many a thanks to you and I'll buy you a pint when we return to Bismarck."

As Wild walked away, he heard Malachy yelp and turned to see him sucking on a thumb. "The little whelp bit me! A hairy case, this one, and he cares not a fiddler's fart for the world and its thumbs."

An excerpt from her father's letter:

...I remember the men along the column grew increasingly anxious as we drew closer to the Indians. Many were fearful, as though they could foresee the terrible events that were coming. Even after all these years it pains me to recollect that less than a day later, so many of them would be dead.

JUNE 24, 1876: VALLEY OF THE ROSEBUD, MONTANA TERRITORY

The next day the regiment went on the march by 5:00 a.m., and moved ahead rapidly. Wild figured Custer must feel he was closing on the Indians quickly for he set an unusually rapid pace, one the horses would not be able to sustain.

In mid-morning, as C Company rode past a creek meander, Wild saw several Rees ride in toward the head of the column from far out front. They reined up next to Custer, who halted the column for several minutes as he talked with the scouts. Then Custer rode off with the Rees, taking with him a squadron composed of the two companies that had been riding at the regiment's front.

The rest of the expedition set forth at a slow lope to follow Custer's detachment. An orderly rode back along the regiment to talk with each company's First Sergeant. Word trickled out that some miles ahead scouts had seen fresh pony tracks. They were concerned that there was a hunting party abroad, or perhaps a group of Sioux scouting the expedition's whereabouts.

Momentarily Edwin Bobo turned his horse from the ranks and sat the animal as his men rode past him. "Check your gear, men. See your furniture's tied and your weapons loaded. Look sharp now!"

Twenty minutes later the column's main body, minus the mule train that lagged behind again, caught up with Custer's squadron. The troopers he'd taken with him stood dismounted beside a huge abandoned campsite, the far borders of which Wild couldn't see, for a low rise intervened in the middle distance and blocked a greater view. But the encampment was huge. A wave of murmurs and quiet cursing passed along the ranks.

Beyond the rise Wild saw tops of what looked like a circle of strong poles set vertically into the ground. In their midst stood a taller cottonwood pole, perhaps thirty feet high. It was painted in different pale colors: yellow, green, red ochre, bluish gray. From its top hung small bundles of sticks and red cloth and what looked like pieces of buffalo hide.

Then Bobo shouted, "Sergeant Wild," and gestured to him to come forward. "Go on up to Bouyer's people and help them walk this camp."

When he got up to Bouyer, the scout said, "Young sergeant, git on line with us and we'll walk this ground to see what we can see. These folks had them a Sun Dance here, and not long ago."

Wild remembered hearing of such a ceremony before, a ritual dance of sacrifice and prayer designed to display a man's endurance and strength of mind, and to foster visions that could guide his people through coming trials.

Once he and the other searchers walked across the rise where the circle of vertical poles was sunk in the ground, Wild saw that the dirt and grass had been trampled by thousands of moccasins. The circle was perhaps a hundred fifty feet in diameter, and several rows of red and blue painted buffalo heads had been arranged to face the east. Long rawhide and buffalo hair lariats hung from each pole and at their ends dangled short bone awls smeared with blood now dried to black. The flesh of many warriors had been pierced as they'd danced at the end of these tethers. Spatters of dry blood lay all over the ground and flies buzzed everywhere.

Shortly the regiment rode on, each man watching the trail ahead. Two men in front of Wild asserted the plowed trail they followed was over half a mile wide. When he looked far to the left and then to the right of the column he figured he couldn't argue with them.

Several hours later Mac heard a rumor that raced back along the line. Up ahead the Rees had found yet another huge Indian trail coming in from the east. Before they could see it, word was passed that it was broad and deeply furrowed. Moments later, standing in his stirrups and squinting across the long-shadows of late afternoon, Mac saw an immense section of torn earth that marked the converging track. Gradually it merged with the expedition and the original trail they'd already followed; the earth was plowed several inches deep from thousands of people on the move.

How could he have gotten himself into this? All he'd been trying to do was find Sophia. Now here he was about to account for himself against forces over which he had no control. It wasn't even his fight. Yet, when he looked around at Holley and Malachy and Wild and the others his resentment faded. They were all here together, each with his own reasons--none of which probably seemed good enough in light of their present circumstance. But who among them could've predicted they'd find themselves in such a spot? He spit mud, then slapped futilely at the dust on his chest and shoulders.

The long formation of men, horses, and mules left Rosebud Creek and the valley floor and picked its way westward, up toward a cleft in the Wolf Mountains. The commanders increased the intervals between their companies and led them along a winding route where more grass grew, a route by which they could minimize the regiment's dust cloud. Like many of the other troopers after such a long day, Mac was dozing in his saddle when just before sunset quiet word to halt traveled back along the column. They'd arrived in the shaded cover of a low bluff that rose toward the Wolfs' divide.

He and the other troopers were allowed to dismount but not permitted to unsaddle their horses. A freshening breeze bloomed from the northwest and began to break the heat. The sun lay just above the jagged hills ahead, and as it quickly sank Mac watched radiant light slant slowly upward onto thin clouds, turning them a soft rosy hue.

The regiment's progress since leaving the Sun Dance camp had been slow, with much halting and waiting as scouts went ahead to follow the trail which was said to be surprisingly fresh. Word came back that the Indians were thought to be only a few hours ahead, perhaps only twenty or thirty miles away.

In the gathering twilight, commanders ordered sentries out on foot to the regiment's right and left. Mac saw a dozen vedettes from another company ride out to take up posts along the rolling land above the valley floor. Sitting his horse alone in the dark so far beyond sight and sound of the camp--particularly now with the Sioux so close--would be a fearful thing. He licked at raw, dry lips, anxious but relieved not to be among the mounted sentries.

⌘

After the regiment had halted behind the butte, Wild dismounted and loosened his saddle girth. As he picketed his mount he heard Edwin Bobo call his name.

"Thomas, walk with me for a minute," Edwin said. They strolled away from the dry bivouac full of dusty troopers and into the looming twilight and growing night sounds. Both men carried their loaded Springfields. Wild waited for his cousin to speak.

"We don't have a lot of time," Edwin said. "Sometime tomorrow the fat will go into the fire."

Wild nodded. "I imagine whatever's waiting isn't far." He knew his cousin well, and there was something else on his mind. But, whatever the nature of it, the subject had to work its way out on its own.

"You're a long way from home," Edwin said, "And you've not seen Margaret in many a year."

"Yes, but I'm among my friends and comrades." He looked at his cousin. "In fact, I've been thinking about going home after this, maybe even getting out of the army. Burden has told some others about me having been a Confederate officer--and probably about me abandoning my men. He's done me a favor of a kind; it's made me think. He set my worst fear before me, but maybe it's not so bad as I've imagined it all these years." His words sounded almost casual to his own ears, and he wondered how such immense and prolonged apprehension could so easily pass away. Burden, in wanting to hurt him so badly, had actually done him good.

Edwin's face looked distracted, as though he hadn't heard. Still, he said, "I know that fear and dread often loom worse in my mind than the facts when they finally fall into my lap."

They walked on slowly, taking in the twilit bluffs beyond, then detouring around a broad patch of prickly pear. Looking at the dry land that rose before them, Wild regretted leaving Rosebud Creek behind; its cool, clear current and clusters of fragrant pink roses had earlier lent a soft note to their journey. When called to mount they would move toward the divide--a gap he could see far ahead in the rugged hills. Knowing Custer's driven nature, they'd probably ride most of the night to cross there.

Edwin would have to lead C carefully, trying to stay behind the company ahead, and hope they didn't get lost in the dark. They'd all be dog tired for whatever might face them tomorrow. While some men could easily fall asleep in the saddle, the weight of apprehension that covered the column like a heavy blanket would make it hard to do so tonight.

Edwin said, "Are you feeling all right about tomorrow?"

Wild thought about that for a second. He wouldn't tell Edwin about Burden's threat; the men of C gave his cousin enough other worries. "I've always been nervous since my first fight years ago at Manassus."

His cousin looked at him. "Not knowing when death was coming: that would be best. All these years that I've been in one shooting war or another, I've been wounded three times." He smiled dolefully. "That seems a goodly number, yet at times it doesn't seem so much."

Wild began to understand. "Yes, and you said that you've been largely lucky, Edwin. You know the odds are good in a fight with these people. They aren't as well organized or equipped as we." He gazed at the sunset's afterglow that topped the jagged hills, leaving them in black silhouette, and struggled for the right words. "Those are your words just before the Yellowstone expedition several years ago."

"Lydia has always enjoyed your company, Thomas."

For a second Wild didn't know what to say to this sudden change of direction. Awkwardly, he responded, "And I value the kindness you've both shown me, Edwin. You've both been my best friends."

"A man can't know what will take place in a battle, but it's fairly certain that tomorrow the worst will happen to some of us." Edwin scratched his belly lazily. "If something happens to me, if I don't return home with all of you, I'd like you to look in on Lydia."

Unnerved by Edwin's anxious words, Wild felt his face flush. "Edwin, it's unlikely that will be necessary." But, sensing his cousin's need, he added, "I'd certainly expect to look in on Lydia. She's like a sister to me, but you'll return to her."

They listened to the sounds of the gathering night. A dove called from somewhere above them on the hillside and something rustled the dry grass nearby. A twilit sky to the northwest was turning indigo and a solitary turkey vulture's black silhouette floated, tilting and drifting on warm air that rose off the land. The smell of pipe smoke, horse sweat, and leather wafted on a silky zephyr from the dusty bivouac. The night was still pleasantly warm, and overhead the belt of the Milky Way stood out vividly with other stars against the blue-black vault.

⌘

Mac saw Wild and Bobo return from their walk, Bobo passing among the other men in the deepening twilight. As the First Sergeant responded to questions and requests, his voice was low but commanding. "I want all of you quiet from here on out. Just eat your meal cold, Holley--whatever you have in your kit. No fires. All of you men, they're lighting tobacco up the line, so go ahead." Bobo cast his thumb at the bluff that hid the regiment. "But no more smokes once we leave here." Mac led his horse away, setting the animal's picket pin and tethering it. He wouldn't be able to brush the big sorrel tonight, but he stroked her and talked to her quietly. He heard Bobo say to someone unseen, "I think it'll be a night march. There's an Officers' Call underway up there."

Mac looked toward the front of the column. Burning tobacco flared and ebbed along the line of men and horses that were nearly invisible now in the gathering gloom. A larger white light shown far ahead, perhaps a lantern or a couple of candles. He guessed that, absent the bugler's call, this light was Custer's beacon to summon his officers.

"Mac, you got any biscuit I can have?" Holley whispered. "I got a big hole down here my raw bacon didn't fill."

Absently, he handed a piece of hardtack to the sheepherder. Then, on impulse, he dug around in his gear and found the locket with Sophia's picture. Hefting it lightly, he went to find Wild. Mac saw him with another trooper. The man handed Wild a letter. Mac waited until the man departed then said, "Wild, I need a minute."

"What's up, Durant?"

He felt self-conscious, sensing that Wild was scrutinizing him closely. "I don't have a letter, but I need you to keep this." He handed him the locket. "I just figure if everybody's giving you letters to carry, I don't need to be the only one with no insurance."

"It's sorry insurance, Durant. You know that."

"I know." He felt a little foolish, but also compelled to do something to relieve his worry. "I might as well take a precaution if I can."

Wild tossed the locket back and forth between his two hands. "This doesn't qualify as a precaution. Better to make sure your carbine and revolver are clean and oiled and loaded." He looked at him hard. "Like I told you on another night, make your stand with these men, Mac."

Somehow Wild's use of his first name made a lump well up in his throat and he felt grateful, as though a special moment of connection had prevailed.

⌘

The soldiers sat in small groups and talked quietly, or wrapped themselves in their bed rolls against the growing chill. Many tried to doze and sleep. Wild sat alone, his blanket draped over his shoulders. That Edwin believed he might be killed tomorrow was hard to digest, and though obviously just a foreboding, it brought Wild low to think such a man--his cousin who'd helped him so much at a critical point in his life--could believe he was going to die tomorrow.

Wild looked along the line of troopers, hardly visible in the dark. He heard a muffled conversation not far away, not words but just a halting human tone. Other voices murmured as if in fitful dreams, and in the distance a man began to snore loudly. Another trooper cursed and Wild heard a soft thump, then a snort, and the snoring stopped. Far ahead, at the front of the column, Custer's light had winked out.

Edwin believed he saw his own death approaching; yet he was blessed with the heart and courage to look beyond the veil. Custer seemed one who'd never drawn the curtain aside to look. He'd been promoted to Brigadier at the age of twenty-three. Perhaps from accolades won too soon, he'd not grown much since that day.

Then, through the darkness Wild heard quiet commands passing along the line. They were told to fix their gear and mount up. He squinted at his pocket watch and in the pale starlight saw it was only minutes until 11:00 o'clock. Men groaned and cursed, stood up and stretched and rolled their blankets, then stumbled off into the dark to relieve themselves and gather their horses.

He scanned the sky westward. The moon would set in a couple of hours, and finding their way would be difficult. Stretching, he inhaled deeply and looked around for Holley and Durant and Burden. Assuring himself they were in motion, he went to get his horse. He checked the sorrel's furniture, tightened the cinch and pulled himself into the saddle. Suddenly, from high among the rugged clefts of broken stone above, a stiff breeze bloomed and swept down over the regiment's ranks like a prolonged and chilly sigh. The entire column shuddered like a living being and Wild set his teeth against the cold. A restless ache filled his torso as he heard the distant movement of horses. The forward companies began to pick their way upward through starry darkness toward the divide.

⌘

A rising clamor of stamping horses and clanking gear jerked Mac from a fitful doze. For a moment he had a hard time remembering where he was, then a pervasive dread swept through his mind.

His tongue was dry in his mouth and he shook himself awake, shivering and stretching in the high plains night. He spoke to no one as he threaded between the men and horses to find his mare. He pulled her picket pin, taking a bit of comfort from talking to her softly and scratching her withers. The animal thrust her nose against his shoulder, then rooted under his arm and staggered him back a step. Nearby, men gathered their forage sacks, tied up their belongings and reluctantly mounted. They waited for the long column to move forward in the night.

From the darkness nearby, he heard a man quietly say, "Please don't forget my sister, Sergeant Wild."

Wild answered, "Private, you'll mail these yourself, but for now I'm glad to carry them."

The regiment moved out. Everything had such an unreal quality to it: the relentless movement through choking dust; the disembodied voices of men and noise of protesting animals that commingled in profusion. A thin white haze of cloud diffused the starlight and so dimly lit the rising land that he could barely see the closer elements of the regiment spread out ahead along the rocky slope.

⌘

A couple hours into the march Wild heard Edwin quietly pass back the word to halt and dismount and take a stretch. They would lead their horses for a time to give the animals rest.

Edwin was trying to keep C Company aimed on the sound of a tin cup that clanked hollowly against a canteen somewhere at the tail end of the troop ahead. But twice he lost his way, so he halted C and called to Wild. "Go on ahead, Thomas, and try to pick up the sound of that cup."

Wild started off, and luckily the breeze had slackened, so night sounds were not carried away. Once he moved off from the quiet clamor of C, he immediately heard the lost company ahead. Squinting in the dark he could even see their dust cloud moving along the slope above. He called back to Edwin to bring the men forward, and stroked his horse's neck as he waited for them. C's troopers picked their way back and forth across a series of slopes and ravines, sometimes whistling in the dark, or hallooing to other soldiers ahead of them, stopping occasionally to listen for the distant clatter of horses' hooves and gear.

He clicked the horse forward and regained his set's position at the end of C. Minutes later he watched Durant give Holley a piece of cracker. The signs had not been promising a month ago, but Durant had begun to take care of Holley and that was good. He'd owned up to being seventeen, four years below the legal enlistment age. Wild just hoped the boy would hold up all right tomorrow.

An excerpt from her father's letter:

...I have never felt more alien from authorities and their orders than I did that night we crossed the Wolf Mountains' divide. I felt myself an outsider, trapped in this service with little understanding of its purpose and devoid of any desire to carry it out. I don't know why my constitution is such that I have always lacked a desire to inflict harm or wreak vengeance, though these desires seem at home in many people. Probably, the seeds of my life's work were being sown then and I did not know it.

JUNE 25, 1876: WOLF MOUNTAINS, MONTANA TERRITORY

About 4:30 a.m., Mac's horse lurched a bit, and its broken rhythm dragged him awake. He turned in the saddle to see an eerie light in the east; a blood-red dawn bloomed beneath feathery clouds. Wild saw it too, saying, "Must be smoky air from a big grass fire somewhere." C had overtaken some of the other companies in the dark and now was climbing along a wide grassy slope.

The scattered regiment finally halted, still a few miles east of the divide. Many troopers slipped from the saddle, quickly unsaddled and picketed their horses, then fell to the ground asleep. The horses cropped grass and everyone waited while riders were sent back downslope to gather up straggling units and guide them in at a quicker pace.

Mac brushed out his horse for a time, whispering to it. He was about to lie down when the regiment's First Sergeants made their sleeping men get up and fall into formation so they could count heads. Once these counts were done the men were allowed to fall out, which many literally did, lowering themselves to the ground right where they stood and curling up to sleep. Horses stamped and mules brayed, but mostly silence came from the troopers who'd last risen from their blankets more than twenty-four hours before.

"Can anybody think the Sioux don't know we're here?" he said to no one in particular. "We're noisy as a cattle yard."

Cornelius looked at him from the ground where he sat cross-legged. "I just heard that a bunch of the companies is missin' some of their men. Durin' the night they disappeared."

Shock stabbed Mac and he looked down at Holley dozing in the grass. "How could that be?" He wondered if he'd missed something terrible back there on the night march--or perhaps something terrible had just missed him.

"For certain it sets a man to wonder," Malachy said, "That maybe the Sioux picked off stragglers in the dark. I've heard too many a story of Sioux sneakin' right into camp at night, right under sentries' noses, to steal horses. And who might be the man to deny they could ride our flanks last night and skewer such unfortunates as merely stopped to dangle their bobs?"

"They ain't picked off nobody," Burden scoffed. "Any such notion is pure and simple bullshit. Those boys just decided to take off."

Bobo was within hearing and glared at Burden. "You can stop that kind of speculation. I goddamn' well won't tolerate it."

Burden smiled cynically.

Holley, awake now, glanced nervously at Bobo. He quietly asked Burden, "What makes you think those men skedaddled?"

Though the First Sergeant had walked off along the line to talk to someone else, Burden still lowered his voice. "You look what we're facin'. I seen men leave before, when I was with the infantry down to Kansas. Even when there wasn't no danger from Indians. It was the army itself--and the officers. The damn' officers treated us like dogs, which is what we had to eat more than once. Why wouldn't a man take off, given the army's aggravations and that"--he lifted his chin westward--"full-tilt misery coming on fast?"

Mac knew he couldn't leave Holley and the others like that now. In his mind's eye he saw straggling horse soldiers in ones and twos, sneaking off in the night and heading back northeast toward the Yellowstone. But where could they go? This empty country would swallow them, or the Indians would bend them backwards over a rock and carve them up.

The sun still hadn't risen when word came down that the men could make small fires for coffee, but quickly put out the flames when their water was hot enough. Mac was surprised the officers allowed this, for surely the smoke would be seen by anyone beyond the divide.

Some of the older enlisted men shook their heads in amazed disgust. "Why don't we just let loose a fusillade to let 'em know we're on the way?" Cornelius said.

Bobo looked stunned at the order and simply refused to implement it. Two of his men started to build a fire and he snapped at them, "Nobody in C is going to have a goddamn' fire, regardless of what the rest do!"

A few moments later, they all looked up to see a Ree scout riding down a long slope from higher on the mountain side. As the man rode he zig-zagged his mount back and forth and Holley said, "Look, Wild. Why's he riding like that?"

Wild watched the approaching rider. "He's seen the Sioux. That's a signal, a little early warning of the news he's carrying."

A short time later Mac saw Custer riding bareback around the dry camp, talking to officers who hurriedly gathered around him at each place he stopped. Cornelius said, "That man ain't much for goin' slow and methodical. I'd appreciate him more if I know'd he ever had a careful thought."

Word trickled out among the troopers that Custer would ride to meet the scouts at some vantage point high in the mountains where they claimed to have seen smoke from cooking fires in a large village maybe fifteen miles beyond the divide, over in the valley of the Little Horn. The regiment would wait for him to return before they advanced to the divide.

Bobo came up and told Blosser, "I want you and Hennessey to ride with the mule train this afternoon, Cornelius."

"Me and Hennessey?" The old man looked nonplussed.

"Yeah, I need two men and you're it. That isn't too strenuous for you, is it?"

"Hell, no, Edwin. I just ain't worked with them much."

"I don't think we've got many mule experts as it is. So hop to it, all right?"

Cornelius nodded and led his horse toward the mules.

⌘

Just before noon Custer returned and the expedition went on the march, crossing the grassy divide that was simply a gap in the hills bordered by broken rocky scarps and sharply eroded gullies. Far to the northwest Wild squinted to see the valley where the main Indian camp was thought to be. A pale cloud hung above part of the valley, perhaps just haze, but also possibly smoke from cooking fires.

The day grew hot as the expedition descended at a slow lope for several miles along a small creek bordered by scattered cottonwoods. Wild thought Custer set too fast a pace, for some horses were wearing out. Green foam dripped from their mouths; their withers and flanks were frothed with lather. A number of troopers fell behind the formation, opting to let their mounts move at their own pace, spurring them only enough to keep near the main body of troops and not be cut off if they encountered Indians.

The regiment halted several times to let lagging troopers catch up and to allow time for scouts to reconnoiter and report what they'd found ahead so Custer might make his tactical decisions. Then Custer took a step that made Wild shudder.

The column had come upon a creek and stopped there to water horses and refill canteens. While there, Custer broke the regiment into three battalion-sized units, in addition to the pack train that still struggled along in the rear with one company as escort. One of the three battalions, under Captain Benteen's command, quickly departed toward the southwest, apparently to scout the ridges and gullies in that direction.

Wild watched in gloomy dismay as the column of perhaps two hundred men rode down a broad incline, splashed over the creek then turned up a far ravine. Certainly Custer knew more than he about their current situation, but how could he know exactly where the village lay, except for the haze that hung over part of the valley? And how could he know how many fighters they would face?

But he'd heard little conjecture about the enemy in the last couple of hours, and if Custer had shared any information with his officers and senior sergeants, some version would've spread down the ranks by now, regardless of how tired and hungry the men were.

"Them people got hunters out all the time," Holley said. "They got to know we're here."

Wild looked at the men nearby; their eyes roamed restlessly over the nearby terrain then out toward the far valley. Most were quiet, having turned inward, absorbed in their own thoughts.

Burden said, "If they knew we were here they'd be on our asses already. They'd ride out to attack us as far from their camp as possible."

Wild knew that was true. When given the chance, the Sioux always tried to fight as far from home as they could, to protect their families. How many warriors could they send into such an attack? If their fighters came out in large numbers could Benteen's battalion get back in time? With the noise of his own battalion's travel, Benteen might not even hear gunfire that issued from a battle several miles from him across these rolling hills.

As they awaited Custer's orders to advance, Wild saw Edwin, his face grim, slowly ride the length of C's formation. He knew his cousin would be skeptical about Custer having broken up the regiment, but there was nothing any of them could do. Their eyes met and Edwin shook his head.

Wild nodded, his anger at Custer as intense as any he'd ever felt. The man was so full of himself, yet he betrayed such poor judgment in critical moments like these. How could he not hold the regiment together until he knew more about what they faced? Moments later Custer formed the remaining two battalions side by side in parallel columns, on opposite sides of the small creek where they'd rested. Major Reno sat his horse at the head of the left column while Custer kept C and four other companies under his own command on the right. Immediately he set both battalions forward in columns of four along the creek drainage that descended toward the valley. C brought up the dusty rear, and Wild's set rode C's drags. Malachy rode in the set-of-four just ahead of them in the formation.

⌘

About 2:00 Custer's and Reno's two battalions arrived at an abandoned camp where only a single Cheyenne tipi still stood. Wild felt grimy, thirsty and tired. He wanted to find some shade. If they'd been back on Rosebud Creek by that big willow, he'd have stripped, walked into its shade, and sat down in the middle of the creek.

He glanced toward the rear but couldn't see the mule train or its escort company. Custer's quickened pace since leaving the divide several hours ago had caused the supply mules to fall far behind.

Twenty or thirty tipis had been here. Remnants of several cooking fires still smoldered nearby within tipi rings of stone, and several temporary wickiups still had buffalo hides thrown across them. Wild glanced down; near his horse's hooves lay a small stack of monkeyflower someone had just cut for cooking. Perhaps a hundred people had camped here, but departed in a hurry not long ago.

Officers and noncoms barked orders up and down the length of the two battalions and the men mounted again. Burden climbed on his horse and started to turn it but then, as though having a second thought, he stopped and looked back at Wild. "We're all gonna be in hell soon, right here on earth. Let's see how you handle it."

An excerpt from her father's letter:

...Oddly enough, though I wished fervently to be far away from all this, I was not fearful, not worried about my own life. Certainly, I did not want to lose it, or be buried in that vast wilderness. However, just as some men have prescient thoughts about their own impending deaths, in some not-fully-conscious way I knew I would live through the events that just then began to unfold.

JUNE 25, 1876: VALLEY OF THE LITTLE HORN, MONTANA TERRITORY

The remaining two battalions rode west at a fast trot on opposite sides of the stream for fifteen minutes or so. Mac couldn't shut off thoughts of the men who supposedly had taken French leave during the night march. His thoughts raced back and forth between a longing to avoid what might be coming, and a vague feeling of obligation to Holley, Malachy and Wild.

Maybe last night he should have been more on the *qui vive* for a chance to escape. But somehow that option no longer seemed right. The others: what would they think of him for saving his own skin? Anyway, where could he go?

He was fully awake as the two parallel battalions halted once more. The troopers sat impassively on their horses for a few moments, though several men called out encouragement back and forth across the creek. Custer and several officers from each of the two units converged into a group to confer, then after a couple of minutes parted and moved back to the heads of their two columns.

Mac noticed Malachy's coyote pup try to scramble out of the forage sack, but the Irishman pushed it back down inside.

Burden snapped at Malachy. "You ought to dump that damn' thing before it confuses you any more than it already has."

Mac heard shouted orders up ahead but couldn't understand them. A few seconds later the two columns moved out again, this time diverging from one another. With Custer in front, C's battalion moved northwest toward hills that rose gradually into higher bluffs, while Major Reno's unit galloped westward toward the valley floor and the river that still lay a few miles ahead.

"The man's splittin' us ever finer," another man said. "I truly hope he knows what's out there."

The five companies climbed a steeper slope toward the top of the bluff, then into a wide coulee, then up the other side, their tired horses straining against the heat and rising terrain. A number of men stripped off their field shirts as they rode, wedging them under the bedrolls tied behind their cantles. Mac kept his eyes on the front of the column and as it topped a rise, he saw several men in the forward companies pointing to the northwest.

Then a chorus of yells exploded from the battalion's front. Through the dust and distance the companies at the front seemed to shudder and shrink back on themselves like an awkward worm suddenly flinching from danger. The column's front halted, as though coming against an invisible wall, and many troopers who were coming along behind overrode the men in front, causing a minor melee and much cursing and yelling. Officers and noncoms broke from the ranks all along the battalion's length. Bellowing and swearing, they urged their men forward up the hill, then reined them to a halt at the top as the forward companies regrouped in fours behind Custer and several other officers.

Mac could hear no gunfire or see any resistance to their advance, but as C Company finally topped the bluff, he discovered why the front of the column had shied. Hair rose on the back of his neck, for in front of them, spread across the valley floor for perhaps three miles, stood an immense tipi village.

"Jesus Christ Almighty," one man whispered. "That's the biggest thing I ever seen." Several men nearby moaned and shouted in objection, their faces full of disbelief. Bobo and other commanders repeatedly yelled for quiet, and the soldiers' anguished complaints gradually died out.

"Them fighters down there know we're here now," Burden said, "they'll be swarmin' us like a nest of hornets."

In the relative quiet of the command's halt, they suddenly heard faint popping sounds. Looking to their left, into the valley, Mac saw puffs of gray smoke begin to rise from the village's southern edge, then heard the snapping echoes of intermittent gunfire. Gunsmoke rose here and there along the edge of the huge tipi encampment. Only then did Mac see Major Reno's battalion riding in a column of fours along the valley floor toward the village. They were tiny figures at that distance, puny in the valley's vastness, but he saw them plainly.

He and Wild and the others had parted from these men what seemed only a short time ago, but now they were across the river and a couple of miles away. They'd forded the Little Horn and were attacking the south end of the village.

Across the winding river below, out in the open beyond a large wooded area that bordered several of the river's meanders, Reno's mounted column began to fan left and right across the grassy valley floor, quickly forming a long skirmish line. Mac watched the tiny figures dismount, but they were so small and far away that the whole scene had an unreal aspect to it, as though it was happening in a dream or didn't involve him.

Every fourth trooper held his set's horses, leading the animals behind the line of skirmishers who started to walk forward, firing as they went, moving toward the village as though they meant to advance inside it. The gunfire from both sides began to build.

Somebody nearby yelled, "Yeee-hawww! See how that's done? That's right out of the manual."

But, from the south end of the village, fighters on foot or horseback swarmed to confront the troopers who walked toward them on line. More puffs of smoke rose from both sides and hung in the hot still air. Major Reno's soldiers fired as they went forward, but Mac saw more Indians run to gather horses from the herds that grazed to the west of the huge encampment.

From their vantage point on the bluff, Mac and the others sat transfixed. Most had never seen a shot fired in combat before, and Mac suddenly wondered how well the men around him knew how to use their weapons. Most had never yet fired a live round from their army-issued carbines.

From the village below, greater numbers of warriors began to emerge, running between the tipis toward the sound of the gunfire, pouring from the south end of the village, small dark figures like a swarm of bees, racing toward the soldiers. Other people--he guessed women and children--ran through the encampment in the opposite direction, away from the shooting.

The volume of firing grew louder and the number of Indians who streamed from the village toward Reno's men increased. Larger clouds of gun smoke and dust commingled above the scene and parts of the battlefield became obscured from view.

Mac and the others watched the action in the valley to the West as more and more fighters rode or ran from the village toward Reno's advancing cavalry. Then, just as quickly as the soldiers' skirmish line began to move forward, it slowed, then stopped. But after several long seconds it moved haltingly forward again.

"The Sioux are going to flank those men," Cornelius snapped. "We should be going to help."

"No, Cornelius," Wild said, "It's too far. That's two, three miles from here. We'd have to find a ford for the river then get through those woods." He said quietly, "It'll all be over quickly."

Mac spotted Bobo at the front of the column and saw him look back toward Wild, but the First Sergeant said nothing. Bobo's face turned toward the front of the battalion's column as though awaiting a command, but none came. Several more seconds passed and the body of cavalry just sat, watching. No order came from the front.

"Those men can't hold off such numbers," one trooper said. "They'll be run over."

In the heat of this day Mac felt a chill move through his torso, and he passed a hand slowly across his mouth. He said nothing but watched with a sense of awe. Though in plain view, the men in the valley were a long way off. It seemed as though he were watching some event out of time, some mythic battle in a dream that took place on the earth far below.

⌘

Wild knew all they could do was watch the tragedy unfold. For a second he looked toward the head of their own column, but, though he couldn't see Custer, a murderous anger filled him. The man must know that the decisions he'd made--the series of actions he'd taken this day--would be their ruin. He'd sent Benteen off with a full third of the regiment, then sent Reno into the valley against an enemy whose strength and location he knew not. If his intention was to attack the whole valley, these deployments made no sense.

Hardly able to contain himself, wanting somehow to act, Wild could only shift his weight in the saddle. What ridiculous notion had moved Custer to make such blunders? It'd be beneficial for them all if Custer should be killed today. He'd been lucky for years, had bathed in glory that others had granted him for being a man of action. The newspapers had made him a hero and he'd relished their reports. Now Reno's men faced death--as all of them might--because of Custer's blind arrogance.

Reno's skirmish line quickly slowed its forward movement, then stopped again. Even across the vast distance Wild felt he could see those men's thinking. They were faltering, losing will; terror was creeping in. Soldiers who served as horse holders had become targets, and several now lay on the ground. Terrified horses had torn free, whirled away from the gunfire, smoke, and dust. Some raced toward the rear, but in the bedlam a few animals swirled through the battle lines and ran toward the Indians in utter confusion. Still others that had been hit by gunfire crashed to the ground, legs flailing at the air.

He was stunned at the suddenness of it. Mounted fighters rode to the west then looped southward around the soldiers' collapsing line. At first only a few troops broke formation and started to move eastward toward the cover of timber along the river. More warriors swung around from west of Reno's line, riding flat out, coming in behind and driving the troopers toward the river. Others came from the village and rode or ran on foot toward the retreating battalion, firing and yelling as the harried troopers tried to reach the cover of the woods and the curving bank of a dry meander long ago abandoned by the river.

Some soldiers recovered and remounted their horses, but others had lost their animals completely so ran pell-mell, stopping to turn and fire while others ran for the trees, not looking back at all. The mounted troops raced for the river and the woods, leaving behind those on foot. Soldiers on foot were ridden down one by one and shot or hacked to death.

Bobo exploded in animal rage, "Officers!" he roared toward the front of the column. "God damn it to hell! We're letting them be killed!"

One captain nearby shouted, "Sergeant Bobo! That's enough!"

Bobo flung his arm at the officer in a gesture of disgust.

Wild's heart raced, agonized at the sight of the slaughter below. All of this had happened so fast--the crescendo of firing below, the encirclement and collapse of Reno's line. But why were they waiting here? Gun smoke hung in hazy air over the valley below, obscuring parts of the battlefield. He couldn't understand Custer's hesitation now. Somehow, they had to act.

For a moment Burden had been as stunned as the rest to see Reno's badly outnumbered men collapse so quickly and flee toward the river and the trees. Burden shook his head and grimaced. "It all comes to this. Swaggering while they lived in swank, but with no thought save panic when their pickles hit the grinder."

Wild looked at him. "You sorry son of a bitch. Shut the hell up."

An excerpt from her father's letter:

...It is not hard to understand the forces that bring men into confrontation and war with each other. They want the means to live better--or to live at all. Or they simply want to dominate and control and lay waste. Why more peaceful means of compromise and accommodation are often not the first choice is a consternation.

I have only come to surmise that many men, restless and indolent and loving drama, actually hunger for a righteous battle with forces they deem evil, when in fact those forces often are simply other men with different points of view and similar hungers. They stir themselves sufficiently to lose patience, then yearn to wade in an enemy's blood and kick his viscera in all directions.

Later in life, I saw this blind fury so often in my peace work that it nearly drove me to despair. Both sides were full of rage that bloody Sunday in Everett, Washington and before that in Chicago at the Haymarket riot, and in other places I have been.

JUNE 25, 1876: HILLS ABOVE LITTLE HORN VALLEY, MONTANA TERRITORY

As hazy sunlit air above the valley floor filled with gun smoke and dust, Mac heard shouts at the front of the column. He wiped his gritty brow with his shirt sleeve and saw Sergeant Daniel Knipe ride past toward the rear, spurring his horse hard. Mac said, "Where's he going? Why's he running?"

Wild irritably snapped, "He's not running! Probably he's going after Benteen or the pack train."

Mac heard a shouted command to move forward. Custer set the column northwestward along the ridge top. He'd let the battalion be routed in the valley below, unable to help, and now he was moving even further away from Reno's battered men and Benteen's battalion. Did he plan to attack the village at a different point and draw warriors away from the battle in the valley? Mac looked down at the village; it was a city! The number of fighters they'd soon face was immense, and those men were protecting their families.

He looked around him. How committed to an attack was this group of men? In their training sessions they'd been told, "The government pays you to get shot at." Well, he'd not had a payday, yet here he was! There must be more than enough Indians to destroy Reno's battalion and this one too. Who could stop that now?

The battalion moved forward along the crest of the bluff at a fast trot, the men hushed now, quieted by the daunting sight of the village sprawled across the valley floor below. Someone shouted, "Sergeant Wild, don't forget my letter."

Mac's heart banged in his chest and he wrapped the sorrel's reins tightly in his right fist. He glanced at Wild, whose face was intense and concentrated, unreadable.

Far ahead, the front of the column stopped once more and a young officer galloped back toward them, reigning in his horse near Bobo. "First Sergeant," he said, "Form your sorrels on me!"

Several men grumbled, but Bobo shouted them quiet and led them to form up on the officer. The battalion column broke into two squadrons, with C and two other companies in one unit riding behind Custer, and the remaining two companies in the other. Mac could no longer hear gunfire from the valley, and a long slope blocked their view of Reno's beleaguered men and their retreat. C took up the rear of Custer's squadron in a column of twos, with Mac and Holley riding at the tail end. At the changeover of their formation several horses collided and reared in the excitement and Mac saw that Malachy had fallen back and now rode abreast of Wild, just ahead of Holley and himself.

Custer led them at a gallop across a broad coulee and northwestward toward a higher ridge. Mac saw the other two companies continue down the coulee toward what looked like a river ford at the bottom. Children and women ran away from the river through the tipis. But more and more warriors ran from the huge encampment toward the ford where the other squadron soon would come out of the coulee at the river's edge.

A growing number of Indians thrashed on foot or on horseback in the shallows, ready to confront the other column that approached them. Gunfire exploded from the Indians at the ford, though when Mac looked back he could see that many of the warriors merely waved buffalo hides, shook their fists, shouted at the oncoming troopers. As his squadron moved across the ridge a broad rise blocked his view of the river ford, but suddenly gunfire increased abruptly from there. The troopers in the other column must have begun their attack across the ford and into the village.

Ahead the column began to stretch out and several officers shouted at the men to move faster and close up the gaps. Troopers lashed their horses forward at a gallop, cursing, their exhausted mounts colliding with one another as they descended the steep side of another coulee then ascended its far side and moved toward a higher ridge beyond. The formation seemed on the verge of breaking apart.

Mac couldn't see to the front because of the dust and the shifting heads and shoulders of the other men. He caught a glimpse of a great mass of warriors on horseback and on foot, now making their way up the hill from the river. This sight struck him with fear, for the Indians were on a path that would converge with their own. But what he saw next sent a bolt of sheer terror through him. The warriors were not just moving up hill but were chasing the other two companies that only moments earlier had descended the coulee to cross the ford and attack the village. Now those two companies' formation was completely broken. The shifting mass of men and horses rode in full retreat up the ridge.

A number of troopers in the retreating column had lost their horses and were on foot. They struggled up the hill running, stopping frequently to fire on the fighters who pursued and threatened to surround them and cut them off from those troops still on horseback. Mac saw one soldier fall and two fighters plunged from their horses and clubbed and slashed him.

Mac's squadron was still separated from the retreating column by several hundred yards, but it looked like their paths would converge with one another when they arrived at a high ridgeline to the north.

A sharp ripping sound passed above his head, and he flinched.

Holley murmered, "Oh, God. Oh, God."

Then another round passed close by, followed by popping sounds from far to the left. A horse ahead of him shrieked and went down, throwing its rider onto the ground. Other horses stumbled over it, swarming past the fallen animal where it lay, its legs thrashing air.

The fallen trooper rolled out of the column's path then jumped up and shouted, "Goddamn' son of a bitch!" He kicked at the animal, but blood rushed from a wound in its face and the horse began to convulse.

"Finnegan, let it go," another trooper yelled. "Come up here." He reached a hand down to the fallen soldier, shouting, "Give me an arm." He pulled the other man up behind him.

A ripping whistle zipped past them followed by a boom from below toward the river and someone shouted, "God damn! That a buffalo gun?"

Mac saw Malachy struggling with the coyote pup again. Holding it by its scruff, he shouted, "Wild, take Phinney! Your saddlebag!"

Wild glanced at him, exasperated. "Shit, Malachy!" But he flipped up the flap of his bag and the Irish soldier reached across and stuffed the wriggling pup inside.

Malachy ducked his head at Wild, grinning nervously, then stood high in his stirrups to see their way ahead.

In the next instant Mac saw Malachy's new straw hat lift from his head and disappear behind them. Simultaneously Mac felt a sting like a needle in his cheek and wetness splashed across his face and neck. "I've been shot!" he thought. He glanced at Holley. The sheepherder's face was terror-struck and spattered with blood. Before Mac could think, Malachy's horse drifted back toward him and Malachy sat back in his saddle then sagged sideways and leaned against him. Mac reached his arm under the Irishman's shoulder, grasped him around his chest and tried to keep him on his horse.

"Let him go!" Wild shouted. "He's dead, Durant! Let him go!"

Stunned, Mac held Malachy's torso tightly. His face was drenched with something wet and his cheek stung as though he'd been shot. Malachy's upper torso lay across his front. He looked down and saw that the top of the Irishman's head was gone. In bewildered shock he held onto him as their two horses slowed and proceeded side by side up the hill at a fast walk. The rest of the column began to pull away. Dazed, he looked after Wild, moving forward with the column.

Wild shouted, "Damn it, Durant! Let him go! He's dead! Come on."

"Agghhh, God!" Mac felt the wail tear from his chest and he let Malachy fall. The Irish soldier's corpse slid down between their two horses and onto the ground, but his boot had slipped forward through his stirrup and now was firmly caught. The horse slowly dragged his body toward the rest of the column which continued up the hill, gradually leaving Mac behind. Wild yelled, his voice tinny in the distance amid the growing din of gunfire from the Indians down the hillside. "Durant! Holley! Come on!"

Only then did Mac look to his right and see that Holley had fallen out of the formation with him, his stunned face spattered with Malachy's blood. They looked at one another and without speaking Mac turned his horse back the way they'd come and spurred the animal, quirting it with his reins. His face burned as if slashed with a knife. He heard Holley coming behind him. They dipped back into the last ravine the column had crossed just moments before, then turned uphill. They whipped their flagging horses and kept riding until they finally reached the ridge top, then stopped. Neither horse had much left in it.

Gunfire rose to their north where Wild and the others had gone. At least no bullets were flying past their own heads. Heart jumping, he stared slack-mouthed at the huge village that spread out below them. A half mile to the north a great cloud of dust began to bloom slowly in the air and he saw C's column and the other column of troops from the river converge then disappear within the dust cloud, pursued by large numbers of Indians on horseback.

Reluctantly, he and Holley finally looked at each other. Holley said, "Mac, you got something sticking in your face."

Reaching one hand to his cheek, Mac winced as he bumped something with his fingers. He plucked from his face a pale splinter and for a second was confused, then realized that a shard of Malachy's skull had impaled him. He flung it away and felt the small wound grow warm as blood began to flow from it. When he looked at Holley's stricken face and shirt front, splashed with a fan of Malachy's blood, he realized the wetness on his own face also was part of Malachy. He wiped at it with his bare forearm and felt the sting of the cut from the bone shard, as the warmth of his own blood mingled with that of Malachy.

For long seconds he struggled to think. He looked about. No one was chasing them. Two hundred yards north, standing alone on the side of the ridge, was Malachy's horse. The Irishman lay dead beside the animal with his boot still snagged in the stirrup. The horse moved forward uncertainly for several steps, but Malachy's dead weight slowed it. The animal lowered its head and began to graze.

"Mac, we got to go back!" Holley said. His voice was tremulous, on the edge of tears.

He looked at him. "What? There's no way to go back."

"We shouldna' run off. We left Wild and them."

Mac couldn't meet Holley's eyes when he spoke. "I didn't ask you to come. I was holding onto Malachy."

"Well, I know, but everything happened so quick. Poor Malachy. Dear Lord, he's dead on the ground and we got his blood all over us."

"It'll wash off. We got to figure out what to do." His eyes returned to the Indian village that spread along the river in the valley below. So many people, and here they were, the two of them alone. He couldn't think, but he had to. He wiped again at the blood on his face.

"We got to go back!" Holley's voice was a rising demand.

"Damn it, no, Leo! We got to get back to those others we left before!" He swept his arm southward toward where they had earlier parted with Benteen's and Reno's two battalions. That was their only hope. "We got no way to get back to Wild and them now."

"I got to go back, Mac."

He didn't want Holley to leave him. He tried to dissemble. "That's fine, Leo. Let's go, but that way," and he pointed south again toward Reno and Benteen.

He'd coaxed his horse a step or two southward when Holley said, "No! I got to go back and help Wild and them."

"You're crazy. You'll be cut off and killed. Just listen," and he pointed toward the rising sound of gunfire from the north.

Holley's voice was almost a wail and his hands trembled. "I shouldna' left. I shouldna' left."

"You try to go back, you're going to die."

"Maybe so. Maybe so." Holley mumbled uncertainly, his eyes tearing up. He wiped at the blood and tears on his face.

"Just come on with me now, Leo." He tried to speak in a cool-headed way, but couldn't give adequate words to his frantic thoughts. "Maybe we can make it back to Captain Benteen's battalion, and Major Reno and the others." He desperately did not want Holley to leave him.

Guilty remorse began to creep into his thinking, and he reacted against it. He'd left Wild and the others, but what were they to him? They all knew it wasn't his fight, didn't they? Hadn't some of them treated him badly for running off before, so why should he feel bad now? How could anybody expect to stay calm when a friend's brains got splattered in his face? They just expected too much from a man.

With his field shirt sleeve, Holley wiped at the blood on his face, but it already had started to thicken and blacken in the heat. The look of quiet resolve in his eyes made Mac even more anxious. "Come on, Leo," he said. "You know you ain't got a chance to help those men. Help yourself now."

"I got to go back, Mac."

"You'll die." He wasn't going to ride mindlessly to his death. He didn't have a thing against any Indians. Sure, he didn't like the ones who killed his parents, but he had no bone to pick with the rest.

"I can't live with myself if I don't go back!"

He tried to put reason in his voice, to make a sound suggestion or two. "What about us helping each other to get back to the rest of the regiment down south there?"

For a few seconds neither of them spoke, but gazed anxiously back northward at the large dust cloud. They could only hear the steady roar of gunfire from there.

Then, with quiet resolution, Holley said, "You been my friend. You got to let God guide you."

Mac looked at the valley below, at the hundreds of tipis spread out so far along the winding river. His heart shrank and he wanted to sob at the prospect of being left alone on this ridge. He looked back toward the mountains over which they'd come only hours before. Everything had happened so fast. For several seconds he couldn't bring himself to speak or even look at Holley. Suddenly the sheepherder seemed like the dearest friend he'd ever had. Tears welled in his eyes. Holley was the only person who'd ever called him "friend."

He tried to swallow the knot in his throat. "So you're going?"

Holley nodded. "I hope you make it through, Mac."

His throat so tight he could hardly speak, he reached out his hand and they shook, a grip grimy with trail dirt and Malachy's blood. His voice faltered, but he said, "I hope you make it through too, Leo." He looked past Holley at the empty country. The idea of being left alone terrified him.

Holley turned his horse and Mac watched the skinny sheepherder set the tired sorrel forward toward the huge dust plume and raging gunfire beyond the ridge. He turned the mare and pointed her south. He would try to find Reno's and Benteen's two battalions that Custer had left behind, though from what he'd seen of Reno's men in the valley fight, maybe all were dead.

As he coaxed the horse forward at a slow trot, a searing thought occurred to him: how would he explain to the others why he wasn't with his company? And what would be the consequences from his running when Wild and the others came back and rejoined Benteen and Reno? Perhaps he could get away, just ride away. He gazed at the distant Wolf Mountains and the tiny gap they'd all ridden through only hours ago. His heart sank at the great emptiness of the land, and he moaned aloud. He couldn't survive in this wilderness with no food, and the land full of Indians. Unless he could find Benteen or Reno's men there was no help within hundreds of miles.

He'd be dead for sure if the Indians found him, and could well be shot or hung if the troops he'd just left found him after the battle was over. Wild wouldn't help him, but would turn away, despise him, feeling he'd done all he could to train and get him ready for this situation, only to watch him turn and run.

He looked over his shoulder in the direction Holley had ridden. Just for a second he saw the gangly soldier, elbows flapping, spur his horse across the top of the far razor back, riding toward the gunfire and the great frenzy of dust that bloomed skyward. Then he was gone.

In the foreground all that remained was Malachy's sorrel, small there on the vast land. The animal had drug Malachy's corpse to a dark green patch of grass. As he watched, the animal lowered its head a bit and looked vaguely around, as though waiting for something to happen or someone to come and release it from its burden.

In disbelief, Wild looked back as Durant and Holley lashed their horses back the way the squadron had come. Malachy lay dead and the shock of his head being shattered had been too much for them. There was nothing he could do about it now, so spurred his horse to keep pace with the column. Many Sioux now swarmed up the hill on the left flank but stayed at a distance, riding parallel to the column and firing with little effect.

Wild saw Burden looking back at him. When Wild regained his position at the rear of the column, Burden laughed. "Looks like I'm the only loyal follower you got left, Wild."

"Go to hell." For a moment he thought of himself and Burden alone at the tail end of the column. This might be the moment Burden would choose, but, no, there were still too many other eyes who would see.

Suddenly, from the column's ranks ahead, a horse carrying one of the young immigrant soldiers bolted toward the growing band of Indians who rode their flank still some distance away. The trooper shouted and jerked on the reins, struggling to gather the animal in, but without success. The terrified horse leaped forward and crossed the gap, plunged into the mass of warriors who parted for the animal, but grabbed at the soldier. Wild cursed and fired his Colt twice at them but without result. Pulling the soldier from his horse, the Indians dragged him to the ground in a dusty melee, kicking and clubbing and slashing at him with feet, stone axes and knives.

This seemed to excite them even more, and their yelling intensified. Many more fighters now rose from cover along a deep coulee to the left and directed their fire into the retreating body of soldiers. Some soldiers fired back, then Wild heard Bobo yell a command. C came to a halt and faced left, forming as a ragged line of mounted skirmishers.

Bobo gave the command to charge and C veered away from Custer's squadron and galloped downhill toward the fighters in the ravine, yelling and firing as they went, scattering the Indians who'd gathered there. Wild pulled his carbine from its ring as they dismounted in the gully.

He handed his horse's reins to Ottocar Nitzsche and for several minutes he and the others fired into an ever larger number of Indians who came running or riding up from the river then ducked into nearby coulees and ravines. Methodically, Wild shot and reloaded the Springfield, tried to remember how many rounds remained in the chambers of his holstered Colt. An arrow hissed past his face. Someone shouted, "Jeremiah! On your left!" A horse fell heavily on Wild's left, throwing its rider, but the man scrambled to his feet.

Edwin rode back and forth behind his dismounted troops, shouting and gesturing at them. "Move left," he shouted, "Up the hill!" As C moved out, several horse holders and their charges were hit and fell. Here and there a soldier grabbed at a loose horse or two that a wounded horse holder could no longer control.

A large fusillade exploded from another body of mounted Indians who rode across the hillside toward them from the south. Wild's eye caught a dark, ascending flash in the sky above the river and looked up to see an arc of arrows rise above them, then turn and descend. Several soldiers stood straight up to make themselves smaller targets, but a second later two were hit. Horses screamed in pain. An arrow ricocheted off a piece of field stone in front of Wild, tumbling onto the turf ten feet away.

Suddenly from their left flank, mounted Sioux thundered in among them. Everything was dust and chaos, a melee of shooting, slashing, yelling. A trooper beside Wild fell under an Indian pony's hooves as the mounted warrior thrust his lance at the man, but Wild shot the fighter off his horse. The band of Sioux rode on through C's crumbling line and veered away toward the river into the cover of a deep ravine.

Wild glanced around to find Bobo, for the company was in a bad spot, isolated from other soldiers farther along the ridge. There were too many fighters here and C, having been overrun once, would soon be crushed by the growing number of warriors who now were re-gathering in the ravine below to charge once more. They had to retreat toward the rest of the squadron, but that unit had now moved on, perhaps two hundred yards away. He saw the distant squadron dismount and deploy along the ridge top. Something slapped the side of his face and for an instant Wild thought he'd been shot, but a quick swipe of his hand showed no blood.

He saw Edwin close by, still on his horse, but riding in a stiffened posture, his back rigidly erect. His face was full of pained concentration, as though remembering something far away he'd forgotten to do. The front of his field shirt was soaked with blood and the lid of his bad eye seemed to droop. Edwin shifted his reins to his left hand, and with his right gripped the cantle of his saddle tightly to steady himself. He stayed upright, yelled, "In the ravine there! Right there! Give the bastards heat!" The troopers fusillade kept the fighters from charging back into C once more.

Wild heard his order to mount again and withdraw along the ridge, but several horse holders had been hit and were on the ground, and riderless horses veered away in several directions. Wild and some others were able to re-gather and remount their horses and follow Bobo and the rest of the column while other men scrambled after them on foot.

Horses screamed and men shouted in the heat. Dust boiled around them, obscuring everything close at hand, but as Wild rode he could see through gaps in the dust where the other two companies of Custer's squadron lay prone in line atop the long ridge ahead. The other two-company squadron that'd been chased from the river still fought its way along the ridge toward a high point further away. C had to get to the nearer group of men, but Indians' gunfire snapped all around them. Bullets zipped past, sliced at the grass by his feet, slapped flesh nearby. Men grunted or cried out as they were struck. Something long and dark flashed by his head.

Wild focused all his attention and hopes on reaching the rest of their battalion on the ridge. C's remaining horses, many of them wounded, were nearly spent. They moved slowly, stumbling and lurching across the rough terrain. Then, momentarily, the company's progress was stopped and it found itself in a standing fight with Indians on three sides, though still at some distance. They were nearly surrounded, almost completely cut off from the troops beyond.

Sweat and gunpowder stung Wild's eyes; everywhere was confusion. Someone--not Edwin--shouted to dismount, but his instinct rebelled at the notion. A hot round scorched past, seared the side of his neck and whipped his shirt collar up. He glanced at the long ridge ahead, felt his exhausted horse tremble between his legs, and hoped the animal had the strength to make it. Make it to where, he could not say, except to reach the other men along on the ridgeline.

One company's guidon had been driven into the ground among those men who lay on line, the flag moving listlessly in faintly moving air. Finally, Edwin yelled at the company to follow him and he led a ragged charge through the mass of Indians in their front. These warriors gave way, fled toward C's flanks, but fired back at the charging troopers as they broke through. C's remaining horses and men leaped and stumbled across the sides of a narrow wash, and Wild and several others turned their horses back among the running men to give them covering fire as best they could.

Ottocar Nitzsche moved at a limping run, blood streaming down his neck. Wild turned his horse toward him but then Nitzsche fell and lay still. Wild couldn't tell if he was dead but couldn't get to him. He remembered with a pang Nitzsche's letter; he had it in his saddlebag with the rest. Turning his horse, Wild urged it back toward the high ridge, leaving Nitzsche behind.

He and the remainder of the company reached the rest of the squadron along the ridge top and as C began to dismount to anchor the north end of the ragged line his horse suddenly collapsed. They went down together and Wild landed hard on his shoulder and side, knocking the wind out of him. The horse fell on his right leg, pinning him, and he pushed with his left foot at the McClellan saddle. He strained hard, finally wrenching his leg free, and pulling his boot half off. A bullet had struck the horse behind its right eye and it was dead. He should take the saddlebags with the letters and the coyote pup. But there wasn't time. He left them, pulled his carbine from its ring and glanced back along their path to find Edwin. The ground over which they'd come was littered with C's dead.

He glanced frantically about, couldn't see his cousin, tried to find a way out for them all. There was none. Fighters from the big village had converged now from all directions and in far greater numbers than the soldiers who were still alive. He sensed a movement to his left, and was dumbstruck to see a great mass of mounted fighters ride up over the back side of the ridge and thunder through a few dozen troopers farther down the line. Plunging into the soldiers from their rear, the warriors shot down into them as the men lay on the ground firing.

Many of these troops rose up with a frenzied roar, their faces contorted, some still shooting but others clawing with fingers and fists or swinging their carbines as clubs. Howling belligerence and terror, they were shot or struck down and trampled.

The south end of the line collapsed. They would soon be surrounded. C couldn't defend this position. Wild stood and yelled at the men nearby to move north with him. He gestured toward a high point where the remaining soldiers from the other squadron had gathered after being pursued uphill from the river.

Wild suddenly glimpsed Edwin, still on his horse but disoriented. He shouted to him but Edwin didn't hear him. Only remnants of C remained, and Wild yelled again to his cousin, tried to catch his eye. Edwin didn't respond so Wild roared at the other men, "Get up! Move! Let's go!"

Blood streamed down a German soldier's face. He was on his feet but appeared transfixed by the bedlam, unable to act. Wild struck the man hard on the shoulder with the barrel of his Colt, then kicked him in the rear. Finally the soldier started to move on his own, stumbling northward along the ridge. Wild led them all toward higher ground and the remnants of the other squadron.

Most of the men now were on foot. Many were wounded. Some fired as they went along, but others simply moved at a shuffling trot, as if half awake. A few seemed frozen by panic at being so suddenly overwhelmed. They did little to protect themselves, eyes vacant, resigned to what they saw as their inescapable end.

Wild's eyes raced, frantic to find any opening that would help them live. Surviving troops from the overrun positions to the south ran after them on foot, but no sooner had they begun to move when the Indians on three sides directed their fire along the line of running soldiers. Fighters hidden in the coulees on the left rose one by one or in small groups to fire, then ducked back down again. Others ran or rode along the ravines and hillocks, firing at the beleaguered troops as they scrambled northward.

Wild looked again for Edwin, and saw only his riderless horse cantering away toward the Indians in their rear. Edwin lay on his side in the grass about a hundred feet back, awkwardly scissoring one leg in the air, apparently trying to rise. Wild flung his empty carbine aside. "Get moving!" he screamed at soldiers nearby. "Get to the ridge with the others!" He turned from them and raced back toward Edwin.

Seconds later, as he neared his struggling cousin, he felt a sharp blow to his neck, as though some powerful creature held him with crushing jaws. He fell hard on his shoulder, driving an arrow shaft even deeper into his throat and breaking it off. Dazed, he lay choking, inhaling his own blood.

He struggled to breathe, but had only a terrifying sensation of drowning....*amid the stillness of the snowfall a junco's tiny tracks...with his father he made no sound in the silent white woods...a junco and Margaret and her hat trailing pink ribbon...*and hands struck him things sharp and hard...and he was drowning....

⌘

Burden, whose horse had been killed at the ravine when mounted Sioux first rode through C's lines, was not far away when he saw Wild fall. He sprinted toward him. But Burden looked away from Wild for a second to shoot a huge Indian who ran at him from the side. When he looked back Wild had disappeared; he couldn't see where he'd fallen. Beyond the spot where Burden thought Wild should be, three fighters hacked at Bobo's head and torso as the First Sergeant's legs thrashed in the grass.

Burden saw a movement, then thirty feet away an arm rose from a patch of taller grass. Wild had fallen into a small sink in the land, an odd cleft where he lay in taller grasses that hid him from view. When Burden reached him, Wild looked at him without recognition. A broken arrow shaft protruded from his throat. The cords of his neck convulsed. He was strangling.

"Well, Wild. Here we are." He wrenched the Colt from Wild's hand and looked around, shooting twice at fighters riding past. The third time he fired, the hammer fell on an empty casing and he flung the revolver away, shifted his own Colt back to his right hand. "Wild," he yelled, but Wild's eyes were unfocussed. He was nearly gone.

He shouldn't have waited to kill the man. Now Wild couldn't even hear him. Still, he said, "I ain't going to kill you, Wild. I'm just leavin' you to them." He rose and shot a skinny fighter who hesitated a second too long as he ran toward them.

Burden scrambled to catch up with the others. As he ran he flipped open the cylinder of his Colt and fingered more bullets from his belt loops. He risked a glance back at Wild and grimaced a grin when he saw two fighters were on top of him.

He passed several other troopers and horses that lay on the ground. A bullet whipped past his face, and something dark landed in the grass at the extreme of his peripheral vision, but he didn't glance at it. A trooper on the ground called his name and reached out a hand. He cursed and ran on. He finally caught up with the rag-tail end of the other soldiers as they stumbled toward the hilltop where Custer and the remaining troops were gathered.

Most were now on foot and made no pretense of trying to maintain an orderly retreat. A captain whom Burden didn't recognize yelled at them, telling them to form on him, but they ignored him. Each man ran to save himself, rarely looking in any direction but straight toward the hilltop where their remainder still fought. Many had no rifles, either because they'd lost their ammunition when their horses were shot, or because the fighting was so close that their Colts were a wiser choice.

Two plunging horses slammed against one another, sandwiching one soldier between them. He fell and other soldiers stumbled across him, kept trotting northwestward. Burden saw the fallen soldier struggle to his hands and knees, trying to rise and follow the surging mob as it moved along the ridge. He yelled for help, but no one went back for him. A skinny Indian boy clad in a breech clout leaped from a near ravine and walked tentatively toward the soldier. Burden glanced back at the boy who--finally deciding--ran at the man and hacked at his neck with a knife until the soldier fell forward onto his stomach.

He saw they were nearly surrounded now, but many Indians didn't even shoot. They simply watched, yelling and hooting as spectators, content to prolong the torment, as though to pound home the bitter lesson. His eyes shot around: all of them, herded together to be killed like a gaggle of terrified rabbits.

An excerpt from her father's letter:

…It can be easy for some to relish killing a man, but in truth I think that idea is hard for most to act upon. The fact is that normal men need to be made to kill another through training and dehumanization of the enemy. In my work I have seen hate on the faces of many, but even their outbursts of violence have been limited to the wounding slash, not the killing thrust.

JUNE 25, 1876: HILLS ABOVE LITTLE HORN VALLEY, MONTANA TERRITORY

Holley left Mac and galloped back toward Malachy's caught body and his grazing horse. He passed them, sobbing, "Dear Lord! Dear Lord! Take him up!" He veered left, and after several minutes reached the top of a bluff. The companies he hoped to reach were still a quarter mile north of him on the high ridge. Gunfire from there was a steady din, but the shrieks and screams of men and horses came to him strangely faint in the vastness and distance. He whipped the mare forward across the top of the bluff. Several troopers lay singly at a distance from each other, having fallen where they were hit. A couple of them still moved feebly, but others lay sprawled in the odd positions of death, and he thought of mired sheep who'd died passively while standing in mud bogs, or died on their backs when knocked off their feet by dogs.

As he rode toward the huge cloud he looked left at a large band of warriors that swarmed toward the fight, riding a course that converged with his own. He veered right to stay clear of them, but two changed course and galloped toward him. "Oh, Lord, help me!" he moaned and turned the mare east, whipping her hard down the far side of the bluff away from the battle and the huge village. She took the lash but couldn't run any faster.

To his front, the long slope fell away eastward. Hundreds of yards below, deep coulees drained the bluff around him. Scattered cottonwood trees spread along a bottom some distance away.

Empty country loomed ahead. He whipped the mare forward, and only then did he see the wound in her crest, there at the roots of mane. The wound was bite shaped, through-and-through, a couple inches across. It seeped small amounts of blood and fluid. But foam dripped from the animal's mouth and she trembled from exhaustion and fear. He looked back and saw the two warriors, one of them a boy.

If only he could get home to Yankton, to be with his family, with his father's sheep. It was terrible and he just wished he could be with his parents and his little brothers. If God would just let him go there again he wouldn't ask for anything, and he'd never get upset at not having enough to eat. He'd find his own food and everything.

Wild and Malachy and Mac were gone. Malachy's blood crusted his face. Wild had been good to him, had helped him. Wild had called him to come back, but he'd left them all there in the gunfire on the ridge. There was nothing ahead except wilderness. The two warriors might overtake him at any minute. If only he hadn't followed when Mac fell back. What had made him do that? Now he couldn't take it back, couldn't do it over. He'd tried to get back to C though, hadn't he? Maybe the good Lord would count that in his favor.

Why did he think he wanted to be a soldier? He wasn't much of a one, but he should be back on that hill with Wild and the others. But the darn' Indians...they'd forced him away.

With an urge almost uncontrollable, he longed to make it to that patch of green cottonwood trees ahead. They beckoned, so peaceful and clean and green, yet so indifferent to his danger. Back home he'd spent many an hour just watching the wind blow over the prairie, billowing and turning over the cottonwood leaves to their gray-green side. The wind, it made the grass and trees like ocean waves.

He lashed his horse again, glanced down at his carbine still in its boot, then at his holstered Colt. He'd never fired a shot with either weapon, but now lifted the revolver. The ride was jolting; the exhausted mare couldn't help losing her stride and the .45 was an unfamiliar weight in his hand. He had only dry fired it fifty or a hundred times since it had been issued to him a little over a month ago. But now he turned and fired once in the general direction of his pursuers. The gun bucked sharply and he nearly dropped it. His hand trembling, he tightened his grasp on the revolver, settling it against his thigh as he rode.

He flinched as the delicate zip of two bullets slipped past on his right, and almost simultaneously he heard two gunshots behind him. He entered a network of sharply eroded washouts with steep sides, some ten or fifteen feet deep. The horse had to be goaded hard to keep moving. Three more shots sounded from behind. He glanced at the heavy revolver in his hand, but didn't turn and fire again.

In this most desperate moment, memories overwhelmed him. Not just what had happened today, not just the expedition of the last month, but all of it--his life. He wished he was back in the states, back where his mother and father had started when he was born, not out in Dakota or Montana Territory anymore.

He'd walked from Yankton all the way to Bismarck. He was a good walker. He had good talks with the Lord. But had he lived a good life? He was glad his little brothers had enough to eat now that he'd left home to become a cavalry man.

He wondered why all his life he'd felt hungry. Even when he had all the food he needed he always felt so hungry, like he had a hole in him that biscuit couldn't fill. Maybe his mother and father would know about that kind of hunger. He'd like to go home and tell them where he'd been, what he'd seen. He'd gone from Yankton all the way to Bismarck, then here to Montana Territory.

He flogged the horse along a rise where a cool freshet of air descended suddenly to embrace him. The mare stumbled but regained her footing. He didn't know where he was going, but a glance back told him the two fighters were still there.

He considered the miles behind him and the endless dark that might lie ahead. Was the Lord really with him as the good book promised? Would He still lift up his soul when his body died? The thought of his family was painful; would they ever know where he was, or what had happened to him?

A bullet smashed into a ledge beside him and a rock chip stung his neck. The two were yelling back there. The mare slowed and he struck her flank with the revolver barrel, dug his boots into her. She couldn't respond.

Just then the mare went down over the edge of an embankment, rolling and sliding in a small avalanche of dirt and rock. Holley hit bottom first and the horse landed on top of his hips. He tried to move but his pelvis was pinned beneath her. The big animal shuddered, nickered weakly and wrenched her head up struggling, flailing with her hooves at the base of the vertical wall. She couldn't rise, so settled back. Holley moaned, in exhalation rather than pain for he couldn't feel his arms and legs. His vision was cloudy and he blinked several times to clear it.

The two Indians appeared just above him at the lip of the embankment and dismounted. From where he lay, they appeared to him as through a gauzy curtain. One of them laughed, pointing into the ravine where he and the sorrel lay tangled.

He rested his head in the dirt, panting for breath, just a small creature that lay hurt in a nameless place under the milky summer sky. The eroded soil was cool, the earth rough against his cheek, and from somewhere lower in the draw the smells of water and grass came to him on a rising current of air. At the edge of his vision, he saw the boy on the embankment lift his arm then drop it, just a lifting and falling. Something struck him in the side.

With great effort he turned his head and saw the arrow shaft protruding from his ribs. He couldn't feel it, but couldn't take a full breath. The mare cried out and struggled once more, then lay still, breathing heavily.

Voices spoke close at hand. He turned his head and saw a dusty, moccasined foot beside his face, then heard more laughter. The boy appeared from behind him and picked up the Springfield which had slid part way out of its saddle ring. The young fighter looked the carbine over; twice he opened and closed the breech.

Someone lifted his head roughly, and a frightened animal sound escaped his throat in a horror of anticipation. He caught his breath sharply, gnashed his teeth at the burning, sawing motion--the worst agony he'd ever felt--and inside his head he heard a soft ripping sound, like bubbles popping. He heard a guttural scream full of anguished pain, as though at a great distance, but it was his own. He blinked his eyes through the rushing blood as the warrior thrust a bloody fist skyward.

In that moment a great peace bloomed within him, brimmed over in his mind, a sudden calm like a sprinkling of grace. He would see his family again, in a sunny place with grazing sheep and stands of pine. They would have plenty of food, and they would talk and learn about the things he'd seen.

The deepest kind of satisfaction filled him and he looked about, feeling a quiet gratitude toward the two fighters. Impatient now, wishing to be gone, he turned his head toward the lower canyon, suddenly smelling a waft of cool water.

The older warrior took the carbine from the boy and put the end of the barrel against the mare's ear. The blast echoed off the ravine, was sucked into the sky. He opened the breech and looked for more cartridges. He finally bent and wrenched a slug from one of Holley's belt loops. He loaded the rifle and swung it into Holley's face.

The warrior wailed a tremolo skyward for several seconds. All that remained was to enter the mystery. Holley tried to help, feebly opening his mouth as though seeking the lip of a chalice. He lifted his dripping chin toward the carbine's barrel and in the sudden flash of light something caressed his cheek and brow, and he felt lifted from the dusky earth.

⌘

Burden couldn't recognize most of the troopers around him, layered in gray dust and sweat, their faces contorted by pain and fear. Reddened eyes betrayed panic, or a haunted stoicism, mouths set grimly as they struggled to live. Bullets whined around them and arrows and spears whispered past or found targets.

The fighters were close upon them from every direction now, yelling, firing, ducking into shallow coulees and eroded defiles. Burden fired the Colt carefully, staying his fire until he had a clear target, but finally the revolver's hammer fell on empty chambers. Something hurtled past his head, and he kept moving into the gaggle of men that crowded ever closer together.

He fingered four more rounds from his ammo loops and loaded the Colt's sooty chambers. Running his fingers over the empty belt loops and over his trouser pockets, he thought, "There should be more."

Snapping the Colt's cylinder shut, he thought: "Keep one round back."

Masses of Indians stood or milled on horseback in every direction, some of them only fifty feet to the soldiers' rear and pressing forward. Many had stopped firing, apparently having decided to save arrows and cartridges. They hurled rocks, hooted derision. They knew the men were finished. Some soldiers had stopped firing, and the Indians directed their fire at those who still continued to shoot, for only they posed any threat.

Any second now life would end. There would be darkness, utter annihilation. If only he'd been able to find Donny. Would one of his letters ever find him? Would Donny ever learn what happened to him? That whore in Abilene: she'd been kind to him, helped him. Did she ever think of him?

A bullet struck his upper left arm and he gasped and ground his teeth in pain at the violation, but refused to scream. He ran with the others toward the hilltop, still saving the last rounds in his Colt. Several Indians stood watching. One pursed his lips, lifted his chin and laughed, pointed at the running soldiers whose terror he considered a pathetic, wretched spectacle.

"Be a truth teller," his mother had told him. And his old man: he'd hardly thought of him in years. In what greasy back street or wilderness had his bones finally been scattered? Had he ever felt a glimmer of truth about how he'd lived?

There was no way to hold the hilltop. The warriors were brazenly confident, almost leisurely, as though no exertions were necessary, as though they wanted to give the remaining soldiers more time to contemplate their fate.

Suddenly he saw Custer only fifteen feet away, surrounded by two of his officers. The self-glorifying bastard had brought them all to this; they damn' sure all saw it now.

A few dozen soldiers remained. An arrow struck the withers of a big gray gelding that stood trembling in the mass of soldiers near Custer. The animal lurched forward and raced full out toward the river, accelerating through a cluster of warriors who leaped out of its path.

The Indians taunted the stricken troopers, jeering; a few threw stones. But fewer were firing. Seeing this, many troopers began to lower their weapons, and there arose a peculiar lull in the fighting. For an instant Burden wondered if there was a chance to surrender. But the Indians stood resolute. A few sporadically fired a shot or loosed an arrow, almost casually picking off a man here and there, like shooting into a pen of rabbits.

Near him a tall corporal suddenly began to sob. He cried out, "John! Oh, John!" and made a supplicating gesture to three warriors who stood boldly close on his left. The corporal turned his revolver, took it by the barrel and resolutely strode toward the three fighters. Burden stood transfixed by the act. One of the three, nearly naked, was armed with a bow and several arrows which he held in his right fist. The soldier walked up to him and sobbed, "Oh, John. Please, John," and offered the young warrior his gun. The fighter looked into the corporal's face, casually shifted the bow and arrows to his left hand and took the corporal's Colt. He hefted the piece, cocked it and shot the tall soldier in the face. Like a long pole, the man toppled backward into tangled grass.

The corporal's beseeching gesture and his death seemed to shake both sides from a stupor, for a general firing began again. Only a few officers remained on their feet, including Custer.

Burden glanced at them bitterly, thinking, "The big mouthed sonofabitch isn't saying anything now. Does he realize what he's done?" But Custer was wobbly on his feet and looked confused, slack jawed. His mouth hung open. His shoulders hunched forward, hands on hips and elbows akimbo, weaponless. He shuffled one or two steps forward through the grass, steadied by a captain who tried to support him. He was no longer capable of giving an order. Burden lifted his Colt and shot Custer in the chest. The bullet's impact flung Custer back and he sprawled sideways into a twisted heap and lay still.

Burden heard someone roar "No!" close by and turned to see an officer raise his pistol toward him, but in that instant an arrow struck the man in the face and he fell to the ground, clawing fruitlessly at the shaft that protruded from beside his mouth. His boot heels dug spasmodically at the ground.

Then Burden heard or perhaps saw--he wasn't sure which--something almost musical. It came confused, a scent upon the air. It had a pureness to it and he shuddered at a sudden rush of longing that he normally tied to thoughts of Donny and Lamar. He clenched a fist, instinctively resisting such sweetness, trying to clear his mind of it.

Few other soldiers were firing now. The Indians were emboldened by this and began to walk or ride closer; their own firing increased. A bullet snapped past Burden's face. A trooper screamed and a man beside him fell. Another soldier began to weep. He was consumed now with a yearning for Donny and Lamar. Might he see them again on the other side, a notion he'd long ago discarded as only a disgusting weakness.

Dumbstruck, he watched as first one trooper, then another, and another, bolted downhill, abandoning their comrades. An officer yelled rage at the running men; he fired at them twice. More soldiers broke and ran toward the river.

Something struck him in the side and he saw the pain as well as felt it, like a bolt of yellow light. He looked down. What seemed an oddly thin arrow shaft had slipped between two ribs and poked out just above his stomach. He looked downhill at the blue water and cottonwood leaves, at the gold prairie grass along the lower slope. He felt a strange submission bloom inside, like a radiant light; he sobbed involuntarily, was surprised at himself, as though he were another being looking at himself from close by.

Nearby, more soldiers broke from their comrades' throng. Confused, unable to muster the angry certitude he'd always held so dear, he watched them run toward the river. Fighters drew back as these troopers plunged past them down the hill, then stepped forward and shot them. Some troopers fell while others ran on, leaving the ragged band on the hilltop.

Soldiers' bodies littered the ridge around him. A wounded horse cried out, an awful shrieking; it tried to lift its head from where it lay. He could stand this no longer, had to leave. Fighters lifted their arms toward him and puffs of smoke rose from their fists, and still others rose from the coulees and beckoned to him like shades. Several ran toward him as if they were his fate, but he remembered a flowered meadow near the Flat Lick lean-to where he and Donny took Lamar to get away from the old man. The air in the meadow was clean and yellow-green. Something heavy struck him in the stomach. He staggered sideways, but could still lift the Colt. He pointed the barrel at the side of his temple and pulled the trigger.

An excerpt from her father's letter:

...I have come to know that violence, seeming so necessary to so many people, always ends in agony, even for the inflictor of that brutality. Of course, no one can teach this point with any success to the multitudes so sorely and murderously offended by the incitements of others.

Your mother, Hattie, first helped me understand that even in the face of such violence one has to follow a higher path. I first met her when she came to what is now Livingston to visit her aunt in 1881. Her eyes were intelligent and full of warmth, and I remember how they searched my face when we met.

You were only four years old, but you both took to each other immediately. She turned me to Universalism, and helped me articulate my tendencies toward non-violence. She also introduced me to her uncle, Mr. Gompers, and working with him those few years after her death gave even more shape and purpose to my life.

With all the killing I had seen in the Army during those few months in 1876, Hattie's death at Haymarket Square in Chicago was still the most painful time of my life. She captured my heart and there has never been another woman for me. I do not know what lies beyond this veil, but my heavy heart still hopes to see her again. I have never known another love like I felt--still feel--for her.

JUNE 25, 1876: HILLS ABOVE LITTLE HORN VALLEY, MONTANA TERRITORY

When Holley left him Mac rode away from the battle, southward down the ravines. He finally arrived at the top of a high bank which dropped steeply into the river. He'd hoped to water his horse and fill his canteen, but they were too exposed here. Somebody below, in the trees across the water, might already be lining him up in his sights. He could only reach the river by going left for a couple of hundred yards where they would arrive at a low bank that had been broken down by buffalo trying to drink. He watched the river below and the timbered area on the far shore, his eyes traveling through the stands of cottonwoods, ash, and willow, but he saw no one. Still, he was fearful of going to the water.

He dismounted and set the horse on its picket pin, took his carbine and Dyer pouch full of ammunition and headed back up the ravine on foot. He heard gunfire beyond high ground to the east, a different direction from the one where Wild and Holley and the others in C had last gone. It had to be Reno's and Benteen's companies coming to help Custer. If he could just get back to those men he'd join up with them. He had to leave the horse, for he needed a story. And a story about his horse giving out on him was all he could think of as a plausible reason for not being with C. He felt bad about leaving the animal for she needed water, and the sky was blinding white and hot. On the ridge above, a great dust cloud drifted lazily southeastward above the muffled din of gunfire, and he trotted uphill toward it.

When he finally topped the rise he saw hundreds of exhausted troopers--Reno and Benteen's men?--retreating in disarray along the dusty bluff to his left. Many of the men, like him, were on foot. Dead soldiers and crippled horses littered their trail. Like howling destiny, dark shapes, most of them on horseback, pursued the outnumbered men, raced to reach their front and encircle them. The soldiers moved on a course that converged with his own, but Mac saw instantly he would have to run flat out for a couple of hundred yards to join with them or the Indians would surround them, cut him off from them. He started running.

Riderless cavalry horses swerved away from the struggling body of soldiers and bolted toward the surrounding Sioux and Cheyenne and Arapaho, some of whom stopped shooting long enough to try and catch the animals as they passed by. More wounded soldiers fell behind and the fighters overtook and hacked them to death, scalped them. The other troopers could do nothing to help. More men were killed and more horses shot in a desperate scrambling retreat.

As he ran to meet them he heard hoof beats coming behind. He turned and looked back to see his horse coming at a gallop. She raced past him toward the retreating battalion, the rope trailing behind her and the picket pin skidding and skipping through the grass. He'd never seen a horse pull its own picket pin before and he looked after her in wonder. He shouted and whistled at her but she ignored him and kept galloping toward the other soldiers.

No one acknowledged him as he joined their number. Stumbling and running, turning to shoot then run again, fired upon from three sides, they finally all arrived exhausted at a broadly indented saucer of ground beyond which the land fell sharply away into the valley. Officers shouted orders into the melee, their voices lost among the bawling pack mules, gunfire, screaming horses and shouting men.

But Mac and the other troopers understood: here was a natural defilade and they raced to build a defensive position. All were soaked in the steaming heat, their stricken faces striped with a mud of sweat, gray dust, gun powder. Like frenzied demons they slashed off the mules' packs and threw piles of equipment into line along a wobbly, curved perimeter.

Several soldiers led wounded mules and horses that were still on their feet into crude alignment with the bending circle of equipment and debris. They cut off the terrified animals' crossbucks, shot them in the head and fell down behind them, gasping and coughing in the gun smoke, dust, and heat.

Dismounted stragglers stumbled across the growing barricade in ones and twos; these men--many of them wounded--were crazed, driven by mortal fear to the edge of panic as bullets whined in the windless heat and skipped and sang in the dirt around them. They yelled for shovels, and other soldiers searched frantically in the scattered equipment and threw them chisels and cooking pots, knives and a wooden ladle, a farrier's nippers--anything that might help scrape a shallow pit in the ground for cover.

They were quickly surrounded and received fire from high ground to the north and east. He glanced up to see one soldier on foot, still a hundred feet out, drag two other men behind him toward the growing perimeter, but as the man reached the barricade he was shot through the heart and dropped like a stone. Two other men leaped over the rampart and dragged the two wounded troopers back across, dropping them in the dirt, leaving the dead Samaritan beyond reach.

Panting and coughing, he spit grit and mud and dropped behind a pack saddle and a thick roll of canvas next to Harker, one of the farriers he'd worked with before. Harker had been with Reno's battalion in the valley and had retreated across the river and up the steep canyons to this ridge where Benteen's battalion and the mule train had caught up with them.

A slug splinter from a ricochet buried itself in Harker's left forearm and the farrier cursed and rolled onto his back. Squinting into the sky he pulled out a pocket knife and probed at the bleeding wound. "Dirty bastards," he snapped, wincing at the pain. "Why didn't the officers know what we were coming against? Where in hell's Custer gone?" Harker pulled the piece of metal from his flesh and for a moment watched blood trickle from his arm.

The grime on Harker's face was thick and his eyes--the only thing about his features that seemed natural and alive--focused on Mac as if for the first time. "I thought you boys in C went with him. How come you're here? Where's Custer?"

Mac felt his face grow hot and he shook his head. "I don't know where he is." He had no good answer.

⌘

The fighters' shooting had dwindled at twilight, though a desultory fire continued from a number of places on the ridge. Mac still lay beside the farrier, Harker, who'd lowered his voice to a gravely whisper as he told of the fight in the valley.

"The sonsofbitches turned our flank and our line collapsed," Harker said. "We couldn't hold 'em, but just ran like rabbits." His eyes looked tormented. "I bet we left fifty men dead in that valley."

Mac worked his mind feverishly, trying to think of questions that would keep Harker focused on the Reno battalion's valley fight, and not direct his mind toward Custer's column. "How'd you fellows get up here?"

"After we hunkered down in the woods by the river for a while, the Major ordered us to retreat across the river and up this hill." Harker said he'd looked back several times in their flight to see individual men, their horses dead or run off, standing or kneeling alone on the plain and shooting at the Indians who rode them down. "They was killed one by one. Nobody and nothing could help them." He coughed. "You got water, do you?"

He shook his head. His tongue felt twice its size.

"The bastards shot us like ducks in a barrel when we crossed the river," Harker said. If they'd a come after us climbin' up them ravines there wouldn't have been a one of us get to this hilltop."

Harker raised above the wooden packing crate full of hardtack and shot his carbine once, then hunkered down and placed another shell into the breech. As Mac listened to him, he saw Captain Benteen striding toward them.

Benteen seemed oblivious to the sporadic stutter and pop of gunfire and the occasional round that zipped or sang in the air nearby. He snapped at Mac, "You, soldier! You're from 'C'?"

Mac said, "Yes, sir." He wouldn't have thought Benteen knew him.

"What in hell are you doing here? Were you assigned to the mule train?"

"No, sir. My horse gave out and I couldn't keep up. The others left me behind." He pointed vaguely northward, forcing himself to look the Captain in the eye.

"How'd you get here?"

"I made it back on foot and met up with you all when you tried to get to General Custer," Mac said, and gestured toward the high point some distance away to the northwest.

"What do you know about Colonel Custer's whereabouts?"

"They all rode away when my horse collapsed, Captain."

"You saw no more of them?"

"I saw them go out of sight over a ridge." He hesitated, trying not to make any mistakes. "For a long time I heard gunfire from up there."

"Where's your horse?"

"I don't rightly know, sir." Why'd Benteen concern himself with this right now? He'd heard the man was a stickler, but.... "It was near dead and couldn't get up, so I left it."

Benteen looked at him, and then turned and pointed at the horses and mules that had been assembled near the ravine where a hospital of sorts had been set up for the wounded. There, some of the more seriously wounded animals had been shot as breastworks to protect the doctor so he could crawl around among the wounded men. Benteen said, pointing, "That your sorrel there, the one with C on her blanket?"

Mac looked at the horses who stood together, many of them wounded, and there was his own. His face suddenly felt flushed. "Well, yes, sir. The sorrel's mine."

"Why is that animal dragging a picket pin?"

"I don't know, Captain," he lied. Why didn't the man just go away?

"Well, unload anything you need from that animal. No doubt, John Sioux and his friends will shoot it and the rest as expeditiously as possible."

"Yes, sir."

Benteen looked at him skeptically. "What's your name, soldier?"

"Durant, sir."

"That horse has recovered pretty nicely for an animal that collapsed only an hour or two ago."

Mac couldn't look at the Captain when he answered, "I don't know, sir. It's a strong horse, and I was surprised to have it go down like that."

"You're either very lucky, Durant, or you're a Goddamned liar and a coward."

"I'm not lying, Captain."

"Well, there's no way to skally-hoot from here, soldier. Do your duty with the rest of these men." Benteen abruptly started off along the perimeter.

He looked after him, then cast a quick glance at Harker, but the farrier lay still, as though sleeping, with his head resting in the crook of his elbow. He acted as if he hadn't heard the conversation, which was fine; he didn't want more discussion anyway.

As darkness came on, the Indians' gunfire fell away to a single shot now and then. He hoped Benteen didn't come back. The thought of Malachy dead on the hillside filled him with anguish. Malachy who'd been such an optimist, so curious about everything--and carting around that coyote pup. The Irishman had come from so far across the ocean in search of his father, and now he was dead. His entire journey had ended in an instant.

And Wild. Where was he? Wild had taken the time to teach them all tactics that might help keep them alive. He'd showed them how to use herbs and things to make their food taste better. And what about Holley who was always hungry and happy to be a cavalry man if for no other reason than that the food was regular and tasted so good to him. And Burden so bitter and violent, but he'd also tried to find his lost brother for so many long years. Were they still alive?

Though the hilltop stood faintly illuminated by light that lingered above the western mountains, the valley below was dark except for dozens of fires in the vast Indian camp. Some of the men nearby speculated there was a celebration going on, for a din of shouting and drumming drifted up from the village. But to Mac the noise sounded more grief-stricken--a shrieking and wailing.

Late in the evening, he suddenly heard bugles sounding far away and cocked his head, trying to tell from which direction. "Custer's coming back," someone shouted from down the line. A general murmur arose.

A tuneless squeal of bugle notes again reached his ears, then immediately another then another. They seemed to emanate from different points in the Indian village below. His hopes shot up when he heard someone say, "That's a funny kind of playing, but it's our boys all right."

Mac had been worried about what would happen to him when the others came back, but he'd avoided thinking about that possibility until now. He wanted the other men to come back alive, but if they did he'd be an outcast. And if Custer had his way he might even be hung or shot.

"That ain't troopers calling. That's Indians," said someone up the line in the dark.

"Bullshit," another man said. "Ain't no Goddamn' Indian knows how to make a damn' bugle call."

"That ain't no bugle call. That's just blowing, and it's John Sioux what's doing it."

The last Sioux had departed and the ridge was finally quiet except for the cries of wounded men who called for water. Mac slapped at mosquitoes that buzzed around his ear, but still he hugged the ground. For the first time in quite a while he ventured a word to Harker, "Looks like we got plenty of bugs--but at least there's no more John tonight." He lifted his head slightly, and with his fingertips dug into the itchy grime on his neck. His gaze roved northward beyond the perimeter. Harker was silent and lay still. Mac added, "I guess they'll be back before light."

After a few moments he glanced again at the silent blacksmith. Harker still lay with his head resting in the crook of his elbow. Then Mac smelled the metallic odor of blood, and beneath Harker's arm he saw a small black pool that glistened in the slight afterglow from the far horizon. The blood had already started to coagulate in the tangled grass and weeds beneath the soldier's averted face.

Mac touched the back of Harker's neck. The flesh was clammy and thick, spongy above a stiffening mass of muscle. He'd been talking to a dead man. The cracker box in front of the farrier had a splintered hole through it. The killing bullet had entered the top of his head. Sixty layers of hardtack in a wooden crate hadn't been enough to save him, and he'd crossed over.

There were so many dead and Harker was just one more, but he'd worked for Harker. He rested a hand on the dead man's shoulder for a moment. Harker had been one of the few company farriers who seemed to care about horses.

But then he had a sudden thought and raised his head to look at the cracker boxes. Sure enough, the box in front of Harker had been dumped in such a way that the layers of hardtack were not arranged like a series of shields. Instead the bullet had simply sliced between two pieces of the dry crackers. He looked carefully at the boxes nearby and decided they all were stacked the right way, then flipped Harker's box around, too. How many layers of hardtack did it take to stop a bullet?

He lay there for a long time, thinking about Wild and the others. He should've stuck with them, like Wild had urged him to do. He'd just done what he thought at the time was best for him, so why couldn't he have any peace about it? He might not have run from Custer's squadron if things hadn't come at him so fast, with Malachy getting shot and his blood and bones flying around. And Holley riding back to join them all; he could've got killed for his sentiment. Maybe he was dead right now, like Harker. He glanced over at the dead farrier. Looking at Harker, and thinking Holley and Wild might be dead made his heart feel bad. Doubly tormented and confused, he wondered what would happen when Wild and the others came back in the morning and found him here.

Only hours ago he'd run away, yet that action seemed only the most recent of many similar acts throughout his life. He'd always believed he stood alone, couldn't trust anyone, until Sophia came into his life. Now he might not see her again. She might never know he was trying to come help her.

The fires still burned below in the big valley camp, and the night sky shone pale blue above the crests of the western mountains. He felt so tired. As he slipped into sleep he could hear wounded men calling for water.

⌘

"Get up, Durant!" Mac felt the sharp blow of someone kicking the soles of his boots. It was Captain Benteen. "You! God damn it, move! Get to the top of that coulee," Benteen snapped. "We need more men over there. Move!"

He looked where Benteen pointed and saw the dark shapes of several soldiers sprawled behind a barricade of dead horses and mules. The night had mostly passed and a faint light already bloomed above the eastern horizon.

It seemed he'd only just fallen asleep, and anxiety swept through him as he jumped up, clenched his fists. His mind wouldn't work and he shook his head to clear the sleep and aching stiffness from his body. Confused shame clouded his thoughts as he snatched up his carbine and ran bent over to join those men already at the top of the ravine. Had Wild and the others returned while he slept?

As he threw himself down amid the small group on the ground, a ragged burst of gunfire erupted suddenly from the gully below. He and the others hugged the ground behind the animals while slugs thumped into the bloated corpses and snapped in the dirt beside them. Other soldiers came up, and when he glanced around, he saw maybe twenty men had gathered.

Benteen was there, shouting above the Indians' gunfire. "We're unprotected here, men, and they Goddamn' well know it! They'll come up this ravine any moment and make short work of us all unless you run them out. Check your side arms. Leave your carbines. This has to be done faster than hell fries feathers."

His back and arms ached, and he badly wanted water. His tongue stuck to the roof of his mouth and he could work up only a little spit to loosen it.

The brief moments since he'd wakened clarified memories that made his torso shudder as if from cold. He looked at the soldier beside him and asked, "Did Custer and the rest come in during the night?"

The other trooper squinted intently into the ravine below, then glanced at him. "Hell, no. Nobody knows where they are. Custer said he'd support us yesterday. But, shit! The man's long gone!"

Even in dawn's wan light Mac could see down into the brushy ravine. It swarmed with moving shapes. Bitterness suddenly overtook him, a fierce unreasoning resentment he'd felt many times against his aunt and uncle, against his father and mother for being killed--most recently against the army. But this time his wrath focused on himself. He'd dragged himself to this place, and here he lay: cold and filthy, thirsty, hungry. The fighters in the ravine were trying to kill him. He'd run from Wild and the others only yesterday, left them to fight alone. In a sudden insight, he saw that act simply as a continuation of his entire past. A sudden insight bloomed in him: at what price life? What prices should be paid, what thoughts should be suffered, to go on living?

His heart pounded rage at himself, engorged his throat, almost choked him as Benteen roared, "Now, men! Charge! Run those sons of bitches out of there!"

In a howling, sobbing release of pent fury, he rose with the rest and plunged forward. A scream as from a knife's gash rent his throat and he bayed like an animal, guttural and savage, and surged down the ravine against a clatter of gunfire from below. The Colt kicked in his hand; something zipped past his shoulder and the sound, the assault, deepened his rage. He sobbed against all this, against the choking dust, against life itself, his teeth gnashing against what seemed a great wasting joke. Bitter laughter exploded within him at a thought that goaded him like a pike thrust into his ribs: "Will it be now? Will I die now?"

The soldier to his left said quietly, "Oh!" as though surprised, and stumbled forward, fell hard into the dirt and rolled. Mac didn't look at the man but raced on with the others, howling apocalyptic rage and fear, hurtling pell-mell down the gully, shooting, cursing.

"Those two!" someone yelled. "There! Those two!" He shot at a moving shape in the semi-dark, and the fighter jumped up then turned and plunged down the gully at a limping run. The gathering of warriors below finally broke and ran before the soldiers' onslaught. He and the others did not stop, but staggered onward, chasing them down the wide ravine. Then a vague shouting came from his left along the threadbare line of skirmishers, someone yelling orders. They stopped firing, glanced around, began to withdraw back up the hill.

Panting and coughing in the gun smoke and dust that hung in the windless air, they reached down to the dead and wounded, grabbed fists full of shirt collars, arms, anything they could grasp. Mac dragged one man back to the hilltop, dropped him beside the dead horses and mules. He looked around and saw a dozen or so of them were left. For a long moment they just looked at each other, panting, blank-faced. A couple of men began to laugh hysterically, and another shouted, "Did you see those bastards scoot?"

Then Benteen yelled, "Get the wounded to Doctor Porter's hospital. Lay them there," he said, pointing, "On the low side of those dead mules." Mac looked down at the man he'd dragged back. His lifeless eyes stared at nothing and his skull was misshapen; he'd taken a round below his eye.

Only then in the crisp air of dawn did he feel the chilly wetness on his arm. A rivulet of black blood ran down his right arm through the dirt and gunpowder. It dripped from his knuckles onto the sooty cylinder of the Colt he still clenched tightly in his fist.

Then a burn seared his forearm like a hot iron and he peeled up his sleeve. He'd been shot just below the elbow, a wound that had severed muscle only as deep as the slug's own thickness. His hand felt locked around the revolver's grip, and for some reason this struck him as funny. He chuckled as, with his left hand, he slowly pried his own unyielding fingers from the grip. He laughed at the incongruity of the burning pain and his soaring elation. He looked up to see Benteen watching, appraising. He met the Captain's gaze boldly, grinning, then turned and walked away.

He sauntered among the other men who'd survived the attack into the ravine. In the slow half-light before sunrise, they shook hands, slapped each other on the shoulders, hooted with good humor. Several grinned at him. His mood climbed higher as one man said, "Good job, Durant." He couldn't remember when someone had said something like that to him. He'd survived, stood among men who'd also survived. But then he looked back at the soldier he'd dragged from the ravine, dead there by the bloated horses, from the force of a bullet his life gone. That dark hole beside his nose. Oddly, it'd bled hardly at all.

He fell silent, became reflective at his survival. For a moment he recalled his rage at himself just before the charge into the ravine: what price would he pay to continue to live? Days ago he'd heard Burden sneer at someone: "You love this life so much." Mac looked at the peaceful dead around him, the departed. The price of all his fears had been paid for so long. Perhaps he had not lived. A pang moved through him, and he wondered at the purpose of it all.

He walked back to the dead man by the horses, bent over and brought the man's eyelids down with his fingertips.

He sat cross-legged behind the tumbled barricade of boxes and saddles, and gazed around. Light rose beyond the Wolf Mountains' gap where they'd crossed the previous day. Dusty air now colored that horizon red, and purple-black clouds were paling toward pink. Even amid the bloated dead soldiers and bodies of mules and horses, everything around seemed fresh, untried. He breathed deeply in the dawn chill, savored the air's crispness as his arm began to throb with his heartbeat.

Somebody passed a canteen of whiskey and he swigged deeply then splashed a bit onto his wound. One trooper laughed aloud and said, "Hey, Durant! That's a waste of good liquor! Better let your arm just fall off!" He smiled and rose to his feet, walked about, for no shots came from the Indians and he felt indifferent to the possibility.

There was no water left anywhere, or at least none anyone would admit to having, and the liquor left him even more thirsty than before, and sleepy. He yawned. But as daylight came, more dark shapes came up from the huge valley camp. Gunfire rose again from their positions.

When the first volleys came in, he threw himself down beside one man. Several moments passed before he realized the trooper was

Cornelius Blosser. The old man lay on his back, utterly still, the flesh of his face pasty and mottled gray. At first he thought Cornelius was dead. He reached out and touched the old soldier's arm.

Blosser opened his eyes and murmured, "You made it through so far, eh, boy?"

Mac said, "I guess, Cornelius."

"I knew you'd be all right. You just needed a little time to think--take a few new things into account." His voice was weak and his breath gurgled in his chest.

"I guess." A finger of shame lightly touched the back of his neck at the realization Cornelius didn't know he'd run again--and only yesterday. What was Cornelius doing here? Maybe he'd run too, and a glimmer of consoling hope rose within him. But then he remembered that Bobo had assigned the old soldier to the mule train.

The old man hacked twice. "C ain't come back. That don't sound good." His voice was feeble, his mouth crackling dry.

Mac didn't answer. He hoped Cornelius wouldn't think to ask him why he was here instead of with Wild and the others. The old man's face, like all their faces, was crusted with dried sweat and dirt and gunpowder. Creases formed from many years on horseback in all kinds of weather spread away from his eyes. Squinting and laughing and drinking lines, Mac supposed. Three parallel white scars marred the right side of his cheek, like slashes made by a big cat. Mac realized that he'd never looked closely enough at Cornelius before to see those most obvious marks.

Cornelius whispered, "Got shot twice yesterday. That's a couple times more'n I'd hope." He coughed feebly. "You got a bit of water, do you?"

"I'm sorry, Cornelius. I don't have a drop."

The old man's dry mouth crackled like rustling paper as he whispered, "Ain't no water anywhere on this hilltop. I guess we got some exterminatin' circumstances here."

"Nobody can get to the river." Because Mac wanted to give him some encouragement, he lied, "I heard a couple men been talking about going down. But the Indians are all through the ravines, and have them covered pretty good."

"They can talk forever, but somebody's got to go do it. We don't get no water, some of us goin' to die today."

"Maybe I could get you some." He was surprised to hear himself say this, and he glanced briefly around, fearing someone else might have heard him.

"I'd be much obliged if you could, son."

"I'll get you some, Cornelius, but it might be a little while longer." He felt nervously foolish for making such a promise. Maybe the old man would be dead before he could get him any water.

He remembered what seemed to be Burden's sneering line: "You love this life so much." A realization came to him suddenly: by any stretch he sure didn't like this life much, but he didn't want to die. Maybe he valued his life, but not so much that he wanted to live it like a coward, without risk of harm, avoiding at any cost the possibility of pain or death's annihilation. He remembered the exhilaration of their charge down the ravine.

He looked again at the old man but he was asleep or unconscious. Maybe he could get to the river, and bring back water for Cornelius and the other wounded men. The Indians couldn't be everywhere. Benteen had made him and the others clear out that big ravine. Maybe the Indians had stayed away from there.

Still, he wished he'd not promised the old trooper any water. He'd only meant to make him feel good. Blosser probably understood that. After all, no one could likely get through the damn' Sioux. They were just like vengeful providence sitting out there, taking potshots and waiting.

The Indians' gunfire was still only sporadic. Some troopers lay flat on the ground behind whatever cover they had, while other men, bent over, ran or trotted around the defensive line on small errands, looking for ammunition, seeking a better weapon from one or another of the dead. They asked around for water and whiskey, speculated on their chances for survival, wondered aloud where Custer was, and when Terry's men would come south down the valley to meet them--and would they come in time?

Mac found his empty canteen and ran with it to the hospital area. Doc Porter lay on his belly behind the wall of dead pack mules and horses. The animals' legs stuck straight out into the air, and the mules' cross-buck cinches cut deeply into their swollen bellies. The flies were terrible.

Mac watched while Porter checked the bleeding beneath a bandage wrapped around the stomach of an unconscious trooper.

Porter shook his head. "You can't get water now, son. Forget it."

"I promised a man I'd bring him water. He's been shot twice." He guessed Porter didn't remember examining him when he enlisted a month ago.

"Where is he?"

Mac gestured across the perimeter to a high point where men from H lay scattered along the line overlooking the river. The doctor squinted with red-rimmed eyes, followed Mac's pointing arm, said, "I want him over here where I can keep an eye on him. I've got a bit of water left, and a bit of whiskey."

Mac said hopefully, "Can I take him that water?"

"No, that water stays here. You drag him on over."

"I'll try, sir." Maybe Porter's water would be enough for Cornelius. Maybe he wouldn't have to go to the river.

Porter cursed as blood leaked from beneath the wounded trooper's bandage and he pressed hard on it, squirmed around, still low to the ground, looking for leverage to make a more firm compress. He snapped, "Then get to it, private."

He ran bent over to where Cornelius lay, and told the old man he was taking him to Doc Porter at the hospital.

"Just drag me by this arm, boy," and he lifted his left arm then dropped it. "That bullet broke the other."

He grabbed Blosser's arm and started to drag him, but the old man cried out so he stopped. "Cornelius, I got to try to carry you."

"Go ahead, boy," the old man said meekly. "I'll be still."

Mac tried to lift him in his arms but Cornelius was too heavy so he wrapped his arms around the old man's chest and lifted him, letting his legs drag. Cornelius growled with pain through clenched teeth, his teeth grinding. Mac feared he was harming him, but kept on. Bullets zipped nearby, trying to find them. He ignored them and backed as quickly as he could from the perimeter and down along the broad swale toward Doc Porter's hospital position. A couple of soldiers lay amid the horses by the hospital, and turned to look at him, ducking lower and cursing as balls flew by them. Panting, Mac moved Blosser in among the other wounded.

Dr. Porter acknowledged him with a nod, saying, "That'll be a good thing if you can get to the river, son. Take that with you." He pointed at a lidless tea kettle that lay nearby.

"Yes, sir," Mac said, then to Cornelius: "Dr. Porter's going to look you over."

"If you got some water, son, I'd be obliged." His voice was only a feeble whisper.

He got Dr. Porter's water and gave a bit to Cornelius. The old man didn't remember he'd told him he had no water. Maybe he didn't recall the promise he'd made to get him some. Possibly Cornelius didn't even remember who he was. Still, he'd told Porter he'd get water. He looked at the lidless kettle the doctor had indicated, and at his own canteen. Supposedly, most of the Sioux were not good shots, so maybe they'd shoot at him and miss and he'd be able to get back to the hilltop. Even if he couldn't get to the river, he'd know he tried.

He grabbed the kettle and his canteen and scurried back along the perimeter. He passed several men dragging a dead mule into position to close up a gap in the line. As he approached the head of the ravine, he heard someone yell his name. He looked up to see Sergeant Knipe from C and felt a jolt of anxiety.

Knipe motioned him over. Mac glanced around, suddenly feeling disoriented that maybe he'd missed Wild and the others coming in. Then he remembered seeing Knipe riding toward the rear yesterday just before Malachy'd been shot and he and Holley had ridden away.

"What are you doing here, Durant?"

His spirits sank as he lied, "My horse collapsed. C went on and left me behind." By starting for the water he'd begun to feel somehow cleaner inside, but here he was lying again. It made his heart hurt.

Knipe had a puzzled look on his face. "Did you see what happened to them?"

"No, Sergeant. They just disappeared over a ridge and there was a lot of gunfire and dust."

"I don't know why they haven't come back, and I don't know why

Reno didn't order us to follow them while we still could. Something bad has happened or Edwin and the others woulda got back here by now."

Mac said nothing. He looked at the tea kettle in his hand. He wondered if Wild and the others were dead, and that's why they hadn't returned, but he could hardly give thought to this speculation, let alone words.

Knipe grimaced. "What are you doing, making tea?"

"No, I'm going down to get water for the wounded. Doc Porter gave me this kettle."

"He told you to go? You won't get to the river without getting shot."

"Nobody told me to go, but we ran the Indians out of the ravine earlier. Maybe they stayed out of that area."

"Maybe at this end, but probably not down by the water. They don't want us getting no water. They'll kill you for certain."

"You telling me I can't go?" He almost hoped Knipe would tell him to stay. If so, that would be the first order he ever welcomed since getting stuck in the army.

"No, I ain't. Not if Doc Porter needs water. But I do believe you'll be shot."

The wound in his forearm had started to swell; it throbbed anew and he considered their charge down this same ravine just an hour earlier. The furious exhilaration he'd felt earlier hadn't lingered. He needed it to come back, but couldn't summon it. Peculiarly, what had stuck was his promise to Cornelius and the doctor. The return of Wild and the others, his fear of them exposing his cowardice, his desire to get to Deadwood and find Sophia: those fears and desires paled beside his promise to Cornelius and Porter. Even though going down to that river was the last thing he wanted, he said, "I guess I better get going."

Knipe looked at him. "I'll go down a little ways with you, and if somebody pops up to shoot you, I'll give you some cover."

"Thanks," he said, then took a deep breath and started into the broad ravine. He took several tentative steps and stopped, but, seeing nothing, proceeded again. He hefted his Colt in one hand and the canteen and tea kettle in the other. After a few moments he looked back up the ravine and saw Knipe wave to him. Although some gunfire still sounded from above, the hillside's steepness dampened the noise and heightened his sense of isolation from Knipe and the others. He was solitary, unaccompanied, had to will himself to take each step further away from his fellows. The drainage curved below and he could see neither the ravine's mouth nor the river. He saw two of the river's meanders far away to the north, but their distance oppressed him and he didn't look at them again.

He stepped carefully as he went along, alert to sounds, fearful of making too much noise. Occasionally he heard a muffled yell but couldn't tell if it came from a soldier above or some Indian along the river who was alerting others that he was descending toward them.

He went much further down before he was surprised to notice the marks of boot heels where he and the others had charged earlier in the morning. He didn't realize they'd come so far before retreating back to the top, and this thought heartened him a bit. But, as he continued on, a renewed sense of his own isolation flushed through him and he looked back up the ravine. The top lay around a curve and he could no longer see Knipe.

The coulee narrowed and steepened considerably as it went along, and at one spot he saw where pony prints had torn the ground. A large number of fighters must have gathered and waited here before dawn. Captain Benteen had been right to make him and the others attack them before they climbed the ravine and charged through the weakened battalion's position.

He went on, almost tiptoeing, until he stood just inside the mouth of the ravine where it emptied into the river maybe a hundred feet away. The river bank was a gradual incline at this point. What at some earlier time had been a steep mud bank had collapsed, been worn away to a wide, muddy shore by buffalo and other animals entering the water to drink.

He looked across the river and as far to left and right as he could. The opposite shore was open but heavily wooded to the north. A dozen fighters could already be setting their sights on him. Benteen said they were lousy shots, and he fervently hoped that was true. But it was hard to credit such a claim when so many soldiers lay dead on the ridge above. Being so totally alone was agony, but he forced this idea away for he couldn't just keep standing here.

He lay his canteen on the ground, grasped the tea kettle and made a run for the water. The muddy shore began to suck at his boots. He feared becoming mired so took several giant leaps and landed with a splash in the water, which at this place was only a foot or so deep. He made one huge, surging scoop with the kettle then turned and bounded back uphill toward the shelter of the ravine.

The muddy bank slowed his flight. Two shots--then a third-- exploded from across the woods across the river. He was moving too slowly; he'd be shot in the back. As if in a dream, his leaping steps seemed to last forever; the distance he must cover seemed vast. But the shots only popped into the mud nearby, one spattering him with muck as he bounded back into the ravine, snatching up his empty canteen.

Hands shaking badly, he started for the top. He had to transfer water from the kettle to the canteen. If he did not he might trip or fall and lose all the water. He stopped and poured the canteen full, his hands trembling so bad he spilled some water in the process. A little water was still left in the tea kettle, and he gulped it from the spout, coughing. He looked at the empty kettle with irritable fear: he should go back and fill it again. But when he looked back at the shore he couldn't make himself go back a second time. The fighters who'd just shot at him would be more ready this time; they might take better aim.

Just then, from beyond the river's quiet current, he heard someone shout in English, "Come on back, you yellow-livered, son of a bitching, wasicu bastard! Come on back here!"

Mac turned to look but could see no one. Was it an Indian or one of those squaw men--some white man fighting on the side of his wife's people? His temple pounded, his face flushing hot from the insult. He remembered all the years of insults from his uncle, and the judgments some troopers made when he'd run away weeks earlier. And what of Cornelius and the other wounded men? They needed this water. He hated giving the man a second chance to shoot him, but he looked down at the empty kettle. He had to get more.

He stoppered the full canteen and laid it on the ground. Gripping the empty kettle tightly, he ran for the river. He leapt across the muddy patch, but his feet slipped and he landed hard on his rear in about two feet of water. He heard the first gunshot. The round just missed his kettle as he plunged it under water. Dripping wet, he clambered to his feet then turned and leaped up the hill as three more shots went wide to his left and right, striking the water and popping into the muddy bank. He made it back into the shelter of the ravine, soaked and muddy, but exhilarated.

As he snatched up the canteen he thought to shout a taunt back at the shooters across the river, but decided not when he heard someone crashing through the underbrush on the opposite shore to get to a better position and shoot at him again. He turned and bent over, taking long, quick strides toward the hilltop with the kettle and canteen.

As he scrambled up the gully a sharp stitch gripped his side from the exertion. He glanced back to see if he was pursued. Once more someone shot at him but the round sailed harmlessly overhead. Finally, winded and his chest aching, he came around the last curve and looked for Knipe. For a second or two he thought the Sergeant had left him, but then Knipe waved from the top of the ravine. With new strength Mac plunged up the steep slope, exhilarated, no longer looking back.

Knipe shook his head incredulously. "Those shots. I figured for sure you were dead."

Mac grinned, "I thought so, too."

He left Knipe and ran across the defensive position clutching the full canteen to his chest and gripping the lidless kettle tightly in his good left hand like a trophy. Once back at the hospital position he ducked to the ground by Dr. Porter, who sat with his eyes closed, reclining against a dead mule. The doctor opened his eyes and looked sideways at him.

Mac said, "I got water, sir."

Porter yawned and said, "Good man." He sighed and rolled onto his knees, then asked, "You had a drink?"

"I had a little one at the river. I want to give some to my friend, Cornelius."

"Go ahead, son," and Porter gestured toward the old man who lay between two mules' bloated carcasses.

Cornelius opened his eyes but they seemed unfocussed. Didn't the old trooper recognize him? Cornelius took a swig but then coughed and part of the water came back up. Mac looked over at Porter for instruction, but the surgeon moved away on hands and knees to tend another man. Cornelius whispered, "Thanks, boy. I...."

Mac cradled his head and tried to get him to drink again, but the water ran from his mouth. Suddenly Dr. Porter was beside him. "Don't waste more of that, son. He can't use it." The surgeon crawled away and lay down between two dead mules.

Mac was stunned, could think of nothing to say. The old trooper's glazed eyes stared blindly at the sky. It seemed so long ago, that night last month when he'd run away. Cornelius had been a stranger, but he'd risked punishment to help him. He'd stayed at his post until Wild brought him back in. But even though Mac had shunned the old soldier's acknowledgments for weeks afterward, Cornelius had greeted him with kindness and unspoken understanding. A tightness came into his throat and he shuddered, swallowing.

A bullet zipped past his face and he flinched, but stayed on his knees next to the old man's body. With his fingertips he brushed flies away from Cornelius' open mouth, tried to close his fogged eyes, but they wouldn't stay shut. That the old man still had to look at the sky bothered him. He wondered how long his own mother and father had lain this way after they'd been killed.

He clenched a fist against his chest and choked back a sob, his eyes roving around. Weary riflemen sprawled along the perimeter beside cracker boxes and saddles. A few lay behind the parapets of rifle pits they'd gouged out during the night . All along the perimeter swollen corpses of men and animals lay contorted in odd repose, having dropped wherever bullets had found them.

He looked again at Cornelius. What did the old soldier see now that he was gone beyond? A thought occurred to him: Cornelius had helped him again on this day, a second time, just by needing the water. Getting that water had made him feel different, somehow hopeful and good. Maybe Holley was right and the old man was now in a good place.

Just then he heard Porter call to him. "Come on back here, private."

He looked again at Cornelius. He tried once more to close the old man's eyes, but the lids wouldn't stay. Leaving him like that was a torment, but he went back to where the surgeon lay on his side beside a dead mule.

Dr. Porter said, "I have plenty of other people who need this water, so take a shot or two then I'll keep the rest. I'll get Major Reno to send more men to the river now that we know it can be done."

Mac nodded, "Yes, sir." He took two deep draughts.

"What's your name, private?"

"Mac Durant, sir."

"You did a good job, Durant--a brave thing."

An excerpt from her father's letter:

…I think back on Wild and Malachy and Holley. I learned something from each of them. Wild with all his practicality and skill and encouragement to us in his "set of four," and his help to the other troopers as well. Such a good man, yet so burdened by his past. I always wondered what happened to him on that hillside, for in the initial search for bodies and the identification process his remains were not found. Though I inquired many years ago to the War Department, they never wrote back to me. I know his remains are still somewhere upon that field, though buried now by over fifty years of prairie grasses' growth and withering.

JUNE 26, 1876: RENO-BENTEEN SIEGE SITE, MONTANA TERRITORY

During early afternoon Indian gunfire began to decline. He and the others watched as most of the fighters left the ravines and hillocks and started to walk or ride toward the village in the valley.

Beyond the river and the wooded area in the valley below, other Indians lit the prairie on fire. Smoke billowed up and obscured the troops' view of the village, but through breaks in the smoke Mac could see tipis being broken down. Men and boys brought in horses from the huge herd that grazed to the west of the village, then lashed together travois. Women hurriedly packed food and gear into parfleches and bundles, attaching these to their horses' backs, then loaded tipi hides and other possessions onto their travois.

In late afternoon there began a massive exodus. Thousands of people, pack animals, and the immense pony herd, all partially hidden by a huge dust cloud and dwindling smoke from the prairie fire, moved slowly southwestward toward the snowy Big Horn Mountains.

They traveled in groups of several hundred, and through field glasses one officer said he could see wounded men tied onto travois and dead men lashed across their horses' backs. Some men and women rode, while other women walked and carried babies on their backs. Young children walked beside them, and here and there old people sat or reclined on travois amid their bundles.

After the exodus began, only scattered shots were fired into the soldiers' hilltop position from a rearguard of fighters who'd been left behind on high ground to the north. Whatever caused the Indians' departure, when he looked southwestward before sunset, their vast migration had passed out of sight beyond the green bench lands. But far to the southwest, in the long sunlight that slanted into the valley from across the Big Horns, he saw a golden bloom of dust that drifted slowly eastward marking the peoples' progress.

By dusk all firing had stopped on both sides. Here and there, well out of rifle range, he watched the last fighters, singly or in twos or threes, depart for the valley from along the ridges around their defensive position. As twilight came on, across the river far below, small groups of men rode out of the trees and began to follow in the wake of their families.

The troopers were thirsty and hungry, stiff from the hard ground. Slowly they began to rise and look cautiously around. They stretched and strode tentatively about under the milky evening sky, speculating about the reason the Indians had withdrawn.

"Maybe Custer's coming back and they didn't want to fight him," one man ventured.

"Where is that son of a bitch?" another trooper snapped. "He was supposed to support us in the valley. Is he off somewhere takin' his ease?"

"I don't expect his boys been takin' much ease," one older corporal said. "Where'd the Indians get them bugles they was playin' last night? Something's gone badly wrong."

Mac heard one trooper say, "Maybe the Indians' outriders saw Terry coming from the north." Several others who'd gathered around this conversation murmured and nodded, hoping that was so.

On the hilltop the survivors brought up more water and set about trying to make their wounded more comfortable. They buried their dead in the rifle pits and shallow trenches that had been excavated the night before, then covered them with loose dirt from their hurried breastworks. They gathered and checked the actions of dead comrades' weapons and stockpiled them, made a full count of men and ammunition, made sure every trooper had some shells in case the Sioux came back. They stripped packs from the dead mules and inventoried their food.

In late afternoon he helped bury Cornelius and several other men. By twilight they'd moved the camp farther north along the bluffs to a better position, still concerned the Indians might return. They drank their fill in the river and bathed, then hauled water back up the hill to a dinner of beans and hardtack. Sentry posts were doubly manned to make sure none fell asleep, while many other men sprawled about and slept as if they were dead.

Though exhausted, Mac couldn't sleep. He felt a satisfying weariness, a quiet excitement. His mind wouldn't rest but kept working over the details of the day: the charge into the ravine, going to the river for water. He couldn't figure why he should feel so absolutely good. The throbbing pain in his wounded arm was merciless, probably from the grave digging. He tried to ignore it, but couldn't.

The question of where Custer and his men had gone was still unanswered. Some of the others speculated that their comrades were dead, and although that would save his cowardice from being revealed, he couldn't hope for it--except on some primal level that felt shameful. He tried to push these thoughts away, for in his deepest heart it hurt to think he might escape exposure and punishment only by purchasing it with the deaths of his friends.

He'd take his medicine. He just wanted Holley and them to come back. He wouldn't mind the sheepherder sitting here with him right now, mooching his hardtack and all. He'd like to see Wild reading by the light of the cooking fire, or Malachy playing with the coyote pup. He touched his fingertips to his cheek where Malachy's bone shard had punctured him. The Irish soldier had been dead a day, only an hour before had he finally washed from his face the fan of dried blood.

In the middle of this pained reflection a trooper he didn't recognize came into the circle of firelight. "Ain't you Durant?"

Mac looked uncertainly at the man. "Yeah."

"You went for water this morning?"

"Yeah. Some others did, too."

"Daniel Knipe told me you went first, by yourself."

Mac just nodded. His wounded arm felt hot and he didn't feel like talking.

"Well, I don't know if you're a drinking man, but"--he held up a canteen--"I still got this near full of whiskey and I'd be glad if you'd share a few snorts."

Mac accepted the man's offer and within a half hour fell asleep, flat on his back on the open ground without a blanket. He woke in the dark with dew-wet clothes and his teeth chattering. Every bone in his body ached and his face felt so thick and tight he couldn't tell if he was sick or just hung over. The first pale bud of dawn's light glowed above the Wolf Mountains, and morning birds called from the trees down along the river.

A whorl of breeze lifted charcoal dust from a dead fire into his face and nose and he sneezed. Seeing a small roll of canvas tarpaulin nearby, he rose painfully to his feet. But as he spread the tarp on the ground he found it hard to bend his elbow. The pain seemed kind of bad, and as he crawled beneath the canvas he favored his wounded arm.

He dreamt again of Sophia. He found her in Deadwood, but she didn't remember him and called to two other men who came and stood behind her, laughing at his profession of love and his offer of help. She turned, and with a taunting smile walked away with one man on each arm.

He woke to an anguished question: was that how she would act when he found her?

Well after daylight a Crow scout rode into camp with news that sent the men to whooping and slapping each other on the back. "General Terry's coming, just a few miles north!" Knipe yelled. "Maybe Custer's with him."

Mac watched a small party of officers ride off to meet them. A couple hours later, he and the others learned stunning news: Terry's scouts had discovered Custer's men, over two hundred troopers, all of them dead on a hillside several miles northwest of this hilltop siege site. Their bodies had been found scattered across more than a mile of grassy ridges and coulees. His heart sank and his arm throbbed like crazy and he couldn't help but sit down and bawl like a baby. Wild and Holley had to be part of that--and Burden.

Doc Porter changed the bandage on his wound which had started to swell and turn red at its topmost end. What looked like a red vein had just begun to show above his elbow. The surgeon pointed at it and said, "This is infected. If the redness goes any higher or if the pain gets worse I want you to tell me."

A bit alarmed, he asked, "Is it a problem?"

"It could be."

He nodded and began to walk away, but turned when the surgeon said, "By the way--" Porter gestured around him at badly wounded men who were being loaded on horse and mule-drawn travois made from lodge poles and buffalo hides taken from the abandoned village. "You helped these men, Durant."

"Thanks, sir." But he felt so weak that when he turned away he had a hard time controlling his tears. He knew he'd abandoned those he should have stood with. Now they were dead. He should be with them.

He and Knipe were ordered to help locate and identify C Company troopers' remains. They roamed the hillside and long ridge where the five companies' troopers had died. The Indians had stripped most corpses of their clothing. Some were so badly mutilated and decomposed from lying in the heat that they were impossible to identify, except by a remnant of familiar clothing, an embossed wedding ring or neck chain, a unique scar or a remembered tattoo.

Survivors from Reno's and Benteen's battalions were detailed to bury their comrades from Custer's battalion. There were too few picks and shovels to be had so the men used cooking kettles, knives, frying pans--even farrier's nippers--to scrape shallow graves. They mounded dirt over their dead friends, some of whom's bloated arms still stuck out from beneath the loose dirt and knots of sod.

He helped Knipe roll Edwin Bobo's corpse into a shallow grave. He'd been scalped. Four arrows protruded from his corpse and his left ear was gone. Sobbing quietly, Knipe tried to pull the arrows out, but only two would come. Cursing, he broke the shafts off the remaining two. Mac could only use his good arm at this work, for his other arm had begun to ache along its entire length. He felt his heart throb in the side of his neck, heard its slushy pounding in his ear.

From what he could tell by asking around, Wild's and Holley's bodies hadn't been found.

With Knipe, Mac wandered the western slopes of the high ridge to look for C troopers' remains. Many soldiers worked with wet handkerchiefs tied over their faces, but to little avail against the stench. Arguments sputtered and exploded between the men, for some were certain Custer's battalion had fought to the end in a disciplined, orderly stand. But to others it was clear their fellows had panicked. They'd been routed, these men said, for only at the south and north ends of the long ridge where the battle had flowed did the distribution of men's and horses' bodies and shell casings indicate any organized defense. He heard one of Terry's officers say, "Thank God there's some tide marks among them."

He looked quizzically at Knipe who said, "You see those men there, how their bodies lie in line?" He pointed. "Like twigs thrown up and left by water--a tide mark. They hung together, didn't just scatter like leaves in a wind."

Some soldiers muttered that only a few Indians had been killed, for rumor said only two Sioux bodies were found among the more than two-hundred soldiers' corpses. Knipe pointed to a dead trooper. "I seen a few temple wounds with black powder around 'em--like this one. Some of these boys killed themselves--or each other." Troopers nodded grimly at the long-held army wisdom that it was smart to keep the last bullet for yourself when fighting Indians.

Several troopers asserted that renegade whites had led the Sioux and Cheyenne in the attack. One sergeant said, "It had to been squaw men. No goddamn' Indians coulda done all this by themselves."

Another man scoffed, "Shit, you mean they ain't hard-hearted enough?"

"Hell, no. Their hearts are bad as ours; they're just not as well organized."

He pondered this notion, remembering the bottom of the ravine when he'd gone for water and been shot at. That shout had come from across the water in good English, calling him a yellow-livered son of a bitch, telling him to come on back. That man sounded like he could've been white.

"The devils ate some of these troops after torturin' 'em," Mac heard one man swear. "Down in that village my bunkie says he saw cooked flesh and ax-smashed bones."

A buck sergeant snapped, "That's bullshit, private. These people ain't cannibals."

The private grew angry and swore, "By God, I guess my bunkie knows cooked people when he sees 'em!"

He was stunned to hear that several corpses were found armed with full revolvers and carbines, and full issues of ammunition. He'd only fired a few shots himself during the hilltop fight and those had been poorly aimed. But he couldn't believe that throughout this battle, though they'd been fully equipped to defend themselves, some men never fired a shot. Some of these were recognizable as new recruits. "Their mamas oughtn't to taught 'em so nice," he heard one trooper grumble, "Or their pappies shoulda growed 'em more spine. In this godddamn' world a man best set his mind to do a bit of killin'."

"Too many new men," he heard one First Sergeant say to a Captain. "Beneath the kepis and the yellow-striped trousers, these poor souls weren't no army."

"Just a rabble," the Captain nodded. "Who was the poet? He said, 'In terror's hour they bent their knee to mood, and fled from discipline.'"

The First Sergeant looked a bit flustered. "I don't guess I know that one, sir."

In late afternoon he began to feel cold--even in the day's heat, and he heard the world as through a layer of cotton. Walking toward the river with Knipe, they counted twenty-seven bodies strewn along the slope. Boot prints here and there in the bare earth indicated these men had been running downhill toward the river when killed.

Near the river bank they came upon Burden's body. Beside it three soldiers were digging a shallow grave. Burden hadn't been a friend or even much of a human, but he had searched long and hard for his brother. Mac felt like he couldn't lift his wounded arm or he'd have offered to fill a few shovels full as a gesture to him.

A trooper who stood beside Burden's corpse waved an arm at the disorderly scatter of troopers' bodies strewn like seeds on the slope above. "I don't know why them boys was runnin' down here."

A buck sergeant man said, "Maybe they were trying to get to the river."

The first trooper said, "With the whole damn' Sioux village just across the water?"

"It don't make sense to you and me, but we ain't faced the same straits as these."

The buck sergeant pointed at Burden's body and said, "I know this poor son of a bitch. He was just about the meanest bastard in the regiment--though there's a few others I can think of too."

The other trooper nodded in Burden's direction and said, "He couldn't write, you know, but was always finaglin' somebody or other to copy out a letter to send his brother."

"He was sending out letters trying to find his brother," Mac corrected him. His arm hurt so bad he just wanted to lie down. "He was looking for his brother ever since back in the Rebellion where they got parted somehow."

The trooper looked at him. "He ain't going to find him now."

He just wanted to sleep and not have to wake up. Twice in the last couple hours he'd seen Sophia in her grandparents' gazebo with small birds all around her. They landed in droves, all singing to beat heck like it was early morning. Her peacock strutted past, flaring its tail feathers and jealously squawking sour notes at the other birds. He couldn't tell if it was just in his mind's eye--like in a dream--or if she was really here. Maybe he'd had a nap or dreamt of her last night, but right now he saw her standing beside him and he wanted to shield her from all this. But then she was gone. He figured he ought to go find Doc Porter.

He plodded back up the hill for what seemed the longest time, lifting one tired leg after another, all the while looking for the surgeon or Wild or Holley; he couldn't be sure which. He thought other soldiers looked at him strangely, but they didn't speak. His head felt hot and he remembered that he'd lost his hat, so when a little ways on he found one of the dead soldiers' straw hats, one that the civilian in the mackinaw boat had been selling up on the Yellowstone days ago, he put it on and found it fit just right.

And though his hands wouldn't stop trembling, he brightened when he saw Holley coming down the hill toward him. "I can get you some biscuit, Leo," he told him. Just then a frigid wind hit him and he felt so cold that he couldn't remember if he was looking for Sophia or the doctor or Holley's biscuit. He lay down to sleep and several men wandered over to look at him, but when one grabbed his bad arm Mac saw a white light and screamed. Through a wall of cotton he saw the man drop his arm and heard, "Jesus!" Behind his ribs he felt soft warmth bloom like balmy air and his mind emptied, falling away from the light, sinking agreeably into darkness.

An excerpt from her father's letter:

…Since that day long ago, I know what it is to be ready to die. It is an agreeable state of mind. Once you are close to doing so, and you have decided that it is fine to cross over, it seems like unpleasant work to remain here and carry on. It seems redundant, like you have learned enough from this life. You wish to move on, but you cannot because you are being held back and have to soldier on in this life.

In that process of coming back from death one also loses something, some emotional energy or zest. Since that day I have had many pleasures and many challenges, yet during all these years a quiet current of sadness has flowed through my thinking. I have never discussed this with anyone before, for it would sound too gloomy. But to say that one recovers from nearly dying, is to make the outcome appear to be a boon when, at least in my case, it has required a kind of stoic acceptance.

But it also made me feel I needed to do something useful, something good, with whatever might remain of my life.

JUNE 30, 1876: LITTLE BIG HORN RIVER, MONTANA TERRITORY

They carried him aboard the steamboat Far West with other wounded men. He had no memory of this, except that men were kind and spoke softly as they bent over him and he was carried along through the world on a smoothly buoyant course, as though floating. Sophia came and looked down at him, her mouth a faint smile. His mother was there, her face speckled with dried mud and somewhere nearby, just out of sight, stood his father. Mac strained to see him but could only sense his presence, as though he stood vigil over his son.

The steamboat picked its way carefully back down the narrow Big Horn River to the Yellowstone then on to the Missouri and finally Fort Lincoln where a little over two days later it arrived with direful news and a straw-strewn deck full of dead and wounded men. Mac and others still alive were placed in a barrack hurriedly vacated then set up as an overflow for the Fort's infirmary.

The blood poisoning was expected to kill him, but did not. The doctors didn't know why. At first, in lucid moments he wanted the release of death. He sought relief from physical affliction, but also from his torment and anguish. For his fearful dreams had changed; the Indian boy with the war club who had killed his mother in the slough came no more, but was replaced by other haunts.

In flickering candlelight Holley stood by his infirmary bed, his eyes dark holes, his face crusted with Malachy's blackened blood. He begged for a piece of biscuit. Burden, his face and chest torn with bullet holes, sneered, "You love this life so much." Wild walked toward him angrily, shouting, "I told you to stand with those men!"

He lay in bed in Sophia's rooms in Deadwood while she paced about, unable to recall his name. Benteen raged at him to charge alone down a night ravine with camp kettles toward waiting warriors armed for slaughter. He tried to run, but the kettles were suddenly full and his boots slipped in the muddy river bank. He floated helplessly, then was struck in the back by bullets he couldn't elude. He felt each round smash his flesh and splinter bone.

Over the weeks that followed, he slowly recovered. After his release from the hospital he was amazed to find with his other gear the straw hat he'd found after the battle. He kept it close.

Scattered reports arrived that expeditions led by General Terry and General Crook out of Wyoming Territory had chased the Sioux and Cheyenne around the Powder River country then to the east, but with little success at finding and forcing them to fight. The massive nation they'd faced in the valley of the Little Horn had split into many smaller groups. Some were said to be headed for the haven of Canada while others had melted away into the Big Horns or southeast toward the Black Hills or back to the agencies in western Dakota Territory.

The wound in his forearm and the infection healed grudgingly. At first he had trouble walking and keeping his balance, but by late August he was left with only an indented spot below the elbow of his right arm where scar tissue had formed.

When he finally left the hospital he spent his days on light duty. Word got around among other soldiers how he'd gone for water at great risk. His money quickly became no good. Everybody wanted to buy him drinks. Some mornings he couldn't remember the previous night's events and this frightened him. It frightened him that, though his body was healed, somehow he might lose his mind. He knew he shouldn't drink so much. He'd have to cut back.

When he thought about Wild and Malachy and Holley he wanted to be--struggled to be--lucid and fully awake. Late at night dreams of Sophia came to him. He saw her with the birds in the gazebo, her long auburn hair backlit by sunlight. He pulled out the letter she'd written him more than six months earlier, now dirty and stained with a bit of Malachy's blood that had soaked through his field shirt when the top of Malachy's head had come off.

She'd written that she hoped they'd meet again, but did she still feel that way? Or had her emotions been only fleeting? In reflecting on all that had happened, it amazed him that he had come all the way from St. Paul merely on the strength of her letter. "Things are not going well for me," she wrote. "I wish you were here--or I was there again--that we might talk."

The idea that he had no home, no place among people he cared for and people who cared for him, intruded more frequently into his consciousness. During his life with his aunt and uncle he'd become embittered. That life had poisoned his thinking. He'd found solace only in scorn and cynicism, but over the last few months he felt different. He'd seen terrible things, done things, some of them cowardly. But somehow these events had opened him, made him look at himself anew.

As he recovered he found himself reading Sophia's letter again and again. He felt it strange that he was not driven by the same longing he'd felt for her months earlier. True, she'd been good to him for a time, but she'd left him without even a goodbye. Given the events of the last several months he wondered if his feelings for her had drained away. Still, he felt attracted to her no longer on the basis of his own desire, but what seemed her heartfelt appeal for help.

⌘

In the pre-dawn of a damp morning in early September, he woke alone on the edge of the high prairie above the two forts, his clothes soaked with dew. Near him lay his straw hat and an empty whiskey bottle. The front of his field shirt was crossed with a small stripe of vomit and he couldn't remember how he'd gotten past the Fort's sentries and vedettes, or why he'd ended up in this spot. He coughed and ran his tongue around his dry mouth, tried to work up spit. He raised himself to his elbows, then some moments later sat up. His head logy, he locked his arms around his knees.

Gazing back down at the cavalry and infantry forts along the river bottom, he saw the glow of lanterns here and there among the dark buildings; only the fire watches were awake. Just beyond the two forts, enfolded within the river's broad valley, the turbid Missouri ran silvery blue, reflecting a hint of pale light which had begun to edge the prairie to the east. The waxing moon stood high in the zenith, and sunlight reflecting from the earth's curve lit its dark regions with a pale glow.

Stars still filled the sky in the west, and low in the firmament one bright star was about to set. He gazed at that far horizon, where on a distant plain Wild and Holley roamed. Their bodies had not been found, not been buried, and in his mind they still lived. On one hand he knew the notion was absurd, for no one could have gotten away that day. Yet a longing that they still lived--he could hardly call it hope-- seemed necessary to his own enduring breath. He conceived that they still might be riding with Terry's men, Holley with his Bible and Wild maybe giving him some biscuit now and then. He smiled faintly at the thought.

Though he'd run from the fight just in time to keep on living, each recollection of those moments agonized him. He was haunted by Wild's voice yelling to him and to Holley to leave Malachy's body and catch up with the column. He saw the horse slowly dragging Malachy's corpse through the stiff grass. And Holley: he had to go back, and he'd done so. He had been right.

Maybe Holley had known something about life that he himself was only now beginning to understand. Still, it was hard to give it words. All he could think of was that he wasn't so angry. His heart felt softer toward everything; he didn't feel so afraid, so cynical. He didn't know how to account for it.

He took from his field shirt the small folded packet that was Sophia's letter. He held it in his hand, for there was not enough light to read by. Doves cooed nearby in a brushy gully and something rustled in the stubbly grass. Maybe just a field mouse or a gopher, but he looked around him nonetheless. He strained to see some movement, perhaps a bull snake or prairie rattler. He stood shakily and walked toward the place from which the quiet sound had risen. He turned toward the gully where the doves had called. He wished they would call again, for he loved their soft voices so early in the morning. But they didn't, and though he looked about him for a time there was nothing except her folded letter that grew warm in the callused palm of his hand.

⌘

About a week later on a sunny morning, in a special regimental formation, he received the Medal of Honor which had been created by Congress fourteen years earlier during the Rebellion. When he'd gone from the hilltop to get water for the wounded, Doc Porter had made note of his name and later reported what he'd done. He was told that several other survivors from the Seventh, "water carriers" they had come to be called, also would receive the medal when they returned from chasing Indians.

He shrank at the thought that from the botched campaign the army might want heroes so badly that it would choose him as one. He looked at the ceremony as an ordeal established solely to punish his cowardice, and he numbed his mind to help him get through the event.

He didn't remember much that happened over the next several days, for whiskey flowed freely and he found it hard to resist. He did recall that several times officers saluted him, but even in his stupefied state their show of respect burned him like rock salt rubbed into a knife slash. Though he drank himself into oblivion he held onto the straw hat he'd found after the battle was over, for it reminded him of Wild and Malachy and Holley.

A few days later, news passed through the barracks that a contingent of half-starved cavalry making its way southwest through Dakota Territory toward the Black Hills to get food and supplies had stumbled on an encampment of Oglala Sioux at a place called Slim Buttes. While the soldiers had nearly blundered into the Indians, they did manage to take them by surprise with a charge through their camp at dawn.

Many Sioux were killed. The rest were driven from the camp and scattered. The story swirled around the cavalry barracks and Bismarck's saloons, embellishments being added with each new telling. The time was near when he'd be sent out again. This thought sickened him.

He looked about him at the other men, and all the new recruits. Many expressed eagerness to avenge the deaths of Custer and his men He did not share their sentiment, remaining silent in conversations where these passions ran high. The only soldiers he cared about were dead, gone roaming in the west. What minimal connection he'd ever had to the army was to those few: Holley, Wild, Cornelius, Malachy, Sergeant Bobo--even Burden.

All he had left--all he could think to care about--was Sophia, and he wondered if she was only an idea, a longing, and not a reality for him. He had to find out. He wished he still had her picture and locket, but he'd given those to Wild to keep. If he could see her face he'd be able to tell if she was real to him. Maybe she was just a yearning like liquor was starting to be, and that sooner or later he'd have to give up.

He'd saved his back pay. He went into Bismarck and purchased jerked meat, cornmeal and whiskey, a heavy coat and shirt. He bought an old Henry rifle and two boxes of cartridges from a sutler, then paid the man an extra quarter to keep these items for him in town.

One early morning in mid-September he took the sorrel mare he'd been assigned and got permission to leave the fort for two days in Bismarck. He ferried the horse across the river and rode into town to the sutler's shed and claimed his goods. He packed the gear in two small duffels and lashed them behind his cantle, then turned the mare southwest without a backward look. Half a day downriver from Fort Lincoln he swam her across the Missouri then roamed on south to Fort Pierre. There he learned of an old Indian trail still used by travelers. He followed it west to Bear Butte then down into the Black Hills.

He rode into Deadwood on a morning that was rainy with flecks of wet snow falling. The town was set in a deep ravine, a dank and filthy little place with mud streets and numerous saloons. He wondered why Sophia ever would have come here, for the whole place looked like it could be washed away in a flash flood and the world would be better for it. He asked around, looking for her with no result, wishing he'd not given the locket with her picture into Wild's keeping.

Early that evening he described her to a bartender who'd just started his shift. The man said, "Auburn hair, milky skin. I do believe I remember that woman. Her name's Sophia. I seen her down the street at the Number 10 Saloon. Lives with a man name of Devlin."

This news struck him like a blow and his voice faltered. "I didn't know she had somebody." Embarrassed, he flushed when the bartender looked at him a little more closely.

"To my knowin', he ain't her husband, but for that she oughta be grateful. The man has blacked her eyes a couple times I know of. They been staying up the street at the hotel for a few months now. I'm not certain, but I do believe you might've just missed them. Go on up to the Number 10 and ask for Big Henry."

"What kind of work did she do there?" Mac blurted out. He didn't want to think of what kind of job a woman could have there. He remembered Burden's notion that she was a whore. He would never accept that idea.

"She don't work. Just spends time there." The bartender looked at him. "She a relation of yours?"

"She's an old friend, and she might need some help."

"And well she might, with that Devlin."

How could Sophia be entrapped by any man, if indeed she was. In his view she'd always been independent, able to do for herself. He didn't think she'd kow-tow to a man for long if he didn't treat her right.

"Devlin's a low-life gambler out for himself, but he seems to have an easy way with the women," the bartender said. He pointed up the street. "Big Henry can fill you in."

He went to find Big Henry.

"She didn't work here," Big Henry said. He was a small round man with stubby legs and outsized arms that seemed to hang nearly to his knees. His voice seemed too large for his frame, rumbling like marbles in a bucket of water. "She might's well been on wages, for she was always here with Devlin," he said and pointed at a card table in the front corner. "He made his living right over there--but good riddance, I say."

"They're not here in Deadwood?"

"You missed 'em by a couple days, son." The bartender looked him up and down. "You Sophia's relation?"

"No, I'm a friend." He didn't know why people kept wanting him to explain himself--the church lady back in Bismarck months ago, now these two bartenders--they all seemed to want to know what his interest was in Sophia. "Where'd they go?" He hoped not back to Bismarck.

"Well, she didn't want to go, but Devlin ain't a man to take 'nosiree' from a woman. He wanted to get to Bozeman and into some games there. What with the army still chasin' Sioux everywhere betwixt here and there, more than a few of us told him he was crazy." Big Henry spit on the sawdust floor. "She wanted to go to San Francisco--said he'd promised her. But Devlin, he blew up two nights ago. Said they were going to Bozeman and that was that. Yesterday morning when they left she had a mouse on her eye. Cards ain't the only thing the man's free-handed about."

A surge of anger filled his chest at the idea Sophia had been hurt by this man. Why would she go off with him? "I'll need to go after them. How'd they likely go?" He had no idea if there was a marked route, though he doubted it.

"You get you over to the old Bozeman Trail. Go west from here," he pointed vaguely. "Well out of the Black Hills you'll cross the south fork of the Powder. You'll see wagon ruts and markings, a stone cairn here and there--though the Indians've knocked most of those to rubble. The track'll take you on to the Tongue and the Big Horn. When you hit the Yellowstone, you follow it on to Benson's Landing and then Bozeman's just around the corner 'bout a day beyond Benson's." He swabbed at the bar with a dirty rag. "You get due west of here five or six days, you'll run onto that Bozeman trace. You'll be fine if you keep your hair." He rubbed hard at one spot on the bar. "But I do believe that's iffy."

Early the next morning he used the last of his money to buy some jerky and salt pork, corn meal and wheat flour, but after he'd packed and headed the sorrel westward up a long ravine, he could not rid himself of the doubts that'd gnawed at him during the night. The problems Sophia had written to him about didn't necessarily involve this Devlin, whoever the man was.

If Devlin had hurt her and she'd still stayed with him, she had to be living in a pained confusion. But he felt anxious. What could he do about Devlin, if Sophia favored the man? Still, Sophia had been kind to him--had, in her way, opened up his life. Until Wild and the others came along, she'd helped him in ways nobody ever had. If he could find her, at least his own arrival would give Sophia a choice she might not know she had.

But how would he explain himself when he found her? Maybe she'd forgotten she even wrote that letter; he might look a monumental fool. And no doubt, the man she was with, Devlin, could make trouble. But he wanted her to know that he'd come, however delayed, to answer her appeal.

He tried to keep the sun off his left shoulder but with clouds and occasional rain it still took him the better part of two days to find his way out of the pine covered hills and onto the high plains of Wyoming Territory. There he cut the mare straight west and in four more days came onto the Bozeman trace where a couple of rock cairns had been toppled and scattered.

He saw no one but stopped each afternoon to cook a quick meal and douse his fire. Before dark each night he got well off the trail and made a cold camp. He remembered Bobo's anger at dawn after the night march out of Rosebud Valley when the regiment halted near the Wolf divide. Why had Custer chanced to let the men have fires on the morning of the day when so many would die?

Though Holley and Malachy were rarely far from his thinking, as he rode his thoughts most often went to Wild, for here in the lee of the Big Horns the country was full of late-blooming chokecherries and wild currants. Wild would've used those for something. It was here that he first considered his recent desertion, and a bit of remorse challenged his resolve. But he pushed it away. He would take part in no more killing.

Here and there were signs of other shod horses, but he was no tracker and could tell nothing about their number or when they might have passed. Mightily he feared coming over a rise to see ten or fifteen Sioux or Cheyenne just sitting their ponies astride the trace. He would have no chance. He thought a bit about traveling at night and sleeping well off the trail by day. But he decided against that, worried he might lose the old track in the dark.

Avoiding the more open country to his east, he set the mare along the eastern hip of the Big Horns, a piedmont where there was considerable tree cover. Aspen and cottonwood glowed gold in the early autumn sunlight. Evenings grew colder and chill winds swept down the ravines off the mountains, stripping the aspens' dying leaves into swirling clouds that carpeted the gullies and dappled the water of rocky streams, then were swept along.

After several days he hit the Yellowstone's south shore and turned west. Along the river were the tracks of many shod horses. He couldn't tell how old the tracks were, or if the riders had all traveled together or in smaller groups. It bothered him that he'd ridden fairly hard, but still hadn't overtaken Sophia and Devlin. He tried to envision where she might be right now. Had they even come this way? Maybe he was wasting his time, though he guessed he didn't have to worry on that, for he had no other plan.

There was a small village named Benson's Landing somewhere ahead, still two or three days' ride. Bozeman was only another day beyond the Landing, and certainly he'd find her in one of those two places.

Since the battle, he'd come to feel that although he'd done great wrong, he'd redressed those wrongs in part, even if it were only in getting water for Cornelius and the others. And now by helping Sophia he might do something truly worthwhile for someone who'd helped him. By trying to help her he might do something worthy of Wild and Malachy and Holley.

In a slit in the lining of his heavy coat, snugged inside its flat metal case, he carried the Medal of Honor with its eagle and star and ribbon. He carried it as a conscious weight, felt its heft at odd moments when he picked up the coat, or felt the medal's movement there in the fabric meant to warm him. He carried it not to remind him of his courage in getting water for the wounded troopers back on that hilltop, but to honor the memory of his friends and as a goad to rise above himself.

Just before dusk the next day, across a broad valley on a far slope, perhaps two miles away, two riders--hardly bigger than two moving dots--disappeared beyond a bend of sandstone cliffs near the big river. His heart quickened and he raised himself in the saddle. He did not spur his horse faster for he didn't know who they might be and felt anxious about coming upon them suddenly in the night.

But, continuing on, a couple of hours later he saw a campfire's glow reflecting off aspen leaves in a small ravine some distance from the trail. He dismounted and led his horse off the track opposite the fire. He tied her to a low tree branch so she could graze, then took the Henry and walked quietly toward the fire. He approached it with an anxious stomach, suddenly realizing he didn't know what he would say to Sophia if it was her and Devlin. He stopped to think about this for a moment, and when he did he heard men's voices.

Once he realized the people at the fire were not Sophia and Devlin he relaxed, coughed loudly and "halloed." There came a sudden silence. After a moment, off in the dark to his left he heard the crisp snap of a bolt slapping shut. "Come right in, neighbor," a man said. "Take a seat at our hearth." The man's words were welcoming, but tinged with warning. The figure who came forward from the darkness carried an army Springfield and wore a stove pipe hat. From Mac's right another man emerged from the dark and stood by the fire. He didn't offer his hand, but said, "Jeffries is my name." In the firelight he saw that Jeffries was wall-eyed, one iris lighter than the other, and somewhat askew.

The man with the breechloader and the stove pipe said, "I am Jacob Wessells," and offered his hand. He gestured magnanimously at the campsite. "Our furnishings may be spare, but we are pleased to share a passable rabbit stew and a bit of rather fiery whiskey."

Wessells seemed educated, for he spoke formally and clearly valued setting a high tone with his stove pipe and black suit coat. But when the breeze shifted a bit Mac confirmed that it wouldn't pay to ride downwind of the man; he smelled like a Chicago packing plant in

August. His odd eyes were those of a hawk, fierce and vigilant. It didn't seem wise to get too comfortable.

They all sat cross-legged by the fire and passed a jug of whiskey several times. Wessells told him they'd been in the Black Hills but had tired of gold hunting. "We are embarked on a unique business venture, an unusual opportunity provided by the current Indian wars."

Jeffries looked like a mean little turnip, his face unshaven and pinched in a scowl. He was clad in tatters, like a rag picker Mac had seen back in St. Paul. Jeffries said, "We spent some time lookin' for other ways to acquire our fortune besides gold. What line of occupation are you in?"

From the whiskey he had begun to unwind, embrace that familiar relaxation behind his eyes, but this question jolted him. "I'm just on my way to help a friend," he answered vaguely. He felt uneasy, sensed he shouldn't tell these two very much, and wondering at the wisdom in having joined them at their fire.

Wessells looked at him. "By your boots, young man, you appear to be a member of the cavalry?"

"I've been in the cavalry."

Jeffries grinned cynically. "You don't look old enough to done the army's five years. You take the bounce?"

Anxious irritability flushed through him. Regardless of the fact he wanted no more fighting Indians, a small worm of shame nibbled at him for his desertion. But then he remembered the medal. Fumbling around inside the lining of his coat for a moment, he fished out the small metal case. He opened the clasp and took out the medal and held it in his hand. He looked at Jeffries.

"It's a Medal of Honor."

Wessells looked at him skeptically. He drew himself up squarely where he sat cross-legged, scratched at his grainy neck, then gestured at the medal. "Share with us how you earned this honor."

"I rode with Custer last summer when he and some of his men were killed. The army gave me this for going for water to help our wounded." He paused to let the import of his words sink in. Then, getting no reaction from either man, he said, "Well, I wasn't the only one that went, just the first." At this admission he felt a slash of shame at trying to establish bona fides with these two. What did he care what they thought? The whiskey had colored his thinking, as it always did. It returned him to a mean station where he didn't want to be.

"I thought all them boys with Custer was killed," Jeffries said, glancing at Wessells.

"Not all of us," he said, feeling the whiskey's heat drain from around his eyes. Wessells said nothing and Mac eyed him skeptically. The man gave himself considerable airs, and he felt shamed by his own attempt to impress these men, so folded the ribboned medal and put it back in its case, then slid it back into the lining of his coat.

"You don't look old enough to have completed a five-year enlistment with Uncle Sam's best." He winked at Jeffries. "You may have won the medal. No doubt, as newspapers said, heroics were the order of the day. Perhaps you took French leave after the fight."

"I guess that's my affair," he snapped. He stood and collected his rifle. "I ought to be going along. I got to be looking for my friend in"--he paused for a second, not wanting them to know where he was headed-- "In Deadwood."

Jeffries looked at Wessells then said, "Me and Mr. Wessells here, we was just there last month. We're headed out toward Bozeman ourselfs."

Wessells sat upright again, hunched his shoulders, and pulled the lapels of his coat forward portentously. "We've come upon a business opportunity that could keep us in the region for a while."

He just looked at them.

"We could actually use another man in this venture," Wessells said, "Particularly one such as yourself who has the requisite talents."

Mac looked at him. "Talents?"

"A talent for fighting Indians. I have an arrangement with a very wealthy, very angry man whose wife and child were killed by Sioux marauders two months ago. He will pay fifty dollars for every Sioux scalp we deliver to his agents."

"What's that got to do with a business?"

Wessells stiffened. "I can assert that this sort of depilation is an excellent business opportunity. A man of adequate grit takes advantage of such favorable circumstances when they present themselves."

"I don't follow you exactly," he said. He only wanted to depart from these two. But he needed a delicate way to do it, for he remembered when he'd first heard their voices at the fire and "halloed" to them. The next thing he knew they were out in the dark on either side of him and he hadn't even heard them move away from the fire.

"Certainly, as with most potentially profitable ventures, scalping Sioux for profit is a time-limited opportunity," Wessells said. "If others hear of this fortunate opening, certainly they will rush in and satiate our sponsor's ardor. He might no longer wish to pay for so much hair." He swigged at the whiskey jug.

"We'll have a right bloody harvest for a while," Jeffries grinned, reaching for the jug.

Incredulous, he said, "You're offering me to join up with you?" These two made his skin crawl and he was glad he'd already gotten to his feet and had the Henry in his hand.

"If you're a man of ambition," Wessells said.

"I guess I don't feel an interest in doing that work," Mac said, "But I'm obliged for the conversation and the whiskey." He began to back away, intensely aware of the danger of that moment. "I'll be going on my way." He raised the Henry across his chest, but knew he wasn't ready to shoot these two men; he didn't even think he could do so before they killed him. But he feared they'd come after him in the dark, either for vengeance or out of a misguided notion that they had to protect themselves from him. He was glad it was dark and he'd left the mare in a secluded spot beyond their earshot.

Wessells voice was loud behind him. "We hope you are able to reach your destination safely, young friend." Both men laughed.

Once away from the firelight Mac turned and sprinted straight for the trail. He crossed over it at a full run and passed through the open stand of pines beyond which he'd left the mare. She lifted her head when she saw him and nickered softly in greeting. He scratched her withers with his fingertips and rubbed her ears and nose with the palm of his hand and tried to catch his breath and listen. He whispered to her, then untied her reins and led her deeper into the pine forest that climbed a wide slope between sandstone cliffs. The ground was thick with pine needles and, except for her clicking a stone with her hoof a couple of times, they made little sound as they went along. He stopped to listen every few minutes but heard nothing.

He had to keep moving toward Benson's Landing and Bozeman if he was to find Sophia, but he didn't want to tangle any more with Wessells and Jeffries. He only hoped they'd believed him when he said he was headed east to Deadwood. Would they try to follow him? He didn't know.

Clearly, the two men didn't mind getting bloody, so in the dark he listened for any movement below him on the hillside beyond the pines. But he only heard a slight whisper of branches in the breeze. He decided to head back east a few miles toward a broad creek he'd crossed earlier that afternoon. The stream flowed out of a wide valley from the southwest and emptied into the Yellowstone. He would put the mare into the stream and follow it back into the hills. In a day or so he ought to be able to find his way over a divide or two, get back down to the big river and regain the track that led to Benson's Landing.

That detour might give the two men time to put some distance between him and them. But the wilderness was vast, and the Bozeman trace narrow. Few would consider wandering from it, but he didn't want to see those two again, had to keep his eyes open.

In pre-dawn light he reached the creek and set the horse into the water. She picked her way through shallows and over small rapids for a couple of miles. Gradually, he felt more secure. He progressed slowly all day, but the valley bent back northwestward so sharply he worried the Yellowstone and the trail to Bozeman--and possibly the two scalp hunters--might just be over a low divide to his right.

Jumpy, he made no fire that night. Picketing the horse beside his blanket, he fell asleep listening to her breathe as she cropped grass beside him. Just before sunrise, he departed the creek and crossed a set of tumbled hills above the Yellowstone. Hazy sky shed flat light on the land. He dismounted amid boulders and pines and sat for some minutes watching the river below to see if there were other riders anywhere along the trail. There were none and after a time he remounted and rode into the valley.

Regaining the river, he turned the mare west along the south shore. Several hours later he came upon an abandoned army camp. It was small; perhaps only a single company had stayed here. At one end of the camp the ground was torn with the tracks of cavalry horses and the unshod ovals of pack mules. He wandered the camp to see if he could find anything that would tell which unit this was, though most likely they were from Gibbon's cavalry regiment out of Fort Shaw. He wondered if Wild and Holley might have passed by here, though he knew there was no basis for his thought. It was a foolish notion--like he'd had about maybe his father not being killed long ago in the slough. Why couldn't he get shed of such ideas?

Walking about the small camp all he found was garbage: a dented camp kettle, charred fire pits, a soldier's torn gutta percha and a frayed halter rope, plus other cast-off debris. He examined the torn poncho, then rolled it up and tied it behind his cantle.

East wind had begun to blow harder while he walked the abandoned camp, and finally he mounted and set the horse west again, remaining vigilant about the two scalp hunters. He wondered at the high clouds far to the northwest, that they might signal some kind of change in the weather. That night he was glad for the heavy coat and the torn gutta percha.

At dawn the next morning he dismounted and walked the mare as they climbed across a boulder-strewn scarp above the river. Suddenly he heard the rapid crack of rifle fire, perhaps eight or ten shots off to his left. The mare halted, flicking her ears nervously, and he laid his hand on her withers, whispered to her. Beyond the rocky slope the land fell away into a canyon, but the ground where he stood was not high enough to allow him to see down into it. Suddenly a vagrant whorl of air lifted a sharp whiff of gun smoke from there.

He listened, uncertain what to do, then pulled the Henry from its boot and checked its loads. After the first fusillade he heard nothing. He led the horse forward, staying close to a low cliff near cover. Another shot snapped, and another, smaller sounds from a revolver. After that there was silence.

He tied the mare to a dead pine branch then walked in a crouch to a rise about a hundred feet ahead where he could look into the canyon. Atop a grassy bench on the inside curve of a fast-flowing stream stood two tipis with wispy strands of gray smoke curling from their vent holes. Several Indians' bodies lay in the camp, sprawled in contorted positions, as though they'd been shot while running. A fearful rage burst in his chest and his heart thudded as he saw Wessells and Jeffries moving among the corpses with knives, ripping scalps.

His eye caught movement below him on the left side of the camp. What must be a camp dog limped away into some boulders and brush, though it looked more coyote than dog. Once the animal hit the brush it stopped and peered back at Wessells and Jeffries.

He counted five bodies, one of them a child. A deep bitterness rose within him and he lay down behind a fallen pine and propped the Henry's worn barrel across the tree trunk. Wessells and Jeffries had come a long way to make two hundred and fifty dollars. He took aim at Wessells and fingered the trigger for several seconds. But he felt impotent, unable to act, for though his heart was full of murder, he was not a good shot at such a distance. If he missed, the two son of bitches would hunt him down. Full of impotent rage, he tried to calm himself, and think. He couldn't prevent them from doing more mayhem, for there was no more left to do. Everyone in the camp lay dead, and all he could do was just lie behind the log and watch.

The two men separated, each going into one of the two tipis. He heard them yelling to each other, but still couldn't make out their words.

The camp dog stood off by itself in the brush and trees, watching the two men, not moving. He thought it strange the animal had never barked at Wessells or Jeffries. Their two horses were nowhere in sight. They must have left them at a distance when they set up to kill the Indian family. There were no Indian ponies either. Perhaps they'd been grazing nearby and had run off when they heard the gunfire.

Soon Wessells and Jeffries came out of the tipis with their arms full of items that they dumped into the grass. Jeffries carried two dark bags that appeared to be saddlebags. From the bags he pulled what looked like pieces of paper, shuffled through them, scattered them around. The two men sorted through everything they'd found and after a few minutes gathered together the things they wanted and thrust them into a large parfleche.

Heart pounding in his chest, he rolled onto his back and looked at the mare. He wanted to act, but there was nothing he could do to help the situation now, not without getting killed.

The two men wrapped the scalps in a small hide and stuffed that into the parfleche too. Jeffries shouldered the bag and they gathered their rifles and disappeared into a wooded area south of the camp. He waited.

Five minutes later and a couple of hundred yards west, they reemerged from the woods on horseback and rode west toward Benson's Landing. The smell of wood smoke rose briefly to him from the tipi fires as he watched the two riders disappear beyond a boulder field.

The far clouds had thickened beyond the mountains and the east wind had died as though in anticipation of something. He led the mare down to the camp, but she balked at the smell of blood and he talked to her. The limping dog was nowhere to be seen.

He approached the debris-strewn camp, and reached down and picked up one of the sheets of paper Wessells and Jeffries had strewn around. It was a sealed envelope--a letter actually, for he could feel a slight thickness of folded paper within. He recalled the Indians' sometime habit of keeping white men's letters they found, as though written words had some unrevealed, mysterious power.

Jeffries' bloody hands had smeared this letter when he'd tossed it away. Mac squinted at the envelope and saw it was addressed to somebody in Cincinnati. When he read the return address a lightning bolt hit him: "Private Thomas Coleman, Company B, Seventh Regiment of Cavalry...."

He'd met Coleman! Had shod the man's horse early in the expedition when Wild and Bobo had been punishing him with extra work. When had Coleman written this?

Mac looked about at the other scattered pieces of paper and envelopes that lay in the trampled grass and weeds, their edges lifting like a quiet summons in the softly moving air. His heart beat in his ears as he strode rapidly about picking up the sheets and envelopes. Jeffries had torn open a few of the letters and scattered them, separating them from their envelopes; the scalp hunter's bloody hands had smeared some of the pages.

A sudden thought made him dizzy and his eyes leapt to find the saddlebags Jeffries had carried from the tipi. When he saw them on the ground by one of the bodies, a low moan escaped his throat. He walked slowly to the bags, as if they might take wing or disappear if he moved too quickly or looked away even for instant. Letting the letters fall from his hands in a loose pile, he bent and picked up the saddlebags and saw, embossed in the leather of one flap, the words, "T. Wild, U.S. Army."

He shook the bags gently and something moved inside them, made a soft bumping noise. His hands trembled and an ache rose in his throat as he opened the flap. He reached inside and took out Sophia's dented locket, then opened it and looked at her face for a long moment. He closed the locket and put it into his coat pocket. The saddlebags were fairly light. But one book remained, something called <u>Meditations</u>. It had been in water at some point and smelled of mildew; its pages were damp, puckered and swollen. He set it aside.

The only other item he found in the bags was a small horse figurine, a child's toy, made from bent grass and wrapped tightly with reeds. He'd seen Wild looking at it several times during the expedition. He slipped the small toy into his coat pocket and picked up the jumble of letters, putting them into order as best he could, then placed them in saddlebags. He sat down heavily on the ground and took off his hat, ran his hand slowly through his matted hair, tried to think.

The saddlebag--it held Wild's book and the men's letters, all that was left of the dead soldiers' lives. Those men had seemed so alien to him while he was with them, but since he'd left them they'd come to seem like lost brothers whom he'd let down.

He remembered that instant of Malachy's death when the Irishman had fallen sideways onto him, and he and Holley had slowed down, fallen back from the column. When they parted company Holley had said, "You're my friend, Mac. I hope you make it through." And he'd thought Holley's bravery foolish.

He swallowed the rising ache in his throat. He had to find the pieces of his life, where he should go, what he should do. He somehow had to put things together. Taking the locket from his pocket again, he opened it and looked at Sophia's face, but couldn't decide, didn't know what he felt. He turned his face west again toward the coming cloud front. In his most recent dreams Sophia didn't recognize him, couldn't remember his name. Perhaps she'd think him a fool for coming all this way. If he went forward to find and help her, what of her friend, Devlin? And the two scalp hunters: he might also run into them again.

To his east lay the Yellowstone's long curve, then the big Missouri, and far beyond that the cities of the plain. If he retraced his steps eastward, long miles of hazard stood against him, and to what end? If he went there--perhaps even returned to St. Paul--no one would be there, save a world of strangers.

The air was completely still around him, but a breeze brushed the crowns of pines beyond which the scalp hunters had left their horses in ambush. He turned the little horse figurine in his hand. Dwindling smoke still curled from the tipis' vents, fires these dead people had started in anticipation of another normal day. They'd not known that only moments ahead lay pitch blackness.

What was it Wild once had said--or that philosopher in his book wrote: eventually everything had to be given up, and dying was quick and easeful. Wild had talked about all the tracks of everyone and everything that had ever lived, and how they intertwined. This wilderness camp: just a crossroads, one among all the ancient paths. If only he could find where a good path lay, then walk it, he might find peace.

He put the figurine in his coat pocket and picked up Wild's book, but when he opened it two folded sheets fell out. He opened them and saw a letter from Wild to a woman named Margaret. It had never been mailed, and he began to read.

My dearest Margaret,   *June 24, 1876*

Please forgive my uncertain script for I am writing by starlight. Tonight we are allowed no fires. We are moving fast, having encountered more and more trails of the Sioux over the last two to three days. Time is short and in an hour we shall embark on a night march in hope of surprising them in their camp, probably tomorrow.

We left the Yellowstone River two days ago and our mornings have been vibrant with sunlight and soft winds, but the afternoons sweltering. We now press southward along aptly named Rosebud Creek where small clumps of pink roses are beautifully in bloom. Their fragrance fills this valley. Each evening, the sun throws its green and slanting light, and this immense and lovely landscape seems like paradise.

For many years I have taken refuge in the writings of other men whose clearer minds call out to me and reassure and guide my thoughts. I have read a passage by a man named Seneca so many times that I think I can nearly quote him, though no doubt in somewhat faulty paraphrase. These words have given me great peace over these last years.

It is not possible for us to know each other,
except as we manifest ourselves in
distorted shadows to others' eyes.
We do not even know ourselves; so
how dare we judge our neighbor?

Who knows what pain lies behind virtue,
what fear behind vice? No one knows
what makes a man, for only
God knows his thoughts and joys,
his bitterness and agony, the injustice he
has faced and injustices he commits.

This world is too inscrutable
for our little understanding. After much
meditation I now believe that all lives,
whether good or in error, mournful or joyous,
obscure or of guilded reputation, are only a
prologue to love beyond the grave, where
all will be understood and nearly all forgiven.

I should tell you: recently I have thought of leaving the army and returning home. I don't know if this is wise, given the town's antipathy toward me. I would welcome your advice on this. You appear to me in dreams as you were long ago, so young and beautiful, and loving your older brother so. I have dreamed of a time when I was young and tracked animals in the snow with Father, earnest and eager to please him with my growing knowledge. I have fond memories and I also have hopes that "all will be understood and nearly all forgiven."

We are called to mount soon. This may be my last correspondence until we return to the Yellowstone some days hence. I will always remain-

Your loving brother,
Thomas Wild

Three crows landed near the child's corpse and began to strut around. One pecked at its raw bloody cranium, and Mac yelled and waved his arms. The birds flapped away, cawing. He pushed back against an ache in his throat, gave a bitter sob. What a world. Beauty and mutilation, and birds wanting to eat.

Holley had talked about God's goodness. What'd Holley said to Burden that time--about God giving you pain to draw you near him? God must have wanted real bad to draw these Sioux near. Holley had told Burden this world wasn't the important one, but that made no sense. He looked at the child's bloody corpse, then at the pile of soldiers' letters. He tried to laugh, but only a wet squeak came from his throat and he covered his face with his hands and sobbed quietly. Then inside him something old and guarded fell away and he wept loudly, bent over, clutching himself.

After a time, he grew quiet, wiped at his face with his coat sleeve, swiped at his eyes with both hands. He looked at the whitewater stream. As the sky darkened, the stream took on a certain glow, rippling past on its course toward the Yellowstone which in turn tumbled on, emptied endlessly into all the rivers and seas of the world.

The mare nickered softly as she sometimes did when greeting another horse, and this stirred him to vigilance, but he saw nothing. Still, other Sioux might come. Perhaps one or more people from these families had been out hunting, or maybe others would come, drawn by the gunfire. He shouldn't remain here, but something kept him. He couldn't go.

He looked at the child, saw she was a little girl. He should bury her, but he had no tool to dig even a shallow grave. Next to the bench where the tipis stood stretched a long grassy depression. He carried her and laid her there. But as he went to the river to gather stone he had another thought. He took out the horse figurine from his pocket and walked back and placed it on her chest. He tried to cross her hands over the toy but, as though she wanted nothing from a white man like him, her stiffened arms would not embrace it.

Mac started to the stream again to get stone, but then stopped and went reluctantly to another corpse. He dragged it over and laid it beside the child, then did the same with the rest until all five bodies lay together. He took his case knife and slashed at the walls of the nearest tipi, seeking weak points where the hides had been roughly thong-stitched together, then he dragged the hides over and covered the people. He went to the stream, gathered large stones, worked until the bodies were completely concealed and protected.

When he placed the last stone, he straightened and wiped his forehead, glanced about, increasingly nervous that other Indians might come. He walked back into the camp and picked up Wild's book and put it into one saddlebag, then placed the letter Wild had written to his sister with the other letters. He untied the torn gutta percha and let it fall across the mare's withers. With rain or snow coming he'd soon need it. Lashing Wild's saddlebags behind his cantle he looked around. One tipi fire had gone out but the other still smoldered.

Then he heard the noise. At first it sounded like a small animal whimpering. It came from the wood line beyond the camp. He walked toward the sound, but it stopped. He stepped into the woods, looking around. Then he saw movement in a pile of dry leaves beside a deadfall pine. There lay an infant girl, naked and thrashing, having kicked herself free of a buffalo hide wrap and the dead leaves and twigs with which she had been covered in an attempt to hide her from the scalp hunters. She was so tiny, and shivered convulsively in the cold. For a moment all he could do was stare at her in disbelief, bewildered, not knowing what to do. Finally he went and picked her up, held her awkwardly, looked around, as if to find help. What could he do?

He sat on a deadfall pine and wiped the leaves and debris from her, shook out the hide and wrapped her in it. She was newly born, with a segment of string tied off from her navel, still wet, wrinkled and homely like the two or three other new babies he'd seen before. She shivered and he carried her inside the nearest tipi and looked around. On a hide next to one wall there was blood. Her mother had just given birth, only to be killed by Wessells and Jeffries. What could he do with her?

She began to cry and he looked around, but could find nothing. Her mother lay dead by the stream, beneath the piled stones. He had to get out of the camp. He mounted the mare, put the wrapped infant beneath his overcoat and buttoned it tightly. He wished she'd stop crying. He didn't know what to do.

He looked up to see, not a hundred feet away, the camp dog. It stood watching them from beside a fallen pine trunk. He waved at it and whistled; the animal didn't move. It looked just like a coyote. There would be enough animals rooting at the stones of these people's graves without their own trying to get at them. He took the Henry from its boot beneath his leg.

But, as he pressed the baby to him with an elbow and gingerly raised the rifle, memory nudged him. He recalled Malachy's coyote pup. Malachy had handed the pup to Wild in the last seconds before he was shot. Hadn't Wild stuffed it into his saddlebag? Mac lowered the rifle and looked more closely at the animal. What had Malachy named it?

He called out, "Phinney!" The animal's ears pricked up but it didn't move.

He walked the horse toward it, but when he got within about thirty feet the coyote laid its ears back and limped away. Only then did he see that its right front foot was missing. "Oh, God!" His voice cracked, "Phinney!" The coyote stopped and looked back at him. But when he advanced the animal moved further away and wouldn't allow him any closer. It slipped into the trees and disappeared.

He plunged the Henry into its boot and reached into his pocket, grasping the locket with Sophia's picture, as if it could help him focus his attention. For a brief moment, he wanted to tell her what had happened to him, tell her about the others in the regiment, about what he'd seen, so much killing, tit for tat, all the deaths. Such indifference and fear and hatred among people. He felt he couldn't stand all that anymore, for something in him had broken or changed. He could not give it words, was not sure how. Then, as the metal grew warm in his hand, he realized the only thing to do was to get to Benson's Landing as quickly as possible. There might be help for the baby.

He sat the mare for a moment, scanning the surrounding canyon for the coyote. Its people lay dead beneath the stones and the crippled animal was hardly any better able to survive alone than this baby. Beyond its path falling snow now hid the nearest hills and peaks.

Then he saw the coyote once more, farther to the southwest below the canyon rim, a pale brown spot picking its way up a slope of broken rock toward a line of low sandstone cliffs. Amid that desolation he smiled thinly at the animal as it confronted head-on the early snow and the sting of coming winter.

He released Sophia's locket, then shifted the baby slightly. She had stopped crying. He put the horse forward into the stream and crossed her over a gravel bar as the first snowflakes hit. As the mare clambered onto the grassy slope, the falling flakes came big and sloppy, fell straight down. They muffled the canyon in heavy silence, a silence that must have covered the entire world long ago before creatures lived to contend with one another.

He peered up at the canyon rim to track the coyote's progress, and glimpsed the animal for only a second before it disappeared into a narrow slot that led to the top of the rim rock. He reached back to check Wild's saddlebags, tugged at the ties.

Wet flakes gathered in the horse's mane, melted on her withers, touched his neck like cold fingers. He turned up his coat collar and pulled it close, then shook out the torn gutta percha and draped it around himself. In the rimrock above, where the coyote had disappeared, he heard a hollow echo of falling stone, but when he looked up he could see nothing.

The mare couldn't beat the snow now, or the coming night, and this concerned him a little, for there was a ford somewhere ahead that he'd have to find and cross in darkness. The trail was sparse here, little marked, and he didn't want to lose it. He figured half a day more into Benson's Landing. The child couldn't eat until then. He might find Sophia and Devlin there, or possibly the scalp hunters. But, whatever came, he would just deal with it.

Later, the snowfall ebbed as he rode out of the canyon into the broad valley of the Yellowstone. Across the river, meadows rose to scattered pines and upon the valley's farthest rim, dotted here and there, stood clusters of yellowing aspen. The clouded autumn vista lifted him somehow. Barring the wet and cold and getting a little turned around, they would likely make it through. He put the mare into an easy lope, and every now and then as they went along he quietly spoke to her, and stroked her, to reassure them both. The baby's cries came muffled from his coat and he reached inside to make sure she had space to breathe. It was all he could think to do.

⌘

He made a cold camp and, to keep the baby warm, wrapped them both in his blanket and the gutta percha, holding her against his chest. She cried for long periods through the night, and her cries unnerved him greatly, but he thought maybe she would be all right as long as she could cry. They set out again at first light and he kept the mare moving westward at a lope. The rhythmic gait seemed to sooth the baby and she sobbed quietly, hiccupping, then was still. The mare was breathing hard and lathered when he finally reined her to a walk and hung back to watch two riders in the distance far ahead of him. They didn't look like Wessells and Jeffries, so he clicked the horse forward again.

Both riders turned in the saddle when they heard him coming from behind. His heart leaped in his chest, for one rider was a woman and she had auburn hair. As he drew near he saw it was Sophia. She gave no sign of recognition and he suddenly realized with a shock what he must look like: shabby clothes, stubbly beard, dirty tangled hair. Suddenly, his whole journey to find her seemed unjustifiable, possibly even ridiculous. She would be surprised, maybe even shocked. Would she mock him? What would Devlin's reaction be? All bad things suddenly seemed possible, but he would deal with it all.

He caught up with them. With a dry mouth and effort he forced out, "Hello, Sophia."

A look of confused surprise swept across her face. She looked nervously at Devlin then back at him. Even through the sunburn and trail dust coating her face, he saw her right eye had been blackened some time back. The bruise had turned grayish, fading to yellow at its edges. Anger flushed through him, warming his face. He glanced at Devlin, then at her. "It's me, Sophia. Mac. Mac Durant."

Sophia looked at him, her face incredulous, commingling both fear and a fleeting smile of confusion. "Mac? What are you doing here?" Her voice was disbelieving as she and Devlin reined in their horses.

Even as he said the words he felt they were the most foolish he'd ever spoken. "I've been trying to find you in Bismarck and in Deadwood, but things happened and I got delayed."

Devlin said, "What's all this, Sophia?"

She ignored him. "What do you mean, you were trying to find me?" Waiting for an answer, she looked anxiously at Devlin.

"Who the hell is this, Sophia?" Devlin snapped. The three sat their horses.

"You wrote to me," Mac said. "I thought you wanted me to come, that you were in trouble."

Devlin's face was dark beneath his hat, his features hard to make out.

"You wrote him?" Devlin asked her. "God damn it, Sophia! Who is this?"

"It...it's all right, Axle. He's a friend. We grew up together for a time at my grandparents' home."

"When did you write him?" Devlin's horse crow hopped and turned a step and Mac could see his face better now. He was handsome, with cynical lips and eyes. And he was angry.

"Yes," she snapped. "I wrote him from Bismarck--that muddy hole!" Her voice was defiant, but she was clearly frightened. "I was just feeling low." She turned to Mac. "I can't believe you're here, Mac. You came so far...and...because of my letter?"

"You sounded like you were in trouble."

"I'm not in trouble, Mac." She patted her horse's neck. "I'm with Mr. Devlin." She held up a hand toward the man. "We're going to Bozeman."

"I thought you were going to San Francisco." The baby started to whimper inside his coat; Sophia and Devlin looked surprised at the sound. "I found this baby yesterday. She was born just before scalp hunters killed her family. I had nothing to feed her, and I've got to get her to Benson's Landing." He couldn't take his eyes off Sophia's face and the fading bruise beneath her eye. Tilting his head toward Devlin, he asked, "Did he do that to your eye, Sophia?"

Devlin snapped, "That's between us, boy. You'd better turn that God damned horse around and head yourself home." He pulled his coat back and rested his fist loosely on a holstered revolver.

"Axle, don't!" Sophia said, alarmed. "Let's just talk for a minute. Mac, how are your aunt and uncle?" She forced a smile, tried to look interested.

"I left there, Sophia, and I'm not going back. There has been so much...." He saw Devlin grasp the revolver's grip and said to the man, "I just want to talk to Sophia. I'm not carrying a sidearm." He wanted to calm her, protect her. Help her see there was another way for her than continuing with this man--maybe not with himself, but she could take some other, better road than the one she rode with Devlin. Would she want to hear about the last few months? He fervently hoped....

Devlin's voice was tight and quiet when he said, "Boy, you're not likely to need a sidearm in about five seconds."

Sophia said, "Axle, just wait! I never asked him to come, but give us a minute!"

"You damned slut," Devlin grinned. "You've been having a bit of pleasure I didn't know about."

He put up his hand to Devlin. "Let us talk a minute." He looked at her closely. "Sophia, I want to know if you're all right. I want to know your situation." Strangely, he felt no fear of Devlin. Maybe he'd come too far to be fearful. The baby began to cry loudly now.

Tears welled up in her eyes and she wiped at them with her fingers, making muddy streaks on her face. "I'm fine. Just fine. You shouldn't have come, Mac. I can't believe you did this."

The chastening tone in her voice slashed him like a knife, but he couldn't bear the sight of her tears, which gave the lie to her words of assurance. He coaxed his horse forward and reached for the reins of her horse. "Sophia, are you sure? Do you want to come with...." He fought himself for words. "I think of the gazebo," he smiled. "Your peacock...and that sparrow you coaxed from the birdbath."

Her face suddenly filled with painful recognition. "Oh, God. Mac, I'm so sorry. I...." In that instant Sophia glanced at Devlin and opened her mouth to scream.

Mac heard no sound but felt something heavy hit him in the belly and he toppled from the mare's off side, landing on his back on the trail. He couldn't breathe, but saw the mare bolt away.

He lay on his back in the dusty track, not sure what had happened. The two riders sat their horses but he averted his eyes, couldn't look at them. He heard a scream. "Mac, I'm so sorry! Oh, God!"

They finally reined around and rode off. Through a reddish fog he saw the mare walk back toward him. She stood over him as he gulped for air, and as she lowered her head her reins brushed his face and green foam flopped from her mouth onto his neck. He heard a baby crying somewhere and couldn't remember what had happened or why he'd pressed the horse so hard. A disorienting mix of grief and dread washed through him and he tried to swallow air--bite and swallow it--but he couldn't get any. He twisted his head sideways hoping to get air and his mind registered several bear lilies blooming beside the trail. He thought Sophia would like to see them. He heard a sound like a baby crying.

A chinless man in a black suit appeared above him in the red haze and he looked at the black suit and whispered, "Just leave me be." He wanted to be gone into the night where no thought intruded.

But the chinless man bent to him and pulled his coat open to look, tore his bloody shirt open then ripped pages from a book and wadded them, pressed them against Mac's belly and tied him tightly round with what looked like a purple sash. "Your baby is all right, young man. We'll get you both some help." When the man lifted him and draped him across the mare, agony slashed at him, dumping him into darkness.

An excerpt from her father's letter:

...An old soldier named Cornelius once helped me when I tried to run away from the army. He died during that battle on the Little Horn. It was in trying to help him that I first went to the river for water. Before he died he told me that he was shot twice, and said that was a couple of times more than he'd hoped for. I still smile at that bit of humor, offered in the most dire circumstances, and only moments before his death.

After the Little Horn battle I deserted the army, and I have felt some guilt about it over the ensuing decades. So many men deserted the Army of the West in those years, around a third of the entire army departed early each year, and the army had no resources to track so many of us. I never felt in danger of being caught out on the matter, but felt a generalized guilt about not keeping an oath that patriots consider of utmost importance. But I have spent my patriotism in other ways, in my work among the country's desperate. Those words sound too self-justifying even to me, but there they are.

Around 1919, a year or so after the Great War in Europe, I read an article in the newspaper that made me think they might have found Leo Holley's remains. That was forty-some years after the battle. The article quoted a rancher near Lamedeer who said that after heavy rains he had been searching for stray cattle several miles east of the old battlefield. When he entered one ravine he saw what looked like skeletal remains which the torrent had just eroded from the coulee wall. He found part of a horse's skull, the bones of a human hand and arm and jaw bone.

He thought these things to be part of an old Indian burial, but changed his mind when nearby he found a large fragment of the tree frame from a McClellan saddle and parts of an Army sack shirt that had corroded brass buttons stamped with the letter C.

Each of our company's field shirt buttons was stamped with the letter C. Those remains might've been Holley or someone else trying to get away from the fight. I do not know why it still bothers me that I will never know.

Clotilde stood in the darkened room of her inn, beside the boy's still form, unable to shed the thought that he might know her Jedro. After all, Jedro'd been on the river last summer. Maybe this one had too. It was perhaps a foolish notion, but one hard to shake. She waited most of the day for the boy to wake, walking boisterously in and out of the big room where he lay. It wouldn't do to tip-toe if she wanted him to get a word out before he passed.

She leaned over him and he stirred, moaning in his darkness. In the night she'd searched his goods, dragged a word or two from him about the woman, Sophia, and the man, Wild--and those bloody letters. Now it was the next evening and he wasn't dead yet. But would he wake again? Or would he just drift silently into death like so many did with so many stories left untold?

She looked at his bloodless face. He was simply one more foolish young buck, just another passing rider. Many such an erring man drifted through Benson's Landing, far from a home of any kind. Mostly they were heedless, had gone lost long before. They just rode on, wandered the wilderness and gradually lost their swagger. Then the years scattered their bones for some other lost pilgrim to ponder.

From the kitchen window she saw Caleb arrive in moonlight from the Bozeman funeral. He led his horse into the shed. His return was an intrusion, for she still felt anger at his presumption, bringing the dying boy and the Indian brat to her. But she put water on the stove to heat so he could wash when he came in. Some minutes passed as he brushed and fed his horse. But too soon she heard him come through the outer door and stop for a second on the porch. Then he opened the kitchen door and came in to wash. When he saw her his somber face brightened. "The boy still alive?"

She jerked her head toward the big room. "I've cleaned his wound again, but it's useless. He's past waking up. He'll soon be going over."

She poured hot water in a basin and Caleb washed his hands and arms, mopped his neck with a rag. Clotilde watched him wash himself just as she used to watch Jedro, for she liked to see a man clean himself.

In Jedro's case there was always much that needed cleaning, but not so with Caleb. She couldn't get enthused about him.

He put his flannel shirt back on and buttoned it. "I forgot to tell you last night when I brought him in. I seen the shooters."

She looked at him.

"I'd just left the Landing at dusk to head for Bozeman, but I heard the gunshot just east and turned around to head toward it. The two of them came past me at a gallop. I only got a glimpse."

She snapped, "It was probably them damn scalp hunters that was skulkin' around here yesterday. That one stunk so bad with his dirty neck. Both of 'em with their sack full of Sioux hair."

Caleb turned away modestly, opened his trousers and tucked in his shirt, then buttoned himself. "No, it wasn't them. 'Twas a man, a fancy dresser, though he was trail dirty--maybe forty or so. He was with a woman. She was younger, had auburn hair."

"Pretty careful glimpse of her you had, all that eyeful you collected."

"Now, Clotilde, even a parson looks at a pretty woman."

"She was pretty?" That stung, but he could gander at whatever he wanted for all of her. "So what happened?"

Caleb nodded toward the big room where the boy lay. "Your young man and the baby was what I found on the track east of here, not two minutes after the two rode past me."

"He ain't my 'young man.' You put him on me."

Caleb looked at her, bemused.

"Well," she said, "He's about dead now. You knew there's no doctor in thirty-five miles. You shoulda just took him with you to Bozeman. What am I to do?"

"That wasn't no choice at all. It was either tie him across his horse and bring him a short piece back here or take him thirty miles to Bozeman. He'd have died from the ride. Besides, I couldn't think of anyone who'd give him a better chance than you."

"Don't flatter me. You put him on me and I don't appreciate it." She looked toward the big room. "But he won't be a bother long." She wished Caleb would just go off to his room, just leave her be.

She was tired, wanted to be alone, so stepped away for a minute, thinking to go outside and take a breath of air before checking on the boy. She opened the door to the small porch and saw a straw hat draped on one of the pegs. A shudder went through her and she snatched the hat and came back in as Caleb was standing before the glass combing his hair.

Her heart pounded and her hand trembled violently as she thrust the hat toward him. "What is this?"

"It's the boy's hat. I left it in the barn last night after I brought him in."

"It's one of them soldier hats I made last summer for Jedro to sell. This boy must've seen him. Maybe he knows of him." She went into the big room with the straw hat. Caleb followed and they stood beside the bed.

She touched the boy's shoulder but he didn't stir. "Did you know my Jedro?" She couldn't hear him breathing. His belly was bloated, hugely swollen, and she saw it move the slightest bit. "Do you know him?" He was still breathing. "Did you buy this from my Jedro?" Her voice was almost a shout.

"Let the good Lord do His work, Clotilde," Caleb said, and put his hand on her arm.

She jerked away--"Don't touch me!"--and a sob broke from her breast. If He helps others, why not her? Why not Jedro? She glared at Caleb through her tears.

The boy was still breathing a bit. She looked at him. "You tell me where you got this hat! Where?" She slapped the straw hat on the bed, then bent her head and began to cry in earnest.

Caleb put out his hand, but she seethed, "No!" and shrank back from him. "I'll never marry you! Never!" The boy wouldn't wake. The poisons were taking him. What wrong-headed notions about that Sophia had led him to this wilderness place? What might he know of Jedro? She sobbed, "Do you know my Jedro?" Caleb should have brought her the hat last night, instead of leaving it in the barn! If she'd just had it last night, while the boy could still talk...! She had so many questions, but now they'd never be answered. Not a one.

She was stunned into silence when he actually stirred, moving his right foot and hand. He opened his eyes a little, said, "I saw him--your husband. In a boat." He slowly rolled his eyes toward them, saying, "I'm not going to die."

An excerpt from her father's letter:

...and of course I did not die, and neither did you. After my recovery from the gunshot Devlin administered to me, I realized Montana's Crows would not adopt you, a Lakota baby. I knew it was me who would have to do it, and I did my best for you when you were young. I think you know that.

I had been constructing a career of whiskey consumption before then, but it was a boy's experimentation, more than an illness. Because of you, because of what I had seen and done, and because of what life seemed to offer and require, I gave up the whiskey. Its temptations have never revisited me.

There was war between our two peoples for over a decade after I found you, though those battles finally culminated with the Army's massacre at Wounded Knee. It was painful for me when you left to help the Lakota survivors, though I understood why you had to go. Even now, all these years later, there is still much suffering among you and Akecheta's people, most of it caused by us wasicu. It is hard to untangle, and I feel it will take generations to repair.

FEBRUARY 1931: LIVINGSTON, MONTANA

There was much more, but Anna put the letter aside to read later in the evening, or perhaps back home in Bridger. To be done with this would be a great blessing. She felt she knew more about her father than when she started to read, but it would take time to absorb. She wished to be with her husband, to walk among their horses there among the cottonwoods beside the winding Cheyenne.

Just then, someone tapped lightly at the front door. Someone from her father's congregation, no doubt. She rose, grunting softly at the painful swelling in her ankles, and went to open the door.

A very old woman stood before her, a stranger. She was bent nearly double and stood supported by a cane in each hand. The woman said, "Hello, Anna."

"I'm sorry, but do I know you?"

"I reckon you do. I just look some different after all these years. So do you."

She was stunned. "Clotilde. I...." This hateful woman--what was she doing here? Her father, when she was young, had sometimes left her in Clotilde's care when his work took him away. The woman had never hit or hurt her physically, but had treated her coldly and let her know in many small ways what she thought of Indian people. She justified her condemnation by a belief that they'd killed her husband Jedro on the Yellowstone years before.

"You thought I was dead, if you thought of me at all. And if you had a thought it prob'ly tasted bad."

"What are you doing here?" She had never complained to her father about the way Clotilde treated her. She had just put up with it, just as she had often put up with similar treatment from other whites. Her father certainly had known in general about their attitudes, but only told her they were blind and ignorant, and repeatedly told her she was strong and good.

The old woman looked uncertain, as though struggling with what she might say. "I'm the one what got you here. Told the doctor where to find you."

Anna's heart sank. "All right, but why?" This mean woman was the instrument that enabled her to come back to Montana for her father's service. "There were bitter feelings between us when I left here forty years ago."

The woman's mouth trembled a bit. "Anna, I ain't the same person you knew when you was young."

Anna shook her head. "You were just one of many." She didn't want to show her old rancor, not sure that it might even give Clotilde a measure of satisfaction. So she changed the subject. "My father, he traveled to so many places in his work. I don't know why he came back here to live last year."

"He didn't come back here to live. He came because we was friends and he was sick. I didn't know it at first, but the infection had set in again. He knew he was dying, and he had no one, and he remembered peace here. He didn't get much of that in his work." Clotilde paused and looked at Anna. "I think he came back here because he had started here with you in such a long-ago time."

This was painful to take in. She and her father had not been close for years, but no hardness of heart separated them. He could have come to her in Bridger when he realized he was sick, but he had not. "Clotilde, thank you for having the doctor contact me. But I've come a long way. I'm very tired." Sighing, she looked at the woman; just had to say it clearly. "Clotilde, you hated my people back then, spoke of us in the most terrible terms. And you treated me poorly." She shook her head. "I was just a girl."

"I ain't got no excuse, except I was a fool, and hurting. Your people killed my husband, Jedro. But your father's kindness gradually helped me put all that aside over these many years."

"And two white scalp hunters killed everyone in my family, a family I never knew."

"I guess we both had wrongs done us." The old woman worked her face around a bit and said, "I followed your father's work off and on, and I read some things he sent me that he wrote. Durin' the course of time he changed my thinking 'bout lots of matters."

Perhaps it was the exhaustion, but she felt her heart soften a bit. Also, she knew how little it took for her righteous anger about white people to boil up. At such times she considered how Akecheta would deal with this. He would say, "Forgiveness, Anna. Forgiveness." She lifted a loose strand of hair back over her ear, gazed for long seconds at the gnarled hands that gripped the two canes. "I want to forgive the past, Clotilde. Certainly there are many things I need to be forgiven for, as well." She took a step toward the door. "I'm really tired from my trip. I assume I'll see you at the church service tomorrow."

"I never been much for churchin,' I ain't been in one since I was young and married my Jedro. I don't spect I'll be there tomorrow, but it don't matter. Your father died with me sitting beside him, and he already knowed what I thought of him."

She looked at Clotilde then, as if for the first time, and felt her bitter thoughts start to crumble. "That was good of you to take care of him at the end," she said, and a pang of regret touched her heart. "He never even told me he was sick."

Tears welled up in the old woman's eyes and, fumbling, she transferred one of her canes from her right hand to her left, then shuffled a foot forward to retain her balance. "I wish to have your forgiveness, Anna, and I wish for peace between us." She reached out a palsied hand.

Anna looked at the gnarled, world-worn hand, then took it in her own. "I do forgive you, Clotilde." They talked for a few moments more, then when Anna helped her to the door she saw that late afternoon was falling into twilight. "How will you get home?"

"I still got old Caleb, the preacher; you remember him. He's always watched out for me since my Jedro was killed. Wanted to marry me long ago, but I wouldn't have him--which I expect was to his good fortune."

Anna heard a motorcar start up and watched it slowly pull forward along the margin, then stop in front of her father's house. The chinless old man in the driver's seat lifted his hand in greeting and Clotilde struggled forward on her two canes to meet him. Anna followed and opened the car door for her, nodding to the old man.

"Welcome, Anna," he said. "I'll be conducting the service tomorrow for your father. I did not see him often over the years, but he was a good man who was of great use in the world."

"Thank you, Caleb." She looked into Clotilde's eyes for a couple of seconds. "I appreciate you both greatly."

An excerpt from her father's letter:

...You know that my work was always driven by the belief that there is much we all do for which we must seek forgiveness, assuming we are wise enough to seek it. We all are on our way to becoming humans, the beings we were meant to become, though we can never reach that position fully. However, there is no judgment that awaits us in death, only forgiveness and loving acceptance, and that forgiveness is available to us right now. Even with all that we each must face in life, we should understand that all is well, both in the present and forever.

FEBRUARY 1931: LIVINGSTON, MONTANA

The next afternoon, Anna's hands fairly shook as she entered the church for her father's service. This world, so full of contention and violence and struggle: she was not at all certain she would have the courage to stand at some point and say what she wanted to say. She really just wanted to go home, and tomorrow morning at 6:45 she would catch the eastbound bus.

She tried to calm herself as the minister, Clotilde's friend Caleb Turner, offered an opening prayer and a statement about her father. Then he introduced the eulogist, inviting her to the pulpit to speak. She was some famous old white woman, Harriot Stanton Blatch, a suffragette who had known and sometimes worked with her father. The woman had traveled here in winter all the way from Boston to honor him.

Anna breathed deeply several times and pressed her cold palm hard against her cheek, then she reached into her coat pocket and pulled out her father's medal. She felt no pride in it, for such a thing had too many meanings: Bravery and self-sacrifice certainly were two. But this ribbon with the eagle and star also meant destruction and death, vainglory and shame, loss and grief, and mortal agony. Such valorous totems meant all those things and more. Happily, her father also knew that. He told her once that he kept it to remind himself of tragedy and irony, of God's grace and mercy, and the nature of human life in this world.

Akecheta had told her that his uncle, Si Tanka--white people called him Big Foot--just before he was killed at Wounded Knee said to the people, "The time for fighting is done. We have to learn to live together, to find a way to live together." And Akecheta, always he said, "Anna, Mitakuye oyas'in. All my relatives. We all are family." How hard it was to accept his words, yet somewhere inside she knew she needed to do so.

When the white woman finished her remarks and stepped down from the pulpit, Caleb asked if anyone in the sanctuary had anything to say about Mac Durant. Trembling, quite terrified before this room full of strangers, Anna raised her hand. Caleb looked at her. "Anna, would you like to say something?" He said to the congregation, "This is Anna, Mac Durant's daughter from South Dakota."

She got to her feet and pulled a piece of paper from her overcoat pocket. "Long ago," she halted briefly, coughed once, "My father found a piece of writing, something written by a Roman Emperor." She looked around her. Faces: intrigued, scowling, indifferent, sorrowful, drowsy, harsh, smiling. "We, all of us," and she swept her hand in a tiny arc, indicating the crowd, "Have a hard time caring about each other, or even understanding each other. My father always kept a copy of that Emperor's words with him wherever he went. The words he valued so much are as follows:

> It is not possible for us to know each other,
> except as we manifest ourselves in
> distorted shadows to others' eyes.
> We do not even know ourselves; so
> how dare we judge our neighbor?
>
> Who knows what pain lies behind virtue, what fear behind vice?
> No one knows what makes a man, for only God knows his thoughts
> And joys, his bitterness and agony, the injustice he faced
> And injustices he commits.

This world is too inscrutable for our little understanding.
After much meditation I now believe that all lives,
whether good or in error, mournful or joyous, obscure or of
guilded reputation, are only a prologue to love beyond the grave,
where all will be understood and nearly all forgiven."

When she was done, she sat down without any further words. The minister thanked her and called on another person to speak. As Anna listened, she gazed around the room at the people, most of them whites, but several Blackfeet and Crow people. Several people said nice things about her father, and this warmed her.

She thought of Akecheta, what they had been through in their life together. In a few days she would be at home with him, and there beside the frozen Cheyenne she would pray as together they built a fire to heat the stones. She would pray toward the East, ask for understanding and wisdom, for a good heart and for courage to do good. She would go into the lodge, sweat out her angry fears and confusion and darkness. She would clarify her mind, purify herself.

Folded within the funeral's "Order of Service" was the mimeographed sheet she and others had been given when they entered the church. She had read it silently before the service began, and it had sharpened her resolve to stand and speak about her father as she had done.

She opened the sheet once more, gently smoothed it on her thigh, then gazed at it. It was a simple summary of her father's life, prepared by Clotilde with help from her minister friend, Caleb. Anna read it once more.

--Life of MacArthur "Mac" Llewelyn Durant--
"Let men see, let them know, a man
who lives as he was meant to live." (Marcus Aurelius)

Born: Boston, Massachusetts to Ben and Anna (Nordvik) Durant, July 14,
1859
Orphaned: Dakota Sioux War, Lake Shetek, Minnesota, August 1862
Hostage: held by Dakota Sioux with others; released September 1862
Raised by relatives: St. Paul, Minnesota, 1862-76
Enlisted: U.S. Army of the West, Seventh Regiment of Cavalry, Fort Abraham

Lincoln, Bismarck, Dakota Territory, Spring 1876

Wounded: first water carrier to aid other wounded men, Little Big Horn
        Battle, Montana Territory, June 1876

Brought back from edge of death: Fort Lincoln, Bismarck, Dakota Territory

Award: United States Congress' Medal of Honor for valor at Little Big Horn,
        September 1876

Departed: U.S. Army, September 1876

Found: Sioux infant, September 1876

Shot: by murderous coward Axle Devlin and consort Sophia Spence, September
        1876

Brought back from edge of death: Benson's Landing, Montana, Autumn 1876

Father: raised daughter Anna, Benson's Landing, Montana and Chicago,
        Illinois, 1876-1890

Married: Hattie Clanton, Universalist and women's rights speaker, Chicago,
        Illinois, 1883

Shot: wounded by police, Haymarket Square Riot, Chicago, 1886

Widowed: wife Hattie trampled during police shooting, Haymarket Riot,
        Chicago, 1886

Brought back from edge of death and despair, Chicago, 1886-87

Negotiator: American Federation of Labor, assistant to Samuel Gompers, 1887
        to 1890

Advocate, speaker and pamphleteer supporting non-violence, rights of the
        working man and woman, the Indian, the Negro, the destitute
        (Chicago, Denver, Omaha, St. Paul, Boston, Seattle, Portland, San
        Francisco, Mexico City, Calgary, Dublin, other cities, 1890-1930)

Peace negotiator: Homestead Steel Strike, Pittsburgh, Pennsylvania, 1892;
        Pullman Strike, Chicago, Illinois, 1894; Labor War, Victor, Colorado,
        1903; Ludlow Massacre, Ludlow, Colorado, 1914; Bloody Sunday,
        Everett, Washington, 1916; Battle of Blair Mountain, Logan
        County, West Virginia, 1921

Beaten by police, arrested for disorderly conduct; charge dismissed and released,
        Everett, Washington, 1916

Lay minister: Universalist Church (itinerant), 1889 to 1931

Died at peace: Livingston, Montana, January 1931

--end--